For my friends..

January 1 - Heather

A good way to avoid a hangover is to alternate between drinking a glass of wine and a glass of water throughout the evening. It was with that intention that I set off last night. Something must have gone wrong though, so here I go again, and yet another year begins with a muzzy head, and a digestive system that's revolted by the "hearty breakfast" that is recommended as a cure. I scroll through my messages, which all seem to be about hoping for a better year than the last one . Well, for me at least it will certainly be a very different sort of year. I stare at the blank page in front of me, and see, in its fresh emptiness, the year stretching ahead with a new story, yet to be written. My new book, and hopefully my new life, begin here. It's a rather obvious thing to write about , I know, this fairly recent turn of events,but maybe it will be therapeutic. This time last year I was un-trimming our rather sad little artificial tree, and wishing for life to return to normal as quickly as possible. I hadn't yet admitted to myself that what I was really wishing for, was for Ted to hightail it back to work, so that I could have some much needed breathing space. It was a couple of days later, after the New Year festivities, that the news was broken to me, just as I was bagging up the leftover chocolates for him to take back to his local council office, to share with his colleagues, 'I'm going to be working from home' , he'd announced, casually, as though mentioning that he was just putting the bins out for collection. It was the beginning of the end. Covid. We neither of us caught it , but it's impact upon us was immense, resulting in a rather eruptive ending to our marriage, and a new beginning for me. So here I am, starting a new book, in a new

2

home, in a new country. I continue to stare at the blank page in front of me, and feel slightly queasy . If only I hadn't drunk so much wine at the party last night. I sit here defeated, and devoid of inspiration , and finally scribble the words 'A fresh start' . I cringe as I put the pen down and reach for my water glass. The irony doesn't escape me.

January 2 - Susan

 Soup. That's what springs to mind when I examine the contents of my post-Christmas fridge. Spicy parsnip with a few mushrooms, then cauliflower and stilton, except that the stilton will in fact be roquefort , and the half head of cauliflower that's lurking in the bottom of the vegetable drawer, will be supplemented with half a bag of brussels sprouts. 'C'est la vie', I mutter, as I begin peeling a couple of onions . Eric will arrive soon for lunch and a haircut. Maybe he'll have time to come on a quick dog walk too. My eyes begin to stream, and I wipe them with the tea towel , forgetting that I used it to wipe the chopping board after I chopped some chillies. They feel as though they've been plucked from my head and rolled in pepper when I open them again , so I go to the sink and splash them with cold water. This improves things, marginally, and through the kitchen window I see the blurry outline of a human figure heading up the pathway to my front door. Eric. I fling the door open, and shout for him to take his boots off. They're always caked in mud, as he takes a shortcut across the fields to the little lane that leads here. I wipe my eyes with a fresh towel and blink several times, before turning to greet him properly, and do a double take. In the doorway crouches a woman, unzipping her beautiful, and immaculately clean, leather boots. The writer, who I met at the New Years Eve party, smiles up at me. I immediately regret my sagging leggings and ancient, hand-knitted sweater, but smile back, self consciously. 'I thought I'd take you up on your offer of coffee' she says.

January 3 - Angel

It's no surprise to me when at the end of my first yoga class of this year, I draw Archangel Michael from the Angel cards that Maisie offers to each of us yoginis. My tarot readings have been telling me that I need to stay strong, and Archangel Michael's blue cape of protection fits in well with that. I look across at Frankie and she winks at me. We seem to have formed an even closer alliance in the last few months, as more and more friends and acquaintances have become vaccinated against the Covid. Those like us, who have remained unjabbed are being increasingly pressured into succumbing. Maisie too, gives me a wry smile. She is quietly one of us. 'Vaccinated or unvaccinated, we are pro choice here' she says as we hug goodbye, and Frankie and I head across the road for a coffee in one of the only places where we are still accepted without a 'pass sanitaire' . Frankie has had a good Christmas, since I last saw her on Christmas Eve, doing 'blissfully nothing' , which seems to have included a lot of walking on the beach , and a Christmas Day swim in the sea. She truly is a nutter, and I wind my scarf more tightly around my neck as she describes the 'natural high' she feels after a cold dip. My own Christmas involved a little too much food and wine , and maybe a little too much of my own company, but I guess it's what my soul needed, and I do indeed feel stronger and calmer after so much meditation and a mindful walk in the woods. The coffee zings through my relaxed body with intensity, and I'm ready to focus on moving forward. I look across the road and see the next yoga class beginning to file in through the door, masks firmly in place. 'I think I might actually crochet myself a blue cloak of protection' I say, half to myself, half to Frankie. She doesn't answer though and when I tear my gaze away from the window and back to her, she's busy with a coffee stirrer, drawing an Angel on the table with the remains of her expresso.

January 4 - Charlotte

I pull on my wellies and my coat, to brave the outside weather, so that I can have my first cigarette of the day. It's almost ten o clock, and I've only just got up, which is actually the norm for me on damp, dark days like this one. I glare out of the window at the grey sky and fish around in my pocket for my lighter as I open the door. Tony doesn't like me smoking in the house, so I close the door behind me before any smoke can get in , just as my phone pings , announcing a message. I finish my cigarette before I look at it, knowing that it's probably only Susan. Sure enough, when I click on messenger, it's her name there at the top of my chat list in the bold typeface which indicates an unread message.

'I'll call in later with some soup I made you, after I've been to Heather's for coffee. See you soon ! X'.

What the fuck! I stuff the phone back in my pocket and stomp over to the garage where Tony is polishing the Renault Scenic that he bought a few days ago. He looks up, smiling

'I've got someone interested in coming to look at this one already!' he says, then his face changes to a frown as he rubs away at some blemish or other that he hadn't previously seen.

'Susan is going over to have coffee with Heather!' I say calmly. 'The writer' , I add when Tony's face registers confusion. He shrugs.

'So?' He asks, dismissively.

I spent almost an hour talking to Heather at the party the other night. I bet she barely even noticed Susan. It should be me calling in for coffee, not her. It's just so like her to want to get in first, and then brag about it to me on Messenger . I take out another cigarette, and light up as I think back to the party at the Salle. It was poorly attended really, with many people choosing to stay home and shield from the Covid, and those lacking a 'pass sanitaire' actually being denied entry, and forced to return home. Tony had persuaded me to go , saying it would be good for business, but in reality he sells cars mostly to English expats, not the Breton clientele who frequent local events, and I'm finding it difficult to interest anyone at all locally, in my perfumes and cosmetics, so I failed to see how either of us could benefit from attending, but we went, and I did meet Heather, and we do have things in common. I inhale and reread Susan's message about the soup. 'I hope it's not parsnip again' I mutter to myself, as I return to the house .

January 5 - Frankie

My atelier feels a bit damp, so I light the wood burner and arrange some smallish pieces of driftwood on the rack above it. They are destined to be starfish, dolphins and other sea themed sculptures for my spring exhibition. I uncover the mermaid I've been working on, which I hope will be the main focal point of the exhibition. I'm pleased with the shape, especially her long sweeping tail, which I'm looking forward to finishing off with some beautiful shards of sea glass, as scales. I have a tangle of rope that I recently found washed up, which I plan to use, to make her hair. I examine it, wondering how much I need to untangle before I start, then I put it aside, and armed with my art journal and a handful of pencils, I flop down on the old sofa, by the fire, and swing my legs over the armrest, immediately attracting the attention of Harper, who jumps down from her spot on my work bench , and up on to my outstretched legs, where she makes herself at home, as I begin to sketch a rather fantastical flying fish , which I may , or may not, end up creating as part of my exhibition, and an extremely curly, fully tentacled octopus , which I almost definitely won't. I'm just wondering about the possibility of using some old fishing net to make wings for the flying fish, when Ross wanders in , with Boris perched on one hand. 'Macron has just said that he's determined to make life as difficult as possible for the unvaccinated' he says, and Boris turns her head to face him as he speaks. Her one good eye seems to open wider in surprise at his words. I chew on my pencil, and picture Macron stamping his feet petulantly. The image makes me smile to myself, and Ross grins back conspiratorially, reading my mind. Together we will stay strong. 'Oh there's a little gift for Boris under that chair' I say, pointing at the decapitated mouse that Missy brought in a few moments ago. Ross takes it gingerly between thumb and forefinger, and offers it to Boris. She immediately reaches out with her left foot and curls her claws around the little body, gripping it firmly. I guess she's saving it for later then.

January 6 - Heather

It's a glorious morning, and fresh from my walk (having closed the exercise ring on the Apple Watch I bought myself for Christmas) , I sit down with a huge mug of tea (rooibos instead of my usual 'builders', in keeping with the new healthy regime) . My book has begun well I think , and I feel quite positive about my writing now, though I am actually a little out of my comfort zone to say the least, in that I'm writing something which is essentially autobiographical, instead of the fantasy and adventure stories that I normally turn out. A dark thought scuds across my mind though, like a heavy cloud. Will it be good enough for publication? I plough on with it anyway. There's no sense in entertaining negativity, and I've promised myself a treat if I've achieved a few pages of writing before lunchtime - A small boutique in the next town sells good quality pre-loved clothes. My wardrobe could do with a bit of a lift, so I'm going to take a drive over there once I'm done with work for the day . It's tough, writing about the messier aspects of my divorce. Sophie is an independent , adult woman, but still my daughter, and the moment when I had to break the news to her was an extremely difficult one. Writing about it brings it all back, and makes me question my decision again. Did I do the right thing? Can I really make it here on my own in a foreign country? Will I spend the rest of my life alone and single, or could I possibly meet somebody to fill the available space that was created when Ted and I fell out of love with each other, a long time before I got the courage to actually leave him? I scribble a few pages about this dilemma, and when I'm done, at least I have something to show for a couple of hours work, and I stop for a breather feeling a tiny bit lighter than I did when I started. Kettle on, I scroll through Facebook while eating a lump of cheese and an apple. The usual food photos, and a few memes and selfies dominate my page. I hit 'like' on a photo of someone's rescued cat, and then notice a friend request from someone called Charlotte Singer. The name is unfamiliar and I almost delete the request, but instead, out of curiosity, I click on her profile. I recognise her right away as a woman I met at the New Years Eve soirée, but I'm baffled as to how she managed to find me on here. Then I notice that we each of us have, as a mutual friend, Susan Matthews. That's odd. I met Susan at that same party, where Charlotte had been completely ignoring her, leaving her to stand self consciously alone, nursing her glass of wine. She had smiled at me when I made eye contact, as Charlotte went outside for a smoke, and I went over to introduce myself, glad to get away from Charlotte's slurry, self centred conversation. Susan was easy to talk to, and soon invited me to pass by for a coffee. I hover over Charlottes profile page, hesitating, but in the end I opt to accept her friendship request. She deserves a chance. After all, both of us were a little worse for wear that night.

January 7 - Susan

I post on Facebook, the recipe for poached pear tiramisu, as it was so yummy when I tried it earlier, and I can't wait to share it tonight with Eric, and Charlotte and Tony. I add a title to the post 'A good way to use up leftover Prosecco' and close down my iPad. I'm going to make a traditional roast, as everyone likes that, and I've bought a chicken from the local organic farm. I'll have to make the stuffing from scratch (Paxo being so difficult to find here), then I'll lay the table once that's done, using the last of the Christmas paper napkins and the crackers. When I check Facebook an hour later, I find that Heather has made the comment 'who has leftover Prosecco?' She has a point I guess, so I reply with a laughing emoji, and a 'not us!' Since Paul went back to England I've cut right down on the alcohol though, and one glass of red wine each night, has become the norm for me, followed by a bath and early bedtime. It's almost a ritual, and I sleep so well with this routine that I'm reluctant to break it. I've asked everyone to arrive at 6.30 tonight, in the hope that they might all leave by 10.30, and I can then go to bed, not much later than my usual 10pm. I'm pondering the likelihood of this when Delilah comes in through the cat flap, and jumps straight up on the table , leaving muddy paw prints in a trail from one end to the other on the white cloth. 'Shit!' I shout , loudly, and she jumps off, claws catching in the lace trim, resulting in a smashed glass and upturned candelabra . Two of the candles roll off of the table and break as I try to rescue everything. I stare despondently at the mess. At least I've plenty of time to start again. Delilah looks apologetic, and I regret shouting at her. She was always Paul's cat really, and I can tell that she misses him still . In a weird way I do too, but definitely not as much as I did.

January 8 - Angel

A wet Saturday is perfect if all you want to do is sit and crochet, while watching a few old movies , so I allow myself the luxury of 'Breakfast at Tiffany's' and begin a kind of spiderweb of teal and royal blue which I hope will eventually form itself into my blue cloak of protection. If all goes well I will make one for Maisie too. The moon is waxing , and so conducive to this kind of creative activity that I find my crocheted square grows very quickly in size, and by the end of the end of 'Roman Holiday' it covers my knees like a blanket, and Lakshmi rubs her face on it as she passes, while pacing the room with an agitated air about her. I decide it must be time for a quick walk, as the rain has slowed to a fine drizzle, so I pull on a coat and usher her outside, closing the door quickly behind me to keep the heat in. The days close in so early at the moment, and with my attention caught by the beauty of the last light on the glistening wet trees, I fail to notice how properly dark it's actually getting. Lakshmi follows a scent that interests her, and by the time I manage to coax her back to me, it's really too black to see my way back through the woods, so I decide to go home by road, though it's twice as far to walk, and the rain and wind have got worse again. I loop my scarf through Lakshmi's collar as a makeshift lead, and turn my own collar up in an effort to keep the rain from pouring down my neck. Five minutes later I'm soaked to the skin and an unfamiliar car draws up next to me. The driver winds down his window , and I notice immediately that it's an English car, with the steering wheel on the right. '

'Can I offer you a lift?' he asks. I vaguely recognise him.

'Tony' he says 'husband of Charlotte'

Apparently I know his wife then , so it's ok to accept , and I apologise for the state of Lakshmi as we both get in the back together so that I can hold on to her and try to stop her from shaking with cold.

'Don't worry , I haven't valeted this one yet ' he drives off smoothly, and I'm grateful to be in the warm car as he chats away about his business.

'Do you have a card?' I ask as we pull up outside my house, moments later.

He scrabbles around under the dashboard.

'I'm on Facebook too', he says as he hands me the card 'Tony Singer' . We shake hands through the car window, and he pats Lakshmi's head.

January 9 - Charlotte

There's nothing worse than a wet weekend. I sit scrolling through the website that I purchase most of my cosmetics from, adding some bath bombs and some shampoo which lightens hair 'naturally'. If I spend enough I'll qualify for a mixed bag of eye pencils which I can sell cheaply, or use as incentives to encourage clients to purchase higher price items. I add some tinted moisturisers, and the total cost is then high enough to get free shipping as well. Free shipping plus the eye pencils makes it a very good deal for me, so I click on the checkout link, and commit to the purchase. The confirmation email arrives instantly, and I decide to use the photo of the 'new and exciting' products to post a promotion on my Facebook business page. When I open Facebook though, on our shared laptop, it's Tony that's logged in, and I swear under my breath as I search for the button I need to click in order to change accounts. I'm about to log out as Tony, and back in as myself when I notice that Tony has accepted a new friend request from someone called Angela Court. I stare at her profile picture while I process this information. It must have been her who Tony rescued last night on his way back from town. Angel. I myself met her a few weeks ago at a coffee morning fundraiser for cancer research. She was offering reflexology treatments in return for a donation, and I took advantage of the opportunity, then had a chat over coffee and homemade cake. Tony must have known it was her, as I've pointed her out to him a couple of times, when she's walked past the house with that dog of hers . Funny that he didn't say that it was someone I knew.

January 10 - Frankie

Angel says nothing when I whip the sheet off of the finished mermaid, and I watch her face carefully as she sweeps one hand over her head in a bid to tame her hair, (we have just finished an early morning Monday yoga class) and then stands back with both hands steepled under her chin. When she begins to nod, I smile with relief, and then I see tears in her eyes and my smile widens to a grin.

'It's just so beautiful, Frankie!' She says.

We both start to laugh, and I hand her a steaming mug of coffee, with Baileys and cream stirred into it.

'Jeez that hits the spot doesn't it!' . It's early , but it's a celebration of sorts and we've already drunk so much water that I had to pee behind a hedge on the way home, even though it's not a long drive.

'How will you transport her?' She asks, and it's a minor detail , but I've been pondering it already. The exhibition is in April, but if I'm going to drive myself there, with all my works, then I guess I will need to buy, or arrange to hire a suitable vehicle sometime soon.

'Something will turn up' . I wonder briefly about karchering Ross' truck and using that with a tarpaulin over the top. We are both quietly lost in our thoughts as we sip our coffee, then Angel puts her mug down and grins at me with the most perfect cream moustache , having tipped her mug up high to drain every last drop. I feel compelled to do the same , and then scoot up next to her in order to take a social media destined selfie.

'Shall I post it?' I ask. She shakes her head.

'Oh I have a card for you ' , she fumbles in her bag , and I wait for her to pull out the tarot deck that she always carries, but instead it's a business card that she hands to me

'might be a good contact if you're looking for a van', she smiles as she hands it over 'Tony Singer' it says 'Quality Secondhand Motors. Reliable and Affordable' I raise my eyebrows at Angel. Clearly, she hasn't made the connection.

January 11 - Heather

12

I read back over what I've written, a little afraid that the tone is too negative. It's cathartic, writing all this stuff , but would anyone actually want to read it? It maybe sounds a little too much like a pity party. Oh well. I put the pen down, and then pick it up again to scribble a few notes in the heavy black diary that I treated myself to, while I was in town last week. It's a French "Agenda", with a whole A4 lined page for each day. I thought it might be therapeutic to write a little each day about my new life here in France. My experiences, the people I meet, and just my day to day life. When I'm done I put my boots on with the plan of getting some much needed fresh air , but just as I reach the door a new idea suddenly occurs to me. Charlotte Singer! She's a writer too! Or at least I think that's what she said during our somewhat drunken conversation. I could drop in for a coffee and a chat. Maybe we could be each others writing support buddy. I scroll through my recently added friends, and send her a quick message to find out if she's home, and where that is exactly. She replies immediately, and I'm soon on my way to Chez Beauté, which is apparently seventeen minutes walk away. I'm just about to leave for the second time when I decide that I ought not to arrive empty handed. My eyes settle on the wine rack and I select a decent bottle of Madiran , and then a plain black gift bag from my drawer of recyclable gift wrappings. When , on my way past the farm, I find that the mimosa tree has begun to bloom , I tuck a sprig of it inside the bag , and it starts to look as if I've gone to some trouble. Feeling optimistic now, and ignoring my intuitive misgivings about whether Charlotte and I have much in common (despite the writing) I follow Google maps on my phone and continue on determinedly.

January 12 - Susan

Boris Johnson's apology is a joke. A pathetic one at that. I don't normally watch Prime Minister's Question Time, but I couldn't resist it today. I wonder if he'll have to resign in the end, when the enquiry is finished. He should, after all Lockdown meant Lockdown, and there were certainly no parties going on around here at that time, though I did hear from Charlotte, that Frankie and Ross had had a 'massive' gathering of campers in the woods behind their place. I think she was just jealous though at not having been invited! I switch off the tv and get ready to take Rhea for a little walk, now that the fog has lifted and there is some blue sky showing. We take the car to the lake at the edge of the village, just behind the Salle. There is a walk that takes you all around it, winding in and out through the trees, and it's perfect for watching the ducks, and even spotting the occasional ragondin. Rhea takes advantage of being let off of her lead, and runs ahead of me into the wooded area, further away from the path and the car park. I walk slowly, checking my phone for messages as I go, and just enjoying being outside, breathing in the fresh air. By the time I get to the corner, where there is a little wooden bridge across the muddy bit, where the ducks gather, there is no sign of Rhea . I call her a couple of times while I lean on the hand rail , and am startled when a dark shape appears among the trees , moving towards me.

'Hiya' calls out Frankie . 'Didn't mean to scare ya' . She holds up a handful of white feathers. 'I'm just collecting these for a project' .

My heart rate returns to normal, and I grin and wave. It's good to see her, and just for a moment I forget about the Covid, and accept a hug. It's then that I spot Rhea, covered from head to foot in mud, chasing wildly back and forth from the ducks to the woods with Artie, Frankie's black labrador. We watch them in silence for half a minute before I call Rhea back. She'll have to go for a proper swim now, to wash the mud off. I've never seen her in such a state.

'We should do this again! ' Frankie says. 'They clearly love each other!' She takes a few photos before she heads off in the other direction. 'Don't forget to post them on Facebook'. I call after her.

January 13 - Angel

I was somewhere else for a while, as I foraged for white feathers in the woods, to help Frankie with her project. I walked in what we have often referred to as 'Harry Potter' country, where the fir trees grow densely together, the narrow pathways between them lightless and endless, though today was a bright enough day, and I was in no danger of repeating my mistake of last weekend. Lakshmi returned from her foray into the blackness.

'Hello you' , I say, as she begins sniffing at the feathers in my hand . She is used to my collecting things from nature , and always takes an interest in whatever it is that has caught my attention. She is soon distracted by some other scent though, and is off again on the hunt for a fox or a deer, or even a wild boar, none of which she will ever catch . I take advantage of the mild, springlike day, and when I find a patch of moss so soft and green that I can't resist, I take off my boots and stand there barefoot, feeling the grounding effects of the forest, and the fresh energy permeating my feet . I breathe deeply, and close my eyes, enjoying the precious freedom of being in nature. This morning I made the unpleasant but very necessary trip into town for food shopping. The contrast between that stressed out and masked up experience, and this one, could not be more apparent. My deep breathing turns into a sigh. Surely this situation cannot go on much longer? I close my eyes again, and know instinctively that it won't.

January 14 - Charlotte

As a general rule I'm not a person who cares much about money but as I tot up the potential profit from the pots of pro-retinol face cream, lash lengthening mascara, and lip plumping lipstick, I can't help but smile to myself. These goodie bags I'm putting together will be a sure fire winner. I arrange them artfully on the table before photographing them for my Facebook page 'Belle j'adore'. I think about sharing the photo to my own personal profile, but stop just in time . I've been using my profile page as a kind of blog of my life. I'm trying to present myself as a writer, first and foremost, and the selling of cosmetics, merely a hobby. When I looked at my page a couple of days ago, some time after Heather passed by for a coffee, I was shocked to see how little content I'd posted on there recently, and how much of what I did post was just shared stuff from the cosmetics page. Of course I then removed most of that, and added a few written posts in order to get back on track. Heather had been happy to share some of her writing habits with me, but when she asked me about what I do when I'm blocked I had to think pretty quickly.

'I read back through what I've written, and then go and meditate on it' I said, somewhat convincingly I hope. She has inspired me to step up my blogging , big style. I particularly remember how her habit of writing something every day, even if it's just her diary, is so important for her. It's a habit that I'm planning on copying. I can write a post for my blog every day, and who knows, maybe I can put together something publishable in book form. With this in mind I begin my blog for today . 'Should Boris Johnson be forced to resign? ' is my chosen subject. I Google that question, and begin making notes.

January 15 - Frankie

I pull up outside of Tony and Charlotte's house, and park my Beetle on the grass verge by the gate. There is a light on in the garage and I can hear a radio playing an old Phil Collins song that I used to love, many years ago. It's a dark morning even though it's a few hours since the sun rose, and apart from the garage radio, the place seems very still and quiet. Tony is surprised to see me. It's been a while since I was last here, but he gives me a friendly grin, and puts down the hoover he's carrying. I speak first, in order to ward off the inevitable 'long time no see' opening line, that I could sense Tony was about to use.

'I need to buy a camper van' I say 'or at least, a van that could be converted into a camper van'

Tony is happy that it's something he can help with, and I remember how he likes to be useful to people, and that we used to get on well together. He has about seven cars, tucked under his hangar.

'They're all for sale!' He says, when I ask. He hasn't any vans at the moment, but he is always on the lookout. He grabs a pen to make a note of what I'm looking for . 'Coffee.?' He offers. I accept, and it's at this point , just as the kettle begins to boil, that Charlotte coughs from the doorway, cigarette in hand.

'I was just going to offer you a coffee. I saw your car ' she explains a little awkwardly, as Tony holds up three mugs.

'So how big a van, and how new?' We carry on our conversation as if Charlotte wasn't there, and I explain that it needs to be big enough for a bed and a few sculptures, and probably quite old, given that my budget is a little on the small side.

'What about that Sprinter you looked at?' Charlotte interjects, albeit helpfully. I give her a friendly smile, pleased that she seems to be making a genuine effort. Perhaps, eventually, it may be possible for us to be friends again .

January 16 - Heather

Well this is weird, I think to myself , as I look at Charlotte's Facebook page. I could have sworn that a few days ago, when I looked at it, there were only a few posts about mascara, BB cream, and something called 'micro blading' . Anyway, now there's nothing of that , and the writing that I was expecting to see, has miraculously appeared. I must have looked at the wrong account or something. I'd had a couple of glasses of wine, so that might explain it. I settle down to read her blog style posts. The one with the beach photo grabs my attention first, but I feel my eyes fogging over before I've read more than a few repetitive sentences. Her writing style is so fussy, and dare I say it ? 'amateurish'….overladen with adjectives, and with no clear narrative. 'Spirituality and the sea' seem to be the vague theme, but I'm not sure what message she was aiming to convey. I skip over a couple of food related blogs, with her recipes for spicy parsnip soup, and healthy fish pie, and concentrate on one about Boris Johnson. This one, in contrast to the others is quite well written, and interesting to read. It lacks the grammatical errors of her other posts, and I find myself reading it from beginning to end, and then going through the comments. One in particular catches my eye. 'This seems kind of familiar, as if I've read it before' somebody called Tink Isaacs says, with a winky face emoji and two exclamation marks. Oh! So that's it is it? That's why it's so much more compelling, and easier to read . It's plagiarised! Poor Charlotte! Having to stoop to that level!

January 17 - Susan

It isn't easy, but I manage it somehow, and the biggest lump of driftwood I've ever seen , lands in the boot of my car, which I've backed up into the hangar, where all the detritus of so many years has found a home. This huge beast of sea smoothed oak, was dragged up from the beach several years ago by Paul, who was maybe going to possibly make something, at some time, with it. That didn't happen, and I was then going to offer it to Charlotte, as I know she's had her eye on it , but changed my mind when I thought of Frankie. Her sculptures are just so interesting and original that I know she will make the best use of this piece, and I can't wait to give it to her. I slam the boot shut, and wipe my hands on a pile of hessian sacks that slump over the old cider press in the corner. It's then that my attention is drawn to something black, that's huddling at the bottom of the press. My heart starts beating wildly, and I freeze with fear, thinking it's a rat. I slowly take a step backwards, and wait for what seems like several minutes, though it's probably only seconds, for the creature to scuttle away. When it does eventually move out of its corner, I see that it's not a rat at all. A beautiful black kitten with blue eyes stares back at me as I begin to crouch down next to it. It blinks, and I am smitten. If only I could keep it!

January 18 - Angel

It's still a bit foggy when I bring my crystals in. They are cold and glistening, shiny and fully charged from last nights full Wolf Moon. I begin placing them carefully back on my altar, and think about the properties of each one as I set them down. I select the tigers eye, and push it into the little silver ball cage pendant, that I wear constantly. The stone's benefits are protection, strength and courage, and for some reason I'm drawn to it today. Next I draw a tarot card. The queen of Wands! Well that's a surprise ! I've been drawing the strength card consistently over the last few weeks, yet this queen is ambitious, resourceful and creative. I stare at her confident expression, wand in hand , with a little black cat at her feet. What is she trying to tell me? My thoughts are interrupted by a knock at the door which sets Lakshmi off barking and jumping up against it. When I open it Eric is standing there, looking a bit mysterious. He has a cardboard box which he carries carefully over to the table before he even begins to speak.

'I thought of you', he says, opening the flaps 'because she's so black' . The most beautiful black kitten stares up at me.

'Susan found her, but couldn't keep her with that terrier of hers' he explains as I lift her out of the box and into my arms, already purring. Lakshmi would be fine with her but unfortunately the same cannot be said for Reiki. Eric's face falls as I tell him this, and we both look over to where Reiki now sits on the kitchen counter, making a low growling noise which ends in a long hiss. A moments silence passes between us , but then inspiration strikes as I remember the tarot card, and with all the confidence of the Queen of Wands with her black cat, I tell Eric not to worry, I will soon find this one a home.

19 January - Charlotte

I am becoming obsessed with Facebook, Tony says, and just maybe he's right. I work in silence for another minute or so on my latest post, 'Nature's Treasures' it's called, and I'm blogging about picking up fir cones, and photographing fungi in the woods. When I've written half a page, I get up to put the radio on, unable to bear any longer the total lack of any sound at all. Tony has gone to look at a car he might buy, and this foggy afternoon is so still and quiet I could scream. Instead I light another cigarette and stand in the doorway with my phone. The photo on Angel's page, of the cutest black kitten is the first thing I saw this morning. Tony said no, of course, but as I scroll down, there it is again, and the comment is from Frankie Stein. 'I would if I could but I already have so many! '. Lots of sad face emojis are tacked on the end of this sentence .

'Such a shame! ', I mutter sarcastically under my breath. We have stayed friends on Facebook, though I never comment on her stuff and I no longer follow her other account 'The curious creations of Francesca Steiner'. If I don't follow it, I can't be accused of trying to copy . I finish my cigarette and start looking through my photos for a suitable one to accompany my blog. Tony's pickup truck rolls into the driveway while I'm still standing there in the doorway. He gets out and waves at me with a silly grin on his face. I keep my neutral expression, 'resting bitch face' apparently, as he goes to the passenger door, and carefully lifts out a box. More car parts I expect. I go in and close the door behind me.

'Put the kettle on!' He calls out , as he enters, thirty seconds behind me. I remain motionless as he places the cardboard box on the table, and opens the flaps, with a mysterious look on his face as his eyes meet mine. After a second or two I step forward and take a peek inside. Staring back at me are the biggest blue eyes I've ever seen. Angels kitten!

January 20 - Frankie

At ten minutes before the 10am deadline I'm done, and I stand back to survey my work as Maisie's first yoga class of the day begins to arrive, each one pausing outside of the door to put their masks on before entering. An older lady first, with white hair tied back from her face with a scarf. She looks at each of the two windows, then goes in , nodding. Next two ladies I've never seen before, arrive at the same time. I watch them both stop suddenly, and then simultaneously stand back to get a better view, while a third one joins them. There is much excited chatter , but I don't understand the language. I think it might be Polish, but I could be wrong. They don't notice me across the street with my camera poised, and Maisie ushers them in, before barefooting it across the road to join me. 'Thank-you so much! It looks so wonderfully amazing!' It does look good, and I'm pleased with my efforts. The dead trees, painted white, one in each window, and both of them strewn with white feathers hanging fluffily from every branch, while a buddha sits under each tree on a carpet of snow made from cotton wool-like wall insulation material.This effect, with the pure white curtains hanging behind, is exactly what I was hoping to achieve. I grin at Maisie, then urge her to go back inside and get on with her day. Now, if only I can get a decent photo or two.

January 21 - Heather

Over coffee, Susan fills me in on the kitten saga. The beautiful black creature, which she sent me a photo of a few days ago, has ended up with Charlotte. Susan couldn't keep her of course, with Rhea being so hell bent on terrorising any cat except Delilah, and so Eric immediately intervened, saying that her silky black coat reminded him of a woman he knows , who lives nearby, and who loves animals. This woman, 'Angel' apparently, who Susan has never properly met, but has long jet black hair , and striking blue eyes , must be the woman that I've seen walking her dog on the road past my house. We've said 'bonjour' and smiled at each other. I thought she was French. Maybe she thought I was.

'So her dog doesn't like cats either?' I ask. Susan shakes her head, smiling.

'No, it's her cat apparently. A half feral tabby thing, with tufts on her ears. Gorgeous to look at but insanely jealous if Angel let's another creature into the house. Loves the dog though. I guess they've grown used to each other'.

Susan's coffee is good. She has a bean to cup machine with an attached frother. I happily accept another cup while breaking off little bits of the shortbread that she made this morning, and feeding them to Rhea underneath the table. I'm procrastinating really. I should be at home, writing, but other than the diary, it's not going too well today.

'So then she put a photo on Facebook' Susan carries on with her story 'and she gets a message from Tony. I'm about to ask who Tony is but she beats me to it .

'Tony Singer, Charlotte's husband…..And next thing there he is on her doorstep, and that's it, job done! I knew nothing about it of course, until I went over a couple of hours later, and Charlotte opened the door with the kitten I found, asleep over her shoulder!'

'Roxy' , I say, referring to the Facebook post of yesterday, in which Charlotte wrote about being so grateful for simple things, and showed off the latest addition to her family. I do love a happy ending.

January 22 - Susan

So it's cold, and I'm justified, having spent the morning cleaning and baking, in spending the afternoon on the sofa with Rhea and Netflix. Eric has invited Angel and I over this evening, for a vegan curry, but I don't need to start getting ready for ages yet. 'Don't look up' is a film that Heather recommended to me the other day. I click on it and scroll through Facebook on my phone at the same time. So many photos of that black kitten! 'Roxy is so happy in her new home' the latest post says. I'm so glad she's happy, and I'm very glad that Charlotte is too. It's good to see her smiling. Further down my page is a photo of the windows of the yoga studio in town. I've never been there myself, but recommended it to Heather when she was here yesterday. The windows have been photographed at night, and the white trees show up beautifully against the darkness. The effect is captivating. As I'm about to forward the photo on to Heather, I notice who is credited for window dressing. Frankie Stein of course! I smile to myself. I never felt it necessary to unfriend her out of loyalty to Charlotte, even when Charlotte couldn't hide her annoyance and irritation about my disinclination to pick a 'side'. It will irritate her further if I share this post. I'm not normally vindictive but I hesitate only a moment before I hit 'share', tagging Heather, and commenting

'this is the place I told you about, you can't miss it with its beautiful windows! ' then I giggle to myself as I put my phone down and snuggle up with Rhea, to watch the film. It's just a little harmless fun.

January 23 - Angel

A brisk early morning walk is necessary in order to clear the cobwebs, and Lakshmi is always up for exercise, impatient to be freed from the leash as soon as we get to the bend in the road where a grassy farm track leads down to the woods. I stop to unclip her, and she runs off to explore all the scents and smells of the local wildlife, and perhaps even other dogs. I take the opportunity to inhale deeply. A few mindful breaths later, my attention is caught by the sound of approaching footsteps. I turn around to see who else has been tempted from their bed at this hour on a Sunday morning, to walk in the forest. A female figure heads towards me, winding her scarf around her neck as she walks. It can only be the newcomer, Heather. I've not met her yet, but recognise her from Susan's description. She spoke about her lots last night, so I know that she's a writer, that she's divorced with one daughter, and that she is trying to make a new life for herself here in Brittany. I wait for her to catch up with me, and realise as she gets closer, that I've seen her before a couple of times , out walking, presumably exploring her new territory.

'You must be Angel' she introduces herself as I open my mouth to speak ' Heather' .

We shake hands as Lakshmi comes bounding over, and a few minutes are spent on the necessary dog greetings before we fall naturally into step with each other, and continue our walks together. She turns out to be good company, and we have a few things in common, including the enjoyment of our single statuses.

'It would be nice just to have some company in the evenings though' she confides, as she finishes telling me about how much of a relief it is to have her own space now. I think about the scarcity of suitable males in the vicinity.

'Maybe you should think about getting a dog' I suggest.

January 24 - Charlotte

I wake abruptly from my dream. I had been an actress, dancer or at least a performer of some sort or other, and was sitting in front of a large mirror surrounded in lights, while a young woman continually pressed a large powder puff over my face.

'You need more makeup'. She kept saying, and the powder puff was swept over my face again and again, back and forth. I gasped as I tried to sit up, and realised at once that the powder puff had in fact been Roxy, brushing past my chin, and then turning around to brush past it again the other way, as she tried to find a comfortable position in which to settle. I sit up and prop myself against the pillows, taking Roxy onto my lap as I do so. She immediately begins to purr, and curls up happily on top of the duvet. That's it then, I can't really get up now without disturbing her. I reach for my phone and take a photo, uploading straight away to Facebook. 'The kitten that nobody wanted' I title it. I guess that's not entirely true but I was the only one prepared to give her a home. It's then that I notice Heather's post.

'Just back from my first early morning yoga class. Thank-you so much Maisie Day, that was fabulous! Namaste!' I throw the phone back down on the bed. I've always wanted to go to that class, but never had the time. If only it wasn't so early in the morning! I can't really afford it either, unless I start to sell a lot more of my cheap makeup. I pick the phone up again and select my 'goodie bag' post to promote on my page. I'll write a blog later. Perhaps I can write about how I'm so busy that my work is getting in the way of my life. Yes, that's what I'll do, a kind of work/life balance post. Roxy purrs and stretches on my lap. I'll let her have another ten minutes.

January 25 - Frankie

The Sprinter van is a blank canvas, mechanically sound, and ready to go. Tony assures me it's a good deal. I stand with my coffee cooling, and try to imagine myself driving it. It's perfect for my needs, but just so uninspiring. Neither of us says anything. I know he has other people who are interested in buying it. He has given me first refusal though, and isn't going to rush me into making a decision. We leave it at that.

'I will let you know by the end of the week' I promise, as I hand back my mug and turn to go.

Charlotte is hovering by the door and I see that she's brought the kitten out to meet me. I take out the present I made for her, (the kitten, not Charlotte) . It's a kind of dreamcatcher confection, made of woven willow, with dangling beads and feathers, and a macrame hanger. Roxy bats a paw at it, then chews a feather enthusiastically, her blue eyes wild. She's a blur of jet black fur, and I drink in her beauty, as I half listen to Charlotte going over the story of her rescue. She's so happy to be able to give this little one a home apparently.

'Not everyone would take in a stray kitten, but I have such a soft heart', she says. I think of all of the animals we have at home. Each one has its own story and they seem to find us as if by magic. 'Well done! ' I say, and Tony gives me a wink. My phone pings as I start to walk back to my car, and Charlotte follows me, trying to engage me in further conversation. I glance at the message discreetly, not wishing to appear rude. It's Heather, who I met yesterday in yoga class. She wants to come over to have a look at my sculptures.

'Home in five minutes'. I send back quickly, then turn to Charlotte as I open my car door 'Gotta go, running late' . I smile apologetically at her, and wave to Tony as I start my engine. When I look in the mirror as I drive away she's waving Roxy's little paw pathetically in my direction.

January 26 - Heather

The day dawns white with frost. I do three sun salutations before I make my coffee, happy with my new regime of early morning yoga class on a Monday morning, to start my week off. Next I settle down to write for an hour or so before heading out for a walk. Inspiration doesn't come easily though, and I find that my thoughts soon wander to my morning with Frankie yesterday. In her atelier, with the wood fire burning, and the smell of fresh coffee brewing, I felt truly at home. Maybe it was all of those animals . There was a dog and at least four cats in there, plus goats and chickens outside, sharing their field with a miniature pony, and when I looked up at their thatched roof, a peacock was displaying his feathers on top of the gable end.

'Angel suggested I get a dog' , I said. Frankie grinned when I told her this. 'Don't worry. A dog will soon find you ' was her answer, though I barely heard her. Her beautiful sculptures had captivated my attention, and as she made us coffee, I listened with interest as she told me about her work - a beautiful blend of metalwork with mixed media , she uses whatever materials come to hand . Natural treasures mainly, but anything that speaks to her can be thrown into the mix. As she spoke she uncovered a couple of sea themed creations, each more beautiful than the last. I focused on a mermaid with a long, driftwood tail encrusted with glass which sparkled in the sunlight shining through the bifold doors. There were further fantastical creatures of old rope, driftwood and rusting metal. Evidence of her immense creativity was everywhere. I stare at my blank page, wondering if my own talents could be channeled in a different way, or if I should just knuckle down and get on with it. Instead, I pick up my phone and scroll through Facebook again. Another photo of Charlotte's kitten stares back at me. I wonder for the third time that morning whether I should get a dog.

January 27 - Susan

Charlotte puts down the brownie she's been nibbling since she opened the Tupperware tub I brought with me. I can tell that she's annoyed about my knowing something about Heather that she doesn't.

'She has to be vaccinated' she says, after a while, with a triumphant tone to her voice. 'How else could she have got in to the Salle for the soirée on New Years Eve? '. She sits back and resumes nibbling on the brownie as she reaches for her mug of tea.

'That's what I said, but apparently, as she had only just arrived in the country, her PCR test was less than forty eight hours old, so they let her in ! '

The brownies are good and we sit in silence for a while, enjoying them. I rub my arm , which is still throbbing from the booster vaccination that I had on Monday. At least I'm feeling a bit better today. The last two days have been horrible, with headaches and nausea. I think that's passed now, as I was up early this morning feeling fine, and happily singing to myself in the kitchen, while baking. Charlotte, I noticed, had only just got up when I arrived, and though she says she's been working, that seems to mean that she has in fact been updating her Instagram page. Red paper bags, beautifully beribboned, and presumably filled with cosmetics, sit lined up on the buffet. The latest goodie bags I assume. I feel a pang of pity when she tells me that she hasn't sold any yet.

'Oh I almost forgot' I say quickly. 'I need to buy a couple of those for my twin nieces' . This is not a total lie. They will be given as presents next time I visit them, but probably not before 2024.

January 28 - Angel

I wake early, and after a quick shower I pull on my leggings, and a loose t.shirt, ready for yoga. I'm sipping a mug of hot water with a slice of lemon in it when my phone pings. Maisie, sick with the flu, is cancelling the class . 'Ok. Take care xxxx'. I type back and add a few caring emoji's. I have an extra hour now. It's a foggy morning, and so quiet and pretty, that I decide to meditate by the window, taking advantage of the peaceful view, of bare branched trees against a white sky. Monochromatic. I inhale all of this peace and imagine it growing inside me into a huge ball which just gets bigger and bigger until it engulfs the whole planet. I imagine each country becoming still, each person becoming thoughtful, each power becoming kind. When I open my eyes I feel an incredible calmness. The fog descends lower, and I sit there, enjoying the moment as if frozen in time. The only sound is Lakshmi breathing loudly as she sleeps, stretched out on the rug. When the fog begins to lift I'm still there. My joints are beginning to complain a little at being in a cross legged position. My feet are tingly and numb. Remembering my yoga, I shift slowly into swan for a few minutes before coming back to sitting mindfully, and beginning some alternate nostril breathing . I end in a long deep 'Om' which wakes Lakshmi, who yawns and stretches in a posture that comically echoes my own yawning and stretching. 'Do you fancy a mindful walk then?' Her tail wags in answer.

29 January- Charlotte

It's more than I expected, and all of it quite good brands, but so many lipsticks in colours that I'm not sure will be popular. It's going to take me ages to add all these to my page. At least the hair colouring products should sell well, and all of the BB cream with the SPF factor too. Roxy is having fun playing in the empty boxes, and diving about all over the bubble wrap. Maybe I'll start with a little blog about holiday preparations, and then a photo of the BB cream, and the bronzer, with a lush lipstick thrown in for good measure, all for nine ninety nine….when Tony comes in he nudges Roxy's litter tray with his foot and wrinkles his nose. I haven't had time to clean it out yet, with all of this stuff to unpack.

'We could think about getting a cat flap' I say . Roxy is probably about nine or ten weeks old, and I've made her an appointment at the vet, for her jabs. Tony bends down and begins trailing the bubble wrap across the floor for Roxy to chase.

'A bit too small yet isn't she?' He asks. We look at each other and shrug. Neither of us really knows that much about cats.

'We can Google it….or maybe ask Frankie when she comes over for the van' I say, reluctantly accepting that her cat know may be superior to ours.

'Oh she's not coming, didn't I tell you? She's decided that she won't be happy with anything that's not a Volkswagen'. He goes on playing with the cat while I sit there quietly fuming. The Sprinter will sell easily enough but that's not the point. I hate that Tony has wasted his time on her.

January 30 - Frankie

When we arrived in France, about seven years ago, we had only one cat, Copper. Gradually we acquired many more, so that there are now nine of them roaming around. Four live, or lived, in the house, while the other five sleep in my atelier or in one of the other outbuildings . Ross helps me make a cage out of some sections of grill that was once part of a large rabbit cage. It needs to be big enough to trap a dog, which we think is a bit smaller than Artie. It's a sad job. This dog, of which we've seen only glimpses, is responsible we think, for mauling poor Copper to death last night. She was about fifteen years old, and very much a 'cat' cat . Sleeping most of the day,appearing for food when she woke up hungry, and minding her own business the rest of the time. Her quiet presence will be missed by us both. When the cage is finished we drag it outside to the barn where we usually feed the cats. Tonight we will bait it with cat food, and hope that the savage dog is heavy enough to trigger the mechanism that will trap him inside. Neither Ross, nor I would ever hurt an animal. The dog will be humanely caught, and then rehomed, somewhere where there are no cats around. On cue, Harper brushes through my legs, back and forth until I bend down to scoop her up. She purrs enthusiastically as I drape her over my shoulder, and I walk her over to the spot where Copper is now buried. She sniffs the ground, and looks up at me quizzically, then scrapes away at the freshly dug soil, preparing to use it as a rather convenient bathroom .

'Harper! ' Ross admonishes her 'show some respect.'

January 31 - Heather

I spend just a few seconds hesitating by the barbed wire fence before I decide to climb through it. It catches my hood, and I hear it tear as I stand back up again. The sheep is on its back, and it seems totally helpless, legs flailing in the air. I talk softly to it as I gently roll it over. It is still for a moment, then struggles to its feet and waddles away. I stand there watching, feeling pleased with myself. My experience with animals is virtually nil. Maybe I am meant to get a pet. Angel, after yoga this morning, told me that it's a new moon tonight, and therefore a good time for new beginnings. I watch the sheep nonchalantly return to grazing with its herd, none the worse for its experience.

'Merci Madame'. I hear a voice behind me call, and a man in blue bib and brace overalls, and heavy boots, waves as he jogs towards me. He catches his breath, and mutters words which I assume are grateful thanks , as he points to the sheep and grins. I understand nothing of what he says , but hold my hand out for him to shake.

'Didier' he says, and then after a brief pause 'English?' I nod, a little too enthusiastically. He is quite good looking, not that tall , and with a bit of a paunch, but long black hair tied back, and beautiful brown eyes. I put all ideas of getting a pet out of my head. It's a man I need!

February 1 - Susan

The mince pies are still a bit too hot to eat, so both Heather and I nibble at the edges and blow on them a bit. It's a bit weird to be eating mince pies at the start of February, but hey ho, I made too much mincemeat at Christmas, and it needed using up. Neither of us speaks for a while, as I check the oven to make sure the banana cake is rising, and Heather studies the calendar on the wall, that the Pompiers brought over just before Christmas.

'That's him! ', she says suddenly, pointing at one of the men in uniform on the front of the calendar. I wipe my hands on the tea towel, and pick up my glasses. The man who she finds so interesting stares back at me from the photograph. Didier. When Paul and I arrived here, around six years ago, Didier knocked on the door here and Introduced himself. He'd pointed to the cluster of buildings in the distance, near the top of the hill , and said to knock on the farmhouse door if we needed anything. Twice I've called on his services. Once in the early days when our fosse began to smell and he came with his tractor towing a big tank on a trailer, and pumped it out for us, then again last summer, when Delilah got chased up a tree and I needed help to get her down.

'He's a really lovely guy'. I say, and Heather smiles, her eyes twinkling. 'He's also married' , I add.

February 2 - Angel

Just before 8pm I sit down with my rose quartz crystal in hand, and a candle burning. There are eight of us in this little group , and together we will set an intention to bring peace to the world. Each of us at home , in front of the fire, by a window, or sitting cross legged on a mat at the foot of a bed, will chant the Ho Oponopono prayer, and send love to the planet, focusing particularly on ending the Covid vaccination mandates. I'm not sure how long I sit there . My eyes are closed, and the planet needs so much love that I carry on saying the prayer, and thinking of Macron, Boris Johnson, and all the misinformation about the current situation. I continue to think about those things, but get distracted by thoughts of other issues that are close to my heart at the moment, such as Syria and it's refugees , and Ukraine . I think of poverty as a whole, and starving children in particular, and the huge numbers of people on this planet who die of hunger. I think about greed and the problem of obesity in the western world, and pollution and whether everything I put in the recycling bin does in fact get recycled. I feel Reiki land in my lap and start to pad her paws up and down, preparing a comfy spot, and I start then to think about cruelty to animals, and that dog next door who hasn't stopped it's pitiful barking all day. When I open my eyes everything is blurry. The dog next door is still making an infernal noise. I've never actually seen this animal as the hedge is so thick. Tomorrow, as soon as it's light, I'll investigate.

February 3 - Charlotte

I should have thought of this before I guess. In writing something every day for my blog, I will eventually run out of anything to write about. And so I have. Run out. Yesterday I rehashed an article about Covid Conspiracy Theorists, and the day before that I wrote about the problems of menopause, using snippets I noted from what the doctor said on the Jeremy Vine show, along with my own recent experience. I've written about animal rescues and house renovations several times, and now here I am with nothing to do today but write , and nothing, absolutely nothing, to write about. I scroll through Facebook again in the hope of finding something to inspire me , and my attention is caught by an article about a new brasserie that has just opened up, about a half hours drive from here. If I can persuade Tony to take me out for a meal , I can perhaps write my blog in the form of a restaurant review. Happy with this idea I put my pen down and head outside in search of Tony. It's a drizzly day, so I hurry across to the garage in my crocs, lighting my cigarette as I go .

'Have you seen this?' He asks, holding up his phone as I enter . It's Angel's Facebook page . It seems she has a dog now that's in need of a home.

'Seriously?' I shake my head, as he looks at me with puppy dog eyes.

'Do you think I have time to look after a dog?'. He puts his phone back in his pocket, and turns away, saying nothing as he picks up a can of black tyre wall spray. I pick up my own phone and quickly find Angel's page. Of course Frankie was the first to comment, but all she writes is 'Heather Warne?'

February 4 - Frankie

'This truly is a gastric experience to experience in the flesh!'

Angel howls with laughter as she reads out Charlotte's post, and I involuntarily spray coffee all over my sketches of a Poseidon type figure that I'm intending to create from the heap of rusting tools and scrap metal, that lies in one corner of my atelier. In that same corner, tied temporarily to an old blacksmiths anvil, sits 'Thug', a rather pretty border collie ish, labradorish mixed breed with a deceptively angelic face , whose penchant for chicken chasing (and killing) got him the punishment of being tied up permanently in the garden next door to Angel.

'I think she meant gastronomic'. Angel says, when she's recovered a little.

'Do you think it could have been him? ', I ask. We still haven't caught the dog that killed Copper, and this one is about the same size as the one we've caught glimpses of and had its freedom up until a few days ago . Angel stares into the dogs eyes for what seems like an age .

'I will find him a home where there are no other animals' she says, and I again think of Heather, though as yet, she's ignored my comment . As if reading my mind Angel checks her phone, then hands it to me saying

'How about this?' . I expect to see an offer of a home for Thug, or at least a glimmer of hope in the search for one. Instead it's a Volkswagen van that she's showing me . An unfinished project. Plain white. A blank canvas crying out for some love and attention. Perfect! This will be my next rescue.

February 5 - Heather

I've got to that part of my story where I begin to wonder if I should have done things differently. A little before I made the big move to this country, I began to have doubts. Was my life with Ted really so bad? Did I absolutely have to move to another country in order to make a new start? And on and on and on…I think I was scared. I'd been over here for a couple of quick visits, while I was buying this little house, but that's all. I had to commit quickly though if I was going to do it at all. Because of Brexit it was necessary to be actually living here before a certain date, to qualify for the Carte de Séjour which allows me to remain here as a French resident for the next ten years. Thankfully I just squeaked in, arriving before the end of December. 'It's a big step', was all Sophie said at the time, and it was, a huge step, but sitting here looking out at this frosty morning, while struggling with a story

35

that is very slowly coming together , sipping a mug of Liptons tea, which is all I could find when my Yorkshire tea ran out, I don't regret it. I have all I need. I've made some friends, and I've plenty of time to write, and to explore the countryside. The word 'lonely' hovers at the edge of the blank page in front of me. I brush it aside without acknowledging it, and focus on the job in hand . So, would I have done better to take my time , and not to have rushed with such alacrity towards this big life change ? The truth is I did the best I could with what I knew at the time . I knew I couldn't go on as I was , and so it was fight or flight, and here I am, looking for about the seventeenth time at Angel's Facebook post.

February 6 - Susan

When I check my account to see if Paul paid me last week, I find that the £3000 he puts in there each month for my living expenses, has now translated into 3500 euros . I smile to myself. Living here has got more expensive over the last couple of years, and lately the cost of fuel has risen alarmingly. I can easily manage on this amount though, and there is always plenty to spare at the end of the month. Charlotte is struggling though, and I'm a bit worried about her and Tony. She has a kind heart underneath that selfish facade. When I hear a faint knock at the door I close my laptop and creep across the kitchen to peer through the window. I'm not expecting anyone this early on a Sunday morning. Eric is standing there on the path looking ghastly. Grey in colour and out of breath, he seems to be struggling to stay upright. I open the door and usher him in, without mentioning his muddy boots.

'Bad hangover?' I say jokingly, though I don't feel like joking, as he does look scarily unwell.

'I think I'm having a heart attack' he replies as he sits down heavily on the chair I quickly pull out for him.

February 7 - Angel

Despite the drizzle I go out early for my walk. Yoga was cancelled this morning, as Maisie is still unwell, so after a few sun salutations, facing a decidedly sunless sky, I head for the track at the far end of the woods. We don't normally go this way, so there are many unfamiliar smells to interest both Lakshmi and Thug. Thug can only be let off his lead once we're safely away from neighbouring farmyards and gardens where chickens roam freely, so we walk along the grassy path and across the field with him straining for his freedom. A black cat streaks across the farm track ahead of us , and Thug whimpers softly. It looks like it's going to be your lucky day, I say out loud, kissing the top of his head as I bend down to undo his leash. The cat is long gone and Thug takes off after Lakshmi, who bears his attentions with stoic patience. I have a feeling it may actually be his lucky day today, the day when he will find his forever home. I stand with my eyes closed for a minute, galvanising this intention. He's such a softy really, though you do have to get to know him quite well before you discover that there is indeed a hug in Thug. The right person is sure to come along for him....when I open my eyes Heather is walking towards us. I am ready with a warm smile, and a word of greeting, as she approaches.

February 8 - Charlotte

'I don't think it's because of the vaccine', Susan says as she unloads several boxes from the boot of her car. She hasn't stopped talking since she arrived, so I've not yet had the chance to ask her what's in them, and I just follow her lead, picking up what turns out to be quite a heavy box, and following her into my house.

'He drinks quite a lot really, and he's actually a bit overweight too…..and at 62, well, it's not that old, but it's not young either'
….

I look at Susan , thinking that she's not that far behind him in years, and then I remember that I'm almost fifty five myself.

'Cat food' she says, suddenly, and there's a momentary silence between us before I realise that she's referring to the boxes.

'It's all the stuff that Delilah doesn't like. She's so fussy now! '. There are tins of expensive cat food, as well as the more usual supermarket brands, plus boxes and boxes of croquettes. It'll save me a fortune, and Roxy is happy to eat anything so there's no chance of it going to waste.

'So I'm on my way to the hospital' she says 'but I'll have a cup of tea first, if you're making one'. I flick the switch on the kettle.

'It's Liptons , I'm afraid . We've run out of English tea bags' I glance in her direction, and she nods.

It's not quite true. Tony has some in the garage, it's just that I can't be bothered to run over there.

'It's not too bad if you mash it well' , I add , as I pass her a cup of piss coloured liquid, and a tea spoon.

February 9 - Frankie

The vinegary liquid seeps through the coffee filter and mixes with the dark stuff already in the jar, turning it almost black. I add some gum arabic to thicken it, then dip the quilled end of a feather into the jar. Oak Gall Ink. I scrawl the word 'Happy' onto a sheet of paper . It's a kind of sepia colour, which darkens deliciously on the page. I hold it up for Ross to see. He breathes out a cloud of marijuana scented smoke.

'Perfect' , he says, and it is. The perfect end to a perfect day. The camper van sits outside in the yard, oozing with potential. A straight swap for the Poseidon sculpture which now adorns the ornamental carp-filled pond of our new friend, Lee. He has been a follower of mine apparently, on social media for a while now, and it seems karma intervened when someone gave him the camper van in lieu of payment for some roofing work. Everyone is happy, and the sculpture has found its ideal home. Poseidon now stands waist deep in the middle of Lee's pond. Giant goldfish swim around his wheelbarrow body as he raises a pitchfork above his rusty colander and flywheel head. His eyes bulge with bolts and washers under his barbed wire crown. He looks absolutely magnificent ! I look at the photos Ross took earlier and smile to myself. The sculpture glows gorgeously in the afternoon sun, and so do my bare legs, white and pimply as I emerge from the pond , having secured it in place.

February 10 - Heather

I'm having a little break from writing, apart from in my treasured black Agenda. Words don't seem to do what I want them to do any more, so I've decided to concentrate on other things for the moment, like getting this little house just how I want it , like planning a vegetable garden maybe…, and like settling in to a new relationship. I look down at the dog stretched out on the rug in front of the wood burner. He seems to feel at home already, and I'm guessing that's it then . Technically he's still on trial, but I don't see him going anywhere, any time soon. Angel was right, he is a sweetie, and I'm pretty sure he's not a cat killer, though I won't risk unleashing him anywhere near houses that may, or may not, be home to somebody's feline favourite. We sit like this for an hour or so, until it's time for his last walk of the day, which we've agreed will be some time in the late afternoon/early evening, before dinner. It suits us both, and when he yawns and stretches, and comes to sit at my feet, with his head on my knees, tail wagging, I get to my feet and pad out to the back porch for my wellies. He nudges me affectionately as I put them on.

'Come on then darling!. You wanna go have some fun? You're a sweet boy aren't you! Let mama put her coat on and we'll be out of here'

Words may not do what I want them to any more, but this kind of gibberish seems to be what Thug understands, so that suits me fine.

February 11 - Susan

'But who takes care of you?' The question surprises me and I don't know how to respond, but Angel sits back and raises her eyebrows, expecting an answer. The truth is that I don't need anyone to take care of me. Paul provides for me, financially. He can afford to, and it alleviates his guilt. My house is comfortable, and I have the company of my pets. There is nothing I need . I tell all this to Angel, who raises her eyebrows even further .

'You run around making sure everyone is ok, and that's beautiful, but occasionally you need someone to care for your needs for a change. Everyone does. You cannot always be the giver. It'll drain you!'

She refers, I think, to the fact that I've been visiting Eric most days at the hospital. Taking him flasks of homemade soup, and fresh fruit. His neighbour, Marie, is going instead of me today, and Angel and Frankie will go together tomorrow. He should be discharged some time next week, so that will be an end to it. The anti blood clotting medicine is doing its job, and he should make a full recovery. The doctor has recorded this 'adverse incident' as a Covid vaccine injury, due to its occurrence, shortly after his booster injection. Angel finishes her coffee, and stands up, rummaging in her handbag. After a few seconds she hands me a postcard. It's a gift voucher for a facial reflexology treatment.

'You can come to me whenever you're ready. It will good for you'.

For some reason tears spring to my eyes at this gesture of kindness. I wipe them away quickly as I thank her, and Delilah rubs up against me reassuringly.

'Cats are such a comfort aren't they!' Angel tickles Delilah on the head before she opens the door to leave.

February 12 - Angel

We eat our croissants in companionable silence on our way back from the hospital. Frankie driving with one hand on the steering wheel of her Beetle, the other one holding half a croissant, that she nibbles at between gear changes, while I'm mindfully chewing the warm flaky pastry, and half-successfully distracting myself from the, frankly miserable, situation.

'It's discrimination' Frankie says suddenly, once she's finished eating and brushes her hands over her jeans. It is. We are banned from visiting the hospital because we aren't vaccinated. It's so ironic that the person we were trying to visit, is in hospital because of a reaction to the vaccination that we refused to have. I do feel though, that things will soon begin to change, and that this madness will come to an end, but at the moment it's hard to stay positive. The woman at the hospital was so demanding, with her little scanning machine

'Pass Sanitaire'! She'd barked loudly, then 'Aller! Aller! ' Ushering us away, disgustedly, when we told her we didn't have them.

'I know what will cheer you up!' Frankie interrupts my thoughts , and moments later, careers off down a long gravel driveway, instead of continuing on to our village. We pull up in front of a stone longère and barn conversion. To one side of this building is a large pond. Almost a lake. I can't help but smile at the impressive figure that looms up out of the water with his trident held high.

'Oh that is a triumph'! I say aloud, once I'm out of the car with my camera in hand.

'Isn't it just!' A male voice behind me makes me jump. I didn't see him approach , and thought it was Frankie behind me, returned from having a wee behind the barn.

'Angel' I point to myself clumsily by way of introduction.

He grins 'Yep! I can see that! ',he replies 'even without your halo!'

February 13 - Charlotte

The weather is so absolutely terrible that I don't mind so much , giving up my afternoon, to visit somebody in hospital who I don't really know that well. I volunteered to drive Susan here, while Tony has a look at her car which has started making a strange noise. Eric is happy to see us, and seems more than happy to look at all of my photos of Roxy , which I show him on my phone. He hopes to be discharged on Tuesday, he says . I notice a look of relief on Susan's face. I feel relieved too. I won't have to make this trip again , even if Susan's car is terminal. Marie will visit tomorrow, and that will be that.

'Did you hear about those poor kids that drowned ?' He asks.

I don't watch the news . My days are depressing enough without that, but Susan does, and she launches into a long story of how it was somebody she knows, that called the pompiers. Apparently their car skidded on black ice in the early hours of Friday morning, and ended up upside down in the canal.

'What a dreadful thing to happen' I say, shuddering at the thought of it.

'Those poor parents' Susan adds, and we are all then quiet for a moment. Neither Susan, nor I, have any children, and I know that for Susan it's definitely too late now. For me too, I suppose, and for a moment I wonder about what might have been. I think maybe I'd have made a good mother, Susan too, possibly . I watch her gather up the empty vacuum flask, and the Tupperware boxes that held sandwiches and homemade cookies . She looks at me, as we walk out along the corridor.

'Do your coat up! ' she says 'it's getting cold out there'.

February 14 - Frankie

'Careful you don't trip over all of those valentine cards'! Maisie says, as Angel and I arrive at the same time , and wipe our feet on the empty doormat.

'Seriously though, did you read it?' Angel continues the conversation we started on our way across the car park, and I've never seen her so incensed.

'She literally bangs on and on about being grateful for being able to visit a friend in need when others could not, and then preaches about how we should all care for, and protect each other, by getting ourselves vaccinated.'

'Lay in butterfly' Maisie calls out, and all six of us follow her lead, and begin to breathe deeply.

'Sorry Maisie, it's just that I cannot stand to be called selfish, and uncaring, when that's not at all what this is about. Anything else I can cope with' Angel takes a deep breath, and I breathe a sigh of relief.

'Try to forgive' Maisie answers 'Remember we are all love'.

All is quiet then, and I focus on the word 'love', as it is Valentine's Day after all, and even though Ross and I never bother with cards and all of that commercial rubbish, it is nice to think of the whole world celebrating love, instead of worrying about war and Covid. It gives me an idea for the huge piece of driftwood that Susan has given me, and for the rest of the yoga session I am lost in my thoughts, creating in my head, a sculpture worthy of such a luscious lump.

'So did anyone get a card this morning?' Maisie asks, after we've ended the session with some alternate nostril breathing. I shake my head, and look around at the others all doing the same. All except for Angel that is, who is smiling mysteriously.

February 15 - Heather

I have a guilty secret. I'm not proud of it , but I've begun to actually look forward to reading Charlotte's posts. It has been blatantly obvious to me since I first started following her on Facebook, that she is no writer. However, her overly wordy, heavily opinionated and Ill informed bursts of prose, which she classes as 'blogs', make for strangely compelling daily reading. The lack of grammar, and the questionable spelling, show that she never bothers to proof read her articles before posting them, and she must be a total stranger to the spell checker. Despite this, there is something entertaining about what she writes, though this is obviously not her intention, and I'm sure she'd be mortified if she knew that I , and probably others are viewing her efforts in this way. What is equally interesting is that sometimes she deletes her posts the following morning, as if she's suddenly changed her mind about whether or not it was worthy of posting. I scroll back to her post of Sunday evening, and find that it's been removed. I wonder if that's because of Angel's comment, if she decided the tone of the piece was a little too ensconced in the moral high ground, or if she merely discovered that she'd misspelled vaccination, inconsiderate and Djokovic. Wow! I'm being pedantic now, I realise, Just because I'm not actually writing anything myself at the moment. I rarely post anything on Facebook, but I wonder if now is a good time to start. It might rekindle my spark, and get my creative juices flowing. With this in mind I snap a pic of Thug lying on his back on the sofa, with his back legs splayed. I title it 'Thug, lying in Butterfly'

February 16 - Susan

For a moment or two I just sit and watch Frankie stretching and pulling at her lump of clay, transforming it effortlessly into the eight legged creature which will eventually become an octopus. It was kind of her to invite me along to her pottery class, and rather unexpected! When I called in on her this morning with a car boot full of old tools, which were part of the clutter that's taking up space in the barn, the last thing I expected was that I'd end up spending the afternoon here. I'd driven over to her place, having seen on Facebook a photo of her Poseidon sculpture, with all the scrap metal I could cram in the car, thinking she might be able to make use of it. I'd hoped for coffee, ended up staying for lunch, and when I mentioned that I'd done a few pottery classes, years ago. She persuaded me to join her here. Lesley tells me to start with something easy, just to get a feel again for the clay. I pretend I'm in the kitchen, and roll my ball of clay out flat, before using cookie cutters to cut out shapes that will eventually form a mobile. Two hours flies by, and I have enough star , sun and moon shapes on my board for at least one hangy thing, plus a plaque with a bumblebee on , and the words 'bee happy'. It's been one of my happiest afternoons in a long time, and I find myself asking Lesley if she has space for me next week.

'I'm hooked' I tell Frankie when we get back in her Beetle. 'It was so kind of you to treat me. Thank you for that!'

It's what I've been missing I think - spending time in the company of other women, doing something creative. I've been in a rut, but now I think I see a way out.

February 17 - Angel

It's a glorious morning. I forego the hot water with lemon, that I usually take first thing, and opt for coffee instead, which I take outside on the sunny terrace. Lakshmi stays close to my side, unsure of this change in her routine. Her wet feet have left footprints across the polished wood floor. She must have been out for a bathroom break then. I thought I heard the door open earlier, when I was still only half awake, and vaguely aware of my surroundings. She watches me closely as I sip the hot liquid.

'Yes, we'll go home soon' I say, reassuringly. Reiki will need feeding, and I have a client at eleven. Frankie's 'Poseidon ' reflects the sunlight beautifully across the pond, and there are snowdrops on the bank behind it . I snap a random photo, and am pleased with the result. Lee's Cherokee jeep pulls up outside and he jumps out waving a brown paper bag.

'Croissants for my lady' he calls out theatrically.

Lady! I'm hardly that! I point this out to him. All the things we did last night, and the night before that, flash through my mind. Not very ladylike at all. I balance my coffee cup on the wall as he comes up behind me, kissing me on the neck, bunching my hair up in one hand as he does so. I reach back to grab his backside, and he guides my hand to his groin instead.

'Have you got time to be rather unladylike again, before you go home?' He asks.

Insatiable! How long can this last?

February 18 - Charlotte

I thought the party might be cancelled because of storm 'Eunice', but no. I click on Messenger and see that Vanessa's latest message to the group 'party peeps' , simply states that tonight's party will storm ahead, regardless of the weather. I look outside at the raindrops bouncing off my car bonnet , and the puddles forming on the driveway, and I really don't want to go. I check messenger again to see who has been included in the group invitation. A few names I don't recognise, but mostly it's the usual crowd of locals, French and English. Heather's name isn't there . That's a shame. But neither are Frankie or Angel's, so that's ok. I don't fancy running into either of them after I heard from Susan,that Angel wasn't happy about my Facebook blog about the importance of Covid vaccinations. Oh well. I'm about to put my phone down when I notice a message from Susan that pops up on the same thread.

'Happy Birthday Vanessa. Looking forward to seeing you later. What can I bring?'

Shit! It's actually her birthday. I'll have to take her a present. I look over at the dresser, where my latest cosmetics are bagged up, and labelled 'for your eyes only' . They each contain a mascara and three eye pencils , but I have to admit to myself that they look a bit cheap, and I'm not sure my stuff is right for Vanessa, who spends a fortune on Clarins, and regularly goes for spa treatments, but it'll have to do. I open the cupboard under the stairs distractedly, looking for my cards and wrapping paper, and I spot the little wooden sailing boats that I made for the craft fair almost two years ago. I pick one out. It looks ok. It's body is made from recycled wood, part of an old shed that fell down shortly after we moved here. I drilled a hole in it for its bamboo mast , and the sail is an old cotton handkerchief from a pack that Tony was given one Christmas. I smooth it out and take it over to the table where Roxy helps me to wrap it up.

'Ok we're ready to rock and roll! '

February 19 - Frankie

My hands are blistered from all the chiselling, but when I stand back to admire my own work, Ross silently takes hold of my left one and gives it a squeeze. It really is a massive stump of well worn driftwood. Sea smoothed over several years, so that no rough edges remain. A torso of aged tree trunk, which divides in two , where the branches would have been . It is in this natural gap that I have carved out the shape of a broken heart , with the break following organically the natural break in the wood, and into this heart, at either side of split, I've drilled holes and threaded leather laces through them, so that it appears to be stitched together. I am satisfied with the end result . It is what I imagined.

'You've done an amazing job with that' Ross says.

But it's the sea that has done most of the work, and my upcoming exhibition, which is really an homage to the power of the sea, will be almost complete with this new addition. Ross is taking the van out for a test drive , now that he's finished tinkering with the engine. When he gets back we're going to park it in the hangar, in my outside workspace so that I can begin painting it. I look over at the boxes that will all need moving before I can start work. The blisters on my hands tell me I should put gloves on first, so I go back into my atelier to begin the hunt for a suitable pair. Missy has a penchant for gloves, and will often carry them off, and hide them in unexpected places. I pull out a large box from under my workbench, and am immediately distracted. It contains, amongst other things, the three driftwood sailing boats that I made for an exhibition just over two years ago . The wood is beautifully smooth, and I fondly remember the time I spent whittling down twig like pieces to make the masts , and then attaching antique lace handkerchiefs as sails. It's been a while since I last looked at them and I'm momentarily surprised somehow by their beauty, then I remember the pressing need for gloves, and carry on with my search.

February 20 - Heather

Frankie's sculpture is beautiful. I give it a heart, and comment 'what a triumph! That truly is a piece of fine art!' There are fifty seven 'likes' on it already, and it was only posted an hour ago. I read the comments and they are all spectacularly positive, then I take the banana bread out of my oven. It smells heavenly, but it's appearance is sub standard to say the least. Not a work of art then! However I'm not discouraged from taking it over to Susan so that we can have a slice with our coffee. I am trying to socialise Thug. I have read on the internet that it is a good idea to introduce your puppy to as many other dogs as possible (and other animals, even humans) , so that they will be able to cope with social situations. This should make our everyday life, calmer and simpler. Susan's little terrier, Rhea, is a dear little thing, though she can be a bit excitable around other dogs. It will be good for both of them. It's a two minute drive to Susan's house. Normally I walk across the fields but the car is another thing Thug has to get used to. It takes a while to put his harness on, and strap him into the front passenger seat, but soon we're on our way, and his nose is pressed hard against the window, fogging it up with his incessant panting. As I'm turning into Susan's lane, I stop and wind the window down to greet the familiar figures, that are walking towards me. Angel with Lakshmi, on their way home from a leisurely ramble.

'You've caught me doing the walk of shame!' she says, as she continues onwards, after the usual greetings. I drive on, wondering what she could possibly mean.

February 21 - Susan

49

It's a scrubby little oak tree. Not very thick, with a weird, irregular shape, that lies across the path, just in front of my house, having fallen down in last nights storm, barely missing my car. I've cut all the twiggy bits off of it, and will have a bonfire when we next get a calm day. The main trunk though, needs a chainsaw. I can't ask Eric, who is still a bit fragile from his ordeal. There's Didier of course, but I don't really want to bother him unless I have to. The chainsaw in the barn is quite easy to use. I have tried it before on some small branches and I did ok. It's an electric one, so I plug in an extension lead, and we're good to go. I feel quite empowered somehow, as I opt to do this myself instead of asking a man.

'I've got this'. I say to myself as I begin sawing the tree into manageable sections. It's surprisingly easy. The chainsaw cuts through the wood like a wire through clay, My mind turns to the pottery studio at the slightest provocation now. I've been twice already, and will go again tomorrow. I'm making some garden gnomes at the moment, having got the idea from 'The great pottery Throwdown' that I've been watching on catch -up. It's so therapeutic! Frankie doesn't go every week, as it's an hour's drive away and she can't always spare the time, so Lesley will fit me into classes with other people. Tomorrow I think there will be a couple of younger students in with me, so that could be fun. I'm looking forward to continuing the gnome project, and it's that, that I'm thinking about when it happens. I put the chainsaw down , having released the trigger, so that it stops, except that it doesn't stop, not immediately, and as I step forward to start picking up the logs, it catches the toe of my old Converse trainer, and cuts straight through it.

February 22 - Angel

It feels good to wake up in my own bed alone, and as I slowly become fully conscious of the dawning day, I realise that it's nine thirty already, and I really should get up to let Lakshmi out for a wee. It's a good job she has a strong bladder. It's then that I remember that Rhea is also downstairs. Yesterday evening, after I got the frantic call from Susan , asking if I could possibly pick her up a bit later, from the Urgences, I went to her house , packed away the chainsaw, which had been abandoned in the driveway, still plugged in!, collected Rhea, then drove to the hospital. Poor Susan. It's just one toe, but it's a nasty wound, and she won't be able to walk very well for a few days, so I brought Rhea here, walked her with Lakshmi, and kept her overnight. I shuffle downstairs and open the door for the two dogs, while I fumble with my phone. There is a meditation app which I've started to use, and it will do me good, after yesterday's hectic events. The dogs are busy investigating the garden, sniffing for evidence of any nightly visitors . I go back in for a blanket and a cushion, anticipating a few peaceful moments on the garden swing, concentrating on the breath, but the ping of messenger, three times in as many seconds proves irresistible .

Frankie 'coffee on if you fancy it?'

Susan 'Had an ok night. When do you want to bring Rhea back?'

And finally Lee 'This is officially what's known as a booty call . I miss your sweet ass!'

I reply to Frankie first 'see you in ten!'. I'll drop Rhea off on the way over, and then go to Lee for lunch. So much for peaceful meditation!

February 23 - Charlotte

If money were no object then I would enjoy food shopping. As it is though, I unload the boot of my car and I feel irritated. There is so little to show for the money I've spent. I miss the bargains of the U.K. supermarkets. The meal deals, the buy one get one free offers, and the yellow stickered, short date, cut price, luxury items that I wouldn't normally buy if they weren't so greatly reduced. Tony walks over , whistling, ready to help me carry the bags into the house.

'Those pizzas look nice' he says, in a tone which tells me that he recognises my mood, and is determined to lift it somehow. He takes the heaviest bag, the one with all the cleaning products in it, and the wine box , leaving me with the frozen food and a huge pack of loo rolls.

'At least we are prepared if there's another lockdown!' I can hear the smile in his voice as he says this, and I slap the bags down on the kitchen table.

'Hardly!' I answer 'we'd soon run out of food!'

He grins at me as I go to switch the kettle on 'but our bums would be clean!'

I open the cupboards to start putting things away, and Tony notices the huge stash of cat food.

'Well, she won't starve will she!' He picks Roxy up, and she starts purring loudly.

There really is a lot there, and I won't need to buy cat food for a few weeks at least. It was so kind of Susan, and thinking about it, I really should have asked her if there was anything she needed while I was out shopping, since she cannot drive herself at the moment. Oh well, perhaps I'll call her later to see if there's anything I can do for her.

February 24 - Frankie

I wake to the news that Russia has invaded Ukraine. Ross sits at the table, doodling pictures of tanks on the back of an envelope. He has already rolled himself a joint. I know this mood. It will take a few hours for him to process this information, and he won't speak until he's done that and found some peace within himself. I pull on boots, and go out to the barn where Boris has the whole of the top floor. She is on her usual branch, and turns her head to look at me with her one remaining eye. I pull my sleeve down over my hand, and encourage her to hop on. It takes her a few moments to consider the wisdom of this action before she succumbs to my invitation. Together we walk back to the kitchen where Ross has a frozen chick thawing for her breakfast. She can keep him company while I feed and care for the other animals. In my atelier I feed Missy and Harper some croquettes which I pour into a tray on my workbench, and call out to Skunky and Pasha, who must be out hunting . Artie watches closely, hoping for some of the meaty treats to fall on the floor. I throw one out of the window for him to hunt for, and then we go to the goats and the pony. The chickens I'll do later , when they've all exited the henhouse, having laid their eggs. We head back to the kitchen, stopping on the way, to pour the rest of the croquettes into the tube feeder that caters for all of the wild cats that reside here (there are currently at least five) . Artie accompanies me every step of the way, looking lovingly up at me with an expression of concern on his face. When we arrive back in the house, Ross has the radio on, and he and Boris have moved to a chair by the wood burner. They are listening grimly to a discussion about Putin and the lead up to this war. Artie nudges me, consolingly, and Boris slowly shakes her head from side to side as Ross rhythmically strokes her head.

'Why can't humans be more like animals, eh Boris?' , he asks her quietly. Why indeed.

February 25 - Heather

No two days are the same here, and after a rather raucous yoga class (I have never laughed so much before in downward facing dog) , I dash home to change, throw a few doggy treats at Thug, and I'm outside Susan's house before ten am, ready to drive her to the art shop in the next town . She hobbles out to the car with a smile on her face and her feet in her modified crocs. We decided upon this plan only yesterday, when I walked Rhea and Thug together, and then got the car stuck on the muddy bank outside of Susan's house. With no one to help me but Susan , with her bad foot, and Eric , who is being careful because of his recent scare , we got the car free, by placing a sheet of plywood under the wheel. We then returned to the kitchen to find it full of smoke , and Susan's cake burned to a cinder in the centre of the oven. The plan for today is for some light shopping in the art shop, and maybe a brocante, followed by a sandwich in the car (I'm not allowed into restaurants without a pass sanitaire), then a cheeky trip to the depot vente store on the way home. All in all a rather easy, relaxed , kind of day. What could possibly go wrong? Susan flops herself down onto the passenger seat, and shuts the door firmly. An overwhelming stench suddenly overcomes us, and we stare at her foot in horror. Her bandaged toes, peeping out from the cutaway croc, are slicked with an ominous coating of chocolatey brown.

'Oh no! The dreaded Dog poo shoe! '

February 26 - Susan

Without the bandage I can walk a bit more comfortably, and the sun is out, so fresh air is pouring in through my open windows, ridding the kitchen of that last whiff of smoke , and burnt oven. Maybe things are going my way at last! Sitting at the kitchen table with a huge lump of clay, and the sculpting tools that I treated myself to yesterday, I am inspired to create a chicken, similar to one I have on the kitchen wall in the form of a painting by a local artist. Lesley has agreed, for a fee, to fire anything that I make at home if it's not too big for her kiln, so I begin the chicken by making two thumb pots and joining them together for the body, then measuring them to make sure that the finished piece will fit. Eric arrives just as I've done this, having walked across the fields for the first time since he was discharged from hospital.

'What is it? An egg? ' he says, studying the clay object lying there on a sheet of newspaper, next to Delilah who begins rubbing herself contentedly on Eric's sleeve. I patiently explain to him that this is only the start of the creative process, and that this will in the end, be a chicken similar to the one in the painting. I point to the wall by the larder, where the painting hangs, and he slowly nods, his eyes twinkling with the sense of humour, that he has been sadly lacking in the last few weeks.

'At least it answers the age old question' . He grins, taking the mug I pass him, and sitting down at the table.

'What do you mean?' I ask, humouring him, as I pick up the clay and pull off a lump that will form the head.

'What came first! '. He raises his eyebrows, waiting for me to see the joke. I manage to raise a weak smile, but even Delilah yawns and turns away to begin licking her backside.

February 27 - Angel

'I'm sorry, please forgive me, but I'm so in need, we are so in need of peace in this world'. I hold a rose quartz crystal in my hand, and sit on a stump in the middle of a stand of trees, alongside the lane that leads to Lee's house. Lakshmi explores the undergrowth around me.

'I love this planet. Thank you for listening '. I repeat this mantra several times in full, directing my words at the trees, the earth, and the sky, focussing my energy on the sun, the daffodils that are on the point of blooming for the first time this year, and even the cows in the field beyond. The plight of the Ukrainians is on my mind , and it's so hard to concentrate on positivity and . not to let bad thoughts against Putin cloud my mind. When I feel I have achieved this I shorten the mantra

'I'm sorry . Please forgive me. I love you. Thank you.' The Ho Opono Pono prayer. I keep this up for at least ten minutes. My eyes firmly closed. When I open them everything looks blurry, and Lakshmi is nowhere in sight. I stand slowly and do a few sun salutations before I call her. She appears from nowhere and drops a stick in front of me, expectantly . I throw it a few times for her as we head back to Lee's, there being no sign of any cars or tractors on this quiet Sunday morning, so the road is safe. It's the perfect start to the day, as far as Lakshmi is concerned. She stops for a quick drink, from the pond on the way in, then flops down in a sunny spot by the kitchen table, panting and watching Lee as he breaks off one corner of a croissant he's eating, and throws it in her general direction.

'Dogs are nicer than humans really, aren't they?' He muses. He's right . 'Present company excepted!' He adds.

February 28 - Charlotte

I try to hide my disappointment with a smile. Susan looks so pleased with herself. When she said that she had a little present for me, and would I like to call in for a coffee on my way to town, I felt a tiny bit excited. Now that I'm here though, having unwrapped the rather intriguingly shaped package that she presented me with as soon as I arrived, I'm finding it hard to be enthusiastic. It's a cats food dish . We already have three of these at home, but this one is hand made .

' I actually threw it myself, on the wheel!'

I turn it over a few times. It's a kind of teal blue colour , and shiny, with ROXY imprinted on the outside and what must be a cats paw print on it's base.

'It's lovely, well done'. I put it down on the table next to what appears to be a clay chicken. I think Susan may be getting a bit carried away with all this pottery stuff. 'It's great to be doing something creative' she keeps saying . I sit down with my coffee and get a closer look at the chicken. It's actually quite good, and I can't help but feel inspired.

'I've always wanted to go to that pottery class!' I say, hoping for a positive response , but she doesn't seem to hear, and instead it's Lesley this…..Lesley that…and how she cannot wait to turn up to each class and discover how something has turned out once it's out of the kiln. Delilah jumps up onto the table , and is presented with a similar cat dish , with DELILAH imprinted on its side. A tin of Sheba gets emptied into it.

'You shouldn't let her on the table!' I can't help saying. I'd never let Roxy do that, but maybe it doesn't matter here in this cluttered kitchen, with its clay smeared table.

'Maybe you could come with me one day then' she says suddenly. How kind of her to offer!

March 1 - Frankie

It's so very satisfying to paint. This old wooden board, which I've sanded smooth. It used to be a menu board, outside of an abandoned beach cafe/shack type building. I took it from the debris, long after the sea had done its best to reduce everything there to strips of torn fabric and splintered wood, threaded through with rusted spikes and poles from the old sunshades. The sunflower that I'm painting on it is for Ukraine . I will auction it to raise funds to give to one of the many charities which have sprung up overnight in response to the crisis. This at least is something I can do, though it's not much, in the grand scheme of things . I photograph it as soon as it's finished. The paint is barely dry , but it does look good propped against the camper van with the pony looking over the fence behind it, and Ross standing by with Boris perched on his hand . Walking back to the house, I decide to post it right away. I add it to my page with the simple heading. 'For Auction, For Ukraine' , and let it play out organically. Before I close Facebook though, I observe a notification that Angela Court has changed her status to 'in a relationship' . Wow! That was quick! Things are moving fast for Angel, with Lee . Im happy for her, and just a little bit worried too. I send her a little supportive message, then check back to see if there's any response yet, to my Sunflower Auction post. Facebook is such a time waster, and I can't help but read Charlotte Singer's post about acceptable standards of housekeeping! just 'Why?' I know Angel will be laughing about it too. There is only one comment so far on my own post, and it's Angel herself. 'I will give you one hundred' she says. That's an excellent start .

2 - Heather

'How bloody dare you!' The message says, and I almost spit my lemon water out all over the table. I'm still trying to follow Frankie and Angel's example of starting the day in a healthy way. I laugh out loud as the message is followed by a GIF of a red monster jumping up and down in rage. It's from Angel, and she's referring to the fact that last night I outbid her latest two hundred euro offering for Frankie's sunflower. It's mine at the moment, for a maximum of two hundred and sixty. By the end of today it will probably go higher than that, and therefore be more than I can afford. Angel and Frankie have one of those enviable friendships where it's all banter on the surface , with a deep love beneath. It's hard to believe that they haven't known each other that long . Angel has only been here about a year and a half, and before I arrived, she was the newbie. I look out of the window at the mist and drizzle. It's hard not to think of the word 'mizzle' , and I cringe inwardly. If Angel can move over here, form an amazing friendship, build up a clientele for her reflexology and reiki skills , and find herself a lover, in that short space of time, then it shouldn't really be beyond me to make some kind of a success of this new life I've chosen, and anyway I think, brightening, I've already got myself a dog!

3 - Susan

I peel the plaster off and try flexing my toes. It's still very painful, and a bit red and swollen on either side of the jagged cut which runs from the base of my little toe, across the top of my foot for a couple of inches . With a fresh plaster , and a thick sock though, I can put my boots on, and walk fairly normally. I can even drive.

'Ok, so we're good to go' I say to Rhea, who is staring up at me, and Delilah, who is licking her arse on the kitchen table. I have six sleeping bags, that I bought years ago, when Paul and I brought a team of builders over with us to work on the roof, and do the necessary plaster boarding and plumbing , so that we could move in. They slept on camp beds, dormitory style in the grenier, while Paul and I stayed in a Chambre d'hôte nearby. I roll each freshly washed sleeping bag and stuff it into a bin bag, then along with the two child seats which I've just finished scrubbing (not sure where they came from), and a few boxes of food and hygiene products, that I bought yesterday, I cram them into the boot of my little Peugeot. Boxes on the back seat contain bottled water, crisps and digestive biscuits, plus colouring books and crayons etc....(I'm thinking this might be useful for the journey over, for at least one family). There is just about room for Rhea, who jumps willingly onto the front seat. I feel like I'm doing my bit, but that maybe it's not enough, and again I toy with the scary idea of driving to Poland myself. I could bring back a couple of Ukrainien women, or perhaps one with children. As soon as I put my foot on the pedal though I realise how impossible this idea is , and I wince with pain. I'll make it to the drop-off point, but I probably couldn't go much further.

March 4 - Angel,

As I lie in butterfly a million things run through my head. The Pass Sanitaire will be lifted on March fourteenth . That is such good news, and I cannot wait to go to a restaurant for an evening with friends, in a relaxed atmosphere, or to watch film at the cinema, or even just to a bar for a drink or two. When we change to bridge position I think about Lee , and what I might cook for him this weekend. It's a novelty thing, having someone to cook for, but I don't expect it to become a habit. With each sun salutation I consider the situation between Russia and Ukraine. I send an intention every night now, lighting a candle for peace, but I wonder if there's something I could actually do on a more practical level.....box up some supplies? ......drive to Poland to bring back some refugees? The yoga class passes quickly and before I've had the chance to answer my own question Maisie announces that it's time for relaxation. I have missed out on the usual banter through my daydreaming habit , but now the conversation has begun to filter through, and it seems that the discussion is all about which particular vegetable shape we each resemble. So far we have a cucumber and an upside down butternut squash. In relaxation I can't decide on what to cook tonight, or whether or not I should take in a refugee or two, or even which restaurant I might sample next, now that I'm free to do so, but I do voice my conclusion, that I am in fact a Comice Pear!

March 5 - Charlotte

'Congratulations! ' I comment on Frankie's post. I almost never like, or comment on anything that she puts on Facebook, but I don't want to appear jealous, or give the impression that I'm not supportive of Ukraine's plight , so I grit my teeth and consider adding a little heart emoji to my comment, but can't bring myself to do it somehow, so that solitary word goes out there, amongst a plethora of other, more sincere comments of praise and celebration. Frankie's sunflower painting has attracted a bid of one thousand euros. This will be given to the local group of 'Brittany Buddies ' , who have teamed up to offer transport and accommodation to as many refugees as they can. It will be so welcome I'm sure, to pay for fuel and food. I scroll down Frankie's page to look at her other recent posts. All of them irritate me to some degree or other, but none more so than one from a couple of days ago…A selfie of her and Angel , their feet up on a table, both of them wearing Doc Marten's, and two flutes of champagne between them . 'The end of the Vaccine Pass! ' is the simple heading, with lots of smileys and coloured hearts. There are some people for whom everything always seems to go their way , and Frankie is definitely one of them!

March 6 - Frankie

There's no such thing as a bad day at the beach. Ross relieves me of the lumpen piece of driftwood that I'm struggling with. It's not that big, but it's soaked in seawater so it weighs heavy. We take turns to carry it, on our way back to the car. My pockets are full of sea glass and I have a nice haul of razor shells , which I plan to make a kind of screen with. The sun is low as we head back up the beach, and it's hard to pick out Artie from other random dogs that he's found to play with, as they run circles in the edge of the surf. When Ross puts the driftwood down I take a photo of it with the silver line of the horizon in the background, and in the mid ground an Artie silhouette, airborne as he jumps for a stick. It's one perfect moment in a very uncertain world , where everywhere the whisper of war permeates our conversations , and even those who don't normally watch the news, are opinionatedly discussing the latest updates. My upcoming exhibition seems such a frivolous thing to be thinking of at a time like this , but I can't seem to help it. I pick up the salty lump of log for the last leg of the walk to the car, and see in my head, the metal wheel rim of an old cartwheel that's currently in my atelier, threaded like a loom with fishing line , and hung with razor shells, that shimmer in the breeze. I just know that it's going to look awesome, with all the other pieces I've created.

March 7 - Heather

Poor Thug. He's been out in the garden for a wee, but must wait until Angel arrives with Lakshmi for his walk. I light the gas stove to heat the chicken soup that Charlotte so kindly brought to me .

'It's only a cold' I find myself saying for the umpteenth time. I had to message Maisie first thing this morning to cancel yoga, and since then I've received so much support from all of my new friends that I'm sure they must think that I'm seriously ill. What began as a scratchy throat yesterday morning, has progressed to a runny nose, aching head, and general feeling of malaise today.

'Are you sure it's not Covid? ' Charlotte demanded, from across the driveway, having abandoned Susan's saucepan of soup on the doorstep. 'Because I wouldn't wish that on anybody'

Well, I wouldn't wish this on anybody either, but it's a cold like any other cold, and like every other cold I've ever had, it makes me feel like shit. I pour some of the soup into a mug, and head for the sofa, where I have a box of tissues, a bottle of water, and Netflix on my laptop. Thug joins me, and puts his head on my lap. The love and comfort I get from him , and my friends who have all shown such concern, makes me feel very blessed. I will soon be well I'm sure, and hopefully I will then have a chance to return this kindness, but for now I will continue with my binge watching session , of old tv dramas and sit coms . Who knows what inspiration I may glean from this.

March 8 - Susan

I feel at home now in the pottery studio. The flapjacks I made are on the table for all to share, on the plate I made when I first came here. My chicken is in the kiln, and a new lump of clay is in front of me. I begin rolling it out immediately, with the aim this time of making a butter dish. Opposite me Frankie sits, making waves. Literally waves, out of clay coils which she rolls and shapes effortlessly.

'You've been coming here a while' I say, watching her.

She tells me of how she's been dabbling with pottery since she was a child, from clay collected from the beach, and fired in a home made brick kiln in the garden. I didn't know that you could collect clay from the beach, and I think I actually prefer to simply buy it. She smiles warmly when I tell her this , not judging me. Her expression soon changes though as a spray of orange glaze hits her in the face. Madeleine, next to me, is enthusiastically adding spots of yellow and orange to her vase. It really is an impressive piece, and I'm a bit surprised that Lesley could fit it in the kiln. I look down at my coffee . Swirls of yellow now sit artistically on top of the cream. Lesley hastily covers the flapjacks with a tea towel.

'Hey! Jackson Pollack over there! ' Frankie shouts, wiping her face on her sleeve, but Madeleine takes no notice. It's like that here in the studio, when you're in the zone, you're in the zone

March 9 - Angel

The bucket of flowers becomes gradually emptier, as I place a little bouquet on Heather's doorstep, having dropped one already at Maisie's, one at Susan's, and one at Marie's. I'm enjoying myself, imagining their reactions when they each find the mystery flowers. They were a bargain I couldn't resist this morning, and I'm hoping they will bring joy to many. I park my car in a field gateway, a few yards in front of Charlotte's house, and run the short distance to her driveway before tiptoeing up to the front door. I'm just in the process of tucking the little bouquet of tulips into the boot scraper when the door swings open, and Charlotte jumps backwards in surprise, spilling tea on the doormat, and almost choking on her cigarette.

'Surprise! ' I yell, after we've both stared at each other in horror for almost half a minute. I didn't want to get caught, with three flower stops still to make, but I accept her offer of tea, as I'm sure it would be rude not to, and we sit on her doorstep in the sunshine, making polite conversation. I've never actually been here before, and it is nice to see Roxy again, settled in her new home, though I've seen a thousand Facebook photos of her. Charlotte's tales of woe about their leaky roof and lack of central heating are a challenge for my powers of concentration though, and I find myself looking distractedly around the garden. In the centre of the lawn a coloured glass screen catches my eye. It's made from bottles, threaded end to end, and held in an s-shaped metal frame. The sunlight filters through it onto the white pebble bed that it stands on.

'That's amazing ! Did Frankie make it ? ' I blurt out, unthinkingly. Charlotte merely nods, and lights another cigarette.

March 10 - Charlotte

Angel's tulips inspire me to write about random acts of kindness, so after my first coffee and cigarette of the day , I snap a quick photo of them in the vase by the window, and open up Facebook, only to be greeted by a page full of flower photos! Heather's, with the title 'A mystery admirer?', below that, a photo from Susan , of tulips in a rather obviously homemade vase. I knew she'd received some because she couldn't wait to message me as soon as she'd found them on her doorstep. I had to tell her who they were from , but she titles her post 'lovely flowers from a mysteriously lovely friend '. Sweet. Then Marie, who I don't really know, but I see her on here because she's friends with some of my friends, posts a pic with the title 'Une mystère!!!!' I'm about to start my blog anyway, when I catch sight of Frankie's post further down. Her photo is of her doorstep, the bouquet artfully placed by her plum coloured front door , with one of her cats tentatively sniffing the blooms. The title of her post , predictably, 'A random act of kindness' . Well that's that then . I decide to post my photo anyway, and call it 'The joys of spring' instead. It's easy to write about flowers, as there are so many words that describe their beauty. I'm not feeling it though, and after several attempts, I change my mind , put a couple of bright lipsticks, fully opened, in front of the tulips , take another photo , and title it 'The beauty of Spring' . I may as well take the opportunity to try and sell something at the same time!

March 11 - Frankie

The wet and windy weather drives me indoors early, and I take the opportunity to design some new business cards, and get them ordered in plenty of time for the exhibition. The electricity goes off thirty seconds after I place the order, which has grown, to include flyers and posters. 'Go big or go home', Ross said, when I asked his opinion on whether or not they would be a worthwhile investment. He is a man of few words, and we sit in companionable silence with a selection of animals and a candle or two , until the whistle of the emergency kettle, which we've placed on the wood burning stove, pierces the atmosphere. Ross gets up to make two mugs of tea, while I cut bread into wedges that we can toast on the fire , in the absence of power to our electric oven and hob. A fork, attached to an unravelled wire coat hanger makes an excellent toasting fork, and I do the honours while Ross tunes his guitar in readiness for an evening's entertainment without tv or internet. We are nothing if not resourceful.

'This may, or may not be the most practical thing I ever made', I hold up the toasting fork in anticipation of Ross' approval. I've bent the wire at the end into a zigzaggy kind of shape to hold the bread, and threaded wine corks onto the other end for a handle. Ross smiles but says nothing.

'Ok so maybe it's not quite up to standard but it'll do the job I think! ' I say, a little miffed that he seems so unimpressed by my efforts.

He takes it from me anyway, and passes me the guitar in return. While he toasts, and butters the bread , I strum a few chords, and make up a song about a sad perfectionist. He raises an eyebrow as he passes me a plate.

'Burnt enough for you?' He asks.

'It's perfect!'

March 12 - Heather

Thug and I decide to walk through the woods, taking advantage of the early spring sunshine. So many daffodils! A host? I'm not sure how many would actually constitute a host of golden daffodils, but there are a lot here in amongst the trees, so I pick a few of the little ones, and make a posy with some grape hyacinths and primroses, then continue my walk home via Susan's house with my offering. My cold has gone now, leaving me with just the remains of an irritating cough, but when Susan comes to the door, she takes a swift step backwards, then offers me coffee in the garden, where we sit at opposite ends of the table.

'Are you sure it wasn't Covid?' She asks me for the second time in ten minutes

I reassure her again that it was just a little cold. It never occurred to me to take a test, so I don't actually know for certain, but as I'm over it now anyway, and as I was never very ill in the first place , it seems to me to be completely irrelevant. Even so, it's nice to sit outside, and Thug enjoys sniffing around the garden while Susan puts the flowers in a little pot she made .

'You must be psychic!' , She says, and explains that she only just picked up the little vase from the pottery studio yesterday. I admire it's simple robins egg blue glaze.

'You're getting quite professional!'

She blushes. 'No no, it's just a little hobby'.

She could easily sell her creations though, and I'm about to suggest it when I remember that she doesn't need the money. A dark cloud scuds across my mind then. She may not need to make money, but I do! I resolve to spend the rest of the day writing.

March 13 - Susan

I'm out of clay, and don't want to bother Lesley on a Sunday, so it's back to barn clearing for me. I slide open the big metal door and immediately feel a bit despondent. There's still so much stuff in here. Four ride-on mowers, each in a dubious condition, take up a huge amount of space in the middle, and there's an old trailer which was one of Paul's first purchases, a mini-digger, and various other tools for which I don't know the name or the purpose. I need help I realise. I don't need to keep any of this stuff as the gardener brings his own tools. I stare at the chainsaw by my feet, and notice the fabric from my Converse trainers, still caught in its teeth. That decides me. I open the other door, then stand back with my phone turned sideways so that I can get everything in one photograph. On 'All sorts for sale and wanted' I offer the whole lot , free of charge to anyone who can arrive and clear it all this afternoon, with the only condition being that they must take it all. I count twenty five seconds before the first ping of messenger arrives.

'Please send your exact location' it says ' I can be with you in around half an hour'

I'm not sure why I didn't think of this before. Maybe it's because I had no pressing reason to get on with the clearance, just a vague idea of creating an outdoor space for entertaining, that would allow for social distancing. Now though, I have other plans. With a bit of work this old shack would make a brilliant pottery studio. All Frankie's idea of course.

March 14 - Angel

The Chinese restaurant is one of the only ones open on a Monday evening, so it's there that we arrange to meet for our celebration. The health pass has been lifted. We can eat in restaurants again, and we don't need to wear masks in shops either. The occasion calls for dressing up, and I pick a floaty, silky, kaftan type top in purple, to go with my black silk trousers and spiky heeled boots, then sit down in front of the mirror to apply some makeup. Lee's hand appears on my shoulder, then disappears down my top while I'm pencilling in my eyebrows.

'Are you sure I can't come with you?', he says to my reflection. I put down the pencil and fumble in my makeup bag for mascara. I don't often wear makeup, and the mascara has dried up a bit in the tube. I spit on the brush a few times, then pump it up and down to get it flowing again, ignoring Lee's question. This night has been anticipated since forever ago, and it's girls only. Frankie will pick me up in ten minutes and we will collect Heather on the way. Maisie and Claire will meet us there, and Sylvie will join us a bit later, with her friend Joelle if she's recovered from her cold.

'There is beer in the fridge, and plenty of stuff in the freezer if you want to stay here and wait for me. I won't be late '

Lee pouts, then kisses the top of my head before backing away.

'Ok Lakshmi, it looks like it's just you, me and whatever's on TV.

March 15 - Charlotte

Uninspired, I trawl from shop to shop. I like the clothes shops in England. The quick changing fashions, and the bargain rails. Here, everything is so expensive, and there is nothing I love, and not much I can afford. We need to spend all of our money on the house really, as the roof needs doing and there seems to be a problem with the fosse septique. I'm only in town to try and cheer myself up. The weather is dull and miserable, and Tony hasn't sold anything for a couple of weeks, which means his mood matches it. I myself have sold lots. Lipsticks and mascara's mainly , in a 'Face up to Spring' gift bag. I think they are destined for Mother's Day presents. I've sold so many, but still it doesn't amount to much. When I arrive home with a pair of flip flops and a new bra, Tony rolls his eyes, and asks how much I spent this time. I don't dignify the question with an answer, and merely glare at him until he goes back to staring at his phone. There's a mini-digger that needs a bit of work, which is up for sale on Facebook. He's working out if there's enough of a profit margin in buying it, doing the work, and selling it on . When he puts his phone down and starts totting up the figures he's written on a scrap of paper, I notice the photo .

'That's Susan and Paul's old mini-digger' I say . I recognise it from it's unusual turquoise colour and it's shattered side window. It's being sold by someone called Markandrachel , and it looks like they have the mowers too. I am mystified . Surely Susan would have offered it to us first?

69

'Damn! it's sold already!' Tony slams his phone down on the table and glares at me, as if it's my fault.

March 16 - Frankie

I'm rummaging around in search of bubble wrap when Angel arrives. I'm ahead of the game, wrapping up the smaller items for my exhibition, the things that sell easily, and bring in the bread and butter money. The larger, more originally creative, statement pieces, that draw in the crowds, do of course sell, but less frequently. If I sell the mermaid it will be a cause for celebration. I pull out a half full box of recycled packaging while Angel pours coffee , and I begin wrapping some driftwood wall hangings , of naturally sea smoothed wood, with seagull shapes cut out of them. They hang from pieces of beachcombed rope, and look stunning against a white wall . Angel helps me find the end of a roll of sellotape, and we work together to get the pieces wrapped.

'That's a great start anyway! I put down the sellotape. We've run out of any recycled materials that are good enough to use, and so begin chatting about other things, specifically, Angel's new 'relationship' , which is the word we are using to describe the situation between her and Lee. It seems to be going very well, except that she doesn't like the word 'boyfriend', for anyone over forty, and he's a long way away from being called partner. It's a minor dilemma .

'So there's lover, of course'. …..We both cringe, and dismiss the idea, then suddenly, remembering a conversation we had a few weeks ago about watching reruns of the sitcom, Friends, I have a burst of inspiration ..

'How about'Lobster'? Lee is your lobster! '

It works, and at the same time gives me an idea for a new sculpture. Angel drains her coffee and claps her hands. She loves it! Then her face changes.

'Oh my god!' Something in one of the boxes has caught her eye, and she reaches in and gently pulls out one of the driftwood sailing boats.

'This is beautiful! ' she puts it down and reaches for another 'Exquisite!' She says, holding it up so that the sun shines through its lace sails.

I realise then that I haven't told her the story, and the reason why I can't exhibit them. Ok, now is as good a time as any.

March 17 - Heather

Fantasy and adventure is my 'go to' genre. Limited only by by imagination, I can create worlds where strange creatures inhabit earth and other planets. Often my characters are realistic, but the setting is somehow dystopian, and a little horror-esque. The stories appeal to young teenagers mostly. I have begun this latest one, having abandoned my life story in disgust, because I bored even myself, and have created instead, a rural scene with a couple of farming families and a few odd-ball characters. I'm not yet sure where I'm going with this, but the ink is flowing , and I've outlined a female character, a farmers daughter in fact, who increasingly exaggerates and enhances her life on her social media accounts , to the point that she is blatantly lying. However, due to some super power or other (I haven't yet decided what) the lies that she writes start to become true. The morning sun draws me outside, and Thug sits contentedly by my chair while I write. It's a blissful moment. Inside I still have boxes to unpack from when I moved over, and outside the grass needs mowing, and my car is coated in the Sahara sand from yesterday's wind and rain, but I am happy anyway, to spend an hour or two sitting here, drinking coffee, reading a bit, writing a bit, and sometimes just sitting observing nature. I've avoided the news so far today, and ignored my phone. It's a good way to start the day. A mindful way, as Angel would say.

March 18 - Susan

I catch the girls after their yoga class finishes. I'm on my way back from the bank, and the sound of chatter, and laughter, reaches me as I round the corner, and see them disappearing into the épicerie opposite the yoga studio, their mats hanging over their shoulders. Heather sees me wave, and calls out for me to join them for coffee. This is fortuitous. It's Angel I've been wanting to see, as I've heard that her new man is a builder.

'He's actually a roofer' she tells me as I pull up a chair, and begin to ask some questions,

'But I guess he'll have contacts in the trade' , she adds, when my disappointment registers. I'm wanting someone to insulate, and plasterboard the barn, plus replace the doors I think…..maybe a bit of plumbing to move the outside tap, and out in a sink….

'I'll ask him to pass by and take a look' , Angel says quickly, before I can go into any more detail about the project. Frankie leans forward

'You could always get a 'workaway' ? , I Shake my head. I'd rather simply pay a tradesman to do the job, and get it done properly and speedily.

'What's a workaway? ', Heather looks confused. We explain between us that a workaway is somebody who comes to stay, and does jobs in exchange for their keep. It's a scheme you can join on the internet, and is a good way to get help with DIY jobs, and gardening etc. Heathers eyes get that intense look as she takes this information in. A workaway is my idea of a bad idea. Heather clearly feels differently.

March 19 - Angel

From my window I watch Lee digging a pond. He's weirdly happy with the little mini-digger he bought, and managed to repair himself. Resourceful, like me , he too is a Scorpio.

'Be careful you don't sting each other'. Frankie said, when I told her. Dear Frankie. I look at the wooden boat that now sits on my window sill, and admire the sunlight filtering through the old lace sails. A beautiful gift, and very worthy of a place in her exposition. When she told me the full story, the other morning, over a second cup of coffee, I was sympathetic, and not surprised. Not even a little bit surprised that Charlotte would stoop so low. I see that in her, and I'm proud of dear Frankie for reacting in the way she did, calmly withdrawing some of her own beautiful works from the public eye, in case anybody thought her the plagiarist, and then coolly distancing herself from Charlotte . The thing is though, I've seen one of the offending items that caused this rift. Cheap and nasty. A varnished piece of pine, hastily cobbled together with bamboo for a mast , and a polyester cotton handkerchief sail, stained with tea. It sits in the back bedroom window of one of my clients, Vanessa, next to a vase of silk flowers, and a glass dome thing with some kind of grass arrangement in it. She admitted that she didn't really like it but that it was a present from a mutual acquaintance. I quickly smudged the room with sage before beginning her reflexology treatment, to clear the room of its negative vibe. Lee waves at me through the window, distracting me from my thoughts. I wave back at him, then put my phone in camera mode. This particular creation needs to be made available for all to see.

73

March 20 - Charlotte

'It was one of those March days when the sun shines hot and the wind blows cold. Where it's summer in the sun, and winter in the shade'. I like this quote, and wonder if I can get away with borrowing it for my blog, without anyone having read it before. I decide to risk it, and add it to my 'Host of golden daffodils' photo, then post it to my page. Job done, and it's only ten am. I light another cigarette, and head out to the doorstep with Roxy in tow. Tony has the hoover going, and I watch him thoroughly vacuuming the inside of the boot, of the Peugeot 206 that he bought the other day. The automatic roof doesn't work apparently, so it was a bargain, provided it's an easy fix. When he switches off the hoover and takes out his phone, I watch his face change from the slightly lopsided smile that he usually favours when he's concentrating on something he enjoys doing, to the vaguely irritated frown that he adopts while he scrolls through Facebook. He walks slowly towards me.

'I still can't believe that you didn't know Susan was getting rid of that digger! There can't have been much wrong with it either!'

He shakes his head and walks past me into the house. I wonder what triggered this latest irritation, as the subject hasn't been mentioned in the last couple of days. When I hear the familiar squeak of the bathroom door closing, I go in and find his phone on the kitchen table, still displaying the page he was looking at. It's Angel's latest post . A photo of a driftwood boat sculpture that leaves me cold. I'd hoped that episode was dead and buried. 'The Curious Creations of Francesca Steiner' is tagged of course, and I can only hope that any of my friends who see this post , won't make the connection to my own efforts . I can't see what this has to do with the mini-digger though, and then suddenly I can, as I see the digger in the background, through Angel's window, being driven by that new man of hers.

March 21 - Frankie

Back when we were friends, I was tolerant of the numerous sales-pitch posts, featuring garish coloured nail varnishes, and self tan lotion. I ignored the mis-spelled, grammatically incorrect, pointless blogs about life in general, and nothing in particular. I even teased her a little about the typos, in an effort to get her to edit her posts a bit. Of course I realised that she had issues. I just didn't expect what I got. The boat sculptures were just symbolic of the whole sad situation, as I explained to Angel. It wasn't the obvious plagiarism of the whole thing....(there were other attempts made, at copying mobiles and wall plaques etc) . It was the deceit. The craft stall, set up at a Summer Fair a few miles away, that I wasn't likely to attend, or hear of. The sly attempt she made to hook up with my friend Virginie , in a bid to acquire exhibition space in her gallery, and then that Instagram page, quietly created under a pseudonym so that I wouldn't easily discover it, then quickly hidden from me when I did, as if blocking me would prevent me from discovering what she was up to. It was the final straw for me . Up to that point I had continued with our friendship/pretendship but after that I could no longer excuse her behaviour. I could no longer blame it on her 'issues' . A deliberate attempt at stealing a piece of me is what it was, so I no longer wasted time or energy on her , and simply stopped returning her calls and messages, leaving her to reflect on what she may have done to deserve this cooling of my attentions. I look at the close up of Charlottes nails now, painted 'foxy orange' , and decide that it's not interesting to me at all. I dont unfriend her though, I merely unfollow.

March 22 - Heather

Daisy May discovers her super power when she uses photoshop to erase all of her pimples and blemishes, then uploads the result as her profile pic. The next day, on the bus to school her friends are amazed by her flawless skin. Not quite believing it herself, a few days later she goes back to photoshop and makes her eyes a little bluer, then shaves an inch or two from her waist....I am a quarter of the way through this latest adventure, and Daisy May is beginning to cause a chain of events, where triggered by jealousy, other superpowers begin to make themselves known, in the teenage friends of Daisy May . I'm not yet certain how this will end , but it's going well I think, and I am steadily writing for two hours every day. When I allow myself a break, I decide I need to treat myself to something nice, so I message a girl who I met at yoga, a beautician called Liddy, and ask if she can fit me in for a facial and a brow and lash tint. The spring weather has renewed in me the idea that in order for anyone else to love me I must first love myself. Thug comes over, and places a paw on my knee to distract me from my phone. He probably just wants a walk, but when I tickle his head, and those soulful eyes of his stare up at me with an expression of bliss, I really feel that he loves me, regardless of my pale lashes and neglected complexion.

'Ok Thug, let's go '. I say animatedly. His tail wags. He is so easy to please. Easy to love.

23 March - Susan

The builders arrive promptly at nine, ready to start work. Dave and Ryan, friends of Lee, pull up in a white van with the new doors and window carefully stowed in a trailer . I make them tea while they get started with removing the old barn doors. When Eric arrives , a large pot of tea, and a plate of assorted cookies, stands ready on the garden table, and the three men together heave the old doors onto the now empty trailer. Eric is just here for the company really. He doesn't know much about building work, but he doesn't mind lending a hand , lifting and carrying, now that he is completely well. Once the new doors are in place , and the window fitted in the end wall , the whole barn will be insulated, and boarded out with plasterboard. This will take as long as it takes, maybe a few days, maybe longer. An indeterminate length of time best described, apparently, with outstretched arms and an exaggerated shrug. Dave doesn't know exactly, but if I source some of the materials myself, and if I keep the tea and custard creams coming, then the whole thing will get done a lot quicker. When Heather arrives for a late morning coffee, the doors are in, and Ryan is cutting a hole in the side wall for the window. She eyes the workmen as she sips, and I notice that she's had her brows done , and is wearing makeup for a change.

'They're both married' I say, before she can get any ideas, and together we watch Thug getting more attention than either of us ever do. When Charlotte arrives some time later in the afternoon , the builders have already left, to take the old doors to the tip, and to pick up some insulation for the next part of the job. We stand in the middle of the empty barn. With the new doors and window it's very light in here.

'All this just for pottery!' Charlotte says ' Just think, you could have housed a whole family of Ukrainiens in here!'

'Well, you could probably house two families in Tony's garage I should think!' For once, I give as good as I get.

March 24 - Angel

It's been a glorious sunny day. Lakshmi and I return from a long walk along the canal where I have been mindfully noticing every spring bloom and blossom, and Lakshmi has been concentrating on earthier things, which evidently smell irresistible, and require thorough investigation. Its also given me time to think a bit about my situation with Lee. Things are moving quicker than I anticipated, and we now spend most nights together. I was wondering if I should try to slow things down a bit, but after some quiet meditation this morning, and this, much needed walking therapy this afternoon, I have decided to throw caution to the wind, and just go with the flow. I'll see where this thing takes us. Life is for living after all. My kitchen still smells of the palo santo I used to smudge my space earlier today, before my meditation. Lakshmi stands close by my side, wagging her tail hopefully. It's then I realise that I left her bowl over at Lee's house when I left this morning. I open the huge armoire that serves as my main kitchen cupboard to look for a substitute and the first thing that catches my eye is the giant mug , a favourite of Lee's that he uses for his first coffee each day. No wonder he couldn't find it this morning. Lakshmi barks, and brings me back to the present moment just as I hear someone's footsteps approaching the front door. Her wagging tail tells me that it's a friend, and when I open the door Susan is standing there with a gift for me. I usher her in , and unwrap the bulky parcel .

'I wanted to give you something, after your thoughtful surprise the other day with the flowers.' Susan shuffles nervously from foot to foot.

It's a beautiful dog bowl that she's made, with Lakshmi's name on it. I thank her profusely, and marvel at the serendipitous timing. The Universe is certainly looking after me at the moment!

'I wonder if I could commission you to make a large mug?' I ask, as a thought occurs to me.

March 25 - Charlotte

'I wouldn't walk into a shop without a mask on if you paid me! I know that masking doesn't stop the virus but it does reduce it, to kind of like a cold thing, instead of something serious'.

I begin today's blog having just returned from a supermarket where about half of the people were maskless.

'I know it's not a legal requirement any more, but numbers are still very high, and with so many people still unvaccinated it's pretty unnerving. 'Omicron' is twice as contagious, so there's actually even more need to observe social distancing, continue hand gelling, and yes, mask wearing is still important too! I myself wear a mask out of respect for those who are vulnerable to the disease'.

I end my blog with a jaunty 'stay safe folks' and close down the Facebook app with a satisfied click. That'll show these people who think that getting on with their lives is more important than caring about others. Tony comes in with Roxy draped over his left shoulder

'I've got to test the brakes on that Mazda' he says. I look out of the window at the black MX5 that's parked on the driveway with its roof down. 'So I thought you might fancy a drive down to the coast' ?

'There's all of that recycling to take to the bins' I shake my head slowly as I list all of the things I need to do. It's a huge stash of empty cat food tins and bottles, 'and there's washing in the machine that needs hanging out too.'

'So hang out the washing while I put the bin bags in the car , and then we're good to go' I shake my head again, and stuff the washing in the tumble dryer to save time, before putting my coat and a big scarf on. It will be cold in a topless car. When I step outside though I'm glad that I didn't even try to line dry the washing, as the smell of pig excrement hits me full in the face. The farmer has been spraying the field. Tony laughs at my expression

'So put your mask on! ' he says.

March 26 - Frankie

I stay in the sea for maybe two minutes before my feet get so numb that I can't feel the pebbles as I walk back up the beach. Artie stays in a lot longer, leaping about in the surf, while Ross throws a stick, that was one of the bits of driftwood that I rejected. We will have lunch in one of the restaurants, with tables already placed outside due to this incredibly warm March weather. It's not summer though, and in fact, it's only just spring really. The forecast for the coming week is not so great, and we may soon be reminded that the balmy beach days of July and August are still a long way off. I try to pull my jeans and t.shirt on quickly, to avoid the stares of those walking along the shore, who are not used to nudity in a public place. I wear a costume for the actual swimming, but modesty in changing from that wet clingy item into more comfortable attire, is in my opinion overrated, and not a priority for me, so two older ladies get an eyeful as I search my rucksack for underwear, having discarded my towel on the sand. Ross laughs at their scandalised expressions, and turns his back to put a flame to the joint he just rolled while I was swimming. He takes a long drag , then passes it to me, putting an arm around my shoulder and summoning Artie from the sea at the same time. A perfect moment in a perfect day.

March 27 - Heather

I get out of bed slowly, testing my head as I raise it from the pillow. Not too bad. My stomach is a bit delicate I think, but I'll survive. I open the door to let Thug out into the sunshine, then put the kettle on for a cup of hot water with a slice of lemon. Well, that was an interesting evening! I'd decided yesterday afternoon to spontaneously invite all of my new friends over for aperitifs. Maisie was the first to respond to the open invitation which I posted on my Facebook page, knowing that even if everyone within striking distance turned up , there could not be more than a dozen or so people. It was lovely sitting in the late afternoon sun, with a glass of rosé, and Maisie for company. She had a dinner invitation, so was very happy to spend an hour or so here, on her way to friends who live near the coast . Susan arrived a bit later with Eric in tow. Between them they brought three bottles of wine, and so many bags of crisps and nibbles I was relieved when Charlotte and Tony turned up a few moments later, and it turned into a bit of a party. When it started to get dark, and I went inside in search of citronella candles, I gathered up five empty wine bottles, and Susan and Eric began making noises about it being time they left. Having eaten nothing but crisps and cheese I was beginning to feel a bit wobbly, so had a couple of glasses of water before going back outside, just in time to see Frankie and Ross arrive, fresh from the beach, having had what they called, 'the most perfect of days'..

'Happy for you' Charlotte had responded to this statement, a little sarcastically. 'Not all of us are able to take off to the beach whenever we feel like it'

Charlotte, I realised, had drunk more than any of us. Her speech was slurred , and when she put her glass down heavily on the table, spilling some of the contents, Tony stood up and said they'd better be going, as Roxy would be wondering where they'd got to.

'Yes, perish the thought that we might stay and have some fun' Charlotte had slurred with a glare , as Tony helped her to her feet, and Susan and Eric had quietly stood up too.

'Thank you Heather , enjoy the rest of your evening' Susan said as the four of them disappeared down the driveway, and I poured wine for Frankie and Ross.

As I nurse my hangover this morning, I think about Charlotte's rudeness towards Frankie, and wonder if I should send an apologetic message for the behaviour of my guest , but when I pick up my phone I see that Frankie has beaten me to it.

'Sorry you were caught in the crossfire between Charlotte and I . She's not always quite so openly venomous towards me. Hope I'm still welcome at yours! '

Ok so there's history and a mystery there for sure!

March 28 - Susan

Dave and Ryan arrive again at nine am on the dot, to continue with the plasterboarding. I take their tea over, with the biscuit tin, and am immediately tasked with finding tiles for the floor.

'It'll be the next thing' Dave says, and I feel excited by the thought that soon this old barn will become a smart new studio. It's lucky for me that it's not a sunny day today. I spend the morning researching, and ordering tiles , and also sneakily looking at kilns, then the whole afternoon, trying to throw pots on one of Lesley's wheels, that Ive temporarily borrowed, with most of them ending up in the recycling bin. When Lee arrives to chat to the guys about another job, Angel joins me in the kitchen, so I make coffee while we chat.

'If you are able to take commissions , I would like another bowl, for Reiki'

I haven't glazed the mug I made for her yet, but am happy to make another dish all the same, and it boosts my confidence to be asked. My throwing skills may not be up to much yet, but I can hand build quite well.

'Are you thinking of making tiles then?' She asks, looking at the page I have open on my laptop. There are some beautiful mosaic tiles there, next to the very plain floor tiles that I've ordered for the studio.

'I'd actually really love a panel like this for my treatment room'. She points at a gorgeous mosaic tiled backsplash and it gives me an idea , so I scribble down 'mosaic tiles' , and then , as I hand her an espresso, in a tiny Pyrex cup, another idea hits me about making some prettier ones of my own, so I write that down too. Angel, I decide, is very inspiring company!

March 29 - Angel

Having missed yoga yesterday as I spontaneously stayed over at Lee's the night before, and didn't have my yoga kit with me, I decide to spend an hour on my mat this morning, in front of the patio doors, looking out at an opaque sky. I spend a good while in butterfly pondering things. I missed Heather's little soirée too, and Susan hinted yesterday that it had been 'interesting ' I change to cat position, and think about my visit to Susan's yesterday. Lee had wanted to see the builders about something, a job he has in mind and is being rather mysterious about. Susan herself looks brighter somehow, sparkier, as if she has a new lease of life. I thought at first that it might be a man, but maybe I'm just seeing romance everywhere at the moment , due to my own situation and the fact that spring is in the air. It's her pottery studio plans that have given her this gleam in her eye, and nothing to do with any man, besides, as she reminded me, at the moment she is still married to Paul, and the only man she ever sees is Eric, who's gay. I spent a long time wondering about this last statement. I know Eric quite well now. Not as well as Susan does of course, but we've socialised on lots of occasions , and shared the odd meal. He's a little fussy, and effeminate…..I roll over into sphinx pose, while Reiki yawns and stretches beside me….but he's not gay, not gay at all, and I'm amazed, truly amazed, that Susan hasn't picked up on that.

March 30 - Charlotte

When I go down to the kitchen in search of tea and toast, Roxy has already been fed, and the kitchen looks clean and tidy. I've been getting up later since the clocks went forward, and it's not long before Tony comes in from the garage muttering about taking the Mazda in for its contrôlé tech before lunch.

'I'll come with you' I say, and Tony does a double take. It's not often that I accompany him on such a boring mission, but the truth is it's another dreary day , and I haven't seen or spoken to a living soul since Saturday night, except Roxy, and Tony of course. If I don't get out of the house I might actually go mad.

'Ok then be quick! I haven't got time to wait while you put your slap on'

I give him a withering look, and grab my phone and cigarettes, slipping my feet into my old garden crocs at the same time. Nobody is going to see me.

'You can't smoke in here!' Tony's irritation is not what I need right now , but I wind the window back up , and throw the cigarette packet back down on the dashboard. Someone is coming this afternoon to look at this car. A girl named Amanda. I saw her enquiry on Tony's Facebook page, and looked her up. She's blonde, and smiley. A bit like Frankie but much younger, and shinier looking. The thing is, I know we need the money, but I wanted to keep this one myself. I've always wanted a convertible, and I actually enjoyed going down to the coast in it the other day, when the sun was out. Today is a different sort of day entirely though, and the car roof remains resolutely up, as we drive to the test centre.

'I hope it goes straight through'. Tony says as we pull up outside the test centre. I smile sweetly at him, but in my mind is an image of the lovely Amanda driving off into the sunset in what should have been my car.

'Me too' I answer, but I don't . I hope it fails.

March 31 - Frankie

I can't believe that snow is predicted.

'Seriously? ' I say to Angel who has just arrived. After the glorious sunshine of last week we have now been plunged back into winter again. The van is packed already, with boxes of my smaller creations, and the carefully wrapped mermaid, razor shell screen, and other pieces slotted in between. The wooden heart sits on the passenger seat. On Sunday night I will drive down to the exhibition hall, on the Quiberon peninsula, ready for the opening on Monday afternoon. Monday morning will be spent frantically setting everything up, as long as it doesn't snow. My success depends a lot on good weather. In sunshine, people amble slowly along the seafront, enjoying their surroundings, and taking the time to look at the boats, buy an ice cream, and yes, wander around an art exhibition. In bad weather those who venture out, do so because they have to. They hurry, heads down, from one place to another, and don't care to glance at anything that might slow them down. I am not going to dwell on this. What will be will be. Angel picks up the razor shell screen carefully. It makes a very satisfying rattle as she slots it into a different space in the van , stacking a few boxes in front of it, creating more space . When she goes to the front of the van and gently lifts out the wooden heart, I see immediately what she's doing.

'You're coming with me!'

She nods, tucking bubble wrap securely over the razor shells.

'Lee will pick me up in Monday night, once you're all set up and well established'.

I am so grateful to her. Ross can't come with me because of the animals, and I was resigned to going on my own.

'Of course you know that you'll have to share a bed with me on Sunday night' she adds.

The camper van bed is big enough for two, and I've added plenty of pillows and afghans . All we need is a bottle of wine or two and it will be perfect. I feel so blessed at this moment to have such a friend.

'Angel, you really are an Angel'.

April 1 - Heather

A sleety sort of snow hammers against the window. There is no need to go out, and I give in to the temptation to light the fire. Thug watches me intently as I open the door, and load up the log basket from the stack inside the porch. He's been out for a bathroom break, but seems to agree with my decision against a proper walk, and wags his tail from his position on the rug, as I close the door again. He will be happy to spend the best part of the day snoozing by the fire while I continue with Daisy May, and her super powered friends. The story is going well, and this bad weather will help things along enormously. There will be no aperitif parties this weekend to distract me. My thoughts turn once again to last weekend, and Charlotte's odd behaviour. I hinted to Frankie at yoga on Monday, that I thought Charlotte may have had just a little too much to drink.

'Well, she has issues' was all Frankie would say, and the conversation soon took a turn towards the more general assessment of a 'lovely evening had by all, or at least most of us'

'Where's our love bird this morning? ' Maisie asked then, and the banter that ensued was of a lower tone than I had encountered in other yoga classes. So much lower that our downward facing dogs soon collapsed with laughter and assumed puppy poses similar to the one Thug is demonstrating now.

'Right Thug, let's get some work done'. I make a start on a friend of Daisy May who discovers that when she is sufficiently charged with jealousy she is able to focus her attention on the target of that emotion and freeze their actions completely, taking down their energy until they eventually fall unexpectedly asleep.

April 2 - Susan

I whizz off a quick message to Lesley.

'Could I bring a friend with me on Tuesday please? She's called Charlotte. Is there room? '

Charlotte seems a bit down and depressed , so I thought I'd try to do something to cheer her up, and remembering my promise of a few days ago, I decided to treat her to a pottery session. Ok, so that's one thing I can tick off of my list for today, and I've just got time to make a batch of rock cakes before I'm off to the Brico with Eric, to pick up the floor tiles. The guys are due back on Monday to start the floor, and they do eat a lot of cakes. When Lesley messages back, saying there's plenty of room, I waste no time in messaging Charlotte the good news. A simple 'OK I'll be ready' is all I get by way of a reply , and I can tell by the lack of emoji's that she is still feeling a bit flat, so I send her a GIF of a little puppy cuddling a teddy bear, in a heart shaped frame, and then I get on with the serious business of kiln research, accompanied by the smell of baking rock cakes, and the very English sound of Saturday morning BBC radio 2, courtesy of Alexa. When my inbox pings with a new Email I ignore it, focussed as I am on a large cylindrical metal object that's going to set me back several thousands of euros, but which really has me drooling.........so I add it to my basket, and then I hear Eric's car pull up outside, so I close down my laptop, reopening it again quickly when I remember the email. It's from Paul. Apparently now that England is on France's green list, he's decided to come over. Shit! I wasn't expecting that.

April 3 - Angel

'You be a good girl my darling'. Lakshmi gives me a mournful look as I dump my overnight bag on the doorstep, and come back inside to grab my phone and sunglasses. It's like summer again, which feels weird after the snow of yesterday. I look at Lee. He gives me a mournful look too.

'One night'! I say to them both. Frankie waves as I hold up two fingers as a signal for two minutes. I give Lee a quick kiss and a tight squeeze, before picking up my bag and rushing over to the van . We drive off, with silly grins on our faces as Lee stands there, and I watch him, watching me, until we are out of sight. It's only about an hour and a half's drive away but it feels like a little holiday anyway, and I open the Haribo's before we're even halfway down the road, wriggling around on the crocheted seat covers that I've made as a gift to Frankie, especially for this trip.

'Are you nervous?' I ask. Frankie grins and nods, and grimaces all at the same time.

'Once the expo is set up I'll be fine, I always am, but there's a lot to do first! '

I lean in close to her and take a selfie, which I post immediately on Facebook, with the heading 'Thelma and Louise reincarnated'. I add a little border of flowers and peace signs, to enhance our hippie vibe, then turn the music up, and we spend the rest of the journey singing along to the radio, and waving at anyone who looks our way.

April 4 - Charlotte

'Strawberry sorbet, Amber rush, Smiley summer' ...... I put one of each into every bag, and add a couple of sample products each of tiny perfumes in little blister packs, my business card and a few glittery sprinkles, and I'm done. That's five orders for 'Spring fever' on their way to customers. A message from Susan says that she is going to make the coffee and walnut cake that I especially like , to take with us to the pottery class tomorrow. I'd forgotten about pottery, and wonder if I really want to go. What if I can't do it? I've seen some of the things that Lesley posts on Facebook.

They look really professional. On the other hand, if I mess up, nobody needs to know. Roxy has been playing with something in the sitting room,while I've been working here at the kitchen table. I could hear the thud of her paws running across the parquet floor after having leapt down from the sofa, then the vibration of the glass on the gold coffee table as she jumped up on that for a few seconds before landing on the floor again. It's been quiet for a while though so I decide to investigate. Tiny fluffy feathers float in the air by the window where Roxy is now lying stretched out on the sill.

'Not another one!' I see the tiny, chewed up form of a dead blue tit on the rug. It's the third one in as many days. It makes me want to cry.

'What's this Roxy?!' I shout at her, but I know it won't do any good. I was at least warned about this by every cat owner I know in Brittany. 'Spring fever! ' . Henry the hoover will be working very hard for the next few weeks.

April 5 - Frankie

The campsite is almost empty. Not many people choose to camp at this time of year, especially in this wintry weather. The sea is the coldest I've been in for a long time, and I'm only in there for a minute before wrapping my huge towel around me and making my way back up the sandy beach. A dog walker shouts something about the wind, and I raise my hand in acknowledgment, not wanting to be engaged in conversation before I've had a chance to get dressed and use the bathroom. My exhibition is going well despite the lack of sunshine, and Angel's help yesterday really saved the day, as she was able to continually mop the floor behind us as we unloaded the van and walked in and out with our wet, sandy shoes. She was also amazingly quick to stow away the mountain of bubble wrap as we arranged the exhibits, so that we were done setting up, inside of the two hours

I'd allowed before opening to the public. I'm sure the free glass of wine offered to visitors helped to pull them in out of the rain too, and by the end of the day I'd sold three small pieces (wall hangings and a sailing boat) and I have somebody interested in the razor shell screen. Dressing in the van can be a challenge as everything is crammed into my rucksack, and I can't find what I need, so that when I hear a light tap on my window I'm totally naked with my bum in the air, and my top half elbow deep in harem pants and little tops . A man in a beanie hat asks if I'm the artist, pointing to the exhibition poster that Angel thoughtfully placed in the back window . A short conversation ensues, and I hand him one of my business cards. The nudity doesn't seem to bother him.

April 6 - Heather

Fantasy fiction can transport the reader to any number of fictional realities, familiar, or futuristic, without the restrictions of scientific laws. Daisy May and her super powered friends live in a believable world, similar to rural Brittany, with its farms, villages, and quiet roads. The characters are all relatable to normal teenagers, and I try to keep their issues and concerns up to date and relevant. Once I've established their world, and imagined their personalities, their families and their histories, I throw in a super power or two and see where it leads. It's not long before the book begins to write itself. When I put down my laptop at the end of the morning, I'm satisfied that I've almost reached that point. From here on in, writing this one will be a pleasure. I dash off a quick message to a group of friends about a possible visit to Frankie's exhibition one day this week , and with my phone in one hand and a bag of bread in the other (I've found a tame duck living on its own, on a pond in the woods), I call to Thug, who must stay on his lead for most of this walk, because of said duck, and we head out into the drizzle for our daily exercise.

'Well it's nice weather for ducks at least', I say, trying to remain positive as I clip his lead to his collar'. He doesn't seem impressed though.

April 7 - Susan

'My kiln should arrive on Monday ' .

Lesley looks as excited as I am . The barn is ready. Well almost. It has walls, ceilings and windows, plumbing, insulation, and a tiled floor. It looks like a studio. Lesley throws a perfectly cylindrical piece, which will become a mug, and draws it off of the wheel with a cheese wire, placing it on a board with six other identical pieces. I am trying my best to repair Charlotte's 'cat' . The ears have fallen off (not enough scratching and slipping) and the end of the tail has broken. I use vinegar to try and rejoin the pieces. It's the only thing she made on Tuesday that she didn't lose patience with. Her other efforts all ended in the recycle bin, when she screwed them up before they were quite finished. Lesley and I avoid talking about her, but I know she must be dreading having Charlotte back here again in order to glaze this piece. I don't think it's likely that she will come again after that though. She didn't seem to enjoy herself.

'So how about we shop for clay tomorrow? I could drive over to you, and we could go together to Frankie's exhibition, then we could go to the pottery supply shop on the way back? We could even stop for lunch somewhere? Lesley suggests.

This sounds like a plan, and I begin to feel even more excited about the upcoming studio , than I did before. Charlotte's cat begins to look a little more feline, as a result of my tweaking, and I place it carefully on a board to dry. If only I could just as easily fix Charlotte.

April 8 - Angel

The day is so wet. I come out of yoga and am soaked to the skin by the time I get in the car, teeth chattering as I fumble with the keys. The fuel light is on so I've got to stop at the garage, and then the supermarket for dog food. When I finally reach home, looking forward to a hot shower, I discover that Lee, prevented from continuing with the roof he's currently working on, by the torrential rain, has decided to fit the new smoked glass shower screen that I bought a few weeks ago to replace the clear one that never seemed to look clean. His timing is off though, and when I find that I have run out of the coffee I like, and I'm left with only the decaffeinated version that I bought by mistake, I am sorely tempted to return to bed for the rest of the day . The banging, crashing and swearing coming from the en-suite bathroom puts me off this idea, so instead I pull on my cosy poncho, and go to my mat by the patio doors , to sit and meditate while looking out at the new pond, which is fascinating to watch in the rain. Lakshmi joins me , and together we sit in silence for a few minutes while I concentrate on my breathing and think about the bigger problems in the world and the need to restore peace and harmony. I feel myself begin to relax , with Lakshmi's head in my lap, and I fall into chanting the Ho oponopono prayer again. It seems to soothe both myself and Lakshmi , and as the noise from the bathroom lessens, and the cursing stops, I realise it might be having a calming influence on Lee too!

April 9 - Charlotte

I post the photo of Roxy, sitting by the window wearing her new collar with the bell on it. She has killed five birds this week, that I know of. Maybe there are more outside that I haven't seen. I haven't been out there yet to look properly. The wind is so cold at the moment that I've taken to smoking indoors, then opening the window for a few minutes to let the smell out. I hope Tony hasn't noticed. He hasn't said anything yet.

'Come on Roxy' I move her out of the way in order to open the window and begin wafting, throwing the extinguished butt out onto the flower bed to join the others. My 'Spring Fever' campaign seems to have cooled a little with the weather, and there are no orders today. I begin work on 'Easter Madness' instead. It's a repeat of one I did last year, as I had some bunnies left over. False eyelashes, nail stickers, and lipstick, all in a shade called 'warm chocolate'. The nail stickers have a pattern on them like sugar strands , and a sachet of mini eggs is included. Roxy bats around the little packets of eyelashes while I'm trying to get everything prettily wrapped up, but eventually I manage to get eleven Easter bunnies, sweetly suffocating inside their cellophane cells, and add the photo to my website, then to Instagram, then finally to my Facebook page. I blog a bit about Easter being my favourite time of year , then I scroll down through my feed. The first thing I see is a photo of Frankie's 'successful' exhibition. A mermaid sculpture in the foreground, in front of a window, with a sea view behind it, and ninety seven 'likes' already. I don't add one, but continue scrolling past pictures of restaurant meals, beach walks, and sunset scenes with inviting looking cocktails on outside tables. One is of Heather, with Angel and Maisie at Frankie's 'truly amazing' exhibition. I close it down, and light another cigarette.

April 10 - Frankie

Driving home happy. The traffic moves slowly up the Quiberon peninsula, after a sunny Sunday afternoon, which many families have spent strolling pleasurably on the beach. I am in a reflective mood. What a week.! If I added up the actual money I've taken, and counted that as a measure of my success, then indeed I've exceeded my expectations, and established myself more firmly into the realms of professional artists, but it's been so much more than that. The people I've met. The conversations that have taken place, and the comments I've overheard have been so uplifting. The sea views and the constant sound of the waves, so inspiring. I have had so many moments of meditation, breathing in prana and the salty air, that even Angel will be impressed, and so this afternoon as I was packing up it was with a pang of sadness that it's come to an end so quickly, and I found myself asking if I could be considered as a replacement artist , should anyone cancel their exhibition later in the summer . I'm looking forward now to being home with Ross, and celebrating over a glass of wine or two, a little earlier than expected, as having sold so many of my creations, I had little left to pack up. This afternoon, the razor shell screen finally went, to the woman who had visited it every day and taken hundreds of photos of it in changing light. The mermaid, my biggest sale of the week was reserved on Wednesday evening by a local restaurant owner and and picked up early this morning . Most of the wall hangings have gone, and the ceramic abstract octopuses (octopi?) I can't help smiling contentedly as I think of the boost to my bank balance, and my full sketchbook of ideas for the next exhibition. Pharrell Williams is on the radio, and I sing along to 'Happy' at the top of my voice, with the windows down.

April 11 - Heather

I leave Daisy May at a swimming pool party, and put a coat on before heading out with Thug. The forecast is for clouds and showers, though the sky at the moment is a clear blue, and out of the wind it's actually quite warm. We arrive at Susan's, to find her pacing up and down in her new studio.

'I thought you'd be busy, creating a masterpiece! ' I say, by way of greeting. The new space is airy and light, with the sun streaming through the windows. A long workbench stretches from one end to the other, and metal shelving holds pots of something which I guess might be glaze. Susan explains that she's waiting for her new kiln to arrive, and can't settle to anything until it does. I let Thug off the lead, and Susan makes tea while I look around. Slabs of plastic wrapped clay are piled in one corner, and pots of sculpting tools line a shelf over by the sink . It all looks very new and unused. A potters wheel takes pride of place by the window, and there's a very obvious space in the corner by the wood burning stove , where the kiln will go . No expense has been spared that I can see , and this studio is a far cry from Frankie's atelier, where everything is well used, cluttered, and lived in .

' I hope you've taken some before and after photos' I say, remembering the scruffy old barn that it was, but Susan doesn't hear me , as Thug is now barking loudly, and the sound of a vehicle pulling in to the driveway, causes her to spring excitedly towards the door.

'The kiln!' She squeals, but her face instantly falls when she sees the Land Rover Discovery pulling up outside . A man in a rugby top and jeans jumps out.

'Hello Susan' he says, as both Rhea and Thug sniff suspiciously at his feet.

April 12 - Susan

Paul was surprised, and impressed with the pottery. He walked around it nodding, running his fingers over the workbench, picking up the sculpting tools, and opening and closing the bi-fold doors.

'It's warm in here' was one of his only comments, his hand pressed to the newly insulated and boarded walls . This morning he offered to help me unpack the kiln, which finally arrived at the

96

end of yesterday afternoon. So I suppose all is ok, and having installed him in the guest bedroom without complaint ,I feel I have established the new boundaries . Only one problem remains. I haven't yet broached the subject of how long he will be staying. I look across the table at him pushing bacon and eggs around on his plate, He brought over some English goodies, including bacon rashers and cheddar cheese, (this of course isn't legally allowed any more , but that didn't seem to bother him, and I was very happy to receive it) , it seems to me though that there is something on his mind. I hope, I really hope, that he's not considering moving back over here. He funds it all, so there's not much I can do to prevent him, but our marriage broke down years ago , and though we remain on friendly terms I have no interest at all in rekindling the relationship. I make a second mug of tea. Old habits die hard, and I put it in front of him, having stirred two sugars into it and added milk, leaving him to squash the teabag till the desired tar colour is reached. Delilah is on his lap, just as she always used to be , and it's hard to believe that almost three years have passed. I sit down , nursing my own mug of tea , and a slightly muzzy head. I drank more wine last night than I am used to drinking now. The continual stir and squash of spoon on teabag makes me feel slightly nauseous, and I get a strong sense of déjà vu. I should just come right out with it and ask him what his plans are, but as I swallow a mouthful of tea, I hear him clear his throat as though he's about to speak, and the nausea increases.

April 13 - Angel

The new pond has frog spawn in it. I sit by it with a cup of hot lemon infused water, waiting for my client to arrive for an Indian head massage. Picking up little stones from the gravel driveway, I drop them in the pond, one at a time , observing the circular form of the ripples, and pondering their meaning. In general, concentric circles represent processes , wholeness, a systemic view of nature and the universe. When my pebble touches the surface of the pond,

97

the impact creates a plethora of ever broadening ripples. It's impossible to deny that all of our actions affect the environment, and all are interrelated. I see layers of meaning, encompassing other layers of meaning, like Russian dolls . I see my life, from beginning to end, a complete circle within other complete circles. I drop in stone after stone. There is no need for a water feature here, sitting mindfully like this, I am my own water feature. The spell is only broken when Anita arrives, slamming her car door as she shouts her greeting. She is a regular client, who's stress filled lifestyle overwhelms her at times, and I can already tell that for her, this is not a good day. Perhaps I'll get her to sit here for a while , while I make her a drink. I'm sure it would have a beneficial soothing effect. I look at the stone that I currently have in my hand. Inexplicably it turns out to be a piece of rose quartz . I pass it to Anita, as I coax her to sit down in the warm spot that I've just vacated.

'Rose quartz, for self love', I explain. She palms the crystal, and takes a seat. Almost immediately I see the weight lifting from her shoulders . I throw one last pebble into the pond and leave her to meditate on those rippling rings which are so therapeutic.

April 14 - Charlotte

I've been waiting years for a bath. Ever since we've been here , for nearly seven years, I've made do with a shower. We've had the actual tub, in Tony's garage for about four years already, but with no money for a plumber, that's where it stayed. I look at Tony but I don't smile. I know he's trying his best to lift me out of what he sees as the start of another depression, but it's not that simple. He saw me, a couple of days ago in the spare bedroom, (I'd call it the guest room except that we never have any), going through the little suitcase again. He thinks I'm hanging on to all of the baby clothes because I can't let go of what happened, but I can. I was just remembering, that's all. Just probing an old wound, to make sure it had healed, before moving on. I will be forty eight this year . I'm officially peri menopausal, with all the signs and symptoms. When I was forty two, and pregnant it seemed a miracle. It truly was the most amazing , most wonderful, most scary time of my life, but it was short lived, and I don't mourn now for a baby that never was. I mourn for that feeling. The feeling that I was an amazing, beautiful, vital woman. The plumber, Martin I believe he's called, runs downstairs and out to his van to fetch something or other, and I mechanically put Roxy down , and pick up the kettle. Some of the money we've been saving to fix the roof will be going to pay for this bath installation. Tony comes downstairs and winks at me, before dropping teabags into mugs.

'I hope you've got plenty of candles and bubble bath for tonight'

April 15 - Frankie

It's not often I sit doing nothing for a whole afternoon but today I do. It's full sunshine, and a full moon tonight, so I embrace the holiday feeling. After all it's Good Friday in the U.K., and Susan brought me over some hot cross buns this morning, so it really does feel like Easter. I watch Ross grooming the pony as I lie on the grass at the edge of the paddock, where the sheep have grazed it to lawn level. A jackdaw keeps appearing and strutting about near the field shelter. I watch it fly off after a few minutes, with its beak full of pony hair. From somewhere in the distance I hear a cuckoo calling

'Did you hear that? It's the first one I've heard this year'. Ross puts down the brush and comes to sit beside me, taking out his tobacco tin as he does so. The process of rolling a joint is therapeutic for him, and I love to watch his face as he crumbles the right amount of weed, and licks along the edge of the rolling paper.

'How's the crop?' I ask

He smiles as he lights up and takes a drag.

'All good' , he says, and that's all I'll get from him on the subject. Stoned or sober, he's always been a man of few words.

April 16 - Heather

When the sun comes up I begin writing. It's a full moon today, and Angel has enlightened me of the effects that it can have on sleep. Now that I'm aware of it, I notice that during a full moon I am wakeful, and I've barely closed my eyes since the witching hour. My creativity too, has been heightened, and so I sit here with Thug beside me, having finished one chapter, and gone steaming on to the next without a pause. A week's work probably, done in a few dark hours. Now that I know this trick I can make use of it again during the next full moon, and all the full moons after that. I predict a future of increased productivity.

'Bring it on' ! I say out loud, and Thug mistakes my meaning somehow for 'shall we go out for a walk?' I just want to finish this chapter while I'm in the zone. The sky is a cloudless blue, and I'm pretty sure we're in for a lovely warm spring day. Thug sighs loudly, and settles back down as I continue to write, ending the chapter with a flourish, as yet another angst ridden teenager discovers her unlikely super power. This time it's Charlie, who faced with an angry parent, finds that if she stares directly at the mouth of the person who is shouting at her, she freezes the words on their lips, and renders them temporarily incapable of speaking, and therefore, unable to issue orders or punishment. Ok then, enough for now, pen down.

April 17 - Susan

There are seven pots on the bench now. All of them reasonably tall, fairly symmetrical, quite nicely shaped, the clay not too thick, the bottoms firm and free of holes. I'm getting the hang of throwing. The night before last, after Paul left, I found I couldn't sleep at all, and so instead of tossing and turning, and scrolling aimlessly on my phone, I came out here. The moon was full, so I just padded across the garden without a torch and allowed myself to do just what I wanted, and what I wanted, it turns out, was to sit here at my virgin potters wheel, and teach myself how to throw pots. There's a lot of clay in the recycling bin, that will need pugging before I can reuse it, but here in front of me , these seven pieces will be the first ones fired in my virgin kiln, and I'm more than happy about that. It seems odd that while Paul was here we so quickly fell into an old routine. Him in the garden (he was a little dismayed that I had got rid of most of his tools) , me in the kitchen, coming together at the end of the day for wine and TV. Now that he's gone I can enjoy my freedom again. More freedom than I had before in fact, as Paul's reason for showing up here was to ask me in person for a divorce. He's met someone else , and so I am now firmly, and officially, unattached. I'm not at all sure how I feel about that, but I'm strangely relieved that he's gone. I get to keep this house, while he keeps the English one, and all should go smoothly. I cheese wire off another lump of stoneware clay , and begin rolling it out . I'm making lids , while thinking everything through. My monthly living allowance will disappear, but we have negotiated a lump sum in lieu of that so that financially I should be ok.

' And you've always got Eric!' , was Paul's parting shot.

'Yes, it's a shame he's still gay! ' was my quick retort. We've parted reasonably amicably I guess, which in the end is the best I could hope for.

April 18 - Angel

A Facebook meme about throwing out anything that doesn't bring you joy, rears it's head again. I've come home from Lee's early this morning , determined to get my admin organised. A job I hate, and when I finally get around to opening the electricity bill that arrived last week, I realise that it's definitely a thing which doesn't bring me joy , and I wish with all my heart that I could just throw it away. It's hard to scrape a living here. Every expense seems to be greater than it's English equivalent, and my holistic treatments don't really earn me enough to keep up with it all. I could work harder , but then my whole reason for moving over here was for a better quality of life, and some breathing space, and time for myself. There is no easy answer to this conundrum, so I pay the electric bill on line, and while I'm about it I organise a regular payment to transfer from my dwindling English bank account to top up my French one. I then decide to meditate with a huge green aventurine as my focal point. A green aventurine is a beautiful crystal with many qualities which include the ability to increase financial wealth. I place the crystal on a stone by the pond, and put my mandala shaped mat in front of it. When Lee arrives to take me out for an Easter Monday lunch, at a restaurant in town, I'm still sitting there, cross legged on my mat, having passed a good hour visualising wealth, instead of getting myself ready to go out. Lee eyes the aventurine quizzically.

'Looks good by the pond'! He says, 'Emerald?'

April 19 - Charlotte

Susan calls in for the first time in what seems like ages. We drink our tea in the bathroom, which is of course a tiny bit weird , but at the moment there's only a bath in here, and I thought she might have ideas about how to decorate the room. The loo and the basin are in our ensuite with the shower, so this tiny room is purely for the bath.

'I wouldn't have carpet' she says 'and if you paint the room a dark colour it'll make it appear even smaller' .

There is a dark patch on the ceiling where the roof has leaked . We have to remember to empty the buckets frequently when it rain's heavily.

'That was a quick visit!' I say, of Paul, who I didn't see even once when he was here . I was a little bit offended when Susan didn't invite us over, so I make her feel guilty by suggesting that maybe I'll host a dinner party next time he comes.

'There won't be a next time' she says, flatly, then goes on to tell me all about the upcoming divorce. Poor Susan. To be over here , and all alone , knowing that your husband has started a new life for himself at home in England, must be the worse feeling ever. I tell her how sorry I am, and offer her another cup of tea.

'Some really nice tiles would make all the difference' she says, ignoring my tea and sympathy. 'And some kind of shelving for your spare towels, and bath products' she goes on. I don't think the reality of her situation has really sunk in yet.

April 20 - Frankie

'Mon atelier est un bordel!' I say, as Marie and Jean pick their way through abandoned boxes and bubble wrap. I clear some sketches off of the sofa and invite them to sit down while I put some coffee on. They've been wanting to visit for so long , they tell me as I hand them each an expresso in a tiny cup , two of the

103

minuscule cups I made in pottery especially for this purpose. What they want is a sculpture, maybe two , for their front lawn . I picture the immaculate but uninspiring sweep of grass in front of their Neo Breton house, and wonder how much of a free rein I'll be given in the design of a statement piece. Marie is flicking through some photos on her phone while Jean's attention seems to be caught by my slate cutters, which I've been using to cut hundreds of triangle shapes out of old roofing slates, which will eventually, when strung together, form the shimmering sails of a large ghost ship that will form part of my next exhibition. After a moment or two, Marie starts stabbing at her phone and saying

'Something like this, perhaps?' I look at the image of two deer facing each other, some kind of metal made to look like it's woven together, and sort of bronzish in colour. It's very classical and conservative.

'Well I could do something a bit like that but sort of different?' I sketch out some ideas in my head as Marie nods at me. I gesture the height with my hand

' It would be big though!' I say, waiting for them to catch on. Marie nods again, looking at Jean for confirmation.

'Expensive!' We all say at once.

April 21 - Heather

So it's the Queen's birthday. Even so, I can't help but frown as I scroll through my feed which is exceptionally full of photos of the Queen standing between two fell ponies. Who knew my friends were such royalists! The noise outside has prevented me from writing today . An entourage of yellow vested men with diggers, and reels of cable , has been working its way gradually down the road. After coffee I pluck up the courage to approach them, and try out my French in an attempt to find out what they're actually doing here. I take Thug with me, on his lead, and head for

104

the one who doesn't seem to be doing very much. He has a stop/go board in one hand, and a cigarette in the other. I have rehearsed , in my head, what I'm planning to say, but before I can get the words out he's started a conversation with Thug, and his attention is entirely taken up with how beautiful Thug actually is, then he looks up and adds, rather unexpectedly, 'comme sa maman' . What I say then, comes out as nothing remotely intelligible , and not at all what I had planned to say. He cocks his head to one side, looking thoughtfully at me. I try again, and he grins and points over to where the digger driver, and the other men are busily getting on with their work. I nod hopefully, thinking he means to explain what their mission is. He doesn't . Instead he puts down the stop/go board and goes over to an empty cable reel, which he begins rolling across the road and into my driveway. 'Voila'! he says, triumphantly. I think about trying again, but I'm strangely happy with the giant cotton reel thing, and wonder what I'll do with it. I wonder also (briefly) if he actually fancies me . I decide to quit while I'm ahead, as he's smiling encouragingly at me. 'Merci beaucoup' I say, and then retreat back to my house.

April 22 - Susan

The new studio is the 'in place' for girly gossip and advice, and Frankie shows up shortly after Heather , which means that Thug has a playmate, as Rhea isn't that keen on him, but Artie is. I am making a lamp base out of coils of clay which I've pulled through the new extruder that I treated myself to. It's an expensive piece of kit, but it means that I can make lots of evenly sized, smooth snakes of clay in minutes. Heather makes the coffee while Frankie experiments with the extruder, making lots of tiny spaghetti like strands, and one triangular profiled one, that looks like a Toblerone. I finish telling them about Paul and I.

'Can you support yourself?' Heather asks, as Frankie rocks back on her chair, singing 'Freebird' and flapping her arms gracefully . She comes back to earth with a bump when I confess that I'm not sure. The lump sum Paul is giving me is generous, and I won't contest it, but without the security of a regular income I'm not in a comfortable situation for sure. I tell them that I might have to downsize. Both of them look horrified.

'But this gorgeous studio!' Frankie says, while Heather opens her mouth and then closes it without uttering a word. I'm not happy about the idea myself, but I've wondered about getting a job as an alternative plan, and there's nothing I can really see myself doing.

'You could take in a lodger….or maybe airBNB one of the bedrooms?' Heather suggests, and Frankie nods enthusiastically.

'It's a good idea but I'm not sure I'd be comfortable sharing my space with a stranger' we are all silent for a moment as I continue coiling.

'Have you thought about selling your work?' Frankie asks.

April 23 - Angel

I don't normally take clients on a Saturday, but it's Lee's birthday next week and I want to buy him something nice, so I need to work all I can. My treatment room is prepared, and once I've showered and changed , and done a small meditation, I'll be ready to receive Marcia, for her reflexology and Indian head massage. I look out of the window when I hear a noise. Lee has started the mower , and is preparing to get to work on the bit of grass directly in front of the treatment room window. I tell him that my client will be here in fifteen minutes. He says it will take him ten at most to mow this little patch, and he'll stop as soon as her car arrives if she's early. After my shower I go to the window again, and survey the newly cut lawn. I have to admit that it looks so much better, and the smell of freshly cut grass wafting in through the window is pleasant, and will give an impression of freshness to my new client, who evidently is used to the good things in life , living as she does in a chateau, twenty minutes from here . I meditate while I wait for her to arrive, with my crystal ball in one hand and my goddess stone in the other, sitting cross legged on the floor of the treatment room. I only look up when Lee taps on the window and mouths the words 'she's here'! I open the door then to a woman who at first glance looks like Marine Le Pen, with her coiffed hair and trowelled on makeup. I recognise the smell of Ellnet hairspray, from years ago, when my gran used to wear it. The smile on my face is fixed, and even with her obviously botoxed forehead , and the questionable energy radiating from her, I'm determined to make this experience a positive one.

'Right, let's get you comfortable' I close the door behind her as she sits down elegantly on the massage couch without bothering to remove her shoes. It's going to be a long morning.

April 24 - Charlotte

We don't have a vote of course. You need French nationality for that, and so I don't take much interest in the election today, but as we drive through the village on our way to look at a Smart car that's been accident damaged, there are people standing around outside of the Salle where the voting takes place and portrait posters of both Macron, and Le Penn adorn the windows.

'Christ, I hope she doesn't get in!' Tony says as I take in the crowds and the air of impending doom.

'Why?' I ask. For me there's not much to choose between them but Tony explains that she's very 'far right' and that she has it in for the foreigners in this country.

'Would we have to leave?' I leave that question hanging in the air , as he is clearly unwilling to elaborate further. He would hate to have to return to England. He just loves it here 'in the countryside' as he always says, though all he ever seems to do is tinker with his cars, stare at his phone , or charm potential customers into buying from him. It could all be done equally well in England . He may well love the countryside, but he never goes for a walk. The idea of a French lifestyle appeals to him, but somehow all of our friends are English, and we both struggle with the French language.

'We couldn't afford to'. He says eventually, in answer to my question. This I know is true. I've watched the property prices in England rising up and up, while here they are almost the same as they were when we arrived. Ok, there may be a slight increase in value, but if we sold our house here, with its leaky roof, and dodgy fosse septique we'd be lucky if we could afford a tiny flat anywhere close to where we came from, just outside of Birmingham . Black clouds in the sky threaten a rainstorm, and the day does begin to feel very dark indeed.

April 25 - Frankie

It's a fair trade. Tony will give my little Beetle a service and in return I will sandblast four steel wheels. He brings them into my atelier and dumps them in the corner before having a good look around.

'No!' He groans, when he sees the pieces on the floor. It was a chopper bike. I stripped it down with the intention of using the handlebars as antlers for the deer that I'm making for Marie. I'm using the forks and the frame too, and possibly the wheels, as part of the body. Only the long wedge shaped saddle is as it was. The other bits have all been sand blasted, ready to assemble.

'Do you know how much these sell for now?' He seems totally dismayed as he picks up the saddle. I don't know, and I don't care . I have a vision in my head, and a fair idea of how I'm going to achieve it. I hand him a steaming coffee as if it's a peace pipe, and wait for his next comment, but he just shakes his head and changes the subject.

'Great result from the election eh? That's a relief for sure! '

It is, though I never thought I'd be pleased to see Macron come out on top, after his treatment of us over the Covid fiasco. I tell him this , and he's quiet for just a moment …

'Oh yes I'd forgotten that you're one of those anti vaxers'.

I smile at the opportunity he gives me to use my latest most favourite phrase.

'Well yes actually! , I'm a Pure Blood! '

April 26 - Heather

Susan looks at my design and nods. 'Did you remember to measure it exactly?' She asks . Well it's one meter in diameter, give or take. I figure the grout gaps can be adjusted wider or smaller to make the tiles fit. I'm not sure about the hole in the middle, but it's about the size of a ping pong ball.

'I think it would be best if I make a template by drawing around it ' . Susan is a bit of a perfectionist. I have commissioned her to make tiles for the top of my new cable drum. It will be an outdoor drinks table. The hole in the middle is perfect for a parasol, and I'm going to coil rope around the core , and add a ring of rope around the bottom, so that bottles can be stored there without falling over. I will probably plan a little drinks party once it's finished, to celebrate the completion of my new book, which I hope will reach its conclusion in the next chapter . The workmen are at the end of the road now, near Eric's, and once I've finished here, I plan to walk Thug in that direction.

'You look nice, are you wearing makeup?' Susan asks, somewhat bluntly.

'Well I thought I'd make a bit of an effort on this sunny spring morning!'

Susan eyes me suspiciously, but says nothing as she continues sticking masking tape on the lamp base that she's made, to form a stripy pattern. I make ready to go, putting Thug on his lead, and gathering coffee cups up to put by the sink.

'I'm thinking of joining a dating website' Susan says, as I pick up my phone . She looks at me expectantly, and I realise that this is an invitation of sorts.

'Ok! Let's have a drink tomorrow evening, and we can both have a bit of a browse!' I walk away, wondering what on earth I'm getting myself into.

April 27 - Susan

There is, it turns out, a Facebook website for dating, where you put in the radius of the distance that you're willing to travel, and off you go. Your profile is kept private, and you're known only by your first name, and the name of the town nearest to where you live. This seems to suit our purposes, so Heather scrolls through it, while I draw around the cable drum onto a huge piece of cardboard, part of the box that my kiln came in.

'We need to put some profile pics up of course' Heather says, grimacing. Charlotte has very kindly offered to do our makeup especially for this purpose, but though I appreciated the offer, I felt quite horrified at the idea, and said that I'd let her know. When I tell Heather this she begins giggling uncontrollably. I've had one glass of wine already, and find Heather's laughter infectious, so we're both laughing hysterically, with tears in our eyes when Eric arrives, with a long coil of rope that he's just found in his garage.

' For Heather's drum?' , he says, looking hesitant as he stands in the doorway. For some reason this just makes us worse. I explain, as I pour him a glass of wine, about the dating site, and Charlotte's offer, and he smiles weakly…

'How funny that Charlotte should think that anything she could do with foundation and lipstick would be an improvement' he muses.

I keep on laughing, but I'm not really sure how to take what he just said. In the end I decide to take it as a compliment.

April 28 - Angel

Tomorrow it's Lee's birthday. I lie in bed trying to come up with an idea for the perfect present. I see in my mind's eye, Lee, on the morning of his birthday, his eyes twinkling with excitement as he opens a big box, a gift from me! The trouble is I've no idea what to put in that box. What do you buy for the man who pretty much has everything already? There is simply nothing I can think of, that he wants, so I settle on the idea of treating him to a really special meal at a restaurant not too far away, that has earned itself a Michelin star. Satisfied, that it's the best idea I can come up with, I swing my legs out of bed and do a few sun salutations before making myself a drink. Lee was up, and out of the door at the crack of dawn today. He wants to get the roof he is working on entirely finished before the rain that is forecast for tonight. That way he can have a day off for his birthday. I take my drink outside in the sunshine, and scroll through my phone. A couple of people requesting appointments, one of them a friend of Marcia's, so that has worked out well I guess! And then some new posts in 'Items for sale in Brittany'….somebody, it seems, has a lot of rose bushes for sale . I click on the photos. One of them, a bushy tea rose with large soft yellow flowers, splashed with pink, happens to be called 'Love and Peace'. So that's it then, the universe has intervened once more, with the perfect present suggestion.

April 29 - Charlotte

Susan squints into the mirror , and I say 'voila!' in my best French accent.

'I need my glasses' she says, but I shake my head. It'll spoil the look. Instead, I get her to smile, and I take her photo so that she can then get a proper look with her glasses back on.

'Oh my god!' The smile turns into a laugh. She actually looks quite good. The lipstick in 'Mexico' and the 'Blackjack' mascara and eyeliner, lift her rather lifeless skin tones , and give her a youthful wide eyed look. I've covered her lines and blemishes in a BB cream simply called 'natural'. She rubs a finger along her jawline as if to blend it in further.

'What's this? Pancake? ' she asks, dabbing at her cheek.

'It's actually called 'desert rose' I mumble, unable to hide my disappointment that she doesn't seem to like it. After a while she puts down the mirror and smiles naturally.

'Ok then, let's take a proper photo' she says, with a bit more enthusiasm.

This time I take my time and get a better angle. I catch her with a natural smile on her face and the result is more acceptable to her. Adding a filter, in a pale beige, which softens her features subtly, we upload it to her dating profile. As soon as it's done Susan begins rubbing at her lips with a tissue.

'Sorry, I never could bear that stuff for long'

April 30 - Frankie

I'm pleased with the deer. It's quirky, and funky. …And it's big! The chopper bike handle bars I transformed into antlers with the addition of old cutlery. This has dictated its size . Standing there with its head thrown back, and it's nose in the air, it's taller than me. A rust hole ridden animal feed bin makes up the bulk of its body, and everywhere there are bike chains , fused to make limbs , with cogwheels and bolts and washers, welded on to give it joints and angles, shape and texture. The thing is though, I can hardly move it, it's so heavy now. I've just about finished spraying it with the peroxide mix I use to speed up the rusting process, and soon it will look fabulous on Marie's lawn, if it ever reaches its final destination. Having man handled it on to sack trucks, and wheeled it over to the van , the job of getting it in there, and then out again at the other end of its journey, requires more man power than I've got. Ross isn't here, having chosen today, of all days , to drive across to the west coast to dismantle a fruit cage with his friend Robin. Desperate times call for desperate measures, and I find myself picking up the phone and calling Tony.

'Your wheels are ready. Any chance you could come over this morning and pick them up? They're kind of in my way…'

So, he'll be here in ten minutes. Perfect! I hope his back is strong.

May 1 - Heather

If I'm honest I'm a little bit scared of the dating website. Several messages have pinged my way. I'm known simply as Heather, Loudeac. My profile pic is a selfie I took after my walk the other day. I haven't improved it in any way other than to add a filter which offers a 'dreamy glow' . It seems to attract enough attention as it is. I'm guessing that Susan's inbox must be constantly pinging. Her photo is Charlotte's creation . Heavily made up and airbrushed in photoshop , it looks like Susan's daughter might have looked if she'd had one. This thought reminds me to look again at a message I got from Sophie. She is planning on coming over for a visit, now that all she need do is one test, and there's no requirement to isolate. She hopes to come soon, and suggests several dates that she could travel on later this month or in early June. I tell her to come as soon as possible. My book is almost finished and I will have lots of free time to spend with her. We can explore parts of Brittany I've yet to see. Another message arrives on my dating page just as I finish replying to her. This one from Serge, a charpentier from Lorient. I click on his photo . He doesn't look very tall , and his neck is as wide as his head. I decide to remove myself from the dating site for a few weeks. I will soon be too busy with Sophie for that kind of thing anyway. Thug wags his tail hopefully as I put my phone down and go to the window to assess the weather. It's another gloriously sunny day, and Denis, the cable drum man might still be working down the road. I smile at myself in the mirror as I slick on some tinted lip balm, then I remember that it's Sunday.

May 2 - Susan

Ok, so it's my first date, if you can call it that, tomorrow morning. It's just coffee in a bar in town with a man called Roger, who lives a little over half an hour away. It feels weird to be doing this. Paul and I were together for over twenty years, so it's a long time since even meeting a man for coffee was something I'd consider doing. On my bed lie several possible choices of outfit. I'm making a decision now in case I need to shop for anything. I'm drawn to plain black trousers and a floaty ethnic style top. I put this ensemble on the chair, and everything else back in the wardrobe, before heading down to my studio, where there are now at least five lamps that are waiting to be glazed. I am thinking about selling them, or trying to. I need to make a little bit of money. Not a lot. Just enough to justify the expense of buying all the clay and glazes . I'll never get back what I've spent on the studio itself, but if this little venture could pay for itself from now onwards, I'd be happier. I think again about the lodger idea, and dismiss it quickly, with a shudder. To share my kitchen with a stranger is unthinkable. The guest bedroom is large, and has its own en-suite bathroom, so that wouldn't be an issue. I wonder briefly if a kitchenette could be put in one corner of the bedroom, It's a big room, and it might convert quite well to a studio flat . I mull over this idea as I paint the toenails of the Betty Boop figure I've made as a lamp base, then suddenly I remember my own toenails, which will need attention if I'm going to wear sandals with my outfit tomorrow. I grab my phone. An emergency pedicure is called for.

May 3 - Angel

Back to earth with a bump, after a blissful weekend. We got back yesterday, having spent two nights on the south coast as a birthday treat. Lee insisted, over the amazing restaurant meal on Friday night, that he whisk me away for two nights in a swanky spa hotel. His birthday. His treat. It truly was a perfect weekend break, with romantic beach walks, cocktails and sunsets, and sex of course. Lots of it . But now here I am, faced with a day of laundry and food shopping. Reiki still isn't talking to me , since I left her alone, with Frankie popping in and out each day to feed and fuss her. She walks past Lakshmi and nudges her grudgingly.

Lakshmi is content to be home , and so am I really. I shove a load of white stuff into the washing machine, then take my coffee outside while mentally making a list of essentials that I need to buy. My thoughts are interrupted when a white Mercedes pulls into the driveway. My mind's a blank until I see that immaculately styled white blond head emerge from behind the wheel. Marcia !

'Oh shit' I can't help saying , spilling coffee onto my T-shirt. I'd forgotten all about her appointment, and the treatment room hasn't been cleaned since my last reflexology client on Friday morning. I smile and wave as she approaches.

'I've made you some coffee' I say, handing her my cup.

'You sit here and relax for a moment while I finish preparing the room. She stares at my T-shirt as she sits down, and I pretend not to notice.

'I'll just be a moment!'

May 4 - Charlotte

I cannot believe how much the grocery bill comes to. I accumulated a trolley full of incredibly boring things, no luxuries at all , not even wine, and it's almost one hundred euros. I hand over the bank card, and pray that it's not rejected, before throwing everything off of the checkout area and back into the trolley. This is what I hate. What a waste of time. You put it all in the trolley as you trudge around the supermarket, then unload it all at the checkout, chuck it all back in once you've paid for it, unload it again into the back of the car, then repeat the process once you reach home and need to stash it away in various cupboards and shelves. By the time I've completed this process the sun has gone in and I'm left with nothing to do this afternoon but work out how I can economise a bit. Tony comes in while I'm I sitting at the table staring at the till receipt. The shopping I've bought will barely last us one week, and I realise on top of that, that we've almost run out of cooking oil and I didn't manage to buy any. I tell him this, adding that there's no sunflower or corn oil to be found anywhere. He flicks the switch on the kettle, and shrugs

'We can't afford to stay here!' I say, eventually, putting the receipt down and folding my arms.

'Well we can't afford to leave! ' is his quick reply.

Roxy brushes past me meowing. She wants her dinner. We both look at her, and I'm sure we're thinking the same thing. She is actually a luxury we cannot afford.

May 5 - Frankie

On this bright, sunny morning I take photos. Now that the lawn is mowed and the hedge trimmed, I have permission from Marie to photograph her garden , with the deer sculpture, for my art page. I've been asked to do a feature too, for our commune magazine, of sculptures in local gardens, so I will begin with this one, and then head over to Lee's where hopefully I can have a quick coffee with Angel if she's there . I send her a quick message before getting back in my car, and she replies immediately. She will be there until about eleven. I stop for croissants in the village, buying three in case Lee is there too, and Herve gives me a big bag full of stale baguettes for the animals. He asks after Ross. They are unlikely friends, Herve being the life and soul of the village , and Ross preferring a quiet life and his own company most of the time, but they've bonded over a love of animals, and a dislike of the chasse . When I arrive at Lee's, Angel is sitting on the top doorstep with Lakshmi at her feet. She is wearing a long white shirt with nothing underneath it and her feet are bare. Her black hair is sticking up in all directions, with the sunlight filtering through it. I can't resist taking a few shots of her.

'I thought you said the sculpture!' She screams, in mock horror.

'Can I help it if you look like a work of art?' I snap a few more.

Lee is at work, and the coffee is ready, so we both sit on the steps, and I take a few photos of Poseidon from different angles.

'Are you going to include the screen from Charlotte's garden?' She asks. I put the camera down and take a bite of a croissant. I hadn't thought about that.

May 6 - Heather

All the way upstairs the house smells like a restaurant, steaming with the aroma of coriander, ginger, garlic and cumin. Eric is helping me to prepare an Indian meal. This is my second attempt at inviting everyone I've met here , to join me for an evening meal. There will be fourteen of us in total, and with this sunshine I'm hoping for a happy little gathering of friends. Susan will arrive early to help me set the tables. I've placed three in a row to accommodate everyone, and thrown linen sheets over them to look like a banqueting table.

'I can't believe you make your own naan bread!'

I was relieved when Eric offered to do this for me, along with the sag aloo that he loves to make. I'm making a huge vegetable korma , some dahl out of canned lentils, which I'm hoping will work out ok, and a prawn curry which I'm making up as I go along. It's a celebration of sorts. I've finished my book. It needs a bit of editing, but on the whole I'm extremely happy with it and I know that it's exactly what Corinne, my publisher, has been wanting from me. I can now take the rest of the year off, and maybe think about writing something a little more personal to me. I think again of my abandoned autobiography as I stir the lentils doubtfully.

'When is Susan coming?' Eric asks , as he smoothes his hair back with one hand and turns the naan bread with the other. He's taken extra care with his appearance today, protecting his white shirt with a striped apron, and wearing new trainers, instead of the muddy walking boots he normally favours. Susan walks in moments later, before I can answer his question , carrying an enormous raspberry cheesecake in one hand, and a box of wine in the other. I'm pleased to see that Charlotte hasn't done her makeup for this occasion.

'Gorgeous!' Eric puts down his spatula and takes the cheesecake from her. I wonder if he is referring to the dessert or to Susan herself.

May 7 - Susan

I wake with a slight hangover, and I am relieved when I remember that I emailed Roger last night to cancel our second date tonight. He's not for me , and I've been having niggling little doubts ever since our coffee date on Tuesday. He's nice enough, and we do have a few things in common, but there's no spark, and the thing is, that I just don't fancy him. An English widower called Jim has been sending me messages, but he seems a bit lacklustre and uninspiring , and his photo looks like a passport one. No smile. My thoughts turn to last night in general, and more specifically, of Eric . We had fun together over the poppadoms, but then I mentioned that Andrea will be coming over soon, for a few days, and his smile disappeared entirely. I'm sure I didn't imagine it. Did I imagine it? I must have. Everyone likes Andrea. She's attractive and confident, and she really likes to party. She lived here in Brittany for a few months, in a rented gîte near to us, while she was deciding whether or not to buy a house in the area. It was a bit too quiet for her though, and she left to try Spain for a while. Now she lives in England, and says she will enjoy a little holiday over here. When I got her message I was happy, and began to look forward to seeing her again, and then I remembered that Charlotte doesn't really like her, and now I'm having doubts about whether Eric does either. Oh well, I plump my pillows up, send a quick 'Thank you for a lovely evening' message to Heather, then roll over for another hour or two's sleep, before I need to get up and let Rhea out.

May 8 - Angel

Lee and I have been a bit weird with each other for a couple of days. On the surface all is well, but I sense some brooding going on underneath the smile, when he kisses me hello, after having spent the day apart, with him looking at a job a couple of hours away, and me walking in the woods and meditating. The roof of a manoir, quite high apparently will need lots of scaffolding, he tells me.

'I quoted high' he says, over a glass of chilled wine 'because I don't really want the job'

It's a bit too far away for him, and he didn't really like the guy, who spent a lot of time talking about how he needs to keep the costs down. The reason for the awkwardness between us is because of the beginning of a discussion, on Friday, about whether it would make more sense to think about maybe one day, possibly sharing our living expenses by spending our time at one house, rather than to-ing and fro-ing between the two, as the bills and other expenses are rising all the time . We were getting ready to go out, and neither one of us tried to take the conversation further, so it ended with my saying how it was 'food for thought'. I have been thinking about the situation ever since, and all of my time in the woods yesterday was spent meditating on the question. Should we move in together. I am being driven towards facing my fear, and giving it a go. The only thing is I don't know how Lee really feels about it. He seemed to be trying to steer the conversation in that direction as we drove over to Heather's, saying how he'd never been so happy as he is now, with me, but then we arrived at the party, and further discussion was halted as we greeted everyone. If only Susan hadn't then called out

'Look at the love birds! Isn't it about time you guys started planning a wedding!'

May 9 - Charlotte

So Andrea arrives on Thursday. I, for one won't be rushing over to greet her. Susan thinks she's lots of fun, and the life and soul of the party, but I remember her as a bit of a drama queen, and a bitchy one at that. Also she left, owing Tony money for fixing her car. I wonder if she'll bother to sort out that little situation. I start a Facebook post about not being able to live with debts on my conscience , but abandon it halfway through, when Roxy jumps up on my lap. She won't eat the cheap cat food I've bought, now that the stuff Susan gave me has run out, and keeps demanding something better. When I get up and go to the fridge she runs to her bowl and looks at me expectantly. I pour a little milk in and she glares at me in disgust , before heading outdoors to hunt. She has moved on from the baby birds, to field mice from the hay field across the road. I watch her from the window as she crouches low in the hedgerow at the edge of the field, before pouncing suddenly on some poor unsuspecting creature. She is fast becoming an expert, and though I pity the mice, I'm happy that she is at least capable of feeding herself. I look over at Tony, polishing the Audi Estate that he hopes to sell this afternoon. He's made the price lower and lower over the last weeks. Nobody seems to want such a big, thirsty car. Hopefully the woman who comes to look at it today, will be sufficiently impressed by its shiny bodywork, or alternatively, sufficiently charmed by Tony.

May 10 - Frankie

The blank look on Charlotte's face tells me that she's forgotten that she agreed to me photographing the sculpture I made for her garden, to include in my magazine article. It's true that she'd had a bit to drink by the time I asked her. We all had, but Charlotte more than most. I cringe as I remember her asking Eric why he didn't join a dating website like Heather and Susan , and then adding that 'there are special ones for gay men'. Eric's expression was similar to the one now on Charlottes face . One of total incomprehension. I explain for a second time about my being asked to provide photos of my work for an article in the community magazine, featuring local gardens. We both look across at the screen which is partially hidden now by nettles, and looking a tad unimpressive as the sun shines through it, illuminating the dust and cobwebs. Ok, so we have a little work to do before I can take a decent photo.

'Have you got any gardening gloves?'

Charlotte points to the garage in a vague reference to Tony, and shrugs . I need to pull those nettles out before anything else so I wander over there to consult Tony. He has some rather ineffectual disposable gloves that he uses for oil changes . I put them on and do my best to avoid getting stung. Charlotte turns the hose on the unsuspecting spiders and blasts the cobwebs away. It doesn't scrub up too badly, and I'm on the way to getting a nice portfolio together of my work within the commune, when Roxy jumps on top and poses beautifully for the camera, with her tail in the air. With the clear blue sky, and the long grass of the hayfield in the background, it's the perfect cover photo.

May 11 - Heather

Susan doesn't seem to know what I'm talking about, when I refer to what she said the other night, to Lee and Angel. That rather awkward moment, when she mentioned wedding planning, seems to have been forgotten by her. She stares at me from the top of the little stepladder as I hold the basket out towards her. The elderflower heads have a strange smell. A little bit heady, and intoxicating. A little bit cat urine. She is helping me to make elderflower cordial, as I've not done it before. After a while she shrugs and climbs down.

'Was just a little joke' she says, then changes the subject, and starts to tell me all about Andrea, who arrives tomorrow. Apparently I'll love her, though I'm reserving judgment. Sophie arrives too, at the weekend, and I'm just a little worried. She's coming over on the ferry, and there are storms forecast. She's never been a good traveler, and an overnight trip on a boat, in the middle of a storm, will be too much for her I'm sure. I try not to imagine the boat tossing about on the water, and people crashing from one side of it to the other. I know it's extreme, but when I think about Sophie traveling, I always envisage the worst case scenario, and an image of the Pont Aven going down like the Titanic, rears it's ugly head .

'We need to make sure that all of their heads are underwater' Susan says.

It takes me a minute before I understand that she's talking about the elderflowers.

May 12 - Susan

Eric is a confident driver, and we make quick progress on the route to the airport . I'm so glad I asked him to drive me over to pick up Andrea. I could have driven myself of course, but I would have been a nervous wreck by the time I got there. Heather would probably have taken me, but I know she has to drive to Saint Malo at the weekend to pick up her daughter , and so it didn't seem fair to ask her to do such a long drive today. When we stop for fuel I leap out of the car quickly with my card in my hand. The price of fuel has risen sharply and I don't want Eric to be out of pocket. He won't let me pay him for his time , but there's a million things I know he'd rather be doing, so I must think of a way of returning the favour, after Andrea has been and gone. While she's here we will be too busy catching up with each other, laughing and drinking, On our own tonight, then tomorrow with others that she used to know. I've invited Charlotte, who actually said yes she would love to come, and Frankie who declined, Eric of course will come, though I'm pretty sure now that Andrea isn't quite his cup of tea, and Tansy and her friend Mel will drive over, and possibly camp in the garden. I do have another room, but I didn't offer it, thinking it might be better if they stay in their own motor home. Heather may come for a couple of drinks , as may Didier, since he remembers Andrea from when he found her at the side of the road, apparently asleep, on her way home from a party one night. I think about my full wine rack, and the boxes of Chardonnay in my fridge. Maybe I should ask Eric to stop at the supermarket before we get to the airport. If he continues to drive at this speed we'll have plenty of time.

May 13 - Angel

It has come to light, that the mysterious job which Dave and Ryan have been working on over at Lee's, is not in fact the 'games room, come bar area, come general party room' that Lee said it was going to be. The former pig shed, which is attached to the house on its left side, is quite a big space now that it's been emptied of its debris, re floored, insulated, and plaster boarded. All that remains to be done is the plumbing and tiling, once the doorway through from the kitchen has been knocked out and made good. Lee explains all this to me as he shuffles nervously from foot to foot, and it slowly dawns on me, that what he's actually saying is that all of this is for me if I want it. A treatment room twice the size of the one I have now. My own space in his house, in what could become our joint home, but only if I'm comfortable with it. He puts his arm around me and kisses the top of my head. I can't believe that I had no idea about this. That it never even occurred to me . I've even sent him links to pool tables for sale on 'stuff for sale in Brittany', and hinted that an official opening night party might be fun when the room is finally finished. The noise of a big drill going through the wall from the kitchen side, as Dave and Ryan start work on the doorway, drives us outside, and I realise that it's about time I said something by way of an answer. There is only one answer I can possibly give. I look over at the pond, where the sun shines on the rose quartz crystal that I left there a few days ago, and I begin almost involuntarily nodding my head .

'I'll make us some coffee then' he says 'unless you'd prefer champagne' ?

May 14 - Charlotte

When I head out for my first cigarette it's already midday, and my head throbs in time to the Church bells as they strike twelve. I sip my coffee, knowing that I really should be drinking water instead. It makes me feel a little queasy. I had to drink a few glasses last night in order to be able to stomach Andrea. She was the same as she always was . Loud and a little bit rude. She had us all up dancing in the pottery studio. I hope Susan wasn't too fond of that lamp that fell off of the bench. We were just girls. Tony dropped me off, as he said he couldn't stand an evening with 'that lot', and Eric went home after one drink. I think the farmer passed by at some point, but I never talk to him as he doesn't speak a word of English, and then Heather came for a while, and must have driven me home.

'Did she mention the money she owes me?' Tony looks slightly irritated as he brushes past me as I sit there on the step. I must look a mess. I've an old T-shirt on that I slept in, and nothing else. My eyes feel gritty and I know it's because I didn't remove my makeup. I haven't even brushed my teeth.

'She said she thought that you'd come to some deal or other with that fridge'. I try to remember her exact words, but my memory is a bit hazy. When she left the gîte , she'd broken the fridge door off and had to buy a new replacement fridge to take its place. She'd got Tony to take away the broken one , and as it was a big shiny American one, Tony repaired the door, and it stands now in our kitchen, next to Tony who is slowly shaking his head.

'It was four hundred euros! ' the head shaking continues. There is nothing I can say. I sit there watching Roxy who is over in the field, hunting, and begin to feel as though I might be sick again.

May 15 - Frankie

On our way to the beach we count the people we see who are still wearing masks. There are only three. Last week we counted seven. It's a kind of straw poll. A random way to see how much has changed since they began to relax all of the rules. Covid is not so prominent now in the news, and people have really begun to live normally, and to think about other things. Even so, there are people having a fourth jab. Mostly the elderly I guess. Maisie teaches a yoga class of older ladies, and most of them have had three or four vaccinations. Many of them have been sick too, with Covid itself, a bad cold or flu, even shingles.....I breathe in the sea air. If everyone could just walk on the beach each day, and swim in the sea, I'm sure there would be far less illness . Ross agrees, though he is content to just sit on the beach , rather than venturing into the chilly May ocean. It's a few degrees warmer than it was a couple of weeks ago, so to me it feels tolerably warm, and I stroll in easily up to my waist, past the shrieking children , and dive into the next wave. There is not much surf today and the calm sea has attracted families, and groups of girls with body boards, instead of the surfers, and kite boarder's that usually abound. I stay in for maybe ten minutes, and feel invigorated when I get out, picking my way across the pebbles to where Ross sits taking photos.

'Lunch at the Sunset Bar?' He suggests , as I pull on shorts and a kimono . This makes me smile. Last summer we weren't permitted there, or indeed at any restaurant, officially. They needed to scan your vaccine pass before they would admit you. I remember walking past, and feeling sad for the restaurant owners with their empty tables. This year there is a lot to make up for.

May 16 - Heather

Sophie still looks a bit jaded but assures me that she slept well, and that she feels the country air is doing her good. We will go for a walk this morning, and then take in another brocante in the afternoon if she's up for it. The sea was fairly calm for her trip over, but despite this she was still a bit green when I picked her up on Saturday morning and I had to stop the car in a hurry on our way home. I'd had a weird feeling of déjà vu actually, as I'd had to do the same thing for Charlotte the night before. At least the need to take her home early on Friday night gave me the excuse I needed to leave the party. It would have been fun. It was fun, sort of , except that I took an almost instant dislike to Sally's friend, Andrea. The other two girls that came over to camp in the garden were just party girls having fun and enjoying a drink or two in a very 'English ladette' kind of way , but Andrea, I'm not sure what her game was, It's clear that she wanted to be the star of the show, but when she knocked that lamp over I'm sure it was deliberate, and I really didn't like the way she kept referring to Susan as her 'little grey friend'. Susan does have grey hair. Very beautiful thick grey hair with natural streaky white highlights, and darker strands that weave through it.

'Grey is very fashionable now' Sophie said, when we discussed my plans for growing out my reddish brown dyed locks. I will give this idea some careful consideration . My hair is not as thick and luxuriant as Susan's. I look at my reflection in the mirror above the fireplace, and catch Sophie doing the same thing. We both smile and I notice that there is more colour in her cheeks this morning, so that's good. I take her mug from her and go to the sink. I don't dare put these mugs in the dishwasher as they were a recent present from Susan's studio, and I'm not sure if they're dishwasher safe. I think again of the broken lamp, Andrea's general unpleasantness, and all of that teasing….Not the gentle good natured banter that goes on between friends, there was something almost malicious about her mockery of Susan's latest venture into the world of internet dating. Susan seemed to take it well enough though, and as Andrea is presumably on her way back to England at this very moment, no real harm has been done.

May 17 - Susan

Frankie tells me that yesterday was a full moon, and therefore a good time for saying goodbye to that which no longer serves you. Well it couldn't have come at a better time, with Andrea thankfully on her way home, having organised a BlahBlah car for the return journey to the airport. Now my home has blissfully returned to normal, as Tansy and Mel had already left, on Sunday afternoon, Tansy driving home in her pyjamas while Mel took a nap in the back of the motor home. When Andrea went, I was able to catch up a bit on some much needed shut eye, and now here I am again in the studio assessing the damage to my favourite piece. There seems to be nothing I can do though. The lamp is beyond repair, and that means that the best thing I've ever made is gone forever. I sit down and start again, extruding big fat sausages of clay, coiling them neatly to the shape of a flower pot, then making the circles smaller and smaller, bringing the pot in to the shape of an ali baba laundry basket. I continue to work on the structure, leaving the coils defined, rather than blending them in , and working on every layer until it looks flawless . Once glazed, hopefully this lamp will be as good as the other one, and with luck, nobody will be around to accidentally destroy it. I hesitate for a moment on the word 'accidentally' , as I tell Frankie what happened. She picks through the pieces of broken stoneware , with the 'azure, 'peacock', and 'rock pool ' glazes glinting in the sunlight. Listening quietly she looks up when I pause

'You think she meant to do it?' Frankie knows Andrea, and has never bothered to hide the fact that she doesn't like her. It's the one thing that she and Charlotte have in common.

'Can I make you a little mosaic with some of this stuff?' She asks, not waiting for a reply to her earlier question. I nod .

'If you want! They're no use to me now, so knock yourself out!'

May 18 - Angel

It's a team effort, and the look of concentration on Lee's face
really makes me smile. We manage to syringe quite a bit of the
goats milk into the mouth of the tiny hedgehog we found this
morning. Lee hasn't had much experience with animal rescuing
either, but with Ross supplying goat milk and advice, we've
managed to do ok I think, and it seems hopeful that the baby will
make it through the night . Dave and Ryan are tiling the
barn/treatment room, and what with that and the excitement of the
hedgehog, I almost completely forgot Sophie's appointment, and
pulled into my driveway to find Heather and Sophie waiting there
for me.

'Sophie has been feeling a little off colour since she arrived'.
Heather explains. 'It's been a few days and her travel sickness
usually only affects her until she's had some sleep.

'It's just the moon !' Sophie keeps saying, and I'm inclined to
agree with her . Mercury is in retrograde too, and I think we could
be in for a few surprises up until early June, when things should
begin to settle down again. I tell this to Sophie to reassure both her
and her mother, and they both nod along in agreement, though
Thug seems to disagree and is shaking his head in an effort to try
and tug loose from the lead and escape into the woodland. Heather
takes him off for a walk while I take care of Sophie. We watch
through the window as they disappear and I settle Sophie on the
couch with a cup of tea before beginning her reiki treatment.

'Would you like milk?' I offer, and something about the way
she winces at me queasily, inspires me to ask a different question.

'Sophie you don't think you could be pregnant do you?'

May 19 - Charlotte

'The joys of spring' . I write the title of my post, hoping that readers won't remember that I already used the same phrase a few weeks ago, and add the photo of some wild flowers which are pink, and could in fact be weeds, with some blushers and lipsticks lying on the grass in front of them. 'The joys of spring' I say to myself, scratching around in my head for something to blog about. My mind is a blank though, and I'm reduced to asking Roxy what she thinks I ought to write about. She blinks at me and yawns . She's been out all night hunting, in the field across the road, so she's just a little jaded this morning. A Facebook notification informs me that Andrea Raymond tagged me in a photo. I click on it immediately. There are a few photos in her post . Andrea with her arm around Susan. Andrea with Tansy and Mel , sitting on the bench in the pottery studio, glasses held high while Susan crouches in front. All of them smiling broadly

'Maybe I took that one'….I mumble to myself as I scroll through looking for one of me. There is one of Mel and Tansy dancing a kind of polka, and one of Eric just sitting there with a grin (or possibly a grimace?) on his face, a few blurry ones follow that and then there it is . In the last photo I am grinning lopsidedly, and looking like I may have had a stroke. Somehow I have a red wine moustache (I don't even drink red wine) and Andrea is sitting beside me, supporting my chin with one finger, a victorious smile on her face. The cow. I hastily untag myself , then read through the comments.

'One of us unfortunately peaked rather too soon ' she's written, with a smiley emoji, followed by a green, nauseated one.

Inspiration suddenly hits me and I reply to her comment.

'And one of us rather jealously smashed a rather beautiful work of art!'

May 20 - Frankie

'So would you sell your house?' I ask. Angel puts down her coffee. She is struggling to make a decision. The lump of money that it would bring in would surely be more than welcome , and if things for whatever reason didn't work out between her and Lee, then she'd still be able to buy another..

'Or should I let it? the rental income would mean regular money coming in …..' Angel trails off without finishing her sentence, so I finish it for her

'And you wouldn't have to work so much , so you'd have more time for other things'. She nods. The hoglet is in his box with a hot water bottle and straw. He begins to squeak, so I pick him out of his nest. He is still being fed every couple of hours, and we stop talking as Angel prepares his milk.

'It looks like he's going to make it' I say , after he's greedily suckled three full syringes and been placed sleepily back in his bed. She has a client arriving in thirty minutes , so I get ready to leave, draining my coffee and picking up my mobile phone. It's a tough decision that Angel must make. This little house up has been perfect for her, but Lee's is twice the size, and her new treatment room there will be so much bigger and better.

'The Ukrainians want to be in the towns' she says thoughtfully as we walk out together with Lakshmi in tow. It's true that a couple of the gîtes that were housing the refugees are now empty. The Ukrainian families prefer to live within reach of each other, in the towns, where they can be independent. I look around at the green fields and the banks covered in foxgloves

'But this place is so secluded and idyllic , it would soon be snapped up' I say 'lots of people seek isolation'

'Including me! ' Angel answers ironically. We hug goodbye, and in that hug I feel the full weight of her dilemma.

'Trust your gut! Remember?' I blow her a kiss as I drive off with my roof down. I know she'll make the right decision in the end.

May 21 - Heather

The clear blue sky couldn't be any bluer. The sun burns bright and hot, and it's still only mid-morning. We decide that we'll walk in the woods later, but that it's just too hot, and too far to go to the beach. In the kitchen I make a lentil salad to have with grilled sardines on the barbecue for lunch. In the stillness the birds sing loudly in the trees, and the blue tit babies can easily be heard if you stand outside my door by the stone garden wall where they made their nest a few weeks ago. Sophie sips her glass of fizzy water and smiles at me . I can't believe I'm going to be a grandmother! For the last two days we've hardly spoken of anything else, and we've laughed a lot. It's too much to take in. There is just so much to think about, but for now I think we are both content to be quiet, relax a lot (Sophie sleeps but I am too excited for that) , and eat healthily, with no caffeine or alcohol. We've told nobody except Angel , who was of course entitled to be told first as it was her idea to do the test. I had no suspicion at all , when I picked Sophie up after her treatment. She was quiet in the car, but Angel always says that her treatments can make you sleepy, so it wasn't until the next morning, when Sophie asked me to run her to the pharmacy, that the penny dropped.

'I need to buy a pregnancy test' she'd said, and we'd stared at each other across the kitchen table. It was one of those moments that will stay with me forever.

May 22 - Susan

I think Eric is upset with me. I haven't seen him all week, not since the party, and he didn't stay long at that, making some excuse about it being a 'girly' night and that we'd have more fun without him.

'Ah we think of you as one of the girls!' Someone said, I think it was Andrea, as he was leaving. I'll make him some shortbread later, and take it round to him. He's a good cook himself, but he loves my shortbread. It's raining at last , but I'm snug in my studio looking out at the garden, playing with a lump of clay. The only thing is , I've not been able to make anything decent. Not since the broken lamp episode. Two similar lamps stand side by side on the work bench. Similar, but not the same. I've been unable to reproduce the effect of those glazes that merged together serendipitously to form that beautiful piece, and so I've realised that I've still a lot to learn, and maybe I'll never be any good. I thought I was really getting somewhere, but now I'm beginning to doubt myself . I look around the studio at the expensive kiln, the wheel, and all of the glazes etc. and I realise that I've spent a fortune on this enterprise, and for what. I look at the two uninspiring lamps on the bench and I'm tempted to sweep them off with one wave of my hand , just as Andrea did to the original one, so that they too will smash to smithereens. I ignore the temptation though, and instead I head back to the comfort zone of my kitchen, to make shortbread, this at least I know I can do well!

May 23 - Angel

So I need to start somewhere. When I consulted my tarot deck and drew the death card, I realised it was time for a change. I survey the huge empty space with my drill in one hand and a couple of screws in the other. The printers tray , given to me by a good friend a few years ago, will be the first thing I place in this room. It will house most of my crystals. I decide on the end wall, away from the sun, and it doesn't take long to put it up, but I spend a while arranging the crystals in their individual cells. I will take my time getting everything just right . It's my birthday next week , and it falls, for once, at the time of the new moon. I will move in with Lee on that day , and after that I'll decide what to do with my own house. I stand back to admire my work, and my gaze is drawn to the beautiful dappled pink of the rhodonite crystal. I feel I am being urged to take it in my hand. As I do so I think of Susan, and I realise it is she who must receive this one as a gift. The rhodonite stands on its own for being excellent at improving confidence and self esteem. Susan must be in need of it's help. I place it in my singing bowl and strike a note to cleanse it, before placing it in a little muslin bag. I'll take it to Susan on my way home. Home. I must stop thinking of my house in those terms.

May 24 - Charlotte

That woman is back again, for the Audi Estate. I watch from the window. This is the fourth time she's been here, but it looks as if she will actually take the car today. A man has driven her here, so that she is free to drive it home. I watch him scrolling through his phone looking bored, as he waits, presumably for some signal or other from her, that all is well . She tears off a cheque and hands it to Tony . They shake hands and she gets into the car, taking a few minutes to adjust the seat nearer to the wheel, as she's not very tall. I watch Tony bend down to scoop up Roxy who has

135

come over to see what she's missing and at last I hear the sound of the engine . I see her wave at the other driver and Tony and Roxy walk slowly back towards the house. I hope that the cheque is for the full amount. She asked for new tyres to be put on the front wheels, then once that was done the car radio had to be changed for one with a slot for compact discs (she needs to listen to Michel Thomas while she's driving), and after all that she then began bleating about how much fuel would be left in the tank. I watch the other driver throw his arm over the back of the seat of his Peugeot 206 , and reverse smoothly out of the driveway, and then I watch her, struggling with the gears. Tony turns and waves to her, then walks in with Roxy still in his arms.

'Did she pay you the full.....? ' I'm interrupted before I finish by a loud bang . Roxy flees as Tony and I rush to the window. The Audi Estate is in the road with its tailgate crushed inwards . She's reversed it straight into Didier's tractor.

May 25 - Frankie

I am surprised to see Susan back at the pottery. Since she got her own creative space, and all of that equipment, I assumed that she wouldn't need to come here any more. Lesley welcomes her though, and the atmosphere as usual is friendly, and nurturing with lots of banter and silliness. I spend a couple of hours making urchins with lethal looking spines. They will be incorporated into the theme for my next exhibition. I'm calling it (in my head, as I've yet to tell anyone) 'What Lies Beneath'. I got the idea from my last exhibition, as I spent a lot of time staring down at the sea from the harbour wall, and wondering about what was really going on down there in those hidden depths. The pieces will all be fantastical, and tell a story of the mysterious energies of sea creatures. These urchins will be glazed in a rainbow of different colours, and will adorn the rocks which will mark the entrance, and guide the spectators through the exhibits.

'They'll be horrible to fire' Lesley says as she gently moves them on to a board where they will dry out for a day or two before going into the kiln. Susan screws up her ball of clay and starts again to make a thumb pot. Lesley says nothing, but hands Susan some fresh clay, and takes the balled up, dried out stuff away from her.

'I'm not really feeling it today' Susan says. I can empathise. I know what it is like to feel blocked, though these days for me, the ideas seem to flow thick and fast.

'Try going for a walk for ten minutes or so', I suggest, but she shakes her head, and Lesley shoots me a knowing look. I turn my attention back to urchin production, but resolve to try to do something to lift Susan's spirits if I can.

May 26 - Heather

One more day and then Sophie goes home. Time has flown by and I can't believe she's been here almost two weeks. I put the phone down, having rung Brittany Ferries and reserved a cabin for her return trip. It's a day crossing this time , but I feel that if she spends the trip lying down in her own space she will be more comfortable and not feel so sick. Tomorrow morning we will pass by Angel's and also Susan's, so that Sophie can say goodbye. We haven't actually seen much of Susan, but I think that she might benefit from the attention, as she really does seem a little down at the moment. We will tell her the baby news, and take her some flowers. Maybe I can arrange a little girly beach trip or a spa day as something to look forward to. Sophie yawns and stretches on the sofa.

'I'll go to bed I think' . She's been asleep on and off for the last hour or so, and it's still only 9.30pm.

What will I do when she's gone? It will seem very empty here with just Thug and I rattling around together. I go back to the Brittany Ferries site and start looking at booking a little England trip in September. She should have a noticeable bump by then , and we can have some fun shopping for baby things. I'm sure Frankie and Ross would look after Thug for me. With this in mind I pour myself a glass of wine and start looking into Air BnB 's for somewhere to stay, not too far from Sophie's tiny one bed flat in Bristol. My thoughts immediately drift again to the question of the baby's father , and what the situation might be. Sophie is evasive on that subject. I don't think she has yet broken the news to him, and then I think of Ted. We've had no contact at all, and yet here we are, about to be co-grandparents together. Life is strange, no doubt about that , and I wonder if somewhere in all of this there's a book, begging to be written.

May 27 - Susan

The flowers are beautiful. It was so kind of Heather and Sophie to bring them, and share their joyful news with me too. Now that they've gone though, I'm back to feeling a little bit flat. The smell of the white chocolate and raspberry cookies baking in the oven makes me feel at least as though I've achieved something today . I'll take them over to Charlotte, as I've already baked something for Eric this week, and though he was happy enough to see me, and the Tupperware container filled with his favourite shortbread, I felt as though something was wrong, and I found myself wondering if he's feeling a bit low too. Maybe I should take him some flowers. On second thoughts I won't . Flowers are maybe too much of a 'girly' gift, and he's never yet come out of the closet and told me that he bats for the other side. What's weird is that he doesn't actually appear gay in any way. If it hadn't been for Andrea, who gave it to me straight, I'd never have known. I even thought that he might have been a tiny bit sweet on me at one point, as he's always been so attentive.

'An easy mistake to make' Andrea had said at the time, and she should know. She's been around enough!, while I've been quietly married to Paul, living my sheltered life. Oh well. I take the cookies out of the oven . Perhaps I'll give the dating site another go.

May 28 - Angel

I fill my car boot up with the pots of herbs that I've been growing since my arrival in France. Lee has a lovely garden, but there's nothing much there in the way of useful plants. The big planter with the rosemary in it sits in the passenger seat, and the car smells divine. I slam the lid down, once I'm satisfied that the sage, the mint, the tray full of basil plants, the coriander, the lemon balm and the thyme are secure. Reiki glares at me and wags her tail. She senses that somethings afoot, and has been rather aloof , observing me from a distance, and not settling on my lap at every opportunity like she normally does. Maybe she can smell Hagrid on me. The little hoglet (I shouldn't have named him I know) has doubled in weight since we first took him in, and will soon be able to be released. He is no longer fed by syringe, but has teeth, and makes a lot of noise about enjoying the dog food we've been giving him. It will be so hard to let him go. I go back inside for the flared jeans and crochet top that I will wear to Vanessa's party tonight. Vanessa, a former client of Lee's, has invited us to a hippy party. Lee has been fretting about having nothing to wear but I find that most of the clothes in my wardrobe pretty much fit the bill anyway. I'll add a few beaded necklaces and paint some flowers on my face, and I'll be good to go. On a whim I decide to pass by Frankie's on my way over, to see if Ross will let me have some weed. Might as well be authentic.

May 29 - Charlotte

I must stop doing this. It's a sunny day and I should be making the most of it, and spending time outside. Instead I'm curled up on the sofa with Roxy, nursing the hangover from hell. Again. Vanessa's parties always have this effect on me. I get carried away talking to people, and I just lose track of what I'm drinking, and how much of it! and I always forget to eat, so this is the result. A message from Susan asks if I fancy passing by for a coffee. I ignore it. It's really the last thing I feel like. I know from experience that I'm going to feel better after I've eaten something, but I just can't face it at the moment. Bits of last night's conversations and events float around in my mind. Nonsensical small talk and silly innuendos. Drunken antics involving shots and cocktails, and the passing around of a pretend marijuana joint. At least I hope it was a pretend one! I avoided it myself anyway as I didn't like the smell. A fragment of a conversation I had with Lee comes to the fore in my fuzzy brain. He is looking forward to Angel moving in next week. I didn't get the chance to congratulate Angel. They didn't stay long at the party......something about feeding a hedgehog, I'm not sure, but that didn't stop me from asking Lee whether he thought they might get married eventually. I wish I could have heard his answer before Tony whisked me away. I turn over and put a cushion over my head. If only Tony would stop making that infernal racket. He's in his garage, oblivious to my condition, hammering away at the huge dent in that Audi Estate. She doesn't want it now of course. Cancelled the

140

cheque and everything, and It's up to us to bear the cost of the repairs.

'So sue me'! Was her parting shot.

May 30 - Frankie

I enjoy grouting. I choose a dark charcoal grey to contrast with the peacock, teal and azure of the glazed fragments, which arranged creatively , form a beautiful butterfly on the slate slab I've used as a base. I work the grout into the gaps, then polish away to reveal the lustre of each tiny shard. Angel appears at the door as I'm finishing off the outer edges of the wings, smoothing the grout between the butterfly and the slate so that no rough edges remain. It's her birthday tomorrow, and we're having a little celebratory drink together in her almost empty house.

'This isn't your birthday present' I say, before she gets the wrong idea and goes off into raptures about how lovely it is. It is a thing of beauty though . Those colours and the iridescence of the glaze are just gorgeous. The butterfly itself is about eight inches across, and each wing uses about thirty pieces of Susan's broken lamp.

'It's for Susan! ' Angel says, clapping her hands in excitement. 'I love what you did there, transforming something broken into something beautiful. It's a wonderful metaphor!'

Angel understands my intention without any explanation from me. She runs her fingers over the newly smoothed wings.

'Intention is everything…….and all the love that's gone into this. '. There are tears in Angel's eye'This cannot fail to lift her spirits' she says eventually.

May 31 - Heather

We both have a box of bits and pieces to take home. Frankie's is an eclectic mix of old books, glassware and tarot cards. Mine contains a few practical items. The kind of thing I had in England but have yet to get around to buying here. Tupperware, kitchen scales, a lemon squeezer etc. Angel is almost done with moving everything out, and the local brocante will take the remaining few items that no longer serve her. We sit on a wool rug in the centre of the room with a bowl of chips in the middle, and drink champagne. A box of patisserie from the local boulangerie serves as a birthday cake.

'You don't look forty five' I tell her. She really doesn't. Her skin glows, and that beautiful black hair of hers is so glossy. She is the youngest one of us. Frankie is almost fifty, and I am fifty one. We are nothing like the generation that came before us. I remember my mother at my age. A grandmother in the traditional sense. Grey curly hair, dull, practical clothes, and that 'settled' air about her which seemed to suggest that she'd done in life all of that which was expected of her, and she was now happy to just go through the motions , and stay in her comfort zone until the end of her days, her routine punctuated by certain TV quiz programmes, a bit of light gardening, and the weekly shopping. I shudder at the thought of turning into her, but ironically, grey hair is very fashionable now, and after two glasses of champagne I share my thoughts on this , as they relate to Susan, and then as an aside, I can't keep from saying how much I disliked the behaviour of her 'friend' Andrea, and her 'little grey haired lady' comments. Frankie, despite the champagne, listens with interest, but a few moments pass before she actually speaks.

'Fucking jealous bitch' is all she says.

June 1 - Susan

I'm Pulling myself together now. Walking Rhea early in the morning, then coming back home to bake and clean and driving over to Lesley's sometimes in the afternoons for a therapeutic pottery lesson. Some paperwork arrived from Paul's solicitor and I've barely glanced at it, but I suppose I'll have to appoint someone to take care of my side of things, so I make a note to spend some time today researching solicitors, instead of producing baked goods for all of my friends! I took a cake to Angel yesterday (it was her birthday, so I made something special and took it over to Lee's. She wasn't there but messaged me later with a big Thank you) . I've taken an apple pie to Eric, who kindly made me a mug of camomile tea, and gave me a tour of his garden, and cupcakes to Charlotte, who regaled me with tales of Vanessa's party, and the Audi Estate saga. Somehow she makes me feel better, especially when she offers to give me a facial and makeover

'Softer this time, please' I say, and for once she listens, and I leave there looking a bit brighter, then when I get home Frankie's car pulls up and she shouts

'Get the kettle on . I've got something for you!'

I do as I'm told , and watch as she places a bubble wrapped package on the table, standing back and gesturing for me to open it. I unwrap the most amazing present I've ever been given. It's a metal butterfly, standing there on a slab of slate, with its wings spread. I recognise the remnants of my own work, so creatively arranged to make the scales of the butterfly wings. The sun shines through the window and illuminates those gorgeous greens and blues that I've been trying to recreate ever since the broken lamp incident. Frankie makes the tea while I stand and cry happy tears, ruining Charlotte's work in the process. Half a minute goes by before she hands me a mug.

'Now then' she says 'Enough!'

June 2 - Angel

I stand and watch as Hagrid scuttles away across the garden , and feel content in the knowledge that we've successfully raised him to a healthy weight . He doesn't look back , and when he disappears from my line of sight, I say goodbye to him, and turn back towards the house. It hasn't taken us long to settle in, and Reiki seems to be at home too. She's comfortably installed at the moment in my treatment room, surrounded in things which are familiar to her, but she has the run of the house, and ventures to the kitchen regularly for food. It will be a few days before I can let her outside though. Frankie has filled me in on some of the background story between Susan and Andrea, and now I can see what has triggered this episode of self doubt and low self esteem. Andrea, it seems, has always liked to make Susan feel inferior, though Susan herself never seemed to realise it. At the party Andrea excelled herself, ridiculing Susan for joining a dating site, being scathingly critical of her pottery venture and even sniggering at the idea of her maybe selling her works. I didn't actually meet Andrea, but I can feel her bad energy from the effect she's had on Susan. Feeling guilty about spending my last few days so selfishly, having been consumed by the excitement of the house move and my birthday, I pick up the rhodonite that I should have taken over to her last week, and call to Lakshmi. The walk to Susan's is a little longer from Lee's house, but will still take less than an hour.

I'm saving fuel and exercising at the same time. Reiki stretches out on my massage table, and rolls over on her back as Lakshmi and I walk out of the door. The sun is high in the sky and there are no clouds on the horizon. I am feeling truly blessed.

June 3 - Charlotte

I don't understand Angel's comment about how everything will be ok once Mercury is no longer in retrograde, but I nod and smile anyway. We are having coffee in the little bar in town , as I bumped into her coming out of the yoga studio without Frankie. She's a good listener, and I find myself telling her all my tales of woe about the Audi woman, and our poor financial situation, and the fact that our roof leaks so badly that I dread the storm that's forecasted for this weekend . She asks after Roxy, and I can't resist telling her all about the mice and the birds that she's caught, and how fast she is when she's hunting. Angel says she is happy that she found such a good home, and I feel myself blushing! I'm about to ask her again about the likelihood of her marrying Lee, but curb the question, and ask instead about her plans for her newly emptied house. She has decided to sell it. It's a sellers market at the moment, and the money will mean security for her . I feel a stab of envy, and concentrate on my coffee for a moment. I don't want her to think that I'd grudge her that which I don't have myself. She changes the subject then , and asks how Susan is.

'She's fine' I say, feeling slightly irritated that the conversation has taken this turn, but Angel wonders about a recent change in her since her "friend's "visit, and then I can't stop myself from telling all about Andrea, the things she said and did when she lived here, and how jealous she seemed to be, of anyone who had anything, and especially of Susan.

145

'I really can't understand how they're still friends! ' I say as Angel pays for the coffee, and we walk out into the cloudy day.

June 4 - Frankie

'Nothing soothes the soul like a walk on the beach', that's what Angel always says, but for me a swim in the sea is even better. It's really a lot warmer now than it was a few weeks ago, so I stay in the water for maybe twenty minutes or so, and when I walk back up the beach there is reggae music blasting out from the bar, and it feels blissfully like summer. Ross has Artie on a lead. He's not meant to be on the beach at this time of year, so we mostly walk him in the dunes, and Ross takes him to the bar while I swim. I join him for a drink afterwards, and the trials of the day are almost forgotten; those being, the dodgy ragwort ridden hay that a nearby farmer sold us, and the extortionate fee that the exhibition hall wants to charge me for my September event. Add to the mix, the fact that the promised rain has yet again failed to arrive, so our water bill will be huge with all of our animals and the veggie garden and greenhouse full of thirsty plants , and there you have it, a full catalogue of financial woes . When I recounted these problems earlier, in an unusual moment of despair, Ross dared to compare me to Charlotte. That was the end! , and the sole reason for this emergency trip to the coast. It's worked. I meditate as I sip my beer with my spirits lifted. All of our problems are of the first world variety. We are fortunate.

June 5 - Heather

Sophie's baby is due on December eleventh . She's already chosen a name, regardless of its gender, which we don't yet know. I find myself staring at the little black and white photo which is the twelve week scan of baby Willoughby, trying to take it all in. I just cannot quite believe it, and neither apparently, can the baby's father. 'A friend with benefits' is the statement which best describes the status of this young man. She's known him a couple of years. They get on really well, and make no promises or commitments to each other, ever. They aren't exclusive, that's the thing, and Sophie, though entirely confident that the baby is his , isn't certain that he believes it himself. Paddy's tall, with amazing blue eyes apparently. An architect who is working on the extensive plans for the extension of the leisure centre where Sophie works part time on reception, and part time as a swimming instructor. They met when she accidentally stole his phone, in the sports bar/cafe, which overlooks the pool. She had mistaken it for her own when he left it on the counter, and had it in her bag for half a day, before realising her mistake when she answered it and held a strange conversation about a survey that was due to be done later that day. The rest is history, and that is all I know about him, except that he is the father of my imminent grandchild.

June 6 - Susan

I'm not used to so much attention, and it lifts me up in a way that I so very much needed . On Friday afternoon Charlotte arrived with a homemade cake. It was a lopsided sponge cake with shop bought jam, and cream from a jar, but it was so sweet of her to think of sharing it with me, and we spent a very pleasant hour without any of her usual complaints about being broke in Brittany. Then on Saturday morning Heather brought over some of the elderflower cordial she made from the flowers we picked together, and we sat outside talking about life in general, and relationships in particular. She persuaded me to go to a singles night with her, more fun than the dating sites, and not so stressful. She cheered me up no end when she said she was going to let her hair go grey like mine, as it's so fashionable at the moment. On Saturday evening Frankie arrived, bearing a bottle of wine, which we drank as the sun went down, and together we admired the scorching colours as we simultaneously lamented the lack of rain . I put the butterfly on the table between us, to show her how it's wings seemed to change colour with the light, and she told me of how she was inspired to make a butterfly, as something truly beautiful will often emerge after a period of dormancy, and it reminded her of of me when I began my pottery journey, and rediscovered a natural talent that I had completely forgotten about . She hugged me when she left, and I went to bed with tears in my eyes but with renewed confidence in myself. Then yesterday Angel sent me a message asking if I'd mind being a trial client in her new treatment room. I jumped at the chance, and was treated to two hours of reiki and reflexology, in a room scented with lavender and orange blossom. It was heavenly. I swear that I floated home afterwards, and now here I am, back in the studio. Back in the game.

June 7 - Angel

I stand barefoot on the wet grass, feeling the much longed for rain wash over me . Lee watches through the window, from the comfort of the kitchen. He's not roofing today. It's too wet. He doesn't seem to know quite what to do with himself, and he spends the morning wandering around with a tape measure, and tapping away on his laptop. I have a client due here at eleven, and so I go to change out of my wet knickers and T-shirt.

'Aren't you cold?' He asks. But I'm not . I'm so happy that it's raining at last . Mercury is out of retrograde. Susan is feeling better, and dear Sophie has sent me a photo of her scan, saying that no matter if it's a boy or a girl she's decided on the name

'Willoughby Heaven's Angel'. Heaven after Heather, and Angel after me , though I am really Angela. She doesn't say who the 'Willoughby' is after, but I feel a Jane Austen influence at work there. It's sweet of her to think of me, and I'm happy to hear that the morning sickness has eased, and that she's eating clean now. Lee comes up behind me in the bedroom as I peel my T-shirt off, and we both automatically look at our watches. Ten thirty five. It'll be a good fifteen minutes at least before Janice arrives. I allow him to to slide my knickers down as I lean over the bed, shameless as I watch our reflections in the wardrobe mirror, then Lakshmi arrives at the door to investigate what we're up to . The look of distaste on her face, as she turns and walks away makes us both laugh . We stop abruptly when we hear the bang of a car door . She's early. Lee will make her a coffee while I steal a quick shower. We are a good team!

June 8 - Charlotte

I'm tempted to light the fire. It's been raining on and off for a few days now and the house feels cold and damp. Roxy has become an indoor cat once more, and Tony is working in the garage with the door shut again, instead of outside polishing cars. The Audi Estate has been sold for 'spares or repair', and Tony is looking into obtaining an insurance policy which will cover him if someone damages a car before they've even driven it away . Technically the accident happened on our driveway, as the biggest part of the car was still on our land when she reversed into the tractor, therefore it was possible for the 'old bitch' to just 'fuck off and leave me to it ' Tony is still fuming, but a Peugeot 206 that he picked up at the weekend, and an old Mercedes that he's had for just over a week, have both attracted interest, and Messenger has been frequently pinging. Maybe things are looking up. I put a jumper on, light a cigarette, and walk quickly over to the garage to ask him if he minds if I get the fire going. He's on his phone when

I go in and I can tell by the way he's asking questions enthusiastically, about mileage and service history, that he's already spending whatever profit he may have made on the little Peugeot and the old Merc. I wait patiently to ask my own question, shivering a bit and hopping from foot to foot. It's even colder in here than it is indoors . He's still smiling when he ends the call but his face falls when I mention lighting the fire.

'We already used up all the firewood' ! Oh bugger! I'd forgotten that.

June 9 - Frankie

Angel holds out the cards, and I draw the queen of wands.

'Well of course! ', she says. 'The queen of wands is all about creativity, and she sits there at the top of her game'. We both smile at that one, and I ask her to draw one for herself.. She draws the page of cups, and explains to me that it's the card of emotional immaturity, but also of happy surprises, plus a few other interpretations. We agree that for her it's likely to be a happy surprise, and sip our coffee contentedly.. Its eight O Clock in the morning but the sun has been up for a while, and it looks like our summer weather has returned. Still, only Angel would message me at this early hour, and suggest coffee. Ross is still sleeping with Artie by his side in the empty space I left behind. When Angel leaves, in plenty of time for her nine O clock client, I line up some driftwood in size order along my workbench. I'm trying to make, for 'what lies beneath' , an underwater band, and this will become a xylophone for the strange seahorse-like creature I've made, with huge eyes from recycled, oversized sunglasses. He'll play it with a stick held firmly in the curl of his tail next to an octopus I've yet to make , who I think will play the drums, and, maybe another mermaid, with a harp. I haven't quite decided. I will need a soundtrack to go with this exhibit, and for that I may need some help. I may be the queen of wands but I can't do everything on my own. I look over at the old warped guitar I was considering using , sandblasted, and instantly I'm reminded of Henry.. It was his first 'busking' guitar which he left out in the sun for too long. I pick up my phone and bang off a quick message

'Long time no see! Where are ya and watchadoin? xxx Mum.

June 10 - Heather

It occurs to me, after yoga, and as a result of something Frankie said about the rather 'hippy trippy' relaxation text that Maisie read at the end of the class today, that getting stoned might be a good idea. It might bring out some hidden creative energy in me, and get the ink flowing. Purely as an exercise, I think I'll try this . Not for recreational purposes,. I don't need to write anything saleable at the moment, as my angst ridden super powered teenagers are proving to be quite lucrative, but just as an experiment, to see where it leads. With this idea in mind I consider heading over to Frankie's, as I suspect, though we've never openly discussed this, that she has access to the stuff I need. With no plausible reason to just drop in though, I wonder if I should leave it until the next time I see her, to ask for her help. I ponder this dilemma as I stop to buy an almond croissant, for my post yoga, naughty treat. In the boulangerie though I notice that Herve has a big bag of yesterday's stale baguettes up for grabs, and so, there it is! The perfect excuse!, Frankie uses these as treats for her goats. This experimental drug use thing is obviously meant to be!

June 11 - Susan

I look at my dating profile, and decide that if I'm to attract the right kind of man for me, then really I need to look a bit more like my true self. The photo that serves as my profile pic doesn't look like me at all. I snap a quick selfie by propping my iPad up against the kettle, and setting the timer. The result isn't too bad. It's a good light in here, and my streaky grey hair looks highlighted. I've no makeup on but my skin is clear and my neutral expression looks like the one I see when I look in the mirror. It will do. Then I look at the wording I chose, and change 'I enjoy cooking and pottery' to

' I know my way around a kitchen, and can rustle up a mean madras in no time, or even a devil of a chocolate cake, but mostly I'm found in my pottery studio , where I create the many unique pieces which I sell at local events'.

I click 'save' and then go on to reply to Frankie's email about an event in a few weeks time, which involves music, fireworks, and a craft market. I take a deep breath and summon up the courage to send off an application for a stall. I have nothing to lose, and it might even be fun.

June 12 - Angel

It's rare to spend a day doing nothing, but this is what we decide to do . After a quick check on emails and social media, over our first cup of coffee, we switch off our phones and spread blankets on the back lawn. Lakshmi immediately assumes a very relaxed position, on her back with her legs akimbo. We do the same. It's a clear day with a gentle breeze, and for a couple of hours all we do is lie around on the blankets, talking and giggling

152

like school children, drinking lemon water from a jug that we stash under a hydrangea bush to keep it cool. When Lee needs to pee he walks the few steps to the compost heap and relieves himself there. He seems quite astonished though when I do the same.

'I thought you were a lady!' he exclaims in mock horror. When the heat becomes too much we move to a picnic bench under the trees, and It reminds us both that we are quite hungry, so I shoot back to the house to raid the fridge of olives, cheese and hummus and bring it back to the table with half a loaf of yesterday's bread. The day is quite perfect, and when it ends in a spectacular sunset, it's as if we are on holiday and it's hard to believe that tomorrow we must both get back to work. The week ahead is due to be hot and humid.

'We need more days just like this' I say, and Lee flings his arm around me, kissing the top of my head as we go inside.

'Yep, I love this life, and I love you', he says . Perfect.

June 13 - Charlotte

I've never liked Mondays . I bag up the sun creams with their accompanying lip balms and refreshing face mist sprays, and stick the address labels on them, so they are ready for shipping. This particular promotion is called 'Feeling hot hot hot' , and I am. If fuel was not so ridiculously expensive we'd probably go to the beach today. It would be nice to take some time off. Tony is having a clear-out in the garage , while there aren't any cars in there. When he is ready to drive to the déchèterie I will go with him and stop at the post office to get these packages on their way, without having to put petrol in my own car. I watch him flinging old exhaust pipes and used threadbare tyres into the back of the truck.

'Are you sure Frankie wouldn't want any of this?' He asks again. I'm not sure at all , but I don't see why she should benefit from free art materials, when everything I myself want, I seem to have to pay so dearly for, so I shake my head and watch as he struggles to lift some old bucket seats, from one of the cars that he ended up scrapping. Susan has a date tonight, and I've offered to do her makeup for her, so after I've been to the post office, I hear the ping of Messenger, and I ask Tony to drop me at Susan's on the way back. Then I retrieve my phone from the depths of my handbag, to check the message.

'No Thankyou' it says 'I am going Au Naturel this time' . Jesus! Does she want to get a man or not?

June 14 - Frankie

It's not often I make something purely to please myself, but today I have a vision in mind and if it takes me all day to achieve it, that's what I'm going to do. The huge iron inner wheel, from an old cartwheel has finally arrived home. Ross found it a couple of weeks ago on a walk with Artie. It was in the woods, half buried so that you could only get a hint of it's size and shape. He managed to pull it up out of the undergrowth so that he could wheel it along. Each day he's gone back to it and wheeled it a few yards nearer to home, leaning it against a tree or a wall every few paces as he grew tired from its weight. Yesterday he wheeled it up the driveway , and I was amazed at its size . I can just about stand up in it. It will form a portal between the garden and the lower paddock. I plan to weld two cable wires to it, which will be fixed to the concrete fence posts , and then I'll wedge it at the bottom with rocks, so that it can't move. The spindly hedge which is struggling to grow there, will be cut back to reveal its circular shape, and my singing ringing tree (A sculpture I made a few years ago, inspired by a children's TV program) will stand a few

154

feet behind it , framed by the newly created portal. This may well take me all day today, but it will be worth it when I can stand here and enjoy the view of my tree, with its copper and aluminium leaves twinkling in the light, and tinkling musically in the breeze, through a perfect circle of iron, backlit by tonight's full moon.

June 15 - Heather

I'm not sure if it was the weed, or the strawberry moon. It was my second attempt last night. My first go, on Saturday had no effect. Maybe I didn't inhale enough, but I was mindful of Frankie's warning about not overdoing it, and Ross telling me to just sit quietly and give it time to hit. Last night though, I put a good pinch of it in the pipe they gave me and drew on it strongly a couple of times, and yes, I felt it kick in then, and I began to write down whatever came into my head. An hour or so later I think it was, that I went to bed and slept an incredibly good night's sleep before waking this morning as fresh as the proverbial daisy. So here I am now, with hot coffee and clear eyes, eager to discover the inspirational masterpiece that I began in my marijuana enhanced state . It's a disappointment of course. Not creative or insightful at all . Mindless drivel, with some of the words repeated several times. For some reason I've written 'look up 'Lothario'. I've no memory of why I wrote it or even if I meant 'Look up, Lothario! ' or something else. Anyway I Google it.

'A man who's chief interest is in the seduction of women'. That must have been wishful thinking.

June 16 - Susan

So Heather and I will go there together. I put down my mobile, having confirmed with her, our rendezvous for tomorrow night. It's a once per month event, and each time there is a different theme, so that it's not the same people attending every one. Tomorrow's speed dating soirée is 'English speaking night' , aimed at English people, and French people who would like to meet English people, so we are going to give it a try. Last month's theme was 'over fifties', and even though I briefly considered it, I am only a little over fifty, and I felt I was still a bit young for that age group. This month's event is for all ages , and ought to be perfect for Heather and I . We're both keen on the idea and I'm sure we'll have fun. Three butter dishes sit on the bench in front of me and I'm deciding on glazes when Eric walks in.

'Good to see you're back at it!' He says. I'm confused for a moment about whether he's referring to the pottery or the dating, but all becomes clear when he asks if he can pick up one of the bisque fired lids that I'm about to paint in 'Tahiti Grape' glaze . He picks up the piece gingerly in his manicured fingers, turning it this way and that before saying how perfect it is, and placing it carefully back on the bench.

'Would you like to have a go?' I ask impulsively, wondering why I've never asked him before. He grins, and reaches for an apron.

June 17 - Angel

It's so unbelievably hot. Lee goes to work early every morning , leaving home at five thirty am. The slates, so dark that they are almost black, actually burn the skin in this weather. He stops work at nine thirty , and then goes back for a couple of hours at around seven in the evening. When Frankie messages me about a swim in the river over at her place, he is getting ready to leave for an evening stint, where he will hopefully be finishing off the roof of a longere not far from us. He drops me off at the bottom of Frankie's lane, on his way over, with Lakshmi on her lead, so that we can walk back after my swim . Ross is unaware of my arrival until I unclip her and she bounds over to him wagging her tail excitedly. He is completely naked as he drives back and forth on a ride-on mower. I see him before he sees me , and from my sideways-on view he looks like he could be a calendar model, with his body taut and tanned like that. He turns in my direction, and grins and waves, unashamed of his naked state. Frankie and Artie are already down by the river apparently, so I stroll over that way , through the new portal that leads to the paddock which borders the river. The sweat pours down my back and I wonder once again if this could be the onset of menopause. I've been sweating a lot lately, more I think than could be attributed to the rise in temperature. When I reach the river I see that Frankie too is totally naked as she swims . I look down at my black costume, with the sarong tied around it, and suddenly feel a little overdressed.

June 18 - Charlotte

Susan gives me a meaningful look as I hang the mobiles from the front of my stall. It's a car-themed event though, and Frankie isn't even here. (I checked on the list of stall holders when I arrived) . The mobiles, made up of car wheel trims hanging on brake cable, are in keeping with the event, as are the little driftwood cars with their wheels cut from old tyres and glued on, with other recycled materials.

'My stall would look a bit out of place otherwise' I say, as she raises an eyebrow. The other stalls turn out to be mostly art and sculptures, handmade jewellery , soaps, and vintage clothes . My cosmetics stand out as the most colourful items on offer, and I attract the ladies who, bored with accompanying their petrol

157

headed partners, are on the lookout for something a bit more girly. Susan offered to help me sell a few things and even to drive me here, a good idea as it turned out , as my fuel was running very low. I didn't appreciate this offer though when she was outside my house this morning at stupid o clock with her engine running. I'm doing a roaring trade on a skin spray which smells divine but which is supposed to ward off biting insects (I'm not sure if it does) , and the little goodie bags containing lip balm, a mini fan and a cooling facial mist , which I've labelled 'Southern Comfort' . I'm in the process of putting an Azure eye shadow in a gift bag with with a French Navy eye pencil for a lady who is buying them as a present for her daughter, when Susan suddenly lurches forward and removes the mobiles from the front of the stall , quickly scooping up the cars, and dropping them into a box underneath the table. Seconds later Frankie walks past and gives us a wave as she disappears into an art gallery further along the road. Smiling, I hand the package to my lady customer who waits patiently with her money in hand during this flurry of activity. Susan catches my eye. She's shaking her head slowly.

'That was close!' She says.

June 19 - Frankie

A wet day, and there is no excuse for not catching up with the boring stuff. I choose a photo to put on Facebook, of an amusing character I just finished making out of an old exhaust pipe and some defunct garden tools. Mower belts sprout from his head in dreadlocks and his rusty socket eyes stand out on stalks. He holds the skeleton of an umbrella over his Rastafarian locks, and smokes an oversized pipe made from a socket spanner. I caption it 'At least this weather will make the grass grow!' and it gets seventeen likes in the first five minutes. I am happy to be cheering up a dull Sunday. Susan posts a photo then, of Charlotte's stall yesterday. I

158

notice the 'wheel adornments ' aren't visible in this picture and I smile to myself as I remember them being rapidly removed as I approached the market. Seriously, she cannot think that she's any threat to me with her obvious attempt at copying. The childish and amateur attempts are really quite laughable. I give Susan's post a little heart, then move on to more important things. I need to update my website with a photo of the portal, and a tiny taster of my next exhibition, planned for the end of the summer. A sudden thunderclap sends Artie under the table, and I rush to switch off the internet, fearing that the live box might blow up. The storm doesn't last long , and when after fifteen minutes or so I log back in, my post has seventy two likes already, and lots of amusing comments and questions. I decide that I'll come back to it later and instead I get ready to walk Artie in between the showers. Maybe I'll drop in on Charlotte and tell her what I actually think about her pathetic efforts. I daydream a bit about how this confrontational conversation might play out, but then I let it go. It's not worth worrying about.

June 20 - Heather

Ok so I'm not hungover. That's good, but I still feel the need to detox . The Fête de la Musique is in full swing and I have been to local events for the last three evenings. Not really drinking, at least not very much, but still enough to make me realise that I can't do this any more, not at my age, and not without some recovery time in between sessions. Today I'm going to drink nothing but water with lemon, mint, and cucumber. I'm going to eat a little fruit, and maybe a probiotic yogurt, but that's all. Tomorrow I've got a date with a man called Andre , who I matched with at the speed dating evening. He's French but speaks quite good English, so we will at least be able communicate. He owns a brocante somewhere not far away, and we will meet at a cafe in Baud, a public place that is equidistant from where we each live, as advised in the guidelines emailed to those of us who were lucky enough to match with someone. We will spend an hour or two, not more, having a drink and chatting, and if we like each other, we will meet again for a similar date or maybe dinner at a restaurant. Anyway, at the moment it's just drinks, and I'm looking forward to it, in the way I might look forward to a trip to the dentist.

June 21 - Susan

I didn't really like anyone at the speed dating thing. Well I'm not sure if I didn't like anyone really, or if I just didn't like the whole thing. It was too fast! I guess the clue was in the title of the event, but just five minutes with each person meant that we never got past introductions. There wasn't time enough to find common ground and I found myself feeling a bit stressed, and clamming up . Delilah rubs against my leg , reminding me that she hasn't had a treat yet this morning. She has become very affectionate lately, and if I hadn't had her sterilised I would think that she was about to come into season . I pick her up and she purrs, and pushes her face against me.

'We are probably destined to grow old together on our own' I say , and wonder if she'd ever be acceptable to my taking on more cats, and becoming a mad old cat lady. Eric's pots, just out of the kiln , are on the bench waiting to be glazed. I message him to let him know, then stand looking at the array of vases, butter dishes, lamps and salad bowls that I've made. I did mention to Charlotte that I would have quite liked a stall of my own at the show last weekend, but she didn't take the hint , and seemed reluctant to introduce me to the organisers as they circulated. Oh well there will be other events .....Funny that's exactly what I told myself after the speed dating.

June 22 - Angel

Last night's summer solstice was special. My first one here in
this house. My first one with Lee. He enjoyed the idea that we
would sit out in the garden quietly taking a glass or two and
watching the sunset . When it began to rain , he didn't even
mention it. When it began to thunder, he stroked Lakshmi's head
and gently lead her away, back to the house. Her fear of thunder is
something we must live with. He watched then, from the window
as I walked naked around the garden, touching plants and trees,
feeling the wet grass between my toes and observing the ripples on
the pond as as the huge summer raindrops break the surface. When
the light disappeared altogether, except for the occasional sheet of
silvery lightning briefly illuminating the whole house and garden, I
went inside to find him waiting with one of the big fluffy towels
from my treatment room. We went to bed then, and continued to
celebrate the longest day in a ritual all of our own, and when I look
out of the window this morning now that the rain has finally
stopped , everything thing feels new and different. I pull on a t-
shirt of Lee's, and head for the terrace. With my goddess stone in
one hand and my crystal ball in the other, I settle down to
meditate.

June 23 - Charlotte

Oh my god it's raining again! I know the gardeners amongst us
will be happy, but seriously, enough is enough. I open the window
just enough to blow the smoke out. Roxy looks at me with a
malevolent glare. She blames me for the terrible weather we've
had recently, and resents the fact that she must get wet while she

hunts. Her discontent is demonstrated by the fact that she would rather defecate on the sitting room rug, than go outside for that purpose. When a familiar odour reaches my nose , I stub out my cigarette in a plant pot, and chase her out of the door, before looking for something with which to clean up the offending offering on the carpet. When she slinks back in a few minutes later with her tail between her legs, I point at the rug and scream at her

'Don't you ever fucking do that again!' She flinches and goes to hide behind the sofa. Tony arrives at the door with a spanner in his hand , and a concerned look on his face .

'What's all the shouting about?' A deep rumble of thunder prevents my answer from being heard.

'The live box!' We both say say at once.

June 24 - Frankie

I started the day early and made some brownies heavily laced with canna butter. They smelt so good that I baked some more without the magic ingredient, just so that I can eat one for breakfast without any adverse effects. When I'm done, I wrap half of the ordinary ones in some kitchen roll and place them in a basket by the door while I get ready to go out. I'm trying to follow Angel's example ,and be a little bit kinder to as many people as I possibly can, starting with Charlotte. I can definitely afford to be a tiny bit nicer to her, so my plan is to pass by for a coffee, and offer her these little beauties fresh from the oven . (Not the ones with the marijuana in . She wouldn't approve of that at all!) . My thoughts are therefore full of good intentions as I take the shortcut down the field track towards the road where Charlotte and Tony live. It's a good twenty minutes walk, but I see nobody, except for a farmer in the distance, driving a tractor, until I reach Charlotte's road, where cars take advantage of the long, straight, pothole free

162

surface, and pick up their speed. It's not a main road, but the number of cars using it to avoid the busier motorway route has increased in the last couple of years, and none of them are very considerate of walkers or wildlife. That's why instead of the brownies, my basket now contains a lifeless furry bundle in a velvet collar, still warm, and I'm dreading knocking on Charlotte's door . The tears in my eyes are blinding me , and I almost get run over myself, by a man who hoots at me and shouts 'English!'....something I don't clearly hear, because Tony is already running towards me and calling my name.

June 25 - Heather

'There is no real spark' I tell Angel, as I place coffee on the table outside, and rub the rain off the chairs with the tea towel.

'Give it time' is what I expect her to say . It's what Sophie said on our zoom call yesterday morning. It's what Susan said when I passed by her studio last night. But Angel doesn't say that. Instead she just looks at me and nods wisely. Andre was good looking, is good looking. We understand each other, with his passable English and my increasingly fluent French . He has a serious interest in antiques, and an eye for what people will buy, he says, but mostly he arranges house clearances, and cherry picks one or two items for his shop, while distributing the rest to recyclers and the less discerning brocanteurs of his acquaintance. We agreed that the cost of living has increased dramatically, that there is more to life than work, and that a couple of glasses of wine is enough if you are driving . We then agreed to meet again at the same bar this evening, and to go on to a restaurant for a light supper.

'Are you looking forward to it?' Angel asks. I shrug, and decide to think about it later.

'So how is Charlotte?' I ask, changing the subject back to the sad news that only reached me when Angel arrived unexpectedly this morning.

'Bereft. I'm sending healing from a distance' . I shrug again. I wish there was something I could do.

June 26 - Susan

After messaging Charlotte the obligatory 'Thinking of you. Love and hugs', that I've sent each day since it happened, I load my kiln with a variety of glazed pieces. Little plates and matching egg cups with tiny ceramic toast racks that fit neatly on the plates. They are all glazed with duck egg blue and have comical little chicken decals on them. I think they're going to sell well in my new Etsy shop . The little gravestone goes in last. It simply says 'Roxy' in large letters , with 'RIP little one ' in small handwriting underneath. I have glazed it in verdigris. It's the only thing I could think of doing that might help a tiny bit. When Minx died it took a couple of weeks at least before I could get through a day without crying . It was shortly after we moved here that Paul found her dead in the barn. We think she'd been poisoned. Poor Minx. She was such a character. Delilah is lovely but it's not the same . I think again of taking a second cat, then decide again that it's a no no….maybe it's a man that I need . So I'm back to that, wondering whether it's worth trying the online dating again. Rhea looks up hopefully as I close the kiln. Maybe I'll walk her over to Eric's. I have two pots, nicely finished and glazed in a mix of Garden Mint and Purple Heather. I think he'll be happy with his first pottery efforts .

June 27 - Angel

'I could give them a day' Lee says, when he gets home after a full days work, and I'm chucking a pizza in the oven with one hand while throwing a salad together with the other . I put the tea towel down and pour two glasses of wine. We take it in turns to cook. Me, producing very basic fare and trying to make it look like something you could actually eat. Him, favouring the more exotic, spicier creations, of a much more cosmopolitan menu. Last night we had Turkish flatbreads with spinach and feta, and a spicy lentil salad with pomegranate. We stare at each other over the table.

'You mean on the roof?'

He nods. 'Maybe Friday' he says, decisively, and I walk around the table and kiss him. The kiss leads into something more while the pizza burns to a crisp in the oven. I whip it out, smoking, and frisbee it out of the window, onto the lawn, putting a second one in, in its place, before he can offer to cook again himself.

'That's so kind!' I say, picking up the conversation as if we hadn't stopped talking.

'Well, it would just be a patch up job , replacing the slipped slates and broken ridge tiles, but it would be good for a couple of years or so, and they'd be dry'

I pick up my phone to message Tony . I'd offered to pass by and give Charlotte some reiki over the weekend but she didn't respond. I was trying to think of anything that might lift her spirits and Lee's offer should be just the thing. Charlotte is always saying how desperate she is for the roof to be fixed but they've never been able to afford it . I look at Lee as he eats his pizza contentedly, and feel an overwhelming surge of love.

165

June 28 - Charlotte

I see Frankie's car at the end of the driveway when I step outside for my first cigarette. The car is empty, so she must be in the garage with Tony. I decide to creep over and catch them talking about me, but they stop their conversation, and turn towards me, smiling as I approach, too noisily, despite my efforts not to crunch the gravel in my old crocs. I did hear something about 'the straw that broke the camel's back ' though, and I guess I must be the camel that they are referring to.

'I brought you some brownies' Frankie says, holding up a little Tupperware box, 'and this' . She gestures at a plant in a pot on the bench behind her . It's a little rose bush .

'I thought maybe ......' she stops speaking when she notices that I'm not responding to her at all, and I wonder then if she thinks I blame her for what happened. I'm not sure , but she looks as if she'd prefer to be anywhere other than here, standing in front of me . She looks uncomfortable, and maybe even afraid of me. Tony takes me by the shoulders and looks into my eyes then, concernedly.

'Frankie came by to check that you're doing ok' he says, nodding so that I begin to nod too , and finally manage to say 'Thank you' . She looks relieved . The miniature rose is pretty, and I rub a petal between my fingers.

'It can go on her grave' I say, before I turn away and go back to the house, leaving them to finish their little chat.

June 29 - Frankie

I take off my welding mask and gloves when I see the post lady walking up our driveway. She only does this when there's a parcel for us, that's too large to go in the box, or if there's something that needs to be signed for. I wave, in greeting as I walk towards her, and she stops to fuss Artie, who has a bit of a thing for her. She's been our post lady for a couple of years now, and I really must ask her name. The unassuming, brown cardboard package that she hands me contains packets of glass. Delicate strands of glass in various colours, for fusing . I've been longing to have a go at this, having watched loads of YouTube instructionals and pinned some ideas on Pinterest. I scrawl my signature excitedly on to the little hand machine thingy that she passes to me, exchanging my first name for hers as she tries to pronounce 'Steiner' . She is called Élodie, and lives near the coast, almost an hour away. We chat for a couple of minutes before she hands me the rest of the mail.

'Congratulations for the article' she says, as she walks away , and I shuffle through the various letters and publications to find the local magazine which will be delivered to every house in the area this morning. There, on the front cover is Charlotte's garden, with the screen I created for her. Sitting on top of it, posing professionally for the camera, is Roxy. Fuck! I'd better warn Tony.

June 30 - Heather

It's the last day of June. I've officially lived in France for just over six months. I have friends. I have a social life. I have a dog, and I've written a book (not exactly high literature, but hey, it pays the bills) . It's just a life partner that I'm sadly lacking. Andre repeatedly said 'we stay friends' . I was relieved, and I think it was obvious to him. It's not just the language that's different, it's the culture too. We share nothing in common by way of books , films or music. And the humour! Well it just doesn't translate. I need an

English man, or at least a man who speaks good English and enjoys a good laugh. Someone to have some fun with . I'm contemplating this over a thermos of coffee , as I sit alone by the river, throwing sticks for Thug. He loves to run after them, venturing occasionally into the water when he dares, but abandoning them to their fate if they float too far from the edge or too fast towards the weir. Whenever a cyclist appears on the tow path he rushes over to protect me , barking furiously. I'm pouring myself another coffee when a Lycra clad figure appears on the path, pushing his bike instead of riding it. Thug stops short and wags his tail. This guy obviously speaks doggy language.

'Bonjour' I say amicably. It's customary to speak to everyone you see when out for a walk.

'Bonjour!' He replies, then tentatively 'Hello even!'

July 1 - Susan

The problem with shipping ceramic items, when they are sold in my Etsy shop, is a rather obvious one. What little profit I stand to make, soon disappears when I need to buy so much bubble wrap and strong cardboard boxes. I've made a lot of mugs this week . The ones without handles are popular. I put a little notch in the rim of these, to hold the string of a teabag , and glaze them in duck egg blue and beige, with a golden halo around the top, in sunset orange. I'm proud of how they look in the photos, which I've taken using the new light box I bought especially for this purpose - another expense!

'A shop is what you need' , Lesley says, 'a bricks and mortar shop, not just a virtual one!' . She's popped over to look at my studio for the first time and seems impressed. I hand her one of the mugs with a teabag string notch.

'This is such a great idea!' she says, then surveys the shelf full of lemon squeezers, some of which are destined to be sold on my first craft fair stall tomorrow, along with some mugs , butter dishes, lamps and various other items. Lesley surveys the lamps critically .

'These would be better in an art gallery' she says quietly, as she takes a photo, and I feel myself glowing with pride. I hand her a coffee and as she reaches for the sugar bowl, her gaze falls on the community magazine that lies on the bench next to it. On the front cover Roxy stares back at her from the top of Frankie's beautiful screen .

'This kind of publicity wouldn't go amiss either!' She says. I know. I've thought of that myself, though I've never voiced the idea.

July 2 - Angel

I'm not used to being interviewed. Lee grins at me as he stuffs a chocolate digestive in his mouth, then leaves me to it, closing the kitchen door behind him. Eloise scrolls through the photos she's just taken of my new treatment room.

'So it's holistic therapies mainly?' She asks. I'm sure I've gone through this with her already, but I start again, outlining the treatments that I offer, reiki, reflexology, facial reflexology, Indian head massage etc.. she is half English, half French, her mother having met her French father in England before moving here where Eloise was born, and she is therefore fluent in both languages. It is for this reason that she interviews the proprietors of English businesses for the community magazine which comes out every two months . I'm only doing this because Frankie told her about me .

'It's maybe better if you write your own text though' she'd suggested, but I don't feel confident enough to do that. My writing skills are negligible, unlike Frankie's , whose cleverness with words almost matches her artistic abilities. Eloise takes out another tissue and blows her nose again. She has a cold, not Covid, she keeps telling me. We finish up the interview with a discussion about my special offer for August. A relaxing facial will be offered with every reflexology treatment booked. This will add a half hour to every reflexology treatment, but August is always a quiet month as most people take their holidays then, so I should easily be able to give extra time to those who need me . When Eloise stands up and prepares to leave , Lee comes back in.

'All done already?' He asks. There are still a few chocolate biscuits on a plate on the table, and he takes another. It's a weakness we share . I see Eloise scribbling something quickly in her notebook as she gets in the car. I'm not sure why, but she doesn't really inspire confidence.

July 3 - Charlotte

It's sweet of Susan. She means well . I stare at the perfectly formed ceramic cross with the words 'Roxy RIP' on it. It's filed to a point at the bottom, so that it will easily stick in the ground .

'A bit much for a cat really' I say. I'm not really sure why I say that. Susan looks a tiny bit hurt so I add 'I'm really grateful though. Ok, let's stick it in'.

We stand there then saying nothing while Susan picks the dead heads off of the rose bush that Frankie brought, and I try to remember how much I cared about this little cat when she was alive, but I absolutely can't. My feelings are numb, just as they were when I miscarried that baby. The loss of a life seems to affect me like that. I wonder if I've always been this way, and whether any death could ever truly affect me. Tony comes down from the the ladder from where he's been clearing the gutters of slate shards and rusty crochets. It was kind of Lee too. He came over on Friday and replaced all the slipped and broken slates. It took all day .

'You are water tight now! ' he said, as he was leaving, and I thought it was a reference to the fact that I didn't cry at all over the cat.

'That looks really nice' Tony says 'Thank you Susan!' He squeezes my arm and I pretend at first not to understand that he's prompting me to thank her too. Eventually I give in to the pressure and repeat my earlier phrase .

'I'm really grateful' . It's easy to say, but not so easy to feel . Susan gives me a hug though, and it does warm me up a bit .

'Look, the sun's coming out' she says.

July 4 - Frankie

The yoga class stretches me awake, and I feel ready to face the day. The week even! Clouds scud across the sky but the forecast looks good, and I send a quick message to Angel to ask if she fancies a cheeky beach trip later . She missed yoga again , and I'm guessing she was probably having a steamy early morning love-in! Good for her. I drive home anticipating a quick cup of coffee and then a spot of welding before I head for the coast, for a driftwood hunt and an invigorating swim. When I pull up in our driveway though, Ross is standing there talking to a woman who is holding a leading rein attached to what appears to be an old donkey. He grins at me guiltily. I know that expression.

'This is Madison' he says, as I gaze upon the most soulful eyes I ever saw.

'Her owner died…' I don't hear the rest of the story as the woman starts to speak to me in very fast French that requires all of my concentration if I'm to understand anything she says. It's the usual story of neglect and homelessness, and when I notice the poor creature's overgrown feet my heart goes out to her. She can barely walk, and she's so thin! She probably needs to see the horse dentist as a matter of urgency too.

'I said we'd take her' Ross says, unnecessarily. I take the lead rein from the woman, and hear her audible sigh of relief.

'Come on Madison , let's see if we can make you a bit more comfortable' . Slowly she puts one foot in front of the other, and follows me meekly to the paddock . 'Bye bye beach day' I mutter to myself.

July 5 - Heather

'She needs bolstering a bit' Susan says, of Charlotte. Well it's only been a few days really since Roxy's fatal accident , and she was an 'only' cat, so I can imagine how Charlotte must feel.

'She will get over it soon enough' I answer 'it goes with the territory when you have animals' . I look at Thug, on his back in the doorway, catching some rays . I would hate to be parted from him now. Funny that I'd never considered getting a dog before Angel suggested it all those months ago. She was right though it seems, and as Susan tells me for the third time about Charlotte needing support , and how Tony doesn't seem to understand, I find myself drifting away, back to the riverside where it seems those with dogs go to meet others with dogs , or even others without dogs , such as the cyclist I met the other day. Alan is his name . He doesn't have a dog himself, though he really likes them. He likes a glass of wine of an evening too, and he can't stand people who drop litter . He reads, at least one book per week . He hasn't read any of mine, not surprising really , seeing as they're usually enjoyed by teenagers and tweenagers. We met again by the river last night , and agreed to have a drink together at the bar tabac, just up the hill . We walked together, chatting and throwing sticks for Thug. Him pushing his bike, me rather enticingly dangling a poo bag. He's maybe just a little young for me. I'm not too sure. We have agreed to a walk together next weekend….Susan wonders if Charlotte is in fact clinically depressed, and I'm back in the room, nodding and trying to look as though I've been listening.

'So how can we help?' I ask.

July 6 - Susan

I look at the two community magazines in front of me. One was delivered to my mailbox last week, in the conventional manner, while the other was thrust into my hands by Tony as I

173

pulled up in their driveway. I decide to take one down to Eric , as I haven't seen him for a few days . It's just an excuse to drop in on him really. He probably received his own copy already , but if I take him this one I'll probably be offered a coffee or a glass of wine, and at the same time I can update him about Charlotte. He doesn't really know her that well , and he's probably not that interested, but anyway Rhea could do with a walk and as it's just across the field and down the lane......we set off when the heat of the afternoon has died down a little, and he greets me from his garden gate, where he stands with two banana trees in pots , which he says were going cheap as they were a bit dehydrated.

'Are you expecting bananas to grow here' ? I can't help but be totally bemused by his optimism when faced with the Brittany climate . I remind him of the date palms that he bought a couple of years ago which withered and died, never producing any dates.

'Speaking of dates' he says, 'I actually have one this weekend. I'm meeting someone called Michel. A blind date, friend of a friend, kind of thing! '

'That's fab news!' I say, thinking miserably about my own unsuccessful attempts at finding a love life. I try my best to look cheerful as I hand him the magazine I brought, then focus on the banana trees.

'At least it's a south facing wall' I say.

July 7 - Angel

Michel runs his hands through my hair a few times. Since Covid he's avoided washing it. He doesn't have to disinfect the

174

whole basin area between customers if he doesn't . He looks at me in the mirror. 'Something's different isn't it? ' He asks . It's the first time I've seen him since I got together with Lee, so I fill him in on the details.

'So it's lurrrve! ' he says 'lucky you!' Michel and I usually spend a good while chatting about his love life, or lack of it , so it makes a change to have the tables turned , and to talk about mine. I try to share, without over sharing, while he snips away at the ends of my hair, and enthuses about how thick it is and how lucky I am that I still have my natural dark colour.

'It's almost blacker than black' he says 'where is the grey? Are you a witch or something?' He asks this every time, and I just smile at him in the mirror without ever answering the question. Lots of my female friends come to him for their hairdressing needs, and he has a different line for each of them . We are all flattered. Everyone loves a gay hairdresser. When I stand up, brushing hair off my skirt as he flicks through his diary to make my next appointment, he tells me he has a date this weekend.

'That sounds exciting!' I say. He winks at me as he takes the money I give him

'I'll tell you all about it next time'. He ushers me out of the door after the obligatory air kisses.

July 8 - Charlotte

So we no longer have Boris. I think about this for a minute or two, but it means nothing to me really.

'Who will we end up with next?' I ask Tony, who is sitting in the car next to me, scrolling through his phone. We are early at the

175

restaurant where we are meeting Lee and Angel. It's our treat . A token of gratitude for the roof patching that Lee did for us. We can't afford this really, but a new roof would have been several thousand euros, and we certainly couldn't afford that . When Tony doesn't answer me, I pull down the little mirror in the passenger window visor and start fiddling with my hair . It could really do with a cut, but I don't really like the hairdressers here . They always cut too much off and when they do a colour it's so vivid and harsh. I had to change all of my makeup last time as it clashed horribly.

'That would be another good reason to go back to England ' I say 'for the hairdressers', but Tony isn't listening. He's checking out the cars for sale on Facebook, and considering making silly offers on them so that he can sell them on at a profit . I see Angel and Lee walking towards us, as I push the mirror back up . She's easy to spot from a distance with her floaty clothes and that cloud of black hair.

'I bet she gets it cut in England' I say as we get out of the car to greet them.

'Enough about England already! We can't afford to move back there, and anyway I thought you wanted to go to Spain now!

I'm a little shocked at this outburst. I did mention Spain, but I didn't think he was actually listening to me.

'I hope it's not Priti Patel anyway', he says, and I'm momentarily confused, but then Angel hugs me affectionately by way of a greeting, and tells me how lovely my hair looks, so I instantly forget all about Tony's irritation and begin to look forward to a fabulous evening.

.

July 9 - Frankie

176

It's a last minute thing. Two artists who paint, one in a figurative style, the other more abstract landscape , have asked me to place a couple of sculptures in their new space , which is not to be called a gallery , but is , in effect, a gallery. An old stone barn, attached to a brocante, looks stunning hung with their paintings . Some of the antique furniture from the brocante itself , has been artfully arranged in here, to create a truly beautiful setting. I deliberate for a while over the photos. I don't want to part with any of my 'what lies beneath' exhibits as my own exhibition is only a couple of months away. I do have a couple of lights that I started to make for a restaurant before Covid hit. They are not wanted now as the restaurant failed to reopen, so I could finish them off and they would look stunning hanging from the huge oak beam that spans the barn from front to back. I also have pieces of a female figurative sculpture that would look well with some of the paintings once I put her together. I write my reply , outlining these ideas and confirming that I could have them ready for the opening vernissage on Bastille Day, and send it off to the artist who emailed me, 'Sophie Le Brestec' . Then I set to work. The lights are the barrel like centres of old cartwheels . I have four of them which I turned, one at a time, in a cement mixer with some sharp sand . This resulted in smoothed and weathered, ball like structures , and I then glued frosted glass panels neatly into each hole . I need to pair them up and attach ropes which will allow them to counterbalance over the beam . Then I'll need to wire them up. Artie sighs deeply as I open my studio door, as if he somehow senses that we're going to be in here for quite some time.

July 10 - Heather

Susan arrives with a box of plasters especially for blisters , just as I'm about to sit down with a banana and Nutella sandwich for breakfast. It's about eleven o clock.

'I feel so silly!' I say , as a greeting. Alan and I walked for three hours yesterday. I carried with me, two bottles of water . I wore a hat, and sunscreen, and for much of the time we walked in the shade of the trees. What I stupidly did though, owing to the extreme heat, was leave off my walking shoes in favour of sandals. Flat heeled and supportive, they are usually fine, but after an hour or so of walking in them, on uneven ground, the straps began to rub, and I , not wanting to look silly, kept going without mentioning anything to Alan of my discomfort, so that by the time we got back to the car, two huge blisters had formed, one on each heel, and now I'm not sure if I'm going to be able to walk much today at all, much to Thug's disgust.

' Did you have fun though? Is he nice? Fanciable? ' Susan asks a string of questions as I make us each a glass of cold water with cucumber, mint and lemon. I do like him. He's two years younger than me with a quick witted sense of humour. He's not been in a relationship for a couple of years or more , not since he moved here in fact, from Guildford . Apparently he just drove to Portsmouth one day , got on a ferry and bought a house here before he had time to change his mind. He works remotely for an English company, doing some kind of web design. He knows a few English people , and has a few French friends, but prefers to live a quiet life. That's pretty much all I know really, and all I want to tell Susan at the moment. She smiles knowingly.

' Ok but do you fancy him?' She asks.

July 11 - Susan

Everyone seems to have someone. Even Heather has met a man now, and I don't know but it looks like it might be the start of something. I throw a big lump of clay on to the wheel, and begin centring it. I think of Angel with that glow about her, Frankie and Ross who have such an easy way of being together, and Eric who is being cool and evasive about his date with Michel, not that I've broached the subject of course. I don't want to appear too nosy , and I'm pretty sure that I don't want to hear the details of his love life anyway. Thinking about Eric, I look over at his stripy apron hanging on the hooks by the door, and I long for some company. I've realised that companionship is what I'm truly missing, not romance, not sex. I pick up my phone and send him a message which simply says 'coffee, cake, and clay? '. A positive reply is returned almost immediately so I lay out his apron, put a board in front of his chair with a slab of clay on it, then head back to the kitchen for the banana cake that I made at six o clock this morning. My phone bleeps with a second message. This time it's Charlotte.

'Tony off looking at cars again today, leaving me on my own to sort the garden out, in this heat! Longing for a day of well deserved relaxation, but no rest for the wicked! Anyway I expect I'll cope . Enjoy your day, pottering'

Poor Charlotte. I message back

'Come over for coffee and cake, and I'll help you with the garden later this afternoon' I click 'send' before I change my mind. Eric will be ok in Charlotte's company for a little hour or two.

July 12 - Angel

When I feel the need to change my T-shirt for the second time in a couple of hours, I begin to suspect that I might actually be properly menopausal now. There is sweat running down my back and I dream of making it over to Frankie's for a river swim later this afternoon. However I have a client, Marcia, who comes regularly now for a massage, and likes me to use a lot of pressure. The treatment room is immaculate, and I've just time for a quick coffee before she arrives . I'm looking forward to showing off my new space as I'm pretty sure she suspects me of being a little bit flaky and not strictly professional, so this room, with its airy, whiteness, where everything has its place, and where calmness rules over chaos, should reassure her immensely. I take my coffee out on the terrace and stand there meditating on the row of clean white washing on the line. A sudden arc of water, streaked with shimmering gold, startles me, and I spill my coffee over myself. For the second day in a row, one of the carp has jumped out of the pond. I drop my cup and run . The slippery fish is easy to catch, but impossible to hold on to. For a few seconds I have it enfolded in my T-shirt, but then it sort of squirms, and flings itself up and away from my coffee stained breasts , landing on the grass a few feet away, right in front of where Marcia now stands , surveying the scene with a look of horrified confusion on her face.

July 13 - Charlotte

Susan has done a lovely job of the front flower bed, and it now looks quite welcoming when you drive in and see Frankie's screen amongst the bright bedding plants that she brought over. Karen, the estate agent snaps a quick photo.

'Is it one of Frankie's? It looks stunning there! '. I thank her , and let her know that I too had a hand in its creation. Well why not? I did tell her exactly the kind of thing I wanted , even down to the colours of the bottles she used. I think about offering Karen a cup of tea or coffee, but she stalks off into Tony's garage before I get around to it, and I hear them greet each other like old friends. The market is very buoyant at the moment apparently, and we should have no trouble in attracting a buyer, I hear her telling him.

She actually said very little to me, just nodded and made little notes as I showed her each room.

'This is a great space' was all she said when I opened the door to the sitting room, revealing my efforts. I'd vacuumed everywhere and even rearranged the furniture, so it did look especially nice with the new curtains that Susan gave me . I expected more of a reaction somehow. Tony and Karen emerge from the garage and look deep in conversation as they stare up at the roof . It's obvious that it will need replacing in the next few years

'It doesn't leak!' I find myself calling out as I walk towards them, hoping to reassure her. She smiles.

'That's one of the things that every buyer asks!' She says. 'That, and the condition of the fosse septique. I take it that is up to spec?' Tony looks at me, and shakes his head .

'It works! ' I say , miserably, as it dawns on me that maybe we will need to do some more work before marketing begins.

'Spain will still be there' . Tony puts a comforting arm around my shoulder as we say goodbye to Karen, and goodbye for now to my Spanish dream. Defeated, I walk slowly back in to our unsatisfactory house, to take refuge from the punishing heat of this years Bretagne summer.

July 14 - Frankie

Ross and I decide to take a couple of days off. Well actually, for us, every day is a day off, kind of, but today we're going to spend the day by the river with a picnic, a camera, some books, a sketching pad, and Artie. I'm packing some peaches, and a Caesar salad into a basket when a car pulls up outside. I recognise immediately, from the logo on the drivers door that it's Karen, the estate agent who deals with a lot of the English buyers and sellers around here. I watch her step out of the car . The last time she stopped by, she ruined her 'Manolo Blahnik' heels. I'd had to Google that to discover that her shoe budget exceeded the amount we'd spent on a whole winter's worth of fuel. Today though she is in shorts and flip flops .

'Thought I'd pass by on my way to the celebrations ' she calls from the bottom of the driveway. She is uber friendly, and has an amazing tan and an American smile. I decide to make her a quick coffee and give her a few minutes of my time before sending her on her way.

'I've seen the light!' She says, laughing . I don't immediately cotton on to the joke, so she explains that she's been to the exposition at the brocante and seen the barrel lights that I've hung there. She wants one for her kitchen. The problem, I tell her, is that I don't have any more of the cartwheel centres so she might have to wait a while…

'Also I'd like to create this for my garden'. ….she fumbles in her handbag and takes out a drawing she's made, unfolding it before handing it to me

'I wondered if it would be something we could work on together, as you did with Mrs Singer…'

The rough drawing is of a bottle screen, very similar to the one I made for Charlotte, and I can't help my irritation at the suggestion that she had a hand in it's creation . I look down at the drawing and my head shakes mechanically from side to side.

' I'm sorry, I just cdon't have time I'm afraid, perhaps Mrs Singer could help you!'

July 15 - Heather

We shouldn't have gone to the fireworks. When I arrived home , it must have been around one a.m. , Thug was under my bed, and a large pool of urine greeted me from the middle of the kitchen floor. I could kick myself . I just didn't think! It did cross my mind, when Alan invited me to go with him, that fireworks might not be to Thug's taste , so I left him at home. The party was a couple of miles away, so I didn't worry about him being scared by the noise. But it was Bastille night, and celebrations were happening all over the place, including in villages a lot closer to us. Poor Thug. He seems to have suffered no lasting ill effects though, and having spent the night on my bed . (I didn't bother to walk him as he'd already emptied his bladder on the kitchen floor), he is now sunning himself on his back beside my deckchair while I try to write . It's going to be another balmy day, and I think If I can get a few pages of anything written this morning, I'll take up Frankie's offer of a river picnic and swim this afternoon. It'll be good for Thug. He likes to play with Artie. I look down at him lying there. He has become like my child . I am inspired then , with another book idea.

'How would you like to be a character in one of my books? ' I ask him as I tickle his belly. I get no discernible response, so I go ahead and start to make notes, playing with the idea in my head. It's another children's book though, when I hoped to write something a little more adult. Maybe I'm procrastinating….

July 16 - Susan

My red teapot , and matching cups , come out of the kiln green and brown. Mostly a kind of algae green, turning to a kind of brownish khaki where the glaze is thicker. I don't hate them . Maybe they wouldn't have looked good in red . I turn to Heather, realising that I haven't listened to a word she said. Something about a children's book she's writing, where the children in it turn out to be dogs. I'm not too sure about the idea to be honest.

'Sounds interesting' I say, and go back to emptying the kiln . Two light shades come out next , well not really light shades, but two lattice effect, dome shaped items, that I made to go over a couple of little solar lights in the garden . I'm hoping enough sunlight will get through the holes in order for them to charge effectively. It's an experiment, another crazy idea I had.

'I'm not too sure if it'll work actually'. Heather says, picking up one of my light shades, but still talking about her book idea. I wait for her to elaborate

'Well, children are so much more sophisticated these days' she says, just as I pull out my Magic Roundabout themed mug, shaped like Dougal, with his ears as handles. We both eye it dubiously.

'Shall we have a glass of wine?' I say eventually.

July 17 - Angel

We sleep for a couple of hours in the heat of the early afternoon. I'm enjoying living here with Lee. I'm enjoying life. I can please myself and I have no responsibilities. If I want to disappear into the forest for a couple of hours Lee doesn't mind. Lakshmi can take herself from kitchen floor to sofa, to our bed upstairs, as and when she feels, and Reiki can spend the whole day watching fish jump from the pond if she likes. Everything is beautiful, especially on a Sunday when Lee is home all day. I don't even have to cook if I don't want to. He's quite happy to do that too. I roll over, to watch him sleeping, thinking that he might feel my gaze upon his face and wake up ready to entertain me. He's sound asleep though, so I decide to creep down to the kitchen to make some tea instead.

'Where do you think you're going?' He asks suddenly, and his hand closes around my ankle as I attempt to slide stealthily from the bed. I shriek involuntarily, and Lakshmi comes thundering up the stairs, catching us kissing and giggling as Lee pins me to the bed. She sighs comically, and slinks back down the stairs again. Life is indeed perfect. If only those tarot cards didn't keep telling me that change is on the way.

July 18 - Charlotte

Forty degrees is forecast for today. If only we had a pool! To drive to the nearest beach would take me an hour, and a lot of fuel, and even if I did go, there's only so much time you can spend in the sea, and it's too hot to lie around on the beach, sunbathing. Frankie and Angel swim in the river. I've seen their Facebook posts. It's not for me though. The river has snakes in it, and you can't see what's lurking there beneath the surface. It's also incredibly deep . I sit by an open window, having splashed my face with water and turned on my battery operated fan . Its just like I'm having a hot flush, but I'm pretty sure it's not that, even though I'm that kind of age. When Tony comes in for his lunch I suggest going into town to buy an inflatable pool. I know they're a kids thing, but it would be better than nothing. He shakes his head though

'Too expensive, and I've got more important things to spend money on.'

'But this heat is unbearable! I just can't cope with it! ' I plead

'How are you going to cope in Spain then?' Is his witty reply

But it's a different kind of heat, and I see myself taking siestas in the afternoon, then sitting at some or other sun shaded table, sipping a cocktail. I say nothing more, but later as I'm scrolling through Facebook posts about the 'incredible temperature' accompanied by various photos of thermometers with their mercury levels higher than ever seen before, I glance out of the window and see that Tony has dragged out, from behind his garage, the big black round thing which, I'm told, was a drinking water vessel for cows in a field . It looks like it's about to be repurposed. In the middle of the lawn he stands there in sun hat and shorts with a hosepipe in his hand . I see immediately what the plan is.

'Get your bathers on then! ' he calls, when I go to the door. Oh well, this is as good as it gets I guess.

July 19 - Frankie

Rain at last. There is a huge fire a few miles away, south of us, near Le Mont d'Aree, and I hope this rain will put it out. Artie is in the kitchen with me. The distant thunder disturbs him a bit. We watch through the open door as the rain splashes on the driveway. This is such a relief. The goats shelter under the trees, they're not so keen on getting wet, but the pony carries on grazing, regardless, paying no heed to thunder clap or lightning bolt. Madison, the donkey, stands beside her. Her neatly trimmed hooves have given her a new lease of life , and she seems to have put some weight on too. Donkey's are not supposed to like the rain. Their coats are not waterproof. But she doesn't seem to care at all. Ross stands in a doorway, across from the doorway where I stand . It leads into the barn where Boris lives. Boris sits on his gloved hand watching the rain with interest. Together, we look like the welcoming committee for the much longed for break in the weather. I put my fingers up in the shape of a T, and Ross nods, then turns away to take Boris back to her favourite daytime spot up high in the barn, on a cross beam. It is still incredibly warm. I spent most of yesterday in the river , and I'm tempted to head back over there today , once I've had a cup of tea. The rain doesn't dissuade me from the idea. If anything it encourages me. I should be able to take some interesting photos.

July 20 - Heather

Thank goodness the fires are being brought under control. I look at the photos on my phone . So many acres of forest razed to the ground. The images are depressing to say the least . I click on to Facebook to see if there's anything cheerier, and my attention is immediately caught by Frankie's river pics. She's totally captured the moment when a raindrop bounces off a leaf, and the precise point when the swell of a droplet reaches its maximum before gravity causes it to drip from the end of a blade of grass.

'Beautiful!' I comment, and wish , not for the first time that my own creativity could be expressed visually, rather than through words on a page. My dog children are in the bin . I didn't get very far with that idea, before realising that it was a dud one. It doesn't matter. I'm financially secure enough to not have to work for a while if I don't want to. Today though is the perfect day for writing if I were at all inspired. It's dull, and very much cooler, and I've actually nothing else to do . The house and garden are tolerably tidy. Ive no appointments and I don't need any shopping. Idly, I wonder if Alan is doing anything. We've seen each other a few times, but I'm not sure if it's leading anywhere. I'm not even really sure if I want it to. He's nice though, and I can easily picture us together. Too easily. I'm trying not to appear too eager, but sometimes I can't seem to help myself. When my phone pings, just as I've decided to settle down with a book, it's as if he read my mind.

'I'm off to the garden centre, would you like to join me?' He asks. Funny, I'm now feeling an urgent need suddenly for potting compost and some new gardening gloves.

July 21 - Susan

It's cooler this morning. I put the banana cake in my Tupperware cake box, and pack my gardening gloves and secateurs into my handbag. I'm just heading out of the door, throwing a dog treat to Rhea before I close it behind me, when Eric appears .

'Hello pretty lady! Where are you off to with that cake?' I explain that I'm going to Charlotte's to tidy up the shrubs that border their garden, and to cut back the brambles.

'You do too much for that girl'. He says, and for a moment I consider how nice it would be to not go to Charlotte's, but instead to stay here and have tea and cake with Eric, but then I open my car door and dump the cake on the passenger seat before the idea takes hold. I found out the other day that Angel's gay hairdresser is called Michel. It seems unlikely to me that there could be more than one gay Michel in the vicinity, so it's likely to be him that Eric's been dating. I'm not going to pry though. Eric has stayed very quiet on the subject and I'm pretty sure there has only been a couple of dates anyway, so maybe it will come to nothing. He stands there now, in front of my car, looking a bit disappointed that I'm on my way out.

'You can come and help me if you want'. He backs away a little. He's not that keen on Charlotte, though he doesn't really know her that well.

'Actually I was rather hoping for another go at pottery'. He looks at me hopefully, as I think about it.

'Ok then, Saturday morning'. I say, preparing to drive off. He pats the car roof and gives me a thumbs up sign, and I pull out of the driveway feeling happier than I did a few minutes ago. We get on so well. It's just such a shame he's gay.

July 22 - Angel

The death card again. I stare down at it . It's enough to put the fear of god into some people but it rarely represents physical death. Normally it implies an end to a situation, an interest of some kind, a job maybe, a relationship. I dwell on that for a few moments. My relationship with Lee has an air of permanence. It's so good that I never want it to end. Intuitively I know this card cannot be about that, but it's appeared so often lately that I can't ignore it. I must heed its message. It can of course mean a time of significant transformation or change. A transitional period.

'Is that it Reiki, do you think?' Her beautiful green eyes stare back at me unblinking, mirroring my own , her gaze strong and steadfast as she searches out my soul, letting her eyes roam over my whole body before meeting my eyes once more with her hypnotic stare . That's it! I realise that the change ahead of me is indeed a physical one. I've been feeling rather hot and hormonal lately, and this confirms what I had begun to suspect. The menopause is upon me. There can be nothing more transformational than that. Reiki blinks and looks away . I never cease to be amazed by her perception. Just the menopause. Nothing at all to worry about.

July 23 - Charlotte

'Live your dream' is the meme that I see first when I click on Facebook this morning.

'I'm trying to!' I say out loud to absolutely no one. Tony has gone shopping for some car part or other . There's an old Citroen Dyane he's working on at the moment. They sell for a lot of money apparently. Looking at it I'm at a loss to understand why. I look across at the newly tidied garden, and feel quite pleased with it. Even the pool looks ok, now that Tony's put hay bales around the outside of it , and I've found some outdoor cushions to place on top of them. It's a nice place to sit and dangle your feet. Being black, the water is always quite warm . I ignore the faint smell of something rotten, as I cross the lawn, a mug of tea in one hand and my phone and cigarettes in the other. The grass is a bit spiky on my bare feet . Well it's not actually grass really, just weeds mown short. Still it looks ok even though we've not had much rain and it's not very green. I put everything down on one of the hay bales, carefully placing the mug so that it doesn't spill, and then I sit and swing my legs over, so that my feet are immersed in the cool (ish) water. It's then that I see it . A dead hedgehog is floating on the surface, bloated, and buzzing with maggots. I swing my legs quickly back the other way, knocking over my tea, and soaking my cigarettes. I snatch up my phone before it too gets wet, and take a photo of the scene, posting it immediately to my Facebook page . The dead hedgehog looks vile .

'When is my luck going to change?' I caption it.

July 24 - Frankie

We get up early. The sun streaming through our bedroom window makes it easy. A day to spend in the garden, picking beans, digging potatoes, cleaning out the chickens nest boxes. Most of the time we work in silence, knowing instinctively what needs to be done , and how best to help each other. When Ross appears around eleven thirty with a large mug in each hand, I know that all of the animals will have been tended to . I'm in the polytunnel picking today's crop of cherry tomatoes, and soaking the ground with the hose pipe at the same time.

'I thought maybe a picnic lunch, later, by the river?' I suggest, as he puts the mugs down on the potting bench, and moves the hose to where the ground is still parched.

' I just need to strim around the edges of the paddock' he answers. The strimmer is a necessary evil . Without regular attention, the brambles encroach upon our pasture, and gradually the grazing becomes less and less. The job takes a long time though, as usually I walk ahead of him with a long stick, looking for hedgehogs, to ensure that they don't get injured by the strimmer line. Artie is a good little hedgehog hunter too, running in and out of the hedgerow, sniffing out any creatures that have made their homes there, and encouraging them to get out of the way. I look down at him lying on his back in the sun as we sip our tea.

'You up for some work Artie?' His tail wags almost imperceptibly.

July 25 - Heather

Susan interrupts my writing. If I'm being honest with myself I'm glad of the interruption. Eloise, from the community magazine

191

has asked if I'd like to contribute a short story every now and then. It's a charitable thing, I won't get paid, but it could be fun and it might help me to meet some new people. I can be as creative as I like, and there lies the problem, with no brief, or boundary, I'm at a loss to come up with an appealing idea. ….I'm toying with a mini murder mystery, about a middle aged couple who move over here from England….She suddenly disappears, and he tells everyone that she's gone back home….I give Susan my full attention. She wonders if I'm doing anything tonight. She plans on holding an 'open studio' event, and is inviting everyone she knows to come and have a drink, and a look at what she does, maybe some can even have a go at throwing a pot or two. It sounds like fun.

'You can bring someone if you want' she says . I immediately think of Alan , and wonder if it might be his 'thing'.

'I'll message a couple of people if that's ok?' I'm not sure if Susan knows very many people to invite. Her face lights up immediately

'Maybe that Eloise girl from the magazine would like to come! ' she says.

Aha! So that's what this is about! , I think to myself, but say nothing and pretend not to notice her rather obvious attempt at obtaining an introduction.

July 26 - Susan

I lie in bed with a silly grin on my face, like someone who's just had sex with a particularly hot partner, but apart from Delilah, who is sprawled across the duvet, I'm alone. The Open Studio was a success. Heather brought Eloise, and they both had a go on the wheel. Eloise has asked me to write something for the magazine about what I do, so that's a bit of a result. Eric came, but without Michel, which was a shame in a way though I felt weirdly anxious at the thought of meeting him. Charlotte and Tony passed by for a glass or two , and Frankie brought two girls who I'd never met before, artists apparently. They seemed to enjoy themselves and one of them bought a teapot and some cups, but they were French, and spoke quickly, so I couldn't really hold a proper conversation with them. The sky outside is a little dark today, There is a huge mess to clean up in the studio, and Eric left last night without even saying goodbye, but none of these things is enough to bring down my mood, so I spring out of bed ready to face the day. I'm even momentarily tempted to follow Frankie's cold morning shower routine, but I don't , not wanting to spoil my good mood. It's only then that I look at my phone , and a Facebook memory pops up , an image of Andrea, draping herself over Eric at a long since forgotten party. He looks stiff and uncomfortable, and I laugh at his expression, but the sight of her leaves me cold, and I realise for the first time, that I'm glad she moved away.

July 27 -Angel

Apparently menopause is not official until a year has passed since your last period. I've a long way to go then , and in this heat I'm feeling quite uncomfortable and I'm sure I've already started to gain some weight. I begin to understand a little of what Janice has been going through, though HRT is definitely not for me, and when she comes for her appointment in about forty minutes time I'll not admit to my own symptoms as I'm certainly not looking for her advice. I smooth a clean sheet over the massage couch and plug in my diffuser which adds soft light in pastel colours and scents the air with lavender and geranium oil. I meditate for a while before she arrives. For some reason I feel myself distracted by my thoughts, unable to simply observe them and let them go. What I'm thinking though, and trying not to think, is just plain ridiculous. I'm worrying that Lee won't want me if I put on weight. I'm just being weird and hormonal I'm sure. He looks at me as though I'm the sexiest thing on the planet and he can't seem to believe his own luck,

'But what if you get fat?' Says the voice in my head, and I see once more the death card that keeps coming up in my tarot readings.

'What if'. I say out loud to nobody in particular, then I shrug it off, and get ready to open the door to Janice.

July 28 - Charlotte

'There's no harm in dreaming' Tony says, as he goes back to loading his truck with sacks of rubbish for the déchèterie. It's an irritating comment. I'd suggested, seriously, that if the Citroen sells we could have a little holiday in Spain, and just have a look around, at the properties that are currently up for sale. If we drove down it couldn't cost too much . We could stay in a cheap hotel, and have picnics on the beach, instead of wasting money in the restaurants. I finish my cigarette, and decide to start doing some serious research. I Google 'Citroën Dyane' and I'm amazed at the prices . They are all a few thousand euros at least! I look on Le Bon Coin. The very cheapest is over five thousand. I figure that whatever Tony makes on this one there ought to be enough to spare for a little holiday. I light another cigarette and wander back over to tell him the good news . He's back in the garage, fiddling with something underneath the car, which I pat lovingly, knowing now what it's worth. He asks me to get in and put my foot on the brake pedal. It's strange inside , and there's an 'old' smell to it . I

194

just can't see the attraction at all, to this kind of thing, but when I tell him how much he could get for it he's not surprised. In fact, he has already advertised it for sale, for seven thousand euros !

'Don't get too excited though' he says, and goes on to confess that he actually paid four thousand for it himself. I grip the steering wheel, feeling a bit sick . We've not got that kind of money , and we never have had .

'I borrowed it'. He admits

July 29 - Frankie

It takes me a while to wade across the detritus of my atelier and find the source of the smell. It's a chewed mouse (rat?) , probably been dead for a couple of days and I didn't notice it because of all this stuff everywhere. I scoop up the little body with a piece of cardboard torn from one of the boxes, my face buried in my sleeve to shield me from the smell, which is sickeningly vile, and probably made worse because of the heat . I make it to the compost heap , fling it on top, and quickly fork some hay over it . Angel stands there looking green . We both apologise , her for her exaggerated gagging reflex, and me for not realising as soon as I opened the door , that something was amiss.

'Ok' I say, opening the door wide, and both of the windows 'I need to tidy up a bit first'

We've come straight from the yoga studio, with the idea of creating something fabulous for Maisie's windows. Angel was very enthusiastic about helping me, but now, I notice, she looks a tiny bit jaded.

'We'll make the basic shapes out of wood , and then pad them out with foam before putting sheeting over the top ' I explain, but realise that Angel could do with a moment or two longer before stepping back into the workshop.

'Come on then, we'll have coffee in the house first, and let this air out a bit '. She shoots me a grateful look as we turn away from the nauseating smell.

July 30 - Heather

Neither of us wants a relationship. We've each made that pretty clear .

'I'll probably be single all my life. I actually enjoy my own company, and I'd be hell to live with I'm sure . I just cannot stand all of the arguments and drama which seem to go hand in hand with a "steady relationship"'. He makes inverted comma signs in the air as he says the last couple of words. I reciprocate.

'I'm happy with my dog' I say 'it's such a relief, after having to please someone else for most of my life , that I now don't have to justify a morning in bed doing nothing. I've nobody to to answer to if I go out in the evening, and don't come home until the early hours , and if I'm honest, I like that the house looks exactly as I left it when I do get home. No washing up left on the kitchen drainer, no dirty laundry strewn across the bedroom, nobody else's mail cluttering up the place, so 'just good friends' really works for me' .

Alan looks at me steadily over his mug of tea. He's standing in front of my kitchen sink, leaning back against it, as we have this conversation. It's been brewing for a while . We've been seeing a lot of each other. His body language suggests that he fancies me, and yet here we are agreeing to take the relationship no further. I'm feeling a bit sad to be honest, and slightly panicking at the thought of him cooling off, and me losing him entirely. So stupid! He's probably too young for me anyway , and Thug really is all I need.

'Are you familiar' he says then 'with the phrase 'Friends with benefits'?

July 31 - Susan

I call on Heather for advice, forgetting that it's Sunday, and that ten am. in the morning may not be the best time to drop in unannounced for a coffee. When I get there though, her friend Alan is already parked outside, so I'm obviously not the one who is getting her out of bed too early . Heather is padding about in her kitchen with her hair loose and dishevelled, wearing denim shorts and a baggy T-shirt, while Alan sits at the table doing something on her laptop. He gives me a guilty look, as if I've caught him doing something he shouldn't.

'Not looking at porn are you?' I say, jokingly, realising a bit too late , that having met him only once before, shopping in the Brico with Heather, that that question may have been a touch too familiar. However, he does laugh , and retort quickly

' No those days are over for me!' A bit of a weird answer, but at least he wasn't offended. Heather hands me a coffee without asking whether or not I'd like one, and I sit down next to Alan.

' The thing is it's Charlotte….' I begin, and Heather rolls her eyes .

'It usually is!' She says . This time it's different though. Charlotte found out that I lent Tony some money. There was a car that he could make a substantial profit on if he bought it and did a bit of work. I gave him the cash , as I thought it might help to get them over a rough patch, so that they could sort out the problems with their house and get on with their plans. Heather frowns.

'Is Charlotte not happy about it then?' She's not. She's annoyed because I didn't offer to lend it to her.

August 1 - Angel

In the U.K. it's a bank holiday, not here though, and so it's a normal day for me. After yoga I grab a quick coffee with Maisie and Frankie, then head home in time to meet my first client of the day. I have one this morning and one this afternoon, so it's an easy kind of day. Lee is working on a roof nearby so will be home for an hour or so at lunch time, in between my two clients. This is what has become my new normal, and it suits me so well. I've got a great life balance now, time to myself, and time to work. Time for love too. Lakshmi rolls over when I walk in the door , and wags her tail expectantly. I rub her tummy with my bare foot . She's put on weight I think, just a little.

'Come on fatty! Up you get!' I tell her, encouraging her to go out in the garden for a while before it gets too hot . She looks me up and down as if saying,

'You're a fine one to talk!' before leaving me to change out of my yoga gear and into the white shorts and T-shirt that I favour as working clothes. I catch a sideways glimpse of myself in the mirror as I'm pulling the T-shirt over my head , and immediately suck my stomach in . Lakshmi is right . On closer inspection though my face looks good , my skin glows and I look relaxed and contented.

'Fat and happy' I say to myself.

August 2 - Charlotte

'I was trying to help', Susan says, 'but I'm sorry if I've upset you. Please let me know if there's anything I can do to put things right' . I take the flowers she's holding out in front of her, and open the door wider.

' I just don't like owing money!' I say

'The thing is' …she explains. '…The money was a gift! It's Tony who insists he must pay it back!' This is news to me, and for a moment I can't think of what to say….

'Coffee?' I offer. She looks relieved as she enters and automatically goes to fill the kettle. I find my voice again while she's filling a vase with water for the flowers .

'That's quite a gift!' I say

'I thought it would get you out of a hole, or at least pay for a new fosse septique, so that you can get the house on the market!'

She brings the coffee to the table and I grab my cigarettes and point to the doorstep where we sit in silence in the sunshine . Tony is is in the garage, tinkering with the old Citroen. He's found a buyer already but needs to do a little more work before it can go .

'Thank you' . I say eventually, and she pats my shoulder. It looks like we may have that holiday after all.

August 3 - Frankie

The yoga studio windows look amazing , with their new simple display . Two yoginis, made from concrete-soaked linen, draped over a construction of wood and foam to form the shape, sit one in each window, with sheer white muslin curtains behind them as a backdrop. Angel and I stand across the road from them in order to appreciate the effect. The street is crowded and noisy , with stall holders selling their wares from trestle tables, while sheltering under parasols on each side of the street. It's an annual event, this Vide Grenier, and it attracts stall holders and customers from all over Brittany. I spot Susan a little further down the road, chatting happily to someone over her table of pottery. I give her an encouraging wave and she smiles back at me. She, like many of the stall holders, will have been here since dawn . Angel and I look at each other and grin, excitedly rubbing our hands together as we begin our little tour of the of the goodies on offer, Angel in search of crystals, me looking for anything which speaks to me of an idea for transformation, old rusty tools, interesting bits of wood, shop mannequins etc.....As usual though the stalls selling clothes distract us from our missions, and we end up spending a girly hour or two trying on harem pants and sarongs, and little floaty tops. I spend more than I should, but it's not often I do this . Angel buys a sarong and a maxi dress .

'I've put on so much weight!' she says. I laugh , because to me she looks as perfect as she always does .

'It's this meno-belly!' She explains, cupping her hands over it and arching her back to exaggerate the effect. In reality, mine is only slightly flatter, and I lift my T-shirt to show her. She shrugs

'Shall we go and get an almond croissant?'

August 4 - Heather

So we set some rules, or, more accurately, boundaries. It's simple. We remain good friends, arrange outings together etc, and see each other whenever we are both free and happy to spend time together, maybe a couple of times a week, and if we both feel like it, we have sex. We don't get romantically involved. We make no commitments, and we avoid being seen as a couple. We agree to be completely honest with each other about what we want , and we are each free to fall in love elsewhere if it happens. That's it! It's exciting, and the only thing we didn't discuss (Susan arrived on Sunday morning before we had a chance to finish talking) was what we are going to tell other people. I feel the need to tell Sophie something at least, but as any mention of my sex life is completely new territory for us, I'm not sure what to say, and then there are our friends, and the whole 'not being seen as a couple' thing. If I say nothing at all it's akin to lying, but if we put it out there then it will be awkward questions to start with and then joint invitations at every turn . We are meeting for an aperitif at the bar by the river later today. If all feels right he will come back here with me for a makeshift supper and maybe stay the night. I smile to myself as memories of last Saturday night come flooding back to me. We haven't seen each other since Sunday morning. We are definitely following the rules, and there has only been one message each day . I think I'll tell Sophie that I've met a 'special' friend , but it's nothing serious. My closest friends over here (Susan, Frankie, Maisie and Angel) can be told that too.

'It's a special relationship that we have, but we're keeping a low profile'. Thug looks shocked.

August 5 - Susan

The drought continues, and this afternoon outside in the sun, the greenware dries quickly, and productivity has increased. My stall was a success and I sold several pieces. Frankie was right, I

201

can do this. My aim next week is to gather up some of my best pieces, and visit a couple of arty crafty shops in the next town, and maybe one that's just opened up, a little over an hour away from here. You never know, they might be persuaded into selling my stuff , and nothing ventured is nothing gained. I've also got to write an article for Eloise, to go in the next community magazine . I've made a start, but everything I write seems to sound a bit cheesy, so I sit here surrounded in pages where I've begun a paragraph, crossed it out, started again , made a few notes in the margin, crossed through the whole thing, and begun again on a clean sheet, only to repeat the process. I look out of the window at the toilet brush holders and soap dishes drying on the bench, and see Thug cocking his leg at the foot of the driveway . Inspiration strikes me then , and I open the window wider.

'How would you like a coffee and a nice piece of cake?' I call as Heather comes into view. Thug arrives at the kitchen door before I've finished speaking, scattering Rhea's food bowls as he checks them for leftovers. Heather enters moments later, scolding Thug as she takes a seat. I hand her a plate with a slice of lemon drizzle cake on it. My scribblings are there in front of her and she takes up a page before I've even said a word.

'What have we here?' She asks, and I hand her a coffee with one hand and a pen with the other.

'Ok, I get it!' she immediately gets to work on a fresh piece of paper which she passes back to me ten minutes later. What she's written, actually makes me look interesting. The bare facts are there , but it's almost like a little story, ending with an open invitation to come and 'discover' me in my studio. I'm so grateful, and I tell her so . She nods, and says mysteriously

'I have a little bit of news, myself!'

August 6 - Angel

I grab my car keys as soon as I see Maisie's message, replying with a quick 'on my way', and calling out to Lee that the old boulangerie is on fire, and that Maisie needs me. When I get there I abandon the car at the top of the road, outside of the area which has been cordoned off by the pompiers. There are red engines everywhere, and smoke. Maisie is outside the yoga studio being comforted by her neighbours. It's just the boulangerie at the moment, but if the fire isn't brought under control quickly, then the yoga studio is next in line. I make my way through the crowd to where Maisie is standing. Lee, who insisted on accompanying me, goes to talk to Didier, one of the pompiers who is standing outside of the danger zone , keeping everyone at a safe distance. Sooty tears run down Maisie's face when she sees me , and I pull her in for a hug. The yoga studio windows look just as they did a few days ago. The concrete yoginis with their heads bowed, continue serenely in their lotus position, ignoring the chaos outside.

'It'll be alright'. I say, feeling confident. There are so many pompiers on the scene that they simply cannot fail to speedily and efficiently extinguish the flames . Lee comes over then to confirm this thought .

'The fire is essentially out' he says 'it's just smoke now, not flames. It won't spread any further' Maisie closes her eyes and sighs deeply.

'I need a drink'! she says, gesturing towards the bar down the road, where people sit outside under parasols as if there was never a raging inferno going on further up the street.

'Ok, do you want to wash your face first, maybe?' I ask, tactfully.

August 7 - Charlotte

Tony wants to sell the Citroen, then look for another one to invest in. We are not on the same page. We could buy a fosse septique, and if we did the work ourselves, we would have enough money left over for a little trip down to Spain. I tell him this often, being careful to avoid using the word 'holiday'. Tony grunts a reply

'We need to pay Susan back first!' . I walk away, shaking my head . I've told him so many times that Susan thinks of giving that money as a gift , rather than a loan, but he won't hear of it. We have ended up arguing again, then drinking our coffee in silence, while he scrolls through his phone . Later on though, he approaches me as I sit with my feet in the pool, painting my nails a glorious shade of sunset orange.

'I think I've come up with a compromise' he says, showing me a photo of a big white van. 'If I buy this and convert it into a camper van, we can use it for a little holiday in Spain , then maybe sell it for a profit when we get back, and give Susan back her money!' I stretch out my orange fingertips in front of my face, smiling a little, but saying nothing. I guess it's better than nothing.

August 8 - Frankie

I stand for a while looking up at the burnt out roof of the boulangerie before going into my yoga class, and Heather quietly joins me.

'At least it was empty' she says.

'That was a close thing!' I say, after hugging Maisie. She steps back with her hands in prayer position, nodding in agreement.

'The universe was looking after me'. Is all she says. I'd found out about the fire later that evening when we dropped in on Angel and Lee, on our way back from the beach .

'Such a shame though! It was a beautiful building'. I put my mat down next to Angel who is already lying in butterfly.

'The windows look amazing!' Heather says, unrolling her mat hastily . I'm so happy with the windows this time . The concrete soaked fabric works beautifully when draped over a structure of some kind and left to dry. There must be endless possibilities for sculptures such as this. I wonder about making some cows for the field opposite us, or even a giraffe . Maisie's voice interrupts my thoughts.

'Frankie' she calls gently 'hip stretch'. I quickly adjust my position, but it's too late , I'm so distracted by this latest idea that I can't concentrate. Angel nudges me with her foot, and I see that everyone else has gone into bridge. This is going to be a challenging class today!

August 9 - Heather

'So when are you coming over?' Sophie's WhatsApp message catches me by surprise. In all of my excitement over Alan, I'd forgotten about my upcoming trip to England . I haven't even booked a ferry yet.

'I'm aiming for early September'. I reply, clicking on to the Brittany Ferries site with one finger on my I Pad while replying to Sophie on my phone. The site takes a while to load, and on my phone I see the words 'Sophie is typing' at the top of the screen. I start to look at the Portsmouth to Saint Malo timetable. Sophie is still typing. An overnight crossing suits me best, and I consider going from the fourth to the eleventh of September....then Sophie's message comes through....she is moving house on September the seventh, to a bigger place . It would be better if I went over the week after the move , then I can stay in the guest bedroom in the new place!

'Perfect!' I type back. I'm guessing that the 'guest bedroom' is the room which will soon become a nursery, so I'll make the most of it for the time being. WhatsApp pings again , only this time it's Alan

'I have a little job to do in Paris on September the sixth . Would you like to come with me? It's just for two nights'? .... This day is starting well. I think the universe must be looking after me.

August 10 - Susan

Before I lose my nerve, I slip the simple navy silk shift dress over my pretty new underwear, and with a last look in the mirror I grab my handbag and my car keys. It's 8.15. The music begins at 9pm. I haven't booked a table, but I haven't eaten so I may well decide to stay for a meal, or perhaps get a takeaway afterwards. It will depend on many factors - how busy it is, what's on the menu, how self conscious I feel, etc. I am as nervous as anyone on a first date , and I suppose that's because this actually is a first date, of sorts, and a date with a very important person - myself. Following online advice, I'm going to take myself on a date once or twice a week, going wherever I fancy going, doing whatever I fancy doing , for myself, by myself. It's a bit like Heather's 'friends with benefits' arrangement except that there are no friends involved , and the only benefit is that I'm pleasing myself. I arrive at the bar /restaurant as the band are doing their sound checks, and I'm greeted by a girl in a short black dress who leads me to a table without batting an eyelid at my singleness. I order a glass of Bordeaux, and a pasta dish with Parma ham , and as I sit there waiting for my food, making the wine last as long as I can , the music starts and I realise I'm actually enjoying myself. There are a couple of people here that I vaguely recognise . I raise my glass when they look over, and they do the same. When the waitress comes back with my food I order another Bordeaux and settle down to eat, and enjoy the music. This really is ok.

August 11 - Angel

'Is it just me?' I say, as I lower myself clumsily from the jetty into the river 'or is this heat actually unbearable?' Lee agrees that it's pretty hot. He's taken another day off as the tiles on the roof where he's working are untouchable by mid morning, so that it's not worth going to work at all. We are on our way to a reggae festival, that he bought tickets for ages ago, but have stopped for a picnic and a swim on the way. When we get back in the car we are still wet, and the air conditioning keeps us refreshingly cool. I send a quick message to Frankie to thank her again for keeping Lakshmi overnight, and for feeding Reiki. She messages back straight away.

'Be careful. Broceliande is on fire '. No sooner do I see the message than Lee points to the horizon where a smoky haze , like a very low dark cloud, is looming. Another beautiful forest in flames. It's scary, all these fires. I've never known a summer like it. No grass for the cattle or the horses , a hosepipe ban, and Facebook full of posts about how to save water.

'There is a little rain forecast for Sunday'. Lee says, confidently. I close my eyes, and visualise a giant grey rain cloud, with a torrent of fat raindrops pouring down from it, on to the parched earth.

August 12 - Charlotte

I feel a little bit guilty when Heather arrives, and catches me filling my little pool with the hose pipe.

'I used the water that was in there to water the lawn' I say, in my defence when I see her face fall. It's true though. I did. The lawn needs to look green for when Karen comes to take the photographs. The house can be put on the market now that we have the funds to pay for the fosse septique. Tony is hoping to get Lee here next week with the digger, so it could be all done and covered over again in no time at all. In the meantime Karen can begin marketing it, and we can leave her a key while we go to Spain . Heather fans herself with her baseball cap before opening the boot of her car , and unloading a pile of flattened cardboard boxes.

'Voila!' She says. This is great . I can begin packing things now, ready for the big move. It's all coming together. I can hardly believe it! Then I look over at the newly acquired "white" van, which is at this moment a rather uninspiring shade of algae green, and I remember how much work needs to be done before we can go off on our little holiday. Heather follows my gaze, and her eyebrows lift

'Bon courage! ' she says.

August 13 - Frankie

A big stash of linen sheets costs me only a few euros. I stuff them in my car with an old typewriter, and a collection of walking sticks, then go back in to the brocante to pick up the cello that I couldn't resist buying. It has no strings, and I think it's shape has warped a bit in the sun, but for my purposes it's perfect. I strap it into the passenger seat, and head for home before I run out of space or money. It's the perfect day for singing along to the radio with the roof down, and a defunct musical instrument for company. I pass a couple of dog walkers, who grin and point at the cello, then up ahead I spot a figure, with his thumb out, and both a rucksack and a guitar strapped to his back. I slow down, wondering if it's possible to stuff the cello onto the back seat.

'Ou allez vous?' I call out, as I draw level. The man turns and grins at me. He's got a stubbly beard, and a pierced nose, and his startlingly blue eyes peer out from under the floppy brim of his leather cowboy hat .

'Hi mum!' He says. We stare at each other for the first time in what seems like several years, and then he flings his gear in the back, opens the door and gets in, balancing the cello on his lap.

'Thought I'd surprise you!' Well he certainly achieved that. I'm almost lost for words.

'Henry!' I manage 'My long lost son!'

August 14 - Heather

What a perfect morning. I wake to the sound of rain . At last! The air is cooler. I go to the window and look out. There are puddles forming on the gravel. The brown straw mat that used to be a lawn, will soon come green again if this keeps up. The forests can breathe a sigh of relief for the moment at least . What a difference a day makes ! Yesterday I had to swim in the river out of sheer necessity it was so punishingly hot. Today I'm considering a cardigan. Thug thumps his tail eagerly, and yes, I'm also very keen to go out, so before I've even had a coffee, I pull my wellies on and we wander over to the woods. It smells divine. The rain has slowed to a slight drizzle but the sky is dark, promising more. We walk slowly, with Thug finding something interesting to sniff at every couple of paces. In my head I'm writing a piece for the community magazine. I'm considering the idea of a kind of wild fairy in the woods, observer of nature, who kind of narrates a tale or two based on the seasonal changes of the local countryside. Sort of partly fantastical, partly factual and educational......it could work I think, then I watch Thug run off after a squirrel, and I wonder if it might be better if I wrote a similar piece, but through the eyes of a dog.....here we go again!

August 15 - Susan

What a perfect morning! The first thing I see is a post on Facebook by Dazy Doo, inviting people to come and browse the shop today, and one of the photos is of my own works! proudly displayed in the shop window. It gives me such a buzz. Dazy Doo is an hour away from here, and the third, and last, of the shops I visited last Friday. The first one I went to, nearer to home, was unfortunately planning to close for good in the very near future. She loved my work though, and hoped that I'd find somewhere to sell it. I came out of there with an increase in confidence , so I kept going, only to be told by a woman in the second shop I visited that they have a lot of ceramicists already . She barely even looked at what I had to offer, and carried on dusting shelves while I was talking to her . The shop was immaculately clean, but empty of customers, unlike Dazy Doo's , whose eclectic mix of paintings, sculptures, and jewellery, gave the shop the appearance of an Aladdin's cave, and as I entered , breathing in the heady scent of artisanale soap and scented candles, the woman crouching on the floor arranging a display of unruly hand made teddy bears, smiled up at me encouragingly. I found myself squatting down to her level to show her my wares, which she exclaimed over with much enthusiasm, as customers stepped around us, in search of their next purchase, and now this post! I do a little kitchen dance in celebration, then click 'share'. Things really do seem to be looking up!

August 16 - Angel

What a perfect morning! A huge rainstorm followed by brilliant sunshine. No clients to worry about, and Lee is working all day. For the first time since I moved in, I have the house to myself for a whole uninterrupted day, and I know just what I'm going to do with it. Up until now I have concentrated on my treatment room, making it mine with candles and crystals, and colour coordinated towels. The other rooms I left more or less alone, other than clearing space in a couple of wardrobes for my clothes and adding a few bits and pieces to bathroom shelves and cupboards. The house is as Lee lived in it as a single man, a little minimalistic, clean and tidy, but with something lacking. Today I'm going to change all that, not too much, but enough so that each room is given something to make it a bit more homely and not quite so masculine . I haul out two suitcases from under the bed, and a load of bin bags from the bottom the cavernous old armoires, that serve as wardrobes in the guest bedroom. All of my bits and pieces are here, waiting to be put to use in my new home. I empty out the first bin bag . It contains three ethnic style sofa throws . Lakshmi gives them a good sniff while I untie the next bag , and about nine silk cushions burst out of it. I'd forgotten I had so much stuff, as I open more bags and boxes containing elaborate plant pots , macrame hangers, and sculptures brought back from my travels.

'This could take longer than a day' I say to Lakshmi, but she doesn't care. She's found Bington, my old teddy bear. A dirty gold worn out looking thing with a poorly sewn on ear, and odd button eyes, and is carefully carrying it off downstairs.

August 17 - Charlotte

What a perfect morning! Karen has agreed to take photos and begin marketing the house before the work starts for the new fosse . She is coming at lunchtime, and I'm rushing around like a lunatic trying to get each room to look nice for the pics when Angel arrives with a big black bin liner.

'I thought you might be able to use these cushions!' She says, as I explain that I've no time to make coffee or anything. She opens the bag , and a beautiful silky pile of pink and green tumbles out . When it comes to home furnishings I'm not very confident with colour. Everything I have in the house is in a neutral or muted shade . These cushions could change all that, but I hesitate...

'They would look really good on that sofa!' She says, jerking her head towards the sitting room where the hoover reigns supreme in the middle of the floor. She throws a couple on one end , and tucks the rest in a fan shape at the other. They look fabulous and I'd never have thought of doing that myself. I thank her as I'm unplugging the hoover and moving swiftly on to the kitchen. Tony puts his head through the door and I shout at him to not start messing things up in here. He looks at Angel

'Coffee in the garage then?' He suggests.

August 18 - Frankie

What a perfect morning. We woke to a magnificent thunderstorm, and Ross ran downstairs to unplug the live box. Now, here we all are , Ross and Henry strumming their guitars in the kitchen, while Heather and I try to sing along, drinking beer instead of coffee as the lightning struck a power line, and we've no electricity. Heather arrived, soaked to the skin, five minutes after Thug, who, scared by the thunder, had run off during their walk and arrived at our door . He's now asleep under the table with Artie, the rain has all but stopped, and the thunder is a distant memory . Henry grins at my improvised lyrics. He's only been here a few days but it's as if he never went away. I've no idea how long he'll stay so I'm savouring every moment. He's a free spirit , a wanderer , an 'itinerant' as he calls himself. He is my greatest creation that's for sure. Heather stands up, muttering something about home and writing.

'Stay for lunch!' Henry says enthusiastically, then falters as he remembers the power line problem .

'Sandwiches?' He suggests, as he gets up to investigate the contents of the fridge. He takes out cheese, and a jar of peanut butter, and Heather sits back down, grinning.

'I know, not very French is it!' He says.

August 19 - Heather

213

I admit defeat, and put the phone down. It was over twenty minutes that I hung on for, trying to believe the words I was repeatedly being told , that my call was indeed important to them and that they were experiencing a particularly heavy volume of calls at the moment . Bloody Orange! My call means nothing to them. Here I am, with only my canine friend for company....which is ok of course, except that now that the internet has gone down, I somehow feel more alone than I ever did before. It's quite ridiculous really, but that link to the outside world has become the lifeline that I depend upon.

'How did we survive before?' I say aloud, to no one in particular, as not even Thug is listening. I throw a chamomile teabag into a mug and console myself with the thought that if the volume of calls is that high, then surely that means that someone else is reporting the fault . All I have to do is wait. Outside I can get good reception on my phone at least, so I head back to the garden with my tea and my book , ironically titled 'How not to give a fuck', and consider giving Alan a call . It's so tempting to use this woeful situation as an excuse to contact him for the third time this week, but does this minor inconvenience with the internet warrant such disregard of the rules? I'm about to do it anyway when Thug comes over and gives me a big nudge with his head, spilling my tea on my jeans , forcing me to put the phone down, and begin mopping at my legs with an old tea towel which I use to wipe rain from the chairs . It rings instantly. I smile at Thug. It's Alan.

August 20 - Susan

The glass of Prosecco sparkles in the sun and I take a quick photo of it, with the sea in the background, a shimmering teal. The pic turns out well so I post it quickly to Facebook , with the caption 'A tiny celebration'. It is in fact a little treat for myself.

I've sold two candle holders and a butter dish at Dazy Doo's , so a day at the coast, walking on the beach and dipping my toes in the sea, (I'm not brave enough to swim) and now this little glass, with a Caesar Salad , which should arrive any minute, are my reward. It's quite lovely, sitting here people watching, as couples and families stroll past, or stop and peruse the menu board. A woman about my age, with similarly fashionable grey hair, takes a seat at the next table and picks up the wine list. I'm encouraged by the fact that she too, appears to be dining out alone, and I catch her eye and smile. She smiles back, then puts up her hand and waves . For a brief moment I think that she thinks we know each other, and I'm uncertain how to respond, but from behind me a man approaches and takes the seat opposite her. So not alone then. Not at all. With a man in fact, and not just any man. I'd recognise those loose jeans and leather sandals anywhere. It's Eric.

August 21 - Angel

The 'box room' as Lee calls it, is now devoid of boxes. I've unpacked everything of mine, and the house now looks more like a home, with soft furnishings in every room, where before there were none, and plants, paintings, little sculptures and the like, adorning every surface. It's taken me about five days, but in that time I've also unpacked the boxes that Lee had stored in here before I moved in. A box of books, which he never read and didn't want, went to the local brocante, clothes no longer worn, went to be recycled, and old tools went into one of his sheds, for him to sort out later. The room, empty now apart from a chair where my old teddy currently sits, and an old travelling trunk full of blankets , is actually quite big. Big enough to turn into a second guest bedroom, should we ever need one. I wonder about painting the walls and buying the old Breton bed that I saw in the brocante while I was there. Lee comes up behind me and wraps his arms around my shoulders, while I tell him of my ideas .

'I never have any guests though!' He says softly 'I've no family really, and neither have you, so maybe one guest bedroom is going to be enough for us?' I sigh audibly

'I could make it pretty though!' He kisses my neck in response.

August 22 - Charlotte

I can't believe what Susan is telling me. Eric isn't gay? He's always been gay. I don't know him that well but he's always been gay. I think back to when I first met him, three, maybe four years ago, perhaps even longer. Andrea was here then , and there were more parties. We all drank a bit, and it was like something was happening, a party or a soirée of some kind, almost every week . It's so different now, since the lockdowns . Eric had just moved here then , and both Susan and I had been here a few years. I'm sure we all fancied him a little bit then, especially Andrea, and even Susan, though nothing was ever said, and Susan was firmly married to Paul .

' He wasn't interested in women! Didn't he tell us that? , way back when? '. I'm sure he did, but Susan frowns, trying to remember . She doesn't seem very happy about the fact that she's lost a gay friend, and gained a straight one.

'What's she like anyway? This Michelle? '. Susan shrugs before she answers

'She looks a bit like me I guess, similar hair etc…I can't believe we all thought it was Michel the hairdresser!'

I start to laugh , but then recover myself when Susan doesn't seem to find it funny.

'It was Andrea! ' suddenly I remember a conversation we had when I turned up for coffee once at Susan's , not realising Andrea was there. I never liked her, so I used to try and avoid bumping into her .

'She'd taken him that lemon pie!...Remember?' Susan's expression changes and she starts nodding, remembering the occasion. Andrea had made him a lemon meringue pie, and taken it over to him, which actually felt a bit weird, as Susan has always been the one that brings baked goods to friends. She'd then called in on Susan on her way home, with the news that she'd had a 'confidential' conversation with him, and that he'd confided to her that he was in fact a homosexual, but wanted to stay in the closet for the moment.

'Remember?' I ask, when I've recounted the conversation with as much detail as I can recall. She says nothing for a moment or two, and stares at me intently as she processes the information.

'But why would he have told that story to Andrea, unless he wanted us all to hear it. He knew what a gossip she was!' We fall silent, but I begin to wonder then about Andrea's motives all those years ago, with that lemon pie and the excessive makeup she was wearing that day.

August 23 - Frankie

I can tell that Henry is beginning to get restless. He strums a few notes, then picks up his phone and goes outside. I want to delay the inevitable.

'There's a band playing on Friday night at the Barcarella' . I say , when he comes back in . We could all go, ask a few friends, grab a pizza? '. He grins enthusiastically.

'Sounds cool!' He says, picking up his guitar again, then putting it down as Ross comes in with Boris.

'We were just talking about going to the Barcarella on Friday' Boris turns her head and seems to scowl at me . Ross does the same

'As long as Fly Boy aren't playing again !' He says. They're not. Instead it's a band called 'Charm', and to be honest I'm not expecting great things, but you never know. It's their first gig apparently, and it was only a few weeks ago that they were advertising for someone to join them, who could play the drums.

'It's good to support new ventures!' Ross says, unexpectedly, and Boris nods wisely then ruffles her feathers as Henry plucks a few strings of his guitar. He's writing another song I think. He sings a few reedy notes in between the plucking. 'Live your dream or die trying'......Seems to be the general theme of the piece.

'We are all living our dream actually'. Ross says, and kisses the top of Boris' head before taking her back outside . I pull my sketchbook towards me , and begin a quick drawing of Henry, who is now busy rolling up another twist of tobacco and other substances.

'Living the dream!' I sing, quietly to myself.

August 24 - Heather

I don't have the hands for clay. Too warm apparently. Still, I manage to fashion a kind of thumb pot, and keep on pressing it all around, gradually making the clay thinner and thinner till it starts to resemble something that's quite fine, and almost 'arty', though at the same time,decidedly wonky. Susan has asked me over here for a reason, and it's not just to have a go at hand building I'm pretty sure. When she comes back in with a bottle of wine and two glasses instead of the carton of milk that she went back to the house to get, I stop fiddling with the clay, and ask her if all is well.

'Eric isn't gay.' She says, flatly. I know Eric isn't gay. I don't know why she ever thought he was. He's a regular guy, a bit quiet maybe, even a bit moody, but definitely not gay . So, he is fussy about his appearance, and his interests are somewhat on the gentler side , cooking and gardening, rather than cars and football, but no , I've never gotten gay vibes from him. I tell Susan this as she pops the cork and pours us each a generous glass full of merlot .

'But why does it matter?' I ask, as we clink glasses.

'I feel like he's been lying to me, to all of us….He told Andrea that he was gay, but wanted to stay 'in the closet'. I've respected that ever since' . Poor Susan. I see now now where she's coming from, but I'm wondering if he really told that story to Andrea, and if he did, was it purely to stop her from coming on to him. I take another sip before putting this to her. She stares at me, unblinking as we both process this thought.

'That seems quite likely, actually'. She agrees.

August 25 - Susan

I'm on my way to Dazy Doo's with a few items to replace the ones that have already sold, plus a couple of mobiles of Charlotte's, which she begged me to try to sell there. (They aren't up to standard but I couldn't refuse to even try). As I drive, I mull over the Eric situation, remembering something Charlotte said - Andrea had been especially happy to have been told something 'in confidence' - what if Eric had genuinely thought that it would go no further? Poor Eric to have his confidence betrayed like that.

Andrea must have been coming on strong for him to have to resort to such an elaborate story to avoid hurting her feelings. I suppose i should feel happier now that I know how the misunderstanding came about , but I don't. When I saw him and Michelle together it was as if the sun had gone behind a cloud and I'd lost forever the best friend I ever had. We were such good company for each other before, and that's all I ever wanted from him, truth be told, but now it's like he's a different person, and not just a different individual, he's actually part of a couple! When I think of some of the things I've said to him over the last couple of years I cringe inwardly. I'd even suggested a gay dating site! Why did he never put me straight? I smile at my own pun as I pull up outside of Dazy Doo's. She is standing outside of the shop, hanging two beautiful mobiles made from silk scarves and glass beads . They are exquisite. I look at Charlotte's efforts on the seat beside me, and decide that I too must tell a lie, in order to spare someone's feelings.

August 26 - Angel

I stare at the offending articles that are being held up for my inspection, and there's no easy way to say it , but I've been asked for an honest opinion, so I at least try to comply.

'I'm sorry', I begin , ' but they will never sell. Nobody would buy them'.

Susan is nodding resignedly. I've only called in for a brief moment, with my old teddy bear, to see if it's possible for Susan to make two ceramic black eyes and a nose to replace what used to be there, before wear and tear, and Lakshmi got hold of it. The mobiles, made of bits of wood, string, and lace, are a quick and cheap approximation of the sort of thing that Frankie does, only without the attention to detail, without the skill, and without the creativity and imagination that Frankie puts into her work.

'I don't know what to tell her though', Susan says, handing me a mug, and then turning Bington over and over slowly, examining him from every angle .

' I can certainly do the eyes and nose' she says, 'and if you leave him with me I think I can sort him out a bit for you'. Bington looks even worse in someone else's hands than he does in mine. The stuffing protrudes from his belly, where Lakshmi got hold of him the other day, and his blue face , from where I coloured him with a biro, many years ago, is devoid of any features now that his beady eyes and moulded plastic nose are gone . One ear hangs off, and it's the only one he's got . I was thinking of sewing it back on myself, but Susan seems willing, eager even, to take on the job, and she says she has time.

'You look tired' she says , and I'm not sure if she's talking to Bington or to me , as she settles him amongst the cushions. This heat, and the menopause, have exhausted me, and I'm bloated and irritable. It must be bad if Susan notices. I look at her more closely though, and she looks tired too . Maybe it's the light in here .

August 27 - Charlotte

The new fosse septique sits on the lawn, looking like an art installation. The workers will be here at the end of next week to install it, and after that we will replace the turf, and viewings can commence! I look at the photos, taken on a sunny day with a camera that somehow makes the rooms look larger. Karen has done a good job, and there has been some interest already . It can only be a matter of time before the right person comes along and

221

snaps it up. Tony is replacing the headlights on the van, ready for its contrôle technique test next week. It's all happening. When Susan's car pulls up in front of the house, a little after ten in the morning, I'm already on my third cigarette. I can't seem to help it. The nervous excitement gets to me , and smoking is the only thing which calms it down. She gets out of the car carefully, carrying the mobiles I gave her for the shop. Neither of us speaks until she puts them down on the little table by the door .

'It's just that she has so much of this kind of thing already', she says, and I just smile and shrug. Nothing can bring me down today.

'I've brought cake', she adds, and I take the hint, stubbing out my cigarette and going indoors to the kitchen where Susan immediately gets to work with the kettle. I suddenly realise how much I'll miss her.

'You will come for holidays won't you?' I say, picking the icing from the top of the carrot cake she's brought with her. She slaps my hand away.

'Of course I will! Try and stop me!'

August 28 - Frankie

I wake up , feeling as fresh as the new laid eggs that I'm cracking enthusiastically into a bowl, having just collected them from the hen house in order to make pancakes for Sunday breakfast.

'Bit different to yesterday!' Ross says as he walks into the kitchen and notices that it's still only nine am , and yet here we all are 'cracking on' . Yesterday nobody rose before midday, and we

222

were then all a tiny bit delicate, to say the least. The night out at the Barcarella was at the root of it, and so last night I went totally alcohol free for the first time probably since Henry arrived. Henry takes the bowl of eggs from me and adds them to the flour while the oil heats, and I squeeze lemon juice into a little jug that Susan made for me .

'That was a good night though!' Ross and Henry both nod. Neither of them have much to say though about the evening, but I know they enjoyed it as much as me. The impromptu jamming session they enjoyed with the guitarist from Charm, had everyone who was left in the bar, singing and clapping, and lots of people, staff included, stayed after hours to enjoy more of the music, and even more of the wine, before someone banged on the window and threatened to call the gendarmes if the noise didn't stop. Henry expertly flips pancake after pancake, until there is a nice stack of them in the middle of the table.

'Bon appétit!' He says. I try not to look at the rucksack in the corner, with the guitar standing next to it. In an hour or so he will be gone, and I'm not sure how many months or years will pass before I see him again. I raise my coffee cup.

'Oui bon appétit et bon voyage!'

August 29 - Heather

'Are you sure you'll be able to afford to heat it ?' I'm worried about Sophie moving to an actual house, from her tiny flat . It's great that there'll be room for a proper nursery plus a guest bedroom for me to stay in, but the increase in fuel costs in England are alarming, and for a lot of people, not manageable. Sophie isn't worried though.

223

'It'll be fine' she says, stroking her now clearly visible bump, and adjusting the screen on her laptop as she sits back down. She's moving in two weeks time, a little after I get back from Paris, so I'll soon be able to head over for a visit. Seeing her here on screen always makes me miss her so much, but at least I know I'll be seeing her for real very soon, unlike Frankie, who has no idea when next Henry will turn up for a visit, and no clue either as to where he'll head for next.

'That must be worrying!' I said, when I called in yesterday, unfortunately too late to say goodbye to Henry , but not too early for a glass of wine and a deep conversation about family ties and coping with the distance between us mothers and our offspring, especially with the additional pull of impending grandchildren.

'I think I'm a long way from that situation' Frankie said, when I mentioned how exciting it is to be awaiting a first grandchild. On screen, Sophie is checking her watch, and draining the last of her coffee. It's time to end the call. I kiss my fingers and touch the screen where her bump is.

'A bientot!' She says, and closes the lid of her laptop. I'm left behind, alone in my kitchen with only Thug for company. Ok, time to write……

August 30 - Susan

It was kind of Lesley to invite me, and to be honest I could use the distraction, so in the early evening I find myself heading over there with a bottle of wine, some homemade sausage rolls and a couple of basic pots, painted with raku glaze, to put in the raku kiln. There are a few of us. Frankie and Ross stand to one side of a table where a couple of ladies are hastily brushing their pots with oxides, preparing them for the raku kiln. Ross stands ready with a leather gauntlet on, and a pair of tongs. I watch the process from a distance, as Frankie lifts the lid of a metal dustbin, and Ross quickly transfers the pieces from the kiln to the dustbin where flames leap out as the pots are lowered into paper and sawdust. Frankie puts the lid on and stands back , wafting the smoke away. Lesley takes my pots from me and passes me a glass of wine. I don't know any of the other people here, so I edge towards Frankie , and it's not long before I'm telling her all about the Eric saga, and Heather's theory, my theory now, that he told Andrea he was gay just so that she wouldn't be hurt by his rejection of her.

'Well, you know what?' Frankie says, when I finish my story. ' I think she just made the whole thing up! She came on to him, he turned her down, and she invented the "gay confession" to save her own ego, and to stop you from trying, and probably succeeding, where she couldn't . Remember how you both fancied him?'

I remember that I never once mentioned that to anyone. I was married to Paul. Still am, technically. I begin to shake my head in denial, but Frankie has warmed to her theory and doesn't give me the chance to defend myself

'It was obvious to me, that you both wanted him, and that he favoured you, even if you weren't free to be with him. Andrea saw it too, and she was jealous. Jealous and desperate'. Lesley comes over then and tops up the wine that I seem to have swallowed in a couple of mouthfuls. Frankie smiles and squeezes my shoulder.

'Trust me, that's the truth of it!' She squeezes my shoulder before going back to her dustbin duty.

August 31 - Angel

225

I call the group 'Brittany Menobabes' , and use a cartoon of a hot looking woman lying down with a fan in one hand , her bra in the other, as she slumps on the sofa with her bloated stomach peeping over the top of her unzipped jeans. I'm aiming at those women amongst us who suddenly find themselves at that time of life, when they're not really ready for it. I'm keeping it local, so that we can arrange meet ups , and be a proper support for one another. I'm kind of hoping that we can discuss anything and everything, including physical symptoms and psychological changes, in a safe environment. I click the page open, and add a couple of memes before letting it go live, and inviting a few women who I know are at a similar stage, clients and yoga friends. I hope they will be encouraged to join, and to invite their friends to join too. That done, I go outside and stand on the wet grass. It rained again last night and the air smells pure and clean. I gulp in lungfuls of it and give myself a few grounding moments before I have to go and change into my white shorts and T-shirt before my client arrives. She's the only one today, coming for a relaxing facial. A new lady, with the name 'Hope Hill'. A beautiful name! , and I look forward to meeting her. It's impossible, surely, with a name like that, to be anything other than upbeat and inspirational.

September 1 - Charlotte

I accept the invitation to join Brittany Menobabes . It's Angel that started the group, and I guess if she is willing to admit to being menopausal or peri menopausal, or whatever it is, then there's no point in denying that I too am of a certain age, though I'm not going to be around to go to any group meet ups. I close Facebook, and ignoring the rain outside, and the pile of plates and pans by the sink, I scroll through the sites selling property in Spain. I do this each morning now. It lifts my mood for the day,

226

knowing that this is an actual plan now, and no longer just a dream. Today it's a two bedroom bungalow in Sucina that's caught my eye. For less than our budget, which is somewhere around the ninety thousand euro mark, amazingly, it has a pool. I save the page, and add it to the other saved pages detailing apartments, villas, and bungalows in Pego, Punta Prima and Los Alcazares.

'We should decide on the region first!' Tony keeps saying. He's right but until we get down there , how can we possibly know? So in the meantime.......I light up as I head for the doorway, opening it wide enough to let the smoke out, and there on the drive a mini digger is being unloaded from its trailer.

'The workers are here!' Tony calls 'Get the kettle on!' I do as I'm told, and wash up the mugs while it boils. Tony comes in and begins going through the cupboards, looking for custard creams. He stuffs one in his mouth and goes to the window, looking out at the two men who are discussing where to begin digging, or something like that.

'This is really happening!' I say, handing him a tray. When he goes back out with the refreshments, I go upstairs to watch, leaning out of the bedroom window. It would be nice to have a balcony, I think.

September 2 - Frankie

It's quiet without Henry. Ross is out, mending fences. I'm wrapping up pieces for my exposition. Quite a lot of them are on the larger side, especially those where I've utilised defunct musical instruments . It will be a challenge, getting them all in the van. 'What lies beneath' will be a very different exhibition from the last one, if I can pull it off. Suddenly I realise that I've only nine days to go, and I've done nothing about a soundtrack yet. I need some harp, piano, and xylophone notes, with the sound of the sea threaded through it, plus guitar and saxophone, and drums of course, if I'm going to match the music to the sculptures. I don't want it to sound like an actual tune , but I do want it to sound hauntingly beautiful, and kind of muted and magical. I put down the roll of bubble wrap, and bang a quick message off to Henry .

'Help' it says, 'I need something weird and wonderful as background music for next week'

His reply arrives a few minutes later

'Give me a couple of hours. I've got an app!' Phew! That's one problem solved. The next one is the octopus. He doesn't seem to want to go in the van, and I'm going to have to break his legs off, and then reassemble him on site. I should have thought of this before. If he won't fit in the van, the chances are that he won't go through the door at the exposition hall either. The seahorse watches me through oversized glasses as I pack up his driftwood xylophone.

'What are you staring at?' I ask, rather rudely. His unchanging expression makes me giggle.

September 3 - Heather

I put the pen down and rub my eyes. I've been sitting here for over an hour, and written precisely nothing. It's time to admit that I do actually have writers block. There's nothing to be done about it, except wait . Thug isn't being helpful. He's only interested in food and walks.

'You're a bit shallow really aren't you?' I say as he wags his tail hopefully by the door . At least while I'm walking I'm able to think about what the reasons are for this blockage situation. I clip

228

his lead on , and we take off towards the woods while the sun shines. It's been raining this morning, and the earth is damp as I tramp along in my sandals, with the wet grass soaking the bottom of my jeans. At least everything looks a lot greener now. I think it's just a lack of inspiration which is giving me this problem, but it could be the anticipation of the birth of my first grandchild, which does make it so very hard to think about anything else. Then again, it could be Alan. He's a distraction for sure! A very welcome one. I smile to myself, thinking about the evening ahead. We're going to try a new restaurant, very French, but not very local, so he's driving, and then we're going back to his place, where I'll probably stay the night. I pick up a stick and throw it for Thug. I need to wear him out so that he'll sleep well when I'm not there tonight. I could take him over to Frankie for the evening, but she's having him next week while we go to Paris so it wouldn't be fair . Paris! Maybe after that stimulating adventure I'll be able to write again.

September 4 - Susan

I pluck up the courage to behave as if nothing's changed, and I make a blackberry crumble to take over to Eric's house. I'm relieved to see that only his black Saab convertible stands in the driveway. I'm not yet ready to bump into Michelle, prematurely installed there as the live-in girlfriend. Eric opens the door and grins widely .

'Wow! I'm honoured ! ' he says, looking at the crumble 'Do come In!' I step into the kitchen, placing the crumble on the table, and scanning the room for any sign of female intervention, while Eric busies himself with the Gaggia machine. We talk about Dazy Doo's, and pottery in general, and how amazingly well I'm selling. We talk about Charlottes house being on the market, and we wonder if it's such a good idea for them to move to Spain where they don't know anyone, and neither of them can speak the language. I point out to Eric that Charlotte doesn't speak the language here though either. She's the only friend I have here who speaks less French than me. My French may be a little substandard, but at least I try. Charlotte doesn't. Eric places two cups on the table. The ones that have a rubber sleeve around them instead of a handle , and he pushes a bowl towards me that is full of brown, organically shaped sugar. We talk about the fuel prices and the queues at the station where they're selling it a few cents cheaper. We talk about everything in fact, everything except the one thing that's uppermost on my mind. Was it Eric's intention to deceive Andrea? Both of us? Or everyone in Brittany with his pretence at being gay.......or is it just something that Andrea made up in it's entirety . I stir a sugar lump into my coffee, but my courage has failed me, and when we lapse into silence, I merely fill it by mentioning Frankie's exhibition, and saying how I'd like to go.

September 5 - Angel

The Menobabes page is a success! Forty seven women have joined so far, and eight of those are new since yesterday. Clearly the group has been shared far and wide! I have Karen, the estate agent coming for an Indian head massage, and reflexology treatment tomorrow at eleven. I think she's probably about the right age too, so I'll mention it to her afterwards. Lee is extra cuddly as he says goodbye, even though he'll only be gone for a couple of hours. It's pouring with rain again , so he's off to pick up slates from the supplier, instead of clambering about on a wet roof, and he'll be back for lunch. Karen will have left by then so we can have some cosy time together. I take a stack of towels into my treatment room, and hear the ping of Messenger as I'm artistically rolling them up and stuffing them into the pigeon holes where they form a pretty display of heather and mint coloured softness. I hope

230

it's not Karen cancelling her appointment again. She's already cancelled once, and a few months ago she let me down twice when something cropped up at the last minute. It's not Karen though, it's Frankie, saying she missed me at yoga. I woke up too late again for the Monday morning class, and I watch the waves of dots that indicate that she's still typing.

'Are you still able to come with me next weekend?' The message says. Oops! I'd forgotten that I'd said I'd help her again, with the setting up of her exposition.

'Of course I am!' I hesitate just a little before I type back. I want to help her. I really do, but the thought of missing a whole Sunday with Lee doesn't exactly fill me with joy. Oh well. C'est la vie.

September 6 - Charlotte

The fosse is installed, and Tony is out there in the rain, sprinkling grass seed over the patch in the lawn where it's buried. It's hard to get excited about a new fosse. It's a big, expensive thing, hidden in the ground where nobody can see it, and apart from Improving the saleability of the house , it makes no difference to me at all. The old one was ok, or at least functional, so I haven't really gained anything. The holiday is getting closer though, so nothing's going to bring me down at the moment. In the guest bedroom I've laid all of my holiday clothes out on the bed, making sure I have lots of different outfits for every kind of day, plus the accessories to go with them . I've turned out my drawers and my wardrobe upstairs, looking for my favourite swimwear and sandals, things I never use here, and in the bathroom I've emptied the cupboard of all the lotions and potions that I've collected over the years , in the hunt for insect repellent and Imodium tablets. It really is a mess up here, but tomorrow I can start putting all this stuff in the camper van, and then I can tidy up. My phone rings as I'm on my way outside for a smoke. It's Karen. Someone would like to view the house, so could she bring them over in about half an hour.

'Yes of course!' I hear myself saying. Then I put the phone down

'Tonyyyyy! I need your help'. I scream.

September 7 - Frankie

Thug comes hurtling through the door, scattering the cat food bowls across the floor. I sigh, mildly irritated by the inconvenience of having to clean up the splattered mess of soggy croquettes, and then Artie comes in and does the job for me, followed closely by Ross, who inexplicably places a hoof pick, and a pack of new guitar strings, on the table, before flicking the switch on the kettle. I go back to staring at the screen of my laptop. I've shared the poster for the exhibition on Facebook and Instagram, and the response has been overwhelming. The poster has all the information on it. I checked it , and then Angel double checked it . Ross looks over my shoulder as he places a mug of builders tea in front of me.

'Lots of likes !' He says, picking up the hoof pick and examining it.

'It's the questions that are a pain in the arse though'. I say, pushing the laptop towards him. 'What day does it start??' (it clearly says Monday 12th on the poster) 'Are you going to be there around 1pm on Tuesday?' (The poster also states 10-12.30 and 3-7) . 'I'm looking for a small statue of a fairy or maybe an elf, for my garden. Do you have anything suitable?' (Seriously? Go to a garden centre!) . I politely answer all of the queries though, before closing the laptop

'Statue! I hate that fucking word, and how do I know what might be "suitable"?' Ross sips his tea thoughtfully but shrugs when he can't ,up with an answer.

'Come and help me with Madison's hooves'. He says 'then maybe we can go for a swim'

September 8 - Heather

One more night here, and then back to reality. Alan and I stroll through the jardin des Tuileries, and when we reach the Louvre he leaves me with a quick kiss on the cheek. He's meeting a French friend, Yannick, and though I was invited to go and have a drink with them, I declined. The fast French and the web design orientated conversation would be too much for me so I've opted for a little bit of culture instead. I came here years ago, but was in such a rush to see the Mona Lisa , that I all but totally missed out on the other exhibits. This afternoon I take my time, and I wander, staring at statues and paintings, until I find myself so utterly relaxed and in the zone, that surely I can't fail to rediscover the inspiration to create my own art, in the form of another book, a book which this time will satisfy myself, as well as my readers. I leave my phone in my bag, and three hours passes by without my realising it, so that when I head back to the meeting point in front of the pyramid, there's a chill in the air, and my stomach tells me it must be getting near dinner time.

'Have you heard the news? ' Alan asks, looking up from his phone as I approach . 'The Queen is dead.' We stare at each other then, as the enormity of the situation sinks in. It just seems so unthinkable and surreal .

'Wow! Things will never be the same again, will they!' I say as he takes my hand.

'Come on, let's go and get something to eat', he replies.

September 9 - Susan

I push my sleeve up and use a stretchy black hair band as an armband. Should anyone arrive today they will find me in my studio quietly potting away, while listening to classical music. It seems a fitting way to spend the day after our queen's death, in quiet reflection. I'm not really a royalist , but neither am I an anti royalist. For me the queen was always just there, in the background, doing her job, which I never really understood, but there it is. I never met her, or wrote to her, or even listened much to her speech on Christmas Day. Nonetheless I will miss her . It's difficult to imagine England without her. Everything will change, and as I slowly shape this latest lump of clay into a rather whimsical cat shaped tea pot, the spout being a raised front paw, while the handle takes the form of a curled tail, I find myself worrying about the queen's corgis. They will miss her terribly, for sure. Rhea stares up at me from her favourite studio spot, in front of the glass door in a patch of sunlight. Her tail is wagging and her ears are pricked . Someone must be approaching. Moments later the door is beaten open by Thug, who immediately investigates the dog bowls on the floor, before Artie, a few seconds later, joins him. It's a full two minutes later when Frankie arrives, looking just a little disheveled, and apologising profusely for the interruption. I'm glad of it though. Happy to have company. I tug self consciously at my armband

'Sad news eh?' She says, sitting down opposite me, and picking up an odd scrap of clay. Rhea creeps under my chair as the other dogs run back and forth from the garden to the studio.

'It just seems so surreal'. I carry on with my teapot as we chat, and Frankie absent mindedly sculpts a sort of dog shaped creature out of the the spare clay.

'Looks a bit like a corgi'. We both giggle.

September 10 -Angel

There's a definite chill in the air in the mornings. Lee lies in bed, making the most of a day when he has no commitments, and enjoying the home I've made in his house.

'It needed a woman's touch' were the last words he uttered before I began launching the throw cushions at him as he hid under the duvet. I take a path along the edge of the field across from the house. Lakshmi runs ahead, sniffing, and I breathe in the early morning smells, and listen to the birds, and a dog somewhere in the distance, barking. This will be a mindful walk . Tomorrow I am off helping Frankie, and then on Tuesday, I am hosting my first meeting of the Menobabes. Before this busy period I'm going to just take some Me and Lee time. Up ahead Lakshmi sniffs at a white ball, perhaps forgotten by that other dog that I can still hear, faintly. As I get closer though, I realise that it's not a ball at all , well it is, of sorts. It's a puffball. It's a long time since I last found one of these. I put my hands together and thank the universe before I pick it up. I saw a puffball recipe just yesterday on Facebook, that I would like to try. As I look about me , I see that there are others dotted around . Just one of them goes such a long way though, so I turn around and head for home with my foraged treasure, leaving the rest for the next lucky dog walkers.

September 11 - Charlotte

Less than a week now, and all is ready. The house is so clean and tidy, I've taken to spending most of my time outside on the step, just so that I don't mess it up. There have been a couple of viewings, but as yet, no offers . Karen keeps saying 'Early days!' , and I guess that's true, and anyway I don't really care that much at the moment because we're off on holiday on Friday! We're really going! Our passports are in date, and apparently that's all we need. I did try to persuade Tony to have his Covid booster vaccination before we leave, but apparently he doesn't have time. He wants to sell the little Peugeot Expert van , plus another car, a Renault Kangoo, before Friday so that we have some more cash to spend. I can't complain. I don't really want to have to cook every night in the camper van , so the money for restaurant meals is a necessity really. It's just that I keep hearing that Covid is on the increase , and that we're in for a bad winter so I have been encouraging him to get jabbed , just to be safe. I hear him swearing in the garage . Something to do with a steering rack. I'm about to go over there to see what the problem is when I hear his phone ring and he answers it , speaking loudly and launching into conversation in fluent french. I pickup my own phone instead, and ask Google.

'What did the Queen die of?'

September 12 - Frankie

Angel and I sit outside 'what lies beneath' . I watch couples who are obviously on holiday, file through the door , with their rucksacks and water bottles, and I listen for their reactions. It's hard to hear more than the first few words as they get further away, making their way through urchins and octopuses, past mystical creatures and mermaids, admiring seahorse sculptures and ghostly jellyfish lamps. Then they reach the orchestra at the other end, where a haunting soundtrack plays a sirens song, as if created by the underwater beasts themselves, who I've positioned like a rock band, with the drumming octopus at centre stage, flanked by a guitar wielding driftwood dolphin, giving it everything, to the drummers right, and the seahorse with the xylophone on the other side. A little way to the left, an imposing concrete and seaweed draped Poseidon looks on , leaning on his spring tined trident . I rush to stand outside of the exit door, so that I can once more hear their reactions. I hear laughter. I hear people exclaiming loudly, then murmuring and giggling. I hear one small child scream, then start to cry, and one old lady, obviously English, saying repeatedly, 'oh my word!'. By the time Angel leaves me, at the end of the day, I've sold six little urchins, a jellyfish lamp, and the large seahorse sculpture which I can't allow to be actually taken until the end of the week. Angel high fives me as she gets into the car with Lee, and I wave her off, before turning towards the beach, for a little down time.

September 13 - Heather

The message from Alan last night simply said 'Hope you had a good day. Sleep tight xx' I haven't seen him since we arrived home on Friday, but that feels comfortable, and not at all as if something isn't right with us. 'Friends with Benefits' seems to be an arrangement that works well for me. I tell this to Sophie when she video calls to show me her bump progress. She looks happy in her new home , which I will very soon see for real, and Paddy is apparently more than happy with the idea of becoming a father while continuing to live apart , and lead a life that is separate from her and the baby. He contributes financially in a way that means Sophie can live comfortably, and can go to part time working hours if she wants to . So, finances apart, it's a similar relationship to the one I have with Alan. Perhaps it runs in the family, this need for a bit of distance and breathing space, rather than the constant closeness and domestic drudgery that most couples cling to as an ideal. We both smile into our screens, each waiting for the other to speak .

'Have you booked your ferry yet?' She asks. I haven't, but I'll get on to it soon . It's just that I'm a bit worried about asking Frankie to have Thug again so soon . I look at him lying peacefully on the sofa next to me like butter wouldn't melt. Sophie follows my gaze.

'You could always bring him with you'. She says, a little uncertainly.

September 14 - Susan

'Oh my god you're so lucky!' Charlotte says, almost slamming her mug down on the table, and slopping tea over the Indian silk shawl that I bought her, to take on holiday in case it's chilly in the evenings. I've been asked to supply some kitchenware to a concept store in town . They particularly want my butter dishes and lemon squeezers, but would also like some jugs, sugar bowls, and maybe a teapot or two. I am to have my own display stand, and it will pay well, so I have decided to put my online store on hold for the moment, and concentrate on this new venture, as well as Dazy Doo's of course. Charlotte has a funny way of showing how happy she is for me.

'Success comes so easily to you!' She says, frowning and looking like she's about burst into tears. The shawl is beautiful, in purple, black and gold, Charlottes favourite colours, yet she's barely given it a glance. I put the milk back in the fridge , and wipe the table . I'm beginning to wish I hadn't bothered to venture over here for a 'goodbye' cup of tea before she leaves. Tony comes in, just as I'm rinsing the cloth and thinking about going home

'Shortbread!' He says, eyeing the plate I brought with me.

'Shall I make you a cuppa?' I put the kettle back on without waiting for an answer.

'Thankyou!' Charlotte says then, recovering from her outburst, and reaching for a piece of shortbread. Tony picks up the shawl, and holds it out so that the light shines through it .

'Gorgeous, isn't it?' Charlotte says, and I almost do a double take 'so kind of you Susan'. She smiles at last, rather too angelically . I'm truly going to miss her when she finally moves.

September 15 - Angel

I wake, still processing the shared experiences, and the mutual support, of the Menobabes meeting, on Tuesday evening. There were seven of us in the end. A couple of girls that were due to attend, couldn't make it, and most of the others in the online group, live too far away to come to a meeting. Lynsey, Abi, Caroline and Sarah all came together in one car. They knew each other already, from various local groups and events , and from all having teenagers at the local college. Sally came from farther afield, new to Brittany and keen to make friends, older than the rest of us, I suspect she's firmly in the post menopausal category, and then there was Kerry, who I think I gelled with most. Wearing a simple white linen dress, and a rose quartz necklace, I knew immediately that we would have things in common, and I was right! Kerry is a hypnotherapist and very much into a holistic approach when it comes to treating the symptoms of menopause. I offered free reflexology treatments to the women who were suffering from hot flushes, while Kerry spoke at length about turmeric, and the benefits of probiotics, and focusing on gut health to tackle bloating, and muffin tops. Everyone left the meeting on a high, having gained the support they required, and having consumed , some of them, a glass or two of Prosecco at the end of the session. We all agreed to meet again next month, and as I closed the door when finally, at around midnight they got back in their cars, I think I was the only one who still felt a little bit anxious and unsure about the physical changes ahead. I just don't seem to be able to accept the inevitability of the physical changes ahead in the same way as the other women do, and for that reason, I'm just a tiny bit disappointed. Maybe it's because I'm the youngest in the group, that I still find it all so daunting.

September 16 - Charlotte

When it comes to actually leaving, I start to panic a bit. Tony has the bonnet up, checking oil and water levels apparently. I have our passports in my bag, but get them out again to check once more that they are in date. They are, as indeed they were yesterday when I looked. I have our bank cards, and Tony has a wad of cash. I have two packs of cigarettes, and eighteen pairs of knickers, plus eight different 'Evening out' outfits. I've three pairs of shorts and five bikinis. Tony has a pair of swimming shorts, some 'going out' shorts, and a stack of T-shirts in black, white, and grey. We are good to go, and it's not yet nine o clock . In four hours we will stop for lunch. In another four we will stop for the night , probably somewhere near the Dordogne. It's exciting. The engine is running. I take one last look at the front door, and my favourite step, before getting in and wrapping my shawl around me. The van is cold. Tony grins at me.

'Ready?' We drive out past the garage and the garish yellow 'A vendre' sign, and I begin to relax and enjoy myself, thinking of the weeks of sunshine ahead. Tony fiddles with the radio until he finds RMN. Pharrell Williams belts out 'Happy' , and we both sing along.

September 17 - Frankie

I'm tired. Tomorrow is my last day here, and then I must pack up everything that hasn't sold. I've done well, and I was already in profit by the second day of the expo, but I'm so tired now, of talking and being polite to people. My face literally aches from smiling, and my feet ache from standing. All I want to do is go home and sleep for a day, then hang out in my atelier creating stuff. Once again I wonder about giving up the exhibition thing, or even employing someone else to do 'front of house' for me . At lunch time I take my book to the beach, and settle in a sunny spot between rocks, out of the wind, and away from the people, not that there are many of them on the beach today. The summer is definitely coming to an end. I unwrap my supermarket tuna sandwich from its plastic triangle, and unenthusiastically take a bite . It's a bit soggy and tasteless, and a far cry from the sushi I had yesterday, when I still had some life in me, and could face socialising in the middle of the day. I pick up my phone to call Ross, and it rings a few times before going to the answering service. He's probably in the barn, where the walls are so thick that we can never get a signal. I leave a message.

'I'm tired' I say, and end the call, feeling better already, for having shared that information with him.

September 18 - Heather

I watch Alan sleep. He lies on his back , breathing softly, looking like someone pretending to be asleep. I call his name quietly, almost whispering, not loud enough to wake him . There's no reaction, so I slide my legs out of bed and get up, letting him lie there in peace, while I go downstairs to let Thug out. It's a decadent breakfast that I prepare in the end . Having discovered that I have only one egg in the house, I've assembled bagels with cream cheese and smoked salmon, and sliced up a melon. Thug looks longingly at the table , and I take a photo of him peering over with his front paws on a chair, just as Alan arrives in the kitchen, fully showered and dressed, in the time it took me to fill Thugs food bowl and prepare the breakfast feast.

'Are we celebrating something?' He asks, and I give him what I hope is a mysterious smile.

'Let me guess….it's an anniversary of sorts…three months? Either that or you want something!'

He picks up his coffee and takes a sip before fully committing to the act of sitting down at the breakfast table.

'Thug wonders if you would like his company for a week. What do you think?' . Thug shoots him a meaningful look as he hears his name, a line of drool hangs attractively from either side of his mouth.

'How could I possibly resist him!' He replies.

September 19 - Susan

242

Three of us sit on my sofa. Lunch is a casual affair, with the coffee table laden with bread, cheese, salads and quiche, and I've made shortbread, as something typically English. We watch the procession in silence for the most part. Eric with Delilah on his lap. Rhea in between us, and Marie on my other side , dabbing at the occasional tear with a balled up napkin. Odd that she, the only non English one amongst us, should be the most emotional about the death of our Queen. .

'Ninety six is a very good age' I say, pouring her a cup of English tea with milk and sugar .

'I hope I don't live that long' Eric states, and gives me a sideways glance. We are almost back to normal now, though there is still the elephant in the room, that is his girlfriend, who should have been a boyfriend. If Marie weren't here with us I might ask him about that, but she is, and so I'll save that conversation for another time.

'But if you still have your health it's good surely?' Marie says, and I'm momentarily confused because there's been a few long moments since Eric spoke.

'Not many of us reach that age without issues.' Eric answers, and I think about his recent heart attack . A wake up call in many ways. In silence, we watch as the camera then focuses on the children, grandchildren, and great grandchildren of the late Queen, mournfully dressed in black.

'And there will be nobody much left to miss me when I'm gone'. He adds. I shiver involuntarily. The same thing is true for me.

September 20 - Angel

Mabon tomorrow. In the woods I gather twigs, and a suitable branch to make a broomstick. The weather is already autumnal, and I welcome this change in the seasons. Back home, I pick lavender and sage, and form a kind of bouquet with the twigs, which I then bind to the broomstick with ivy, leaving it to trail down at either side of the broom head. Admiring the finished piece, I place it outside of the door, in time to welcome my first client of the afternoon. One of the Menobabes, Caroline, was so happy with the little freebie session that I gave her, that she's booked in for a full reflexology treatment to see if I can help her with the terrible hot flushes that she's been experiencing. Hot flushes are one of those confusing symptoms. I don't seem to get them in the same way as others do. I'm never 'suddenly, intensely hot', just warm . We all have the bloated belly thing, and a couple of the women, myself included, have tender breasts from time to time.

'No two women are the same'. Kerry kept saying, and I know she's right, but it seems very unfair to me that today I feel quite drained of energy, and even fatter than normal. Maybe the cooler weather will help me to shiver some of the weight off. I tie a couple of cinnamon sticks into the ivy trails, to finish off the broom, and as Caroline pulls up outside I stand up, supporting my achy back with one hand and trying not to yawn as Caroline exclaims over how pretty the broom is.

September 21 - Charlotte

They serve a lot of fish and chips here, and all day English breakfasts . We've taken to eating our main meal at lunchtime, then making a sandwich in the van later in the evening. I'm a little bit tanned, but at the same time, a little bit burned, so I put a T-shirt on over my bikini, and head for one of the sun beds by the pool, to lie down and read, while my bacon, eggs and mushrooms are being digested. Tony swims a bit, holding in his stomach as he walks to the pool, and after a while I think about joining him, but decide against exercising on a full stomach . Anyway I need a cigarette, and I can't smoke here at the pool side , so I tie my shawl around me like a sarong, and walk over to the bench under the palm trees where I won't bother anyone. I watch two girls slip out of their sun dresses to reveal tiny bikinis, the bottoms of which are thong like and show off their perfect rear ends. They glance around to see if there is anyone to impress, but we are mainly middle-aged couples on this camp-site at the moment, and having established that nobody is of much interest to them, they flop down on the sun beds for their daily dose of tanning . Tony walks past them with his belly sucked in. It makes me smile.

September 22 - Frankie

A proper gallery asks fifty per cent of the sale price . That's a big hit for the artist. Nevertheless, if I take into account my fuel and living expenses as well as the cost of hiring exhibition space, fifty per cent isn't so bad. I mull over the pro's and con's of both options, but in the end it's academic, as there are no such galleries near enough to me anyway.

'Start one!' Ross says, as he works alongside me in the garden. I'm picking runner beans. He's pulling out the tomato plants that caught blight in the last few days, due to the recent rain.

'Then I'd have to be there to talk to the customers! '. It wouldn't solve my problem at all. I want to create art, but I don't really enjoy the time spent trying to sell it. Well I do, a bit, but being polite and friendly soon wears thin, and I have to keep reminding myself of the money I'm making. I take my basket of beans into the house, and put the kettle on. Maybe if I just stick to one exhibition each year, and the resulting commissions…..but then I'm not sure if that would be enough, financially.

'We'd get by.' Ross says, when I voice this idea. We would, I know.

September 23 - Heather

My case is back on my bed , being packed this time for England. I leave tomorrow on the daytime crossing to Portsmouth. Nine hours on a boat! I should be able to get some writing done, if inspiration strikes me. Sophie seems excited at the prospect of being able to show off her new home. I may even get the chance to meet Paddy. Thug eyes me suspiciously, from the bedroom doorway. He's seen this case on the bed situation before, and he seems to realise that it means I'll be gone for a while. He gives me a hurt look before disappearing again downstairs. Tonight Alan will cook me dinner, and Thug and I will spend a pleasant evening being entertained at his place. Then I will leave in the early hours of the morning, and Thug will stay.

'It won't be too traumatic!' I say, when he comes back upstairs to check on me, and sighs loudly.

'You'll go for lots of walks!' I cram more pretty tops and another pair of jeans in, before zipping up the case, and bringing it downstairs.

'It's just for a week!' I add, as he follows me with his tail down. He's going to miss me, that's obvious, and I'll definitely miss him, and Alan too.

September 24 - Susan

I wake, feeling ok . Looking forward to the day once more. The last few days have been difficult, as a wave of insurmountable loneliness washed over me. I counted my blessings, and there are many, but I struggled to find peace within myself. It started with the Queen's funeral, and all those grandchildren and great grandchildren. I'm too old to adopt a child, and for the last few days that feeling of having no real connection to anyone here on Earth, was overwhelming. Today I feel calm . Before I set foot out of bed, I think of each friend in turn and feel grateful for them. I think about my good health and my financial stability. I think about my cosy home, and Rhea, and Delilah, and I think about my newly discovered interest in pottery, and the creative skill that I didn't know I possessed. Only then do I get out of bed, in a positive frame of mind. A message, from Charlotte, greets me when I pick up my phone.

'We are in Galicia. It's lovely. Wish you were here.'

I don't know why I didn't think of it before. I could book a flight to somewhere near to where they are staying, and go and surprise her. I'm sure Eric would take care of the animals for a few days, and drive me to the airport. It could be just what I need!

September 25 - Angel

'Well here's a thing!' I say, as I stare at myself in the mirror, The Empress tarot card in my hand . I've drawn her for the past three days. I don't know why I didn't see it before, but actually, perhaps I did, and I was just in denial. I lay the card on my bedside

247

table, which is a kind of altar, full of natural offerings, bird's eggshells, crystals, and pebbles with holes right through them. I don't need to look at the little plastic wand that lies there next to it. The Empress card is the ultimate card for femininity and motherhood. I'm not menopausal at all. Far from it. I'm pregnant. The signs have all been there but I haven't seen them, haven't dared to look, afraid to hope for for something so amazingly wonderful as this. Now it's undeniable though, the physical changes, the pleasure I've taken in building my 'nest' , and the cards, that whispered softly at first, but then began screaming out to me, when I wouldn't acknowledge their message. I glance at the strip of plastic and see two blue lines. No surprise there, and then I look back at my reflection in the mirror and I begin to laugh. I laugh hysterically until I start crying, and then I can't stop.

'This won't do!' I say to myself. Lee will be home soon . He's gone over with the digger to help Ross dig a pit for the massive amount of poop that the pony and donkey produce, now that there are two of them. With him unexpectedly gone for a few hours, I used the opportunity to do the test that I bought from the pharmacy yesterday, and now here I am, a sobbing pregnant mess. I run a bath, and add some lavender oil and chamomile flowers .

'Breathe!' I say, as I sink into its scented embrace.

September 26 - Charlotte

Galicia is a little quiet, and I wonder if I'd get bored here after a while. Tony is enjoying snorkelling, and I'm quite liking the pretty little coves and beaches, but preferred the restaurants, and the life, in Barcelona, where we were a few days ago. I need to persuade Tony to turn around soon, and start heading back in the other direction. He fancies Madrid next though, and I'm really not sure. It seems to me that it might be just a little bit too Spanish. Maybe it's ok for a holiday, but I definitely wouldn't want to live there, and that's the point really, we're meant to be looking for somewhere to settle.

'I liked Sitges' I say , and leave it hanging, as Tony takes off his snorkelling mask and sits down on his towel. I really did like Sitges. I enjoyed shopping there, and I liked the look of the houses. Tony raises his eyebrows. There are symmetrical deep red grooves on either side of his nose, where the mask fits so tightly.

'Did you see the prices in the estate agent's windows?' He says. I shrug, and light a cigarette.

'Ok' he says , and looks down. 'We can stop briefly in Madrid, then go down to Alicante. I think you might like it there' He hands me the snorkelling mask. 'But only if you at least try this out first!'

September 27 - Frankie

'Look away!' I say, as I flip the mask back down, and weld another metal rod to one side of what will be a tree trunk , then unplug the machine, and remove the mask from my head. Angel has patiently waited for me to finish this stage of my latest creation. I will bend the branches out next, and then begin adding leaves of metal, and other items to this 'Christmas' tree, that I'm making for the Commune. Angel shuffles from foot to foot. She's not impressed. I can tell that in her opinion , there's something wrong with it. I stand back to eye it critically. The basic tree is a good shape. When I twist the branches and add twiggy bits , it will really begin to look quite special.

'Trust me! , it's gonna look great!' I take a sip of the coffee she made when she arrived and caught me at a stage where I just couldn't stop, and I pass her a drawing of how the finished tree will look. Angel looks at it and nods briefly.

'I love it' she says , handing me back the scruffy piece of paper , and smiling weirdly at me.

'So everything's ok then?' I can't help thinking that she's holding something back. She nods.

'I'm having a baby.' She says.

September 28 - Heather

While Sophie is at work, at the leisure centre, I carry on painting. The little room, which we emptied a couple of days ago, is perfect for it's purpose as a nursery. The walls have been given one coat of a colour called 'dreamboat ' , and I'm starting the second coat while Sophie works. I'm standing on a chair, cutting in a straight line of paint at the top of the wall, where it meets the ceiling when I hear the front door open.

'You're early!' I say as footsteps on the stairs announce her imminent arrival, and inspection of the freshly painted baby space. Except it's not Sophie. I find myself staring under my arm , as I reach upwards with my brush to the outer corners , at a young man with dark eyes and long black hair tied back in a glossy ponytail.

'Paddy?' I ask.

'Heather!' He says, smiling broadly. 'I've come to give you a hand!' Irish then, and very good looking. He explains that he's not actually Paddy at all, but Ryan .

'Everyone calls me Paddy' he says, his accent broad , and his smile infectious. He helps me down from the chair when I've finished the last corner, and together we begin rolling up the blue plastic which covers the carpet .

'What's next?', he asks, looking at the immaculate room, with its striped navy carpet, and helicopter light suspended from the ceiling. In the hallway , the box containing the cot, blocks the way into the guest bedroom where I'm sleeping. He follows my gaze.

'We could maybe bond over an Ikea flatpack assembly session?', he suggests. I like him already.

September 29 - Susan

Charlotte isn't making it easy to plan a surprise visit. No sooner had I researched flights going to Galicia, or somewhere near, than I got a message to say they were on their way to Madrid! I have to stay one step ahead. I don't think Charlotte will want to stay in the city. She's interested in beaches, and living 'la vida loca' with a bunch of expats . After Madrid, they are heading over to Alicante, and that's a place I can easily get to . I put Angel's teddy bear down , and click on the app that gives me all of my flight options. If I go early next week, I should be able to time it beautifully . I can't help smiling to myself as I message Eric to see if he can take Rhea, and feed Delilah. If he can't do it then I can always ask Marie. It takes moments to find a flight from Nantes to Alicante on Monday. I pick up the teddy again. The eyes that I made are a wonderful shiny black, and the nose I'm especially pleased with, matt black, with perfectly shaped nostrils. I've washed the whole thing on a wool wash , and I'm now sewing on some ears I've made from the fabric of the one arm that was left on the old bear. The new arms don't show, as I've given him a smart tuxedo jacket and white gloves. A black bow tie around his rather feeble neck, supports his head well , and goes with his stylish outfit. I hope Angel will be pleased with him.

'There you are! As good as new!' I place him on a chair, by the window, and pick up my phone again, to check for a reply from Eric.

September 30 - Angel

251

We won't do anything yet. Not until after the scan . We won't tell anyone either (except for Frankie of course) . There will be no plans to turn the box room into a nursery, not yet, and there will be no shopping for nappies or tiny clothes. In short, we will not get our hopes up until we've seen for ourselves, on a screen, that all is well, and likely to stay that way. Intuitively, I feel that I already know this myself , but confirmation would be reassuring. We need to be sure that this is indeed a healthy, viable, living baby that we are dealing with. Even so, it's scary.

'I'm fifty two!' He said, when I voiced my concerns about my own age. 'If I can do this, you can.!'

But it's not caring for a baby that scares me. What scares me is the very real possibility that there may be something wrong with it. A normal baby I can cope with for sure , but what if it isn't normal?

'Let's not give that any thought!' He keeps saying, and I know he's right. Next week we will know more, and the good feeling I have, that all is ok , should be confirmed. The temptation to look at baby things on the internet is almost irresistible, and when a knock at the door distracts me from doing this , I open it quickly. Susan stands there with the most beautiful teddy bear in her arms.

'Ta dah!' She says. It takes me a full minute to realise that this is Bington! I thought at first that she had guessed my secret, and that this was a congratulatory gift.

'Wow! I can't thank you enough!' I say.

'Actually you can.' She answers mysteriously.

October 1 - Charlotte

The Royal palace of Madrid is huge. Tony and I splashed out on the admission fee, and it was actually totally worth it . We saw it from the outside and couldn't resist , as it just looked so amazing. We were lucky, as at this time of year there aren't many people queuing. The only thing is I'm not allowed to take pictures, and I really do want to post on Facebook the only bit of culture that I'll probably experience on the whole holiday. So much gold, antiques, and general grandeur. Tony stands in front of weapons, and armour for a long time, just staring, and I start to get itchy . I like the decor and the furniture, but not so much the swords and helmets. I look at the photos that I have taken, of the outside of the palace. Nobody seems to be watching me, so I surreptitiously snap a couple of pics of the paintings on the walls, and get away with it. Not even Tony notices, so I take a few more in the Kings apartment and the Porcelain room. In the vault I try again, with a painting called 'The greatness of the Spanish Monarchy' . A guard screams at me 'No Photos!!' , and Tony looks at me in disbelief. I need a cigarette now, so we decide it's time to leave, and stroll away to a terrace where in dappled sunshine we are served the most delicious chilled Rioja Blanco, with our tapas .

'Should we start looking at property again tomorrow?' I ask.

'Isn't that what we've been doing today?' He replies. Smart arse!.

October 2 - Frankie

I've never been very maternal, preferring animals to children really, and if I'm honest , preferring animals to most human beings. As a baby, Henry was passed around my friends, while I continued to work at whatever project I happened to be working on. I was lucky to have friends who had their feet on the ground. Good people, reliable people. They looked after me and Henry. When we lived in the caravan there was always someone offering to do my laundry, and piling extra blankets and duvets on us so that we always felt warm and loved. We were welcome at so many tables as my single parent status seemed to automatically qualify me as a charity case . As Henry grew older this state of affairs dropped off a bit, and I took more and more part time jobs in order to get by, when he started school. My art didn't earn me much then, though I did make small pieces for friends, to repay their kindness. I bought a house as soon as I could afford the deposit, a tiny bungalow, part of an ex holiday camp, cheap and with the added advantage of being near the sea. There was a nice space in the attic which, enterprisingly, I lined with mirrors and foil, and started a little cannabis farm, the income from which funded the living expenses of Henry and I , and enabled me to make a serious start at becoming a full time artist. I think of Angel's situation now, pregnant aged forty five, with a stable home and a man who loves her, and compare it to my own fearful teenage experience, and feel a stab of envy. There is nothing though that I would change.

October 3 - Heather

It's almost as if I've never been away . It's drizzling rain again, and I'm out walking Thug again, and thinking of calling in on Susan for a coffee again! Thug was well behaved apparently, which I was glad to hear, and I'm happy that the 'friends with benefits' arrangement, covers benefits other than just the sexual ones. Sophie feels the same way. Paddy is there for her when she needs him, and he can't wait to take his turn with the childcare once the baby arrives.

'We are very modern aren't we mother! ' she exclaimed, when I told her of how things are with Alan and I. I kept it vague of course . I'm not about to regale my daughter with the intimate details of my sex life! Suffice to say I told her that sometimes he 'stays over'. We spent yesterday together, my first day back, and now it's unlikely that I'll see him again till about Wednesday. Thug has missed this particular walk, and he spends an age sniffing at every tree and fence post, familiarising himself again. I pick up a cep or two , and then find a few more, making it necessary to find something to put them in. By the time I get to Susan's I'm laden with them, and when she opens the door she seems only a little perturbed to be presented with a full dog poo bag of mushrooms .

October 4 - Susan

'My flight is early in the afternoon, on Thursday' , I wait hopefully for a response from Eric.

I'm already packed and ready to go, the amazonite and rose quartz crystals that Angel gave me to help calm my fear of flying, sit on the kitchen table. I will put them inside my bra, just before I leave. He frowns, and sips his coffee without answering, and for a moment I'm expecting him to say that he can't drive me to the airport . Instead he says

'Ok, if we leave early enough we can get some lunch somewhere before I drop you off' . Phew! I'm all set then, and lunch with Eric will be nice too. I'm looking forward to surprising Charlotte. They've not been gone that long , but I'm missing her .

'How is Michelle?' I ask him then . I've never asked after her before, but feel it's about time I made an effort to accept her presence in Eric's life.

'Actually that's something I wanted to talk to you about'. He says, and I pause, with my coffee cup half raised, as I wait for him to say that it's all over between them. But no, he looks happy as he says

'She'd really like to try her hand at pottery, and I wondered if she could come with me sometime to your studio? She's really impressed with the little bowls I made.'

This I was not expecting, and I'm actually lost for words, so I just nod and, and sip my coffee until I regain my composure

'Ok, that'd be good' I hear myself mutter, after a while. I manage a weak smile , then get up distractedly to fill Delilah's food bowl .

October 5 - Angel

I don't need a scan to tell me how pregnant I am . Now that I'm listening to my body , instead of just assuming what my symptoms point to, I'm pretty sure I can trace the changes all the way back to the end of June, which means that it's likely I conceived around the time of the summer solstice. It takes me a while to do the maths though, and when I look at my swollen belly in the mirror I settle on fifteen weeks . I look fat but i dont yet look gloriously pregnant. There's a long way to go yet. From my tarot deck I draw the Ace of Cups. New beginnings in terms of love and compassion, amongst other things. Lee comes into the bedroom as I'm getting dressed, and stands there watching me.

'I think we could start thinking about decorating the box room ' he says. We could. At the very least we could paint the walls, and do something about the flooring. I think about my recent, brief conversation with Heather. I've not yet told her about my own situation, and was merely asking after Sophie.

'The baby's not due till December' she said, 'but the nursery is already kitted out as if it might be needed tomorrow'

'Ok' I say to Lee, 'We could certainly choose the colours'.

October 6 - Charlotte

I don't know why Tony insists on going to this bar in Torrevieja. It's a kind of Spanish pub that does tapas every weekday, and then 'Sunday Roast' on Sundays. It's ok, but there's nothing special about it , so I'm a bit irritated that we have to walk past all the other bars on the strip , especially to find this one. We sit down and wait ages to be served, while being "entertained" by a live band, who are at best, mediocre. Tony seems a little bit jittery and excited. We've seen three apartments today, that we could easily afford if we get the asking price for the house. Apartments though, not houses. No gardens. No garages. I'm not sure how Tony would spend his time here. I look at him drumming his fingers on the table, and people watching. The waitress brings me a Seabreeze cocktail, while Tony has a beer with a big frothy head on it . I look around at the other people in here. Groups of women with cocktails. A miserable looking couple about our age, and two men who might be a couple too, though they don't look at each other, they look at their phones. Tony too, is now staring at his phone, and tapping away secretively on Messenger, probably enquiring about some car or other that's caught his attention. I look over his shoulder at a woman who hesitates as she comes in through the open door, looking around for a familiar group of friends. She looks exactly like Susan.

October 7 - Frankie

Eloise and I stand together in the sunshine, waiting for the Mairie to arrive. The 'Christmas' tree looks beautiful in this light, and the photograph will be stunning, except that it's for the cover of the December edition, and I feel a wintry scene would be more appropriate. The tree is concreted into a huge iron pot , and it literally, and intentionally, weighs a ton, so that it won't get stolen, but can, with the help of a tractor, be moved into place each December and taken away again every year some time after Christmas . It stands now, temporarily, in the garden of the Mairie, by the shed, and Eloise wonders if it's in the best position . I look up at the clear blue sky.

'Peut être c'est mieux la bas , contre le mur' she says, as if speaking of moving a table or a chair. I am saved from answering as the Mairie arrives, and kisses us both. Eloise gets us to stand either side of the tree , and she takes a few shots.

' Désolée!' She says , and goes on to explain how it would actually be better if it weren't so sunny. We all agree to arrange another photo shoot for a duller day . In the meantime the tractor driver will arrive , and move the tree to a spot, in front of the white wall . I've wasted an entire morning here, but that's life I guess. The soft ping of WhatsApp interrupts my thoughts. It's Henry , with a song he's written that he wants me to listen to. I smile at the title 'Another wasted day'.

October 8 - Heather

The words 'Indian Summer' are being bandied around on Facebook, and the thought of walking Thug along a sandy beach somewhere is too tempting to ignore . It's a shame that Susan's not here , as she would probably have enjoyed a day out. I could ask Alan of course, but we've plans to get together later tonight, and I feel as if I've been spending rather a lot of time with him lately.

'Ok Thug! So It's just us '. I say, as he wags his tail hopefully. I change out of my jeans, and back into the shorts which I thought I'd put away for this year. When I've finished sorting out a bottle of water for me, and one for Thug, plus a dog bowl, I pick up my phone again. There is a post from Maisie, asking if any of her yoginis fancy the beach today. I send her a message to say I'll be with her in twenty minutes. Then I notice a friend request from somebody called Hope Hill. I take a quick glance at her profile and see that Angel and Frankie are mutual friends, so I hit 'confirm friendship' . I don't know the woman, but maybe she's a fan of my writing or something. Thug whines by the door , as I'm obviously taking too long. I look over at him and he sighs loudly, shaking his head. Sometimes he is exactly like a man.

October 9 - Susan

Tony's paunch has got bigger, and even Charlotte looks as if she's gained a little weight. We wait for the young English waitress, who serves us every time we come in here. I have a cappuccino, while Tony and Charlotte take the 'all day breakfast', as usual. Earlier, back at my hotel, which is clean but soulless, I had my usual grapefruit juice, croissant and coffee, before going to the beach for an early swim. It's a little bit cold, and I don't stay in long, but when I come out I feel virtuous. As if I were Frankie, braving the water in all weathers. I watch Tony cutting his sausage in half , then pushing it around in the baked bean juice before eating it. They have done this every day since I've been here . They walk from the campsite, five minutes away, Charlotte smoking her first cigarette of the morning, Tony holding in his stomach whenever they pass a pretty girl, and they arrive here just

260

around eleven. The huge plate of sausage, bacon, eggs, and all that goes with it, lasts them all day, and it's apparently cheaper than shopping and cooking. I'm not entirely convinced it's such a great idea, but they do seem to be thriving on it, and I think the lifestyle here may suit them well. Tomorrow is my last night here, and if I can convince them not to eat too much in the daytime, I will treat them to a nice restaurant in the evening. Charlotte dips a piece of bread into her egg yolk, then sucks at it, pushing her plate away and frowning like a petulant child.

'I don't want any more of this. Maybe we can get some ice cream later?' Tony swaps his empty plate for her half full one, but says nothing.

October 10 - Angel

I shiver a bit as Frankie spreads the cold slippery paste on my belly . This will be the sixteen weeks bump. There will be a twenty four week bump, and another at around thirty weeks, then finally, the full term bump. Each time she will take a mould and create a concrete cast which will become a pregnant belly for a series of trees in the woodland walk part of Lee's garden. Our garden. The trees lead the way to the strangely beautiful tree at the end of the walk, that spawned the whole idea. It's branches are just like two arms cradling a baby, and so a concrete baby swaddled in a concrete dipped , crocheted shawl , will be the final piece of this installation.

'You ok?' She asks, as she tests the set of the rubbery paste. I am actually quite comfortable, which is surprising, given that I'm half naked in Frankie's untidy studio , reclining on a sofa that smells faintly of cat urine, as the tap on Frankie's paint splattered sink, drips persistently onto the draining board next to my head .

She stands up and makes another attempt at closing the tap off ,
then puts a rag underneath the drip to stop the noise.

' I have a Hope Hill coming over, tomorrow night ' she says.
'she's one of your clients isn't she? She might be interested in a
garden sculpture .'

I feel myself grimace. She came to me a couple of weeks ago,
for some reiki . We didn't 'gel', but later, scrolling through my
phone, I noticed that she'd added Frankie as a friend.

'She's an artist, at least she says she is! That's all I'm prepared
to say at the moment!' I answer, tactfully. Frankie grins at me
conspiratorially.

October 11 - Charlotte

We debate whether it's worth taking the long drive down to
Benalmadena. There are a few cheaper properties there which may
be worth looking at.

'The thing is we know they are there.' Tony says . He buries
his hand in the sand and brings it out again, letting a fine jet of
powdery white stuff trickle on to the top of the hill of sand he's
been subconsciously building since we first sat down here. We're
trying to save money today, by eating pasta for lunch, cooked in
the camper van , and buying some cheap wine from the
supermarket. I pinch a handful of flesh from above the top of my
bikini bottoms, and decide that there is more there than there was
before. When I straighten up though, it almost disappears, so
maybe it's not so bad.

'I think we should make our way slowly back up north,
towards home' . I surprise myself by saying this, but I'm
wondering if it would be a better idea now to concentrate on

selling the house, so that we have a clearer idea about how much money we have to spend. Tony looks at me for a long time, saying nothing, but nodding enthusiastically as I speak.

'We'll drive for a few hours this evening'. He squeezes my knee 'take our time' .

Now that Susan has gone I feel that .I'm actually missing Brittany a bit. ' It'll be nice to go home and get the house packed up and sold. ' I tell him .

He hands me my cigarettes and phone , and we stand up, brushing the sand off our legs. He takes my hand as we go back to the van. This holiday has been good for us.

October 12 - Frankie

When I wake, Ross is already pulling his jeans on , and I pull the duvet a bit more tightly around me.

'Tea?' He asks, as always, and as always I say 'yes please'. This is the morning ritual we have fallen into. After my tea , I'll get up and take a cold shower, before checking in on all of our animals. Artie follows Ross from the bedroom, and I reach for my phone. I send a message to Angel,

'May I call you?' I never phone anyone any more without checking first whether or not it's convenient. It's what most of us do now I guess. I want to tell her about Hope Hill, who came over last night. I wasn't sure what to make of her at first. She was plainly dressed in jeans, and a long sleeve T-shirt, about my age and quite attractive, but something about her repelled me, despite her gushy enthusiasm for my works, I was not charmed by her , and felt a need to be on my guard. I have the feeling that Angel felt the same way about her, though she never actually said as much. I get the 'thumbs up' sign from her, so I hit the green telephone icon , and she picks up immediately. 'Hope Hill' I say.

'Yep, how did you get on with her?'

I describe the way in which she admired everything, and the gratuitously long words she used, as though she was trying desperately hard to impress me. She couldn't quite meet my eyes when I asked her what kind of sculpture she was looking for.

'She's a fake.' Angel says , uncharacteristically. 'She came to me under the pretence of wanting a treatment, because Maisie had somehow let it slip that I had a new space with some blank walls. She'd asked Maisie if she could exhibit some of her art in the yoga studio, you see? '

I think about this for a few seconds and then I tell Angel about Hope's insistent way of showing me photos of her own boring creations on her phone, and her suggestion that maybe some of my sculptures would look good with her paintings hanging behind them, in a joint exhibition!

'In her dreams!' Angel says, and we both laugh.

October 13 - Heather

I am mesmerised for a moment, watching Frankie painting yogurt onto a lump of concrete which turns out to be a replica of Angels pregnant belly.

'I need it to grow a mouldy layer, so that it blends in with the tree '. She explains. There isn't much I can say to this really, except that I'm impressed by this very original, and extremely personal gift to Angel and Lee. I wonder if there's anything poignant I could write, that would be equally as special, as a gift to welcome the new baby. I was thinking of buying nappies, and maybe a little babygrow, but Frankie's present is making me think outside of the box. Perhaps a little fairy story, set in Angel and Lee's woodland walk would be a nice idea. Frankie smiles when I suggest it.

'Really like that idea!' She says, and we discuss how it might work as a collaborative gift. A story of a human baby born to an enchanted tree, and raised by fairies might be the way to go. Thug looks up at me with an expression which surely says

'She's really lost it now! Away with the fairies! '

'I've just got to work on how I'm going to attach the bellies to the trees without harming them'

Ross comes in then , smoking a joint which he passes to Frankie. 'How's the baby belly coming along?' he asks, looking over at the lump on the table, which is now white and slimy looking with its yogurt coating .

'Yep, it's done. Just need to wait for it to go green now' she's about to pass the joint to me, but her face changes, and I turn to see what's caught her attention.

'Nooooo!' I shout. Thug is up at the table, greedily slurping yogurt from the concrete replica of Angel's belly. Frankie raises an eyebrow and shrugs.

'Dog slobber will probably work just as well!'

October 14 - Susan

I look out at the persistent rain, while Rhea debates whether or not it's worth waiting an hour or so before venturing outside for a bathroom break. Spain seems a long time ago now, and the sun has not put in an appearance here since I got back on Tuesday . I should really drive over to Dazy Doo's and see how things are going . I might need to restock before the weekend. The thought of driving over there doesn't thrill me. I'm a bit tired, and I wonder if I've picked up a bug or something on my plane journey home. My throat was a bit sore this morning. I hope not. I really hope not. I have Eric bringing Michelle over tomorrow morning for a pottery session, and I'm not really looking forward to it anyway, if I'm honest, and it will be that much harder to bear if I'm not feeling one hundred per cent. I open the door and encourage Rhea to go out. The rain has eased a little. I decide to take a spoonful of honey, and get in the car . I'll pass by the supermarket for some cookies for the guests tomorrow (I don't feel like baking) , then on to Dazy Doo's with the new incense burners that I've made. If I ignore my vague feeling of malaise, perhaps it'll disappear.

October 15 -Angel

Saturday morning, and I wake to more rain. The Menobabes are due here in half an hour so I'd better get a move on. It's the second, and final, meeting that I will host. I feel like an impostor now that I've discovered that my symptoms are not in fact those of the menopause. Kerry will take over from now on. We've had several discussions on Messenger, and last night we met up for a quick drink (gin and tonic for her, and sparkling water for me). Today she will join me in hosting the meeting, and I will tell everyone my big news. I swing my legs out of bed, and shower quickly, as Lee gets the coffee machine, and a tray of cups and cookies ready. I'm still rubbing my hair dry as two cars, one after the other, pull up in the driveway, a little way from the house. The first, containing some of the same women as before, and I watch as

266

Lynsey, Abi and Caroline spill out of the tiny Mini. The other car I recognise as belonging to Sally, and she gets out, chatting animatedly, to the new friend that she asked if she could bring. I open the door, as all five women hurry over to the house in a bid to escape the rain. Sally is first in, kicking her wet shoes off immediately, and stepping quickly aside to allow the others to enter. She turns to her new friend, who lowers her hood, and smiles, waiting to be introduced as the newest member. I am so glad then, that this will be my last meeting, as I smile insincerely back at Hope Hill.

October 16 - Charlotte

What greets us is Autumn. We pull up onto our leaf strewn driveway, and when Tony turns off the engine we both just sit there. I have a strong urge to turn around and drive back to Spain again, but I swallow it , and get out of the van. We are both tired, as when we reached the border, coming into France it seemed that the best thing to do was to keep driving homewards, with very few stops. No point in taking our time once we'd left the good weather behind us. Tony is already anxious to be checking out a couple of motors, and I'm dying to have a chat with Karen about whether or not there's been any interest in our house. We decide that sleep is is the most important thing though, and anything else can wait till tomorrow. We both yawn and stretch, and I walk towards the house as Tony retrieves the door key from the van. The chestnut leaves, which are blowing across the driveway, have accumulated on the step, where they've been trodden down into a pulpy mess. It takes me a moment before I realise what this means. People have been here. Karen must have been showing potential buyers around!

October 17 - Frankie

I leave my clothes at the water's edge, ready to grab quickly when I come out of the cold sea. The people who walk past are mostly of the "couples with dogs" variety , fleecy tops and walking boots. My own fleecy top is lined with towelling, and is just the perfect thing, for after a cold dip. I walk into the sea in my sporty swimsuit, attracting the sideways glances that I always get when I swim on dull, windy days like this. Some people don't take any notice of me, but others point discreetly and smile while whispering their conversations about how crazy I must be. The sea is cold, for sure. It's rained a lot in the last few days , and the sun has been a stranger, so it's no surprise that the water temperature has dropped considerably. I wade in until a wave hits me and soaks me up to my armpits, then I brace myself, and dive over the the next one before it breaks , swimming a few strokes before standing up again, and jumping up and down as my body temperature adjusts. I stay in for somewhere between five and ten minutes , alternating between swimming, and jumping up and down , and then, refreshed, I pull on the fleecy top and leggings just as it starts to rain, and I head back to my car. By the time I get there though, the rain is coming down in rods, and I discover that my treasured towelling lined top sucks it up like a sponge , so I stand there , searching for my keys, weighted down by a sodden mess of clingy nastiness . I've other clothes in the car but I don't want to get in with my wet things on, so minutes later, when the dog walkers return hastily to their cars, with their heads down and their hoods up, they are greeted by the sight of my goose pimpled body standing there naked in the rain. It's time I bought a DryRobe.

18 October - Heather

I find that it's quite easy, and at the same time, rather therapeutic, to write a fairy tale . The whimsical, the supernatural and the fantastical, are all things that I can get to grips with at the drop of a hat. The creative juices flow with ease, and the occasional break for coffee or fresh air is all that's needed to get me over the odd glitch, or halt in progress. The story of a tree who takes on a human soul , and then becomes pregnant during a thunderstorm, writes itself. As fairytales go , this one is a bit dark, but it does have the obligatory happy ending, and the resulting baby, raised by the fairy folk of the woodland , grows to be a human boy with an inherent deep love of nature, who becomes a planet saving eco warrior by the close of the book. I finish the first draft, and take my celebratory glass of wine outside, pondering the ever present question. 'Why can't I write about reality with this same vigour and enthusiasm ?' My autobiography lies on my desk, not nearly finished, and even though I've tried to incorporate the 'friends with benefits /like mother, like daughter' theme, it just doesn't feel like I've enough in my life to justify an autobiographical account. Still I have this longing though, to write something poignant, and personal, then perhaps I myself can live the "happily ever after".

October 19 - Susan

Sitting by the window, with the sun shining, drying the "Green Man" that I've just finished making, as a departure from my usual kitchenalia into something a bit more arty, I look at the dog , and I actually say out loud,

' I could really use some human company right now Rhea'. She doesn't understand of course, and so she's not upset at all by the implied insult. My test this morning still showed two lines, though one was much fainter than the other, and I'm hoping it means that by tomorrow I'll be negative, and free from Covid once more. The Covid, for me, has just been a sniffly cold, and a couple of days of feeling a bit tired. Even so, after three vaccinations I'm a wee bit irritated that I caught it at all! The failure of those three jabs, designed to protect me from the virus is both unbelievable and unacceptable. What was the point of them? Again, I direct my question to Rhea, who wags her tail uncertainly. I have begun to think that Frankie and Angel were right when they refused the vaccine on the grounds that they didn't believe it had been thoroughly enough researched and tested.

'At least you're not really ill'. Eric said, when I had to cancel his pottery session last weekend (and Michelle's too) due to the positive test.

'Think how sick you might have been if you hadn't been vaccinated' was Charlotte's response, when I messaged her that I had Covid. She might be right of course, but this has really got me thinking, and now I just don't know any more.

October 20 - Angel

The colour we chose for the nursery is called Mother Duck. Susan stands in the doorway and stares at the almost empty room. I've invited her over for a free reiki treatment, now that she is clear of Covid. She doesn't really believe in the reiki but that's irrelevant. It will still help her , and I want to do something to repay her kindness in fixing up dear old Bington. The teddy bear sits in a shabby chic Lloyd Loom chair, the only thing in the room at the moment. We'll take our time with the baby shopping, though Lee keeps suggesting a trip to Ikea to look at cots, and I'm finding it increasingly difficult to say no.

'I could make you some curtains?' Susan says 'if you choose the fabric!' The sun glares through the bare windows, and I have to shield my eyes with my hands as I turn to look at her.

'That would be awesome!' I say, leading her back down the stairs to the treatment room, where soft music is playing, and I've turned the heat pad on, under a fluffy towel on my massage bed. I light the oil burner which is next to it, while Susan takes off her shoes and lies down. I use a geranium and a rose oil to scent the room .

'Not sure if I believe in all this!' She says 'but it does feel nice' . I smile to myself. At least she's honest.

October 21 - Charlotte

There is an offer on the table. Tony and I sit there in silence, trying not to reveal our eager anticipation, while Karen updates us on three potential buyers that have seen the house. Ironically, the first to see it , who were a couple, keen to move at the earliest opportunity, loved everything about the house, and went away, saying they'd be in touch later, with an offer, never came back. The second, a man on his own , looking to relocate in this area, from further down south where things are not working out for him, saw the house, and said it wasn't what he was looking for. Tony gives my hand a squeeze as my smile fades a bit. The third potential buyer though, a woman on her own, loves the house and thinks the garage would make a nice gîte . She can't go to the full asking price, but she's offered one hundred and twenty thousand euros . Tony and I look at each other. It's twelve thousand euros short of what we were asking. I'm nodding as Tony looks at his hands and then at me.

'Well if she could make it one hundred and twenty two thousand......' he says slowly, and Karen is nodding, and picking up her phone. Tony winks at me as Karen goes outside. We had already agreed between us that any offer over one hundred thousand would get us enough to move to Spain, but he's a good negotiator , and a little bit extra would be really helpful. Now all I need to do is persuade him to have his next jab. Susan getting ill, has reminded me that Covid is still a big issue, even if, at the moment, all the talk is of Liz Truss resigning, and the possible reinstatement of Boris.

'We won't care about any of that once we're in Spain though. ', Tony finishes saying, just as Karen steps back into the room. 'Ok!' She announces. 'One hundred and twenty two thousand it is!'

October 22 - Frankie

Ok! So even I am fed up now. Rain stops play, again! Eloise cannot take a decent photo in this weather. The Christmas tree cover shoot will have to wait a bit longer. I see now why it was so necessary to begin this winter project so many weeks ago while it was still summer. Poor Eloise, it's her problem now, and I decide to make the most of another wet day by tidying my atelier instead. After a couple of hours I rediscover my workbench, and clear the floor of various lengths of metal, and a collection of watering cans . I look at the cello from my last exhibition, with its half mermaid, half seahorse player, and wonder about asking at the new English pub that's opened up, not too far from here , whether they'd like to exhibit it. The drumming octopus would take up too much room, and I already sold the seahorse with the guitar, but this one really ought to be on show somewhere. I sit on the sofa with my phone, trying to find a Facebook page for the Folly Inn, and when I do, I discover that it's closed for a couple of weeks. Then I notice the faint smell of cat urine. Ok, so I'd better wash all the throws and cushions while I'm in cleaning mode, after all, this is excellent drying weather! Not!

October 23 - Heather

'I feel the earth move under my feet'. I keep singing as I'm switching everything off, and unplugging the live box, before heading off to bed. It's been a bit of a wet day, and there is a storm, strong enough to take a few trees down. On top of that there's been, what was very definitely, an actual earthquake. I felt the house tremble, then looked it up on the internet to be certain, and yes, there was a scale four earthquake, a few miles south of here. Thug looks a little forlorn. He had to make do with a couple of trips outside in the garden, instead of an evening walk. I'm sorry but there's no way I'm going out in that. My phone rings just as I'm wondering about running a bath, for a nice soak before sleep. It's Alan, checking I'm alright.

'I am!' I say, and realise how good it is to feel that I'm being looked after in this way.

'It's just that I thought you might want to come and spend the night here, if you were a bit nervous about the earthquake ', he pauses, then adds 'or maybe you'd like me to come and stay with you?' I smile to myself then, as I realise this is actually nothing more than a booty call! Lucky me!

'Yes ok. I've got yoga in the morning, but perhaps I'll give it a miss'. I put the phone down. It seems our 'couple of times a week' arrangement, doesn't count when the weather's this bad.

October 24 - Susan

Charlotte sits across the table from me, and pulls her chair out so that she's not too close. My last positive test was on Friday, and even then the line was so faint that it almost wasn't there.

'I wasn't really ill'. I say for the third time. I wasn't, and I'm bored now with having to go over it again . It really was just like a little cold. Tired and snotty for a couple of days, and that was it, back to normal, but still testing positive.

'Well it's a good job your jabs were up to date, that's all I can say! I'm trying to convince Tony to have his booster, but he's having none of it! I've an appointment on Friday, but he's refusing to come with me' .

I try to change the subject. My thoughts now, are that after three vaccinations I should have been completely protected against the virus, but I wasn't, so I don't believe a fourth one will be any more effective against the disease.

'Do you need any help with the packing?' I ask, even though they've got ages yet before the move, as they've only just signed the compromis. Charlotte stands, and lights a cigarette as she walks to the door. She opens it and takes a few puffs before the wind and the rain, drive her back inside, and she decides it's ok to smoke in the kitchen .

'There won't be much to pack! She wants to buy everything! Furniture...curtains...' she waves her cigarette around.

'But you could help me do the final clean if you want', she says. I really am going to miss her!

October 25 - Angel

Kerry and I have become friends since we met at the first Menobabes session, and so we message each other every now and then. This latest message, which I click on just as I'm going out the door, on my way to the forest with Lakshmi, to meditate on my New Moon intentions , stops me in my tracks. Hope Hill, is now actually buying a house somewhere in the area. I shiver involuntarily. She was very charming with the group of women gathered in my treatment room, and while Kerry and I made coffee, and arranged cookies on a plate, I could hear her introducing herself to each woman in turn, and asking 'what they did'. This question always makes my hackles rise, as I feel that it's like asking people to justify their existence.

'I'm an artist!' I heard her say, more than once, and Kerry shot me a sideways glance, with her eyebrows raised, as she placed a cappuccino in front of her. The session was a happy gathering though, with much discussion around the various products available for sale on Facebook aimed at menopausal women, and lately quite aggressively targeted to our pages. Hope's own target seemed to be Abi, who lives in a chateau, by the river, not too far from here, and who hosts events there from time to time. She's hosted big wedding parties , a theatre production, and a couple of musical soirées . I heard Hope mention the word 'exposition', and realised immediately what she was up to .

'Blatant networking!' Kerry whispered to me with a wink, as she gathered up the coffee cups.

October 26 - Charlotte

'Ok' Tony says 'If it'll shut you up'. He drains his coffee and scrapes his chair back as he gets up to go back to his garage. I can tell he's annoyed, but I'm just looking after his health. Covid can still be a serious condition for some people and I really don't want anything to go wrong , now that things are finally looking up for us . It's hard not to get excited about the house sale, but we can't , not yet. It's still "early days", and the buyer could still pull out. I'm concerned too, about what could happen to the house prices in Spain, while we wait for this sale to go through. If the housing market continues to fluctuate we could find that even with the little bit extra we've managed to achieve on the sale price, we won't be able to afford to buy what we want by the time we have the cash in our account. Worrying about the possibility of Covid, on top of all that, would just be too much. I send Susan a thumbs up that answers yes to her question about whether or not Tony will go for the jab on Friday, and as I do so , I notice several notifications for items for sale on marketplace, tyres, hydraulic jacks, an engine hoist, a compressor…..the list goes on . I recognise them immediately as the contents of Tony's garage. Somehow this makes it all seem so real , and for a moment I panic, as the question of whether or not I really do want to move to Spain, rears it's ugly head. I squash it like a bug. Of course I do! Who wouldn't?

October 27 - Frankie

'So the thing is……I said I'd ask you.' Angel squirms uncomfortably on the sofa. I had to throw the cushions away as they reeked of cat urine, and without them it feels hard, and lumpy. Another exhibition! But this time at a chateau, and pretty close to home. I think about it for a minute, chewing my lip as I look at the cello player, and the disassembled drum kit of the octopus. I'm definitely interested, but I feel that there is something

276

Angel's not telling me. It's not just the discomfort of the sofa that's making her so fidgety.

'Does she mean a solo exhibition, or is she asking other artists?' I ask, and wait for Angel's eyes to meet mine. When eventually they do, I detect a slight twinkle of merriment there, and the press of her lips suggests that she's trying not to laugh.

'It's Hope Hill isn't it?!' Suddenly I see what this is all about.

'I knew you wouldn't want to exhibit with her, and I could see that Abi was being pressured, and was too nice to say no to her, but the thing is it's a great space, so I said I'd ask you, and it'd be a shame if you missed out on the opportunity'.

Angel is right, but I've seen the 'art' that Hope Hill creates. Abstract landscapes they're supposed to be, but they are flatter than yesterday's beer dregs, with no depth to them at all, an obvious attempt at the style of another artist who I know personally, but so poorly executed that they just look like a canvas divided in half, painted one colour at the top, and another at the bottom, with no focal point, and nothing to capture a viewers attention.

'I can't do it . I won't be associated with her'.

Angel nods approvingly. 'Yep, that's what I thought you'd say'

October 28 - Heather

After yoga, Maisie makes us a cup of green tea, while Frankie and Angel makeover the window dressings with a Buddha sitting on a huge log, in each window, surrounded in leaves which have been sprayed gold. I watch in awe, as it takes Frankie mere minutes to create a spectacular display while Angel hangs new curtains as a backdrop. I feel a bit insignificant. As an entrepreneur

I must declare my earnings for the last three months this weekend, and there's so little to mention, it's as if I've retired or something. Preoccupied with the community magazine, and the fairytale for Angel's baby , I've not written much else. It's a good job my bank account is looking fairly healthy still. I sip my tea, and again feel that familiar urge to write something real, something good, something that will sell. Frankie stands outside across the road, to admire her handiwork. After a few seconds she signs a thumbs up to Angel, and begins taking photos.

'Do you never get stuck for ideas?' I ask, when she comes back in.

She grins 'I just sort of flow from one thing to another'

I decide to try it myself, writing whatever comes to mind at the time with no particular aim, just letting it flow, just a page, or even half a page a day. Then I realise that it's something I do already, in my black agenda!

October 29 - Susan

The pumpkins I've made for Halloween come out of the kiln. They are a bit of fun, that's all . Three of them with faces on like emojis. I put them on the shelf in the window of my studio, where they form the welcoming committee for my guests this morning. At ten o clock, or thereabouts, Eric will arrive with Michelle. I will show Michelle how to make a thumb pot, and perhaps move on to something a little more adventurous. I could have sent them both over to Lesley I suppose, as I'm not really looking forward to this at all, but it would just have been delaying the inevitable. I need to properly meet Michelle at some point, so it may as well be now. I had a bit of time to think about things while I had the Covid. I realise that what I'm feeling are the ugly pangs of jealousy if I'm being honest with myself. All the time I thought Eric was gay he

278

was off limits to me, and that was fine. He made a fantastic friend in a platonic kind of way, but now that I know that he's not gay, I do feel a bit hurt that I'm not the one he's chosen to be 'not gay' with. Maybe we could have got romantically involved with each other. Maybe we could have been good together.

October 30 - Angel

Now that I've allowed myself to believe in the possibility of a baby, pregnancy seems to suit me. I've got a definite bump, not just a bloated appearance, and when I look at myself from sideways on in the mirror, I can't stop smiling. Lee creeps up behind me and cups my belly from behind, kissing my neck. We are having a lazy Sunday. Scrambled eggs for breakfast, from Frankie's chickens, then a leisurely stroll through the woods with Lakshmi, and now, as the heavy drizzle seems really set in for the day , we're planning to chill out and watch a film together, before we think about cooking dinner.

'We need to make the most of this', Lee says, patting the sofa beside him, to indicate that I should go over and snuggle up.

'Soon enough our lives will be turned upside down'

'In a good way though!' I say , and as it's my turn to choose, I click on the old black and white version of 'Rebecca' .

'In the best way possible', he answers, dreamily kissing the top of my head. We are five minutes into the film when the sound of someone knocking on the front door interrupts us.

'I'll go' . Lee shuffles away in the new slippers I bought him. It seems like an age till he returns.

'Bloody kids!' , he mutters, but I catch him smiling, 'Trick or treating! A day too early, and it's not even dark yet! I had to give them ten euros to get them to go away, and they wouldn't even tell me what the trick would be if I didn't!'

He settles back down again on the sofa, and I start to laugh. He's such a softie despite his rugged roofer image.

October 31 - Charlotte

'So she really is just like you!' Susan shrugs, and carries on carving the pumpkin that Tony brought home when he fixed someone's mower yesterday. Pumpkin soup sits bubbling on the stove. It's the first thing she did when she arrived to help with the packing. Now we sit at the table while she creates a Halloween lantern for my doorstep.

'She looks a lot like me , and we seem to like many of the same things, and when she laughs she even sounds like me!'

She seems to be a little bit disappointed at the similarities between herself and Michelle.

'I just don't understand it', she says. I say nothing. We all thought that Eric was gay because Andrea fed us that line. When I think back to those times I remember that Eric did seem quite into Susan, but she was still with Paul then. Andrea used to try and flirt with him at every opportunity. She was jealous of the attention Susan was getting. I always used to avoid Andrea if I could, I didn't like her, and I think the feeling was mutual.

'So maybe Michelle is kind of a substitute for you then!'

Susan shrugs again, then holds the pumpkin head up for me to admire. It has a rather comically crooked mouth, with jagged teeth. I grin back at it, making her giggle. I will miss her when I go to Spain. I get up to pour soup into the special bowls she made for me.

'There couldn't be another you, who is as nice as you though!' I say, as I put the soup in front of her, and that's when she starts to cry.

November 1-Frankie

Grave day again, already! This year has passed quickly for sure. I clearly remember the Toussaints last year. I'd forgotten what day it was , and had been puzzled by the lack of cars in the supermarket car park . We had no milk, no coffee, and no loo rolls, and all of the shops were closed. It's a good job I'm resourceful, and the community magazine came in very useful that day! This time though I'm prepared, and will spend the day quietly in my atelier, feeling smug with the knowledge that I don't need to go out for anything. Ross is out in the barn, splitting logs. It feels like it's time to start lighting the fire now, and tonight we'll be toasty with the wood burner going and a nice bottle of red. I message Angel.

'Hope the Samhain ritual went well. It's a bit wet and wild today isn't it! Have a good one xx'

I haven't seen her for a few days, and I really get the feeling that everyone's battening down the hatches, and getting cosy in their nests. It's a good feeling. I welcome the long dark evenings of chilling out with a film or listening to Ross play his guitar while I sketch ideas or sit cracking walnuts. I switch off the cement mixer and peer inside the drum . The beach glass is being smoothed and polished to enhance its naturally beach sandblasted appearance, so that it's good enough to make into jewellery . I ordered the silver solder from Amazon Prime yesterday, so that it would arrive in time for an experimentally creative session today, but it hasn't turned up yet. I go to the window and peer out, looking for the familiar yellow van, and then my heart sinks when

I remember that there will of course be no delivery today, because it's grave day! Shit! I've done it again!

November 2 - Heather

It's only Wednesday, and due to the Bank Holiday, yesterday, and the fact that like most people I took the Monday off as well to make a long weekend, Alan and I have already spent more time with each other than we agreed to do . It's been good, but I've done no writing at all for five days so I send him a message.

'Having a couple of days at home, getting some work done. See you at the weekend x'

I put my phone down then, and try to concentrate. The weekend seems a long way off, and I'm half hoping that he'll try to persuade me to take a break from the writing this evening, even if that means that we might as well tear up the twice a week rule, and just go with whatever happens naturally. My phone remains quiet, and the ink begins to flow from my pen. I seem to be writing about my thoughts and feelings as they occur. It's not an interesting read, but it is a good exercise, and for half an hour or so I forget about Alan, and I fill a few pages with stuff about transitioning from summer to autumn, and the need to cut down on the amount of wine I drink, and how I feel about living alone through a second winter. It's the kind of thing I write about every day, in the agenda, only there's more of it than usual. The ping of Messenger is a welcome interruption but it isn't Alan. It's a message from my recently added Facebook friend, Hope Hill.

'I can see from your page that you live in the area, quite close to where I'll soon be living! Maybe we can meet for coffee some time? It would be good to make some new friends'.

I'm just working out my reply when it pings again. Alan this time.

'I hope by 'weekend' you actually mean tomorrow night?'

November 3 - Susan

I'm going to have a chat with Eric, I've decided, and I'm going to tell him everything I feel. I need some questions answered, even if I don't like the answers. I need to know his truth, and I need to tell him mine. I prick the shortbread all over with a fork, and put it in the oven, then light the kitchen log burner, before messaging him a simple

'Coffee and cake? There's something I need to talk about', and sending it, before I change my mind. I spend a while wiping down every kitchen counter and cupboard door, then sort the cleaning cupboard out a bit, while I wait for the ping that tells me I've got a reply. An hour passes, the shortbread is out of the oven, and the kitchen is the cleanest it's ever been, when my phone pings. It's not him though, and I'm a little disappointed, but also slightly relieved to find that it's only Charlotte. The lady who is buying her house would love to come to my studio for a pottery session. I write back immediately that I can do Monday or Tuesday next week, and then I put my phone down with a sigh. It pings again almost immediately and this time it's Eric.

'Ok, I'll see you in ten'. It says. I stare at my reflection in the newly cleaned oven door. 'Right then, this is it!' I say out loud, but it's too late now. I've lost my bottle again.

283

November 4 - Angel

Yoga is cancelled. Last night's storm brought a big tree down on the route that most of us take to the studio, and even now, it's still dark and stormy . I consider crawling back into bed, as Lee is considering getting up. Instead I make him coffee, and myself hot water with a slice of lemon. I go outside with bare feet while the kettle boils, and I stand amongst the swirling leaves. It's cold, and for the first time this year it actually feels like winter is on its way. I go back in, feeling grounded. Instead of yoga I will meditate for an hour or two this morning. Lakshmi stays outside, chasing the debris that is blowing about in the driveway. Windy weather seems to give her a lot of energy, and it's funny to watch her enjoying her simple pleasures. Lee sips his coffee, and laughs, as Lakshmi spins in a circle, chasing a twig that has become attached to her own tail. One day I guess we'll stand together like this, watching our own child play. How incredibly, wonderfully weird.

November 5 - Charlotte

We have until the end of this month, to find, and move into, a rental place somewhere in Spain. Anywhere at all will do. We will rent for the winter, and give ourselves time to have a really good look around before we buy.

'I can't wait!' I tell Tony, though secretly I'm not really sure how I feel. I think I'm a little bit scared actually, though I'd never admit it to anyone. There are lots of places to rent over winter, but they all seem to require tenants to vacate by the end of March, and I'm not sure if that would give us enough time.

'Somewhere central would be best'. Tony says, so I keep looking, while he photographs and lists even more items for sale. I will try to find us somewhere nice, as soon as possible, then perhaps I'll feel a little less apprehensive about the whole plan. Tony yawns. He hasn't been sleeping well. The new lady wants to buy almost everything in the house as she doesn't have any furniture of her own. The garage though is another story. She wants nothing that's in there, and so it must be completely cleared.

'Bacon sandwich?' Tony asks, and I nod in reply. There are a couple of messages from Susan on my phone, asking if she can call in for a chat. I click on them, but I don't answer. I've no time for that today.

November 6 - Frankie

I step out of the shower, grab a towel and go downstairs. It's ten a.m. and Ross is already outside in the rain, attending to the animals, with Boris perched on his shoulder. My cold shower each morning leaves me feeling energised, and this morning I was in there for longer than usual, staring at a chandelier I made a few years ago when we first bought this house. It's black metal. Three concentric rings hang, each a little lower than the next , and from the bottom and middle rings, hang chains of sea glass beads . It's perfect in our bathroom, but I now have an idea to create a similar design in ceramic. I'm sitting at the table, still wrapped in my towel as I sketch this idea out in rough, on the fly leaf of a book about permaculture that Ross is currently reading, when he comes back in.

'I'm soaked to my balls!', he states unnecessarily, stripping off his T-shirt and jeans. He stands there shivering with no pants on, so I pass him the towel I'm wearing , just as a face appears at the window. A man, shielding his head from the rain with what appears to be a dustbin lid, gesticulates wildly towards the road. Ross, oblivious to our naked states, opens the door and points to the farm across the road from us and down the lane a bit. I come to the door holding a tea towel in front of me to preserve my modesty. There are about twenty cows in the road outside, and two or three on our driveway. Dustbin lid man's car is parked among them with its hazards lights flashing. I go back to my drawing then, as Ross struggles to put his sodden clothes back on.

'Pointless getting another lot wet', he says, as he heads back out into the torrent.

November 7 -Heather

Susan calls in for coffee and cake at around eleven, just as Alan is leaving.

'Didn't you go to yoga?' She asks, looking me up and down, and taking in my pyjamas with the sloppy jumper thrown hastily on top. We're making a habit of them, these sleepovers. At least it feels that way to me . We're relaxing our rules, compromising our own lives a little bit, in order to spend time together. I don't want to admit that to Susan, don't want her to think that I've smugly become half of a loved up couple.

'A bit too wet and windy to go out that early, I thought' I close the door behind her, and notice that the doormat is now covered in oak leaves. She says nothing, but places a Dutch apple cake on the table while I make the coffee.

'I've got Charlotte's buyer coming over tomorrow for a pottery lesson', she says, ', and thought it might be a good idea for you to come over and meet her, as we will all soon be neighbours'

I nod enthusiastically, as Susan outlines a plan to invite Angel, Frankie, Eric and I for a drink or two in the studio at the end of the afternoon.

'Just a few of you. I don't want to overwhelm her' .

I look at my kitchen table, strewn with bits of paper, and ideas waiting to happen. I'd planned to do so much today, and I've already wasted almost half of it. If I got down to work now, I could still get a serious amount of writing done. Instead I smile at Susan, and ask

'Would you like me to make a few hors d'œuvres ?' I'm definitely still quite good at procrastinating.

November 8 - Susan

It's warm in the studio and I've had a bit of a tidy up while waiting for Charlotte to arrive with our future neighbour. I've asked Angel, and Heather, and Eric, to come over later, but I decided in the end to leave Frankie till another time. She'll understand, as there is often friction between her and Charlotte, so it's better to keep them apart. I watch the car pull up in the driveway . Charlotte gets out with a cigarette already in hand, which she pauses to light while her passenger gets out. I shield my eyes, from the rare winter sun that's put in an appearance today, and wave, indicating for them to come straight to the studio and not the house. Charlotte turns to face the other woman who swings her bag over her shoulder and then stands looking about her . She has long dark hair and a hard, unsmiling face. I open the studio door as they walk towards me, and Rhea runs to greet them.

'This is Hope', Charlotte says, between puffs.

Hope smiles, a sudden twitch of her lips, which doesn't seem to reach the rest of her features. 'It's so lovely to be here!', she gushes, brushing imaginary dog hairs off of her immaculate black trousers as Rhea sniffs her in greeting.

'Ok I'll find you something to protect those clothes!' I turn towards the back of the studio as Charlotte grinds her cigarette butt into the path outside.

'So where do you sell your creations?' Hope asks, as I hand her an apron. I explain that I have connections with a couple of shops , but will sell directly from my studio if someone wants something. She has a lemon squeezer in her hand, that she seems to be scrutinising, but puts it down without asking the price.

'And do they take much commission?' She asks, ignoring my request to take a seat as I put a mound of clay in front of her.

This isn't going quite the way I thought it would.

November 9 - Angel

'We should have seen that coming!' Frankie says, when I tell her about meeting the buyer of Charlotte's house at Susan's yesterday. 'That girl has been hanging around like a bad smell for weeks!'

I must admit that my instincts tell me that Hope Hill is bad news. I've met her on a few occasions now, and every time it's as if she's trying to get something out of me, or out of one of my friends. Yesterday she was quizzing Susan about her arrangement with Dazy Doo's , and then she cornered Heather about her book cover designs, suggesting she take a look at her Facebook page 'Hope Hill Art' .

'God, I wish I'd never said that! '. Frankie says, putting down her soldering iron, and scooping up a cat that's about to urinate against the table leg.

'What's that?' I'm confused, as I open the door so that Frankie can usher out the offending feline.

'That nobody could be worse than Charlotte!'

Oh yes, I remember now the discussion we had when we first heard that Charlotte's house had gone on the market. 'Ironic isn't it?', I say, turning to face nobody at all, as Frankie has suddenly bolted off down the garden.

'Those bloody cows are out again! ', she shouts, and I watch as a heaving mass of mooing black and white gathers around the singing ringing tree. I inhale deeply, and take a moment to reflect on the fact that life is certainly never dull.

November 10 - Charlotte

I watch Tony load up the camper van with bags and boxes . It's a whole load of stuff that was in the garage, and is now destined for the déchèterie. He leans on the van for a moment, taking a breath as I stub out my cigarette and wander over.

'You ok?' I ask, expecting the usual grunt, in reply.

'Just felt a bit dizzy for a second', he says. It's not surprising. All that stuff in the garage he's had to move by himself, and it's not even half done yet. He stretches himself and I follow him back in there. It's a lot tidier, but there are still some of the larger items that need to be sold. I remind him of the moving date , and he fends me off with both hands, not wanting to hear. Hope wants the garage emptied first, so that she can store some of her own stuff in there before the sale goes through. We've agreed to do this, as we don't want to risk losing her as a buyer, especially as she's also buying most of the furniture, albeit at a small price. I head back to the house to get on with my own packing, and think about trying to sell some of my clothes . Hopefully I'll never need the winter things again. Opening the wardrobe door I am faced with the enormity of the job as I stare in at crammed rails, and overstuffed drawers and boxes. I pick up my phone to message Susan . She may like to help.

November 11 - Frankie

It's a sunny morning but I spend it anyway inside my studio. Armistice Day. All is quiet outside, and while rummaging through my wardrobe, looking for boots . (I just ruined my favourite pair, running about on the muddy road, herding cows), I found an old pair of the Doc Marten's I used to wear back in the nineties. They are vintage and in great condition, but this doesn't stop me from painting poppies all over them, surrounded in leaves of green, gold, and silver. I am pleased with the end result, and photograph them for my Facebook page, where they quickly get lots of likes, and enthusiastic comments. Ross is outside with the Karcher when I finally finish fussing about with them , and I go over to see what he's doing, attaching so many extension leads, and a hose that's literally about half a mile long.

'The road!', he says, simply.

I look over at it. Didier hasn't had time yet to clean up, and the cows, having escaped about five times in the last week, have covered it in mud and manure so thick that you cannot any longer tell where the road ends, and the field begins. It's slippery too, as the constant drizzle of the last few days has kept it from drying up .

'Before somebody kill's themselves', he adds, as a car brakes, then slides a bit as it comes to a halt in front of our house.

November 12 - Heather

Sophie's baby is due in one month. I can hardly believe it. I look at the ferry timetables and dither about when I should go over.

'First babies are often late aren't they?' Thug says nothing, but gives me that look again - the one that tells me to trust my gut. It's a bit noncommittal to be honest, as if he doesn't want to be blamed for getting it wrong. I don't want to go to England for a couple of weeks in December, only to spend that time waiting for the baby to arrive. On the other hand I really need to be sure to be there for when it does. When he does. We know it's a boy, and we know that he will be called Willoughby Heaven's Angel, or probably just Willoughby most of the time. I like it. It's unusual without feeling "made up". As if reading my mind, Sophie sends a message asking when I'm coming over. I decide to go for it, and book my trip for December ninth. It's two days before the due date, but by the time I arrive it will be one day before.

'So that's done!' , I say, and Thug raises an unimpressed eyebrow, coolly shrugging off any responsibility for the errors I may have made with the dates. I look out of the window at the fog that's still hanging around.

'So do we go out now, or do we wait for a bit?' This gets a much more animated response. Apparently we definitely need to go now!

November 13 - Susan

I look at Frankie's sketches , that are frankly brilliant. 'Of course!', I say. She wants to make the chandelier that she's designed, here in my studio.

'It'll be easier than going all the way over to Lesley's, and more fun.'

I feel honoured that she would think of coming to my little studio to create one of her pieces, and I waive off her offer of paying for the studio time. When I tell her that Hope Hill has asked if I would like a couple of her paintings to hang as a backdrop to my display at Dazy Doo's , in colours to complement my own creations, she almost chokes on the custard cream that she's dipped into her mug of tea.

' I hope you told her where to get off!'

The look of alarm on her face says it all. I knew that I should have said no to her, but I didn't. I dithered, and said that maybe it might work, and then I looked at the photos she sent me on Messenger, and wished I'd had the courage to say no from the get go. Even to my uneducated eye, they seem very amateur. The bottom half of the canvas painted a purplish grey, while the top is white with a bit of sand for texture. Some have black and gold streaks running across the middle , but they are all very similar, and, despite the sand, depressingly flat, lacking any feeling of joy or spontaneity. It's as if she's tried to copy the style of another artist and failed miserably. I smile weakly at Frankie.

'Just say no!' She says, putting her mug down firmly, for emphasis. I hold my hands up in defeat. Of course she's right, and I should have trusted my gut instinct, but I hate to hurt anyone's feelings. Oh well, perhaps Hope will just forget all about it.

November 14 - Angel

I spend a lot of time standing at the doorway of what will be the nursery. Yesterday, Lee put a curtain pole up, ready for the curtains that Susan has very kindly offered to make. Other than that, there is just the old chair in the corner. Bington's chair. He sits with an optimistic expression on his face, as if looking forward to the baby that is due to arrive in a few short months. Dare we buy a cot yet? No. I'm going to wait until I'm at least six months along before I start making those kind of preparations. I pick up Bington, the only reminder I have of my childhood, which was indeed happy, up until my dad died of cancer when I was thirteen, and my mother wasted away from grief, little more than a year later. This version of Bington has a very different expression to the original one. He used to look slightly fearful and apprehensive, as if he knew our carefree, fun filled days were numbered. Now he looks more relaxed, and quietly confident. I wish I felt the same. Well, I actually do feel quite confident , but I am at the same time aware of my complete lack of knowledge and experience with babies. I've no family left to help me, and neither has Lee, other than a brother, somewhere over the other side of the world, that he never really has any contact with.

'We're on our own!' I say, to Bington, as I put him back down.

'Relax!' , he seems to say 'You've got this!'

November 15 - Charlotte

Hope opens the front door and calls out to me. I'm slightly irritated by her to be honest.

'I just wondered if you would be leaving the curtains?' She says, as she looks up at me coming down the stairs . We've been through this before. I'm not taking the curtains. The chances of them fitting the windows in our next house are very slim. I nod , to let her know, once again, that yes I will be leaving them, and then with eyebrows raised, I stand, waiting for the next, inevitable question, but all she says is that there's another car load of boxes she has brought over, but Tony needs to move an old old engine hoist before she can stash them in the garage . It takes up space apparently in the driest corner, and these are books and paintings, which can't be allowed to get damp. I nod again, and instead of offering to help move it, or her boxes, or even to put the kettle on, I take out a cigarette and go to the door. I watch Hope fussing with each box as she lifts it from her car boot, and I light up, and take a long drag. She removes the paintings one at a time, carefully stacking them as she goes, so that I get to see each one as it joins the pile. I don't try to hide my expression of utter boredom, and as I turn to go back in, grinding the cigarette butt out on the top step, and then kicking it into the flowerbed as I always do, I am pleased with myself for resisting the natural inclination to fawn all over the 'artist' she professes to be. It's then that I hear the crash of something metal, and heavy, hitting the garage floor . Surely Tony isn't trying to move that hoist on his own.

F

November 16 - Frankie

I don't make a fuss about my birthday. Ross has bought me some new boots. Expensive ones. Ones that will last a few years, and I get a call from Henry. He will bring my present with him when he comes over for Christmas. The fact that he is even considering coming over for Christmas is actually the best present of all. Angel arrives, looking a bit pale and washed out. A silver ring with an enormous jade stone is her present to me. I'm so happy with it. I try it on and dance around in front of the window, turning it this way and that .

'And I've brought some champagne too!', she says, placing a frosty looking bottle on the table, as I open all the cupboards looking for the proper glasses. I find them at the back of the last one I look in, behind a fondue set and a yogurt maker. We don't often have champagne. I rinse three of them under the tap, and I'm popping the cork as Ross comes back into the house. The look on his face stops me in my tracks and I put the bottle down.

'What is it?' Angel asks

'It's Tony! He's dead!'

Angel and I sit down while Ross recounts the tale that Didier has just told him. Yesterday evening the pompiers were called out to Tony and Charlotte's . Didier was amongst those who answered the call, but was late getting there, as he was out in the fields on his tractor at the time. He arrived to find Tony being whisked away by his pompier colleagues, with all the blue lights flashing. A pulmonary embolism apparently, he heard later, when he called in at the station . He didn't even make it to the hospital.

'Poor Charlotte!' We all say at once.

November 17 - Heather

I shiver as I step into the kitchen. It's not very warm in here, and I clear cups from the table and put my bag down, filling the kettle before venturing upstairs, softly calling a greeting, in case anyone is sleeping. Susan appears at the top of the stairs.

'The doctor gave her a sedative' , she says.

So Charlotte is asleep for the first time since it happened. 'You go home.' , I say. Susan looks about ten years older than when I saw her last, and she's shivering there in her pyjamas, but keeps insisting on staying, so that she will be here when Charlotte wakes.

I give in, and tell her to put a jumper on while I make some tea. I'm doing the washing up when she next appears in the kitchen, dressed in jeans and jumper, and looking a bit more like her usual self. We speak in low voices, and agree that we'll clean up and light a fire before the funeral directors arrive later this morning. We have a little over two hours before we must wake her for the appointment.

'What do you think she'll do?' The question has been on my mind since I heard the news, and I've been wondering whether it's possible for her to pull out of the house sale, or if it's already too late for that. Maybe she won't want to stay here anyway.

'She has no family.' Susan says, and leaves it there. A feeling of overwhelming sadness washes over me, and I go outside shaking my head involuntarily as I look for firewood.

November 18 - Susan

Eric comes over in the afternoon. He's never been in Charlotte's house before, and looks around at everything, nodding approval as I put the kettle on. We finally had a long chat yesterday, when I went home for a bath and a break, leaving Heather with Charlotte. He confirmed that he had never once said he was gay. That was a fiction entirely constructed by Andrea when he politely, but very firmly rejected her. It was me that he was attracted to, but sadly, I was already taken . When Paul and I split up he was hoping that after a little time had passed there might be a chance for him, but apparently I made it very clear that I had him firmly ensconced in the "friend zone"

'I thought you were gay!' I said then, for the third or fourth time probably. It seemed that it was all I could say.

'Then you started with those dating sites…'. He trailed off, and I filled the rest in for myself

'So you gave up on me, and decided to give them a whirl yourself. '

His eyes then met mine and we stared at each other

'I was looking for someone like you.'

'Well you certainly found her!' I laughed when I said it, and he grinned.

'We are a right pair aren't we?'

We are though. A right pair. Good friends, but that's as far as it goes. I look at him now with his legs stretched out in front of him and his muddy boots still on, and I wonder why I ever believed that he was gay, but I did, and now that I know the truth it's too late. He's in love with Michelle. Charlotte, in pyjamas and a fleecy cardigan, appears at the kitchen door, interrupting my thoughts, and Eric gets up, and wraps his arms around her. I pick up her pack of cigarettes and light one, handing it to her. She opens the door and stands there inhaling smoke. Ironic that I'm now encouraging her in this.

'It brings her some comfort', I say to Eric, as I catch him with a look of disapproval on his face. We both shrug.

November 19 - Angel

Charlotte says nothing as I make her as comfortable as I can on her sofa, while Susan changes her bed linen. Her limp hair sticks to her head, and she looks understandably tired. I want to give her a reiki treatment, but she shakes her head, and reaches for her coffee cup. The funeral is on Monday morning, and arrangements

297

have been hastily made , for Heather to find/write something for Charlotte to read as a eulogy, if she feels like it, or in case she's not up to it, maybe Susan will do it. There is no one closer apparently. Tony has a brother, somewhere in the world, but they've not been in contact for years, and he'd lots of friends too, but most of them were little more than acquaintances when it comes down to it, so we will be few in number, and the service will be a simple one at the local crematorium. The smell of leek and potato soup wafts in from the kitchen, and I go to remove the pan from the stove. We've been trying to tempt Charlotte into eating, but so far she has resisted, so I go back to her empty handed, and mumble that there is soup ready if she would like some. She surprises me by nodding, and uttering a croaky

'Please.....and could you find me a pen and some paper'

I shoot back in the kitchen before she changes her mind. Susan, stuffing the bed linen into the washing machine catches my eye, eyebrows raised. I give her a discreet 'thumbs up' sign. She sighs, a huge sigh of relief.

November 20 - Charlotte

I'm not sure if I feel the blackness lifting slightly. When I woke this morning the sun was shining. I could hear voices. Susan singing in the kitchen, and I found myself almost smiling. The clean bed felt nice when I stretched my legs out. Dear Susan. I'm guessing she'll go home though, after the funeral, and then I'll be completely alone. Raised voices outside spark my curiosity, and I get up, crossing the bedroom to look out of the window. Hope Hill is in the garden, holding a big bunch of chrysanthemums, in purple and white. She is talking to somebody who is out of my line of sight, somewhere near the doorstep. I watch as she takes a step backwards, holding the flowers out in front of her at arms length, to a woman who steps forward now into view, in denim shirt with messy blonde hair, her arms folded in front of her. I recognise Frankie of all people. She takes the flowers and places them on the step

'So you can shove your stuff in the garage or whatever! But you're not to come near the house until you own it, if you ever do. And if I were you I'd stay away from here tomorrow. It's close friends only! '

For once I'm glad to see Frankie. Hope walks backwards to her car which is laden with boxes again, and starts jabbing at her phone, while Frankie stands there on guard, swearing under her breath, loud enough for me to hear now that I've cracked the window open. When Susan comes in to wake me with a cup of tea, I'm laughing uncontrollably, and the stunned look on her face makes me laugh even harder. I don't notice the tears on my cheeks until she hands me a tissue, and guides me back to my bed.

November 21 - Frankie

Well this is suitable weather for a funeral for sure. Ross puts on black jeans and a black shirt, and I do the same. Outside the rain hammers down, flooding the driveway. The singing ringing tree is being blown sideways, and it's familiar soft soporific tones are now a dissonant jangle of jagged metal. My only truly waterproof coat is bright red, and therefore out of the question.

'Wear it to the car at least', Ross says, so I put it on and we dash outside, splashing our way across the drive in unsuitable footwear. The car steams up before we've driven to the end of the road, so that we have to open the windows to the grim weather.

'What do you think she'll do?' Ross wonders, and I realise he's talking about the house sale and the likelihood of Charlotte still moving to Spain, on her own.

'Well if it were me, I'd stay where I was'. As I say it though I think about the differences between us. I'm not sure Charlotte could cope on her own, even in her newly finished and finally habitable house. We lapse into silence as we drive into the crematorium car park. Charlotte, Susan and Eric get out of the car in front of us. The rain has eased a little, and they walk slowly into the building while I take my coat off and switch my phone to silent.

'We'll sit at the back'. Ross says, as I exit the car, and step ankle deep into an icy puddle. I look up at the black clouds overhead, as I shuffle across the car park shaking my leg like a dog, and my mood begins to match the occasion.

'Rainy days and Mondays always get me down', I half sing, half whisper.

November 22 - Heather

'There were about thirty of us maybe' I tell Alan, as we walk, about the funeral of the day before. Charlotte rejected all of the eulogy ideas that I found for her, in favour of her own short speech, which was simple, and on point, without her usual flowery language. Everyone cried. It was so obviously her own heartfelt choice of words, that it was impossible not to feel moved by them. Susan got up to stand with her as she spoke. Alan nods, as I tell the story, and Thug gives me a sympathetic look. It was when she said 'He was my rock' , and couldn't carry on till Susan squeezed her hand and reassured her, that sniffles were heard all around the room. There were a couple of sentences about how they'd shared the good and the bad, then the ending 'half of my heart is gone

300

now'. There are tears in my own eyes as I describe how she hung her head as we all walked past , and patted her back or gave her a hug. I went back with her and Susan, and we had coffee with brandy in it. Very little was said then, and it wasn't until Susan began to tidy up some paperwork that was strewn over the table, guarantees and instruction leaflets for various kitchen appliances mostly, that Charlotte herself began to speak.

'I'm leaving all that here, for the purchaser', she'd said, suddenly, and we waited for her to go on.

'Tomorrow I'll start to look for a gîte to rent , somewhere local , but right now I'm going to have a lie down'

We both hugged her then, and watched her slowly go up the stairs.

'All of her friends are here you see?' I stop walking and bend down to unclip Thug. When I straighten up, Alan puts his arm around my shoulders, and we stand like that for a few moments, lost in our own thoughts.

November 23 - Susan

Lunch was Michelle's idea. She thought I could use a break. I guess Eric's been filling her in on all the events of the past couple of weeks, and Charlotte's subsequent need for care and support . We both take a kir royale as an aperitif, and lift our glasses at the same time. It's uncanny how alike we are in our looks and in our mannerisms . I find myself telling her about Andrea, and the story she made up about Eric's sexuality. She smiles, and laughs in all the right places. She's easy to be with, and confesses to me that she doesn't have many friends around here , and was considering moving back to England , until she met Eric. We naturally fall into a discussion around the importance of friendship, especially when you live alone , as we both do. The conversation trails off , and I can see in her eyes that she is hoping her aloneness may one day be remedied by a move, not backwards to England, but forwards, to a home shared with Eric.

'I've given up on the idea of a romantic relationship', I say, surprising even myself, and adding, as the thought occurs to me, 'I actually prefer female companionship' .

Michelle pushes her plate away. 'I know what you mean! I honestly wonder sometimes why I was never blessed with a daughter!'

She does seem to know what I mean, even more than I myself know. The thought of Heather, off soon to visit Sophie and welcome into the world her new grandchild, fills me with regret that I'll never experience that joy myself. Michelle smiles sympathetically, as though reading my thoughts.

'Everything happens for a reason' she says , and Charlotte is obviously very lucky to have you!'

November 24 - Angel

I open the group message from Heather, which invites any of us (Frankie, Susan, Charlotte or me) to do an online Christmas shop, and have it delivered to Sophie's address by twenty first December, so that Heather can bring it back here with her. She returns to France, hopefully having spent some time with her new grandson, the day after that shopping deadline date. I feel an irrepressible longing to have my own mother here with me for the first few days of this baby's life, and I sit with my head in my hands worrying about how I'll cope with no family around me. My mood perks up though when I click on the Tesco's site, and discover all the Christmas goodies I could buy. There aren't many things that I miss about England, and certainly Christmas commercialism is something I normally try to avoid, however memories of opening a tin of Quality Street after Christmas dinner, or pulling crackers at the table, make me feel a little nostalgic about a traditional Christmas and before I know it I've been hooked into shopping mode, so that by the time Frankie's message appears in the thread, there are already six items in my basket .

'None of this 'buying from local artists and artisans' for us then ! ' (smiley face) 'seriously though we'd like a few cans of Guinness if I could get those sent to you? '

It's a jokey kind of message,with many emojis, but it does get the point across to me, and I stop adding things to my basket. She then sends me a private message.

'You ok honey? Shall we do Cozy Night soon?

This really does lift my mood. Cozy Night is something we started last year when the weather became a bit stormy. It involves a girly sleepover with wine, chocolates and Netflix, by a roaring log fire . We sleep on the sofas in Frankie's sitting room, and toast crumpets on the fire for breakfast the next morning.

'Yes please!' , is my simple reply, though this year I guess I won't be drinking much wine.

November 25 - Charlotte

There are lots of gîtes to rent over the winter months, and I get a weird feeling of déjà vu, as I sit searching the internet . Only a couple of weeks ago I was doing a similar search, but for property in Spain. This is my first morning on my own . Susan went home last night, and I woke, for the first time ever, alone in the house. Weirdly, I feel as if Tony is in the garage, and I have to keep reminding myself that he's not. There's no way I could live here now. I respond to Hope's enquiry on Messenger. I'm not sure that she should be contacting me directly like this but I understand her need to know what is going to happen about the house sale. It will go ahead as planned. I will move out in five days time, and will find someone to clear the remaining garage items. I look at a pretty cottage that's available to rent, some ten minutes away from here. It's chocolate box appeal is what draws me , and it stands alone , surrounded in woodland, unlike most of the places I've found, that are attached to a house or other gîtes . I save the page to show Susan when she comes over later. She's already messaged to ask if I had a good night . I did, and I wrote straight back to her,

'Please can you pick me up some cigarettes on your way over?'

The thumbs up she sent me in reply, let's me know that she'll do it even if it goes against her better judgment. A knock at the door interrupts my scrolling. It's Lee, with another man, who hovers on the driveway.

'We'll get the rest of the garage stuff out of your way', he says, as I shakily light a cigarette, while nodding and trying to smile. I was actually dreading having to set foot in there again, though I haven't told a soul. I'm guessing this was Angel's idea , she's such a thoughtful girl, but actually everyone has been so kind.

November 26 - Frankie

Angel lies back on the sofa with one hand on her rounded belly. We have watched 'Where the crawdads sing' which we both loved, and then started to watch the new 'Elvis' film, but chatted through most of it so that neither of us know what's going on. I'm on my third or fourth glass of red, while Angel is still slowly sipping the one glass that will last her the whole evening.

304

'At least I've got you', she says when the conversation takes a morbid turn and we start discussing what we'd do if either of our partners died.

'And I've got you! , and pretty soon there'll be another family member!'

It seems as if she needs cheering up a bit. She puts her glass down again.

'This baby will have only Lee and I, no extended family. What if we're not enough? Neither of us really knows how to do this!'

And there it is, at the very root of what's been bothering Angel, is this lack of parents and siblings. Ironic really to think of this, when for the first time in a lot of years, she has a steady partner and a precious baby on the way. I put my glass next to hers . We are her family, Ross and I , and amongst her wide circle of friends there are others too who would do anything for her. I attempt to reassure her, by telling her so. She smiles through eyes brimming with tears , and tells me that the tarot card that she keeps drawing now, speaks of help from friends. I balance a box of chocolates on her stomach, and she takes one out, unwrapping it slowly.

'Monty Bojangles' she says, wonderingly, reading the name from the box lid.

'That might be a good baby name?' She looks at me, inviting my opinion.

'Bojangles Court? Or Bojangles Adams ?

I spill my wine as I laugh at my own joke, and mop it up with the sleeve of my red jumper.

'Surely you don't mean Monty?' I say, disappointedly. I was so sure she'd choose something a bit more "alternative", like maybe Chestnut, or Barley.

November 27 - Heather

Thug still needs a walk. Even in this horrible rain, we have to at least go down the road to the fountain and back. I put wellies on, and wonder about an umbrella. It's a bit windy though, so I settle for an old Barbour jacket with a hood.

'Not that way!' I shout, as Thug runs off towards the woods . It's too wet for that. There's a patch of mud at the entrance, by the gate where the cows cross to their field, that's so deep now, that it sucks at my wellies with every step. Instead we stay on the road, and Thug ignores the sad spectacle of a dead cat that's obviously been recently run over, and runs ahead, disappearing behind the fountain into the waste ground where the rubbish and recycling bins are. When I catch up with him he's sniffing at the door of an old corrugated shack, that now stands in a puddle, the size of a small lake. The door is slightly ajar, and Thug, making soft little whimpering sounds, has his nose in the gap . I wade across to him and pry the door a little wider in order to investigate. Inside, on top of an old abandoned cider press, I can just make out a pile of hessian sacks. When my eyes adjust I see the source of Thug's interest. Three kittens sit huddled on the hessian, meowing pitifully. I think back to the squashed feline in the road, and realise they are probably now motherless. Thug looks at me hopefully as I un-pop the hood of my Barbour. It makes a half decent kitten carrier, and so we walk home together with Thug's tail thudding excitedly against my legs.

'Ok but what do we do with them now?' I ask him.

November 28 - Susan

'I thought maybe Frankie might take them' , Heather says, as we stare into the washing up bowl lined with a towel, where three kittens lie cuddled up together, fast asleep. They have eaten some of the cat food that I gave her last night, and have apparently been sleeping in the bathroom next to the heated towel rail ever since.

'I haven't asked her yet though, and she has so many…..', Heather seems to doubt the likelihood of there being room for them at Frankie's. I wish that I could take them myself, but I already have Rhea and Delilah and I'm about to excuse myself as a potential home on those grounds, when Charlotte strokes one of the little heads with her finger.

'They're probably about five or six weeks old', I say, finally unloading the kitten milk, and special food that is our whole reason for passing by this morning on our way back from the supermarket.

'I'll take them!' Charlotte says, suddenly. ' I won't be living by the busy road any more, so they'll be safe.'

Heather looks at me, as if I need to give permission. We are on our way next, to look at a gîte at the edge of the woods, just a short drive from here. It would be the perfect place for a few little cats . I watch Charlotte rummaging for her cigarettes, and realise that she looks almost happy.

'The perfect solution!' Heather says , when Charlotte's gone outside .

'Company for her as well!' We both nod.

November 29 - Angel

'Thug found them' , Heather says. I look out of the window at Thug and Lakshmi racing around on the lawn. Lakshmi and I were just walking past when Heather tapped the window and beckoned me in. The kittens are beautiful of course. One looks almost siamese, and one is grey and fluffy. The other one is black, and short haired with enormous blue eyes.

' I wish Reiki would tolerate another cat'. Heather smiles , and shakes her head.

'Charlotte wants them all!'

I process this information for a few seconds while I let the black one chew on the feather that I've been tickling them with. Their bed is a washing up bowl, placed inside a large laundry basket lined with newspapers. They look so content, and at the same time vulnerable and precious, like all babies are, and I realise I'm subconsciously cupping my belly with my other hand.

'It will be a good distraction for her I think' , Heather adds, when I don't say anything.

'It will', I say eventually, and we both just stand there looking down at the tiny cats for a few minutes, before I decide to tell her something that I read, just this morning.

'Did you know that pulmonary embolisms have been reported as being an injury associated with the Covid vaccinations ? '

She nods slowly, holding my gaze for a moment, before focusing once more on the kittens.

November 30 - Charlotte

It should have been the first thing I asked. I pulled up outside of the perfect cottage in the woods. It stood on its own , just like me now. Maybe that's why I was drawn to it. Susan abandoned the van, full of boxes of shoes and clothes, plus a few other bits and pieces that are all that is left of my previous life, and came over to my car. I lit a cigarette while we waited for the owner to arrive with the key and the contract . The kittens, asleep in their new furry cat bed on the passenger seat, looked cosy and content. I opened the door to show Susan how cute they were, just as a new cream and black Mini pulled up behind us, and a woman of about my age, with a sleek blond bob, got out, smiling and waving as she approached. I quickly stubbed out my cigarette as she came over, and her smile instantly faded.

' I don't smoke in the house.' I said defensively, as she clearly looked unhappy about something

'No pets I'm afraid!' , she said, shaking her head, and shrugging her shoulders at the same time . We all looked at the kittens sleeping peacefully , oblivious to their latest sad predicament, and then she got back in her car, and is sitting there now, waiting for me to make a decision.

'Oh well!, I guess that's that then!', I hear myself saying as I look from her to Susan, and back again. I pick up my cigarette butt, stuffing it back into the empty packet, and as I turn back to the kittens who are just beginning to wake up, the rain that has been been threatening all morning, begins to fall, and I feel as if I might start crying again.

'So what do you want to do?' Susan asks gently, as she looks from the basket of kittens to the cottage, and back again, ignoring the miserable woman in the Mini. The little black kitten yawns and stretches without a care in the world. I smile through my tears .

'Can we just go home?'

December 1 - Frankie

Cold and crisp. A fitting start to the day I guess, as it's the first day of December. Ross has already lit the wood burner in the kitchen when Didier arrives, boots caked in mud, standing in the doorway. He won't have coffee but will take a small glass of wine. It's ten thirty in the morning. He's actually here with the calendars, he explains, shyly. I'd forgotten for a moment about this little tradition . Luckily Ross has some money . I've hardly ever got any cash these days, as I seem to pay for everything by card. Each year at this time we get caught out like this, as a postman or a pompier arrives with a calendar, and unprepared, we scratch around for cash.

'At least this morning I'm not standing here naked!' I say, to Didier, as he sips his wine, and I remind him of a previous encounter a couple of years ago. He doesn't laugh though. Doesn't seem to share my humour at all.

' Alors! Bonnes Fêtés' he says as he puts his glass down. It's a bit early, for both the wine, and the Christmas greeting I think, as we're bound to see him again a few times before the Christmas festivities.

'I like your tree!' He calls over his shoulder, in clear English as he gets back into his very English Land-rover . It takes me a minute to realise that he's talking about my metal sculpture that stands outside of the Mairie , then I look at the calendar he just handed me , and there it is, on the front page!

December 2 - Heather

It's hard to believe that in just one week's time, I will be travelling to England to meet my first grandchild! Me, a grandmother! I look in the mirror, and the person staring back at me says yes, in fact I do look old enough for the role. I get on to Facebook immediately, and send a message to Liddy, the beautician who advertises her services on the Brittany women's page. I've used her before successfully, for facials, and eyelash and brow tinting . She quickly replies to my message, saying that she can fit me in on Tuesday. Tuesday is actually perfect for me. On Wednesday, Alan and I will have a nice evening out, our last evening together before I leave on Friday.

'As long as you're back for Christmas!' Is what he said when I asked if he'd mind caring for Thug again. I will be, of course, but I was a bit worried then, that he thought the idea of having Thug over Christmas would be so terrible.

'Not at all!' Was his reply when I asked this question. 'It's just that I wanted to spend Christmas with you both!'

I am touched by this statement to be honest, and I've decided to bring him back a really special Christmas present. The only question now is what do I bring? Thug looks bewildered when I ask him his opinion, then turns his gaze upon the now empty laundry basket.

'No way, Thug!' I say in mock horror, but it was cute, how he doted on those kittens.

'You're such a big softy really, aren't you!'

December 3 - Susan

Delilah climbs into the basket, and it's not long before we hear purring. I look at Charlotte, and she smiles. A real smile. We have just finished breakfast. I've been making her a soft boiled egg every morning, . Free range, organic eggs, from Frankie's hens, and we've spent our days discussing gîte options , and playing with the kittens. Today will be her turn to help me though for a change, with packing up pottery pieces for tomorrow's Christmas Fair. I like having her here. It's nice to have someone to look after, and she's much better company than Paul ever was.

'I'll make a nice curry, shall I , for our meal tonight?' I offer, knowing Charlotte's love of spicy food . She shuffles across the kitchen in the fluffy boots I gave her to wear as slippers, putting the eggshells in the compost bin and stacking the plates in the dishwasher.

'Ooh yes! yes please! ', she says, in answer to my curry idea, then adds 'I'm never going to want to leave at this rate!'

'Don't then!' I say, realising for the first time how much I don't actually want her to go. She is undoubtedly quite self centred, and certainly she can be lazy at times, but that's really ok with me. She's not that much younger in years, but feels a bit like a daughter somehow. She is, in essence, all I've got really, now that Eric has found the love of his life.

'Stay here!' . I leave it hanging.

December 4 - Angel

I cradle my cup of mulled wine, trying to warm my hands up as I stand listening to the children singing carols in English, and in

French. It's impossible to believe that in a few short years I could be standing here watching my own child singing. The thought brings tears to my eyes, and I look over to where Charlotte is standing, on a cigarette break from helping Susan with her pottery stall. She shuffles her feet up and down, and shivers visibly.

'Come back in!' I tell her , taking her arm, once I've fought my way through the crowd to get to her.

'You'll freeze!'

She stamps on her cigarette butt, then picks it up, following me back into the main hall where most of the stall holders are standing around chatting, while potential customers browse the many arty crafty items offered there. From Susan I buy some tiny ceramic stars which are so fine they are almost transparent.

'I hope Reiki Will leave the tree alone this year!', I say as she wraps them for me.

Susan laughs. 'I hadn't thought of that!' She says, to Charlotte more than to me. 'We'll have to make our tree kitten proof this year!'

There's something about the way she says it that suggests that their home sharing arrangement might be something permanent, and not just a convenient stop gap while Charlotte works out where she really wants to be. Outside, the children are singing 'Joy to the world' , and I begin to feel very warm inside. Of course, that could just be the effects of the mulled wine.

December 5 - Charlotte

We have fallen into a routine. When I get up, Susan has already made my coffee. I stand on the doorstep as usual, with it, and my first cigarette of the day . Next year I will give up smoking, sometime in January, after I've got through my first Christmas without Tony. That'll be hard enough anyway, without further deprivation, so I'm allowing myself to continue until after the New Years celebrations, and then I'll just stop. It will be something to focus on. I come back indoors and we have breakfast, just toast for me now, I no longer need to be cajoled into eating soft boiled eggs , and homemade soup. Then I play with the kittens for an hour or so. They are my therapy, while Susan goes to her studio and potters about for a couple of hours. By the time she comes back in I've cleaned the kitchen and hoovered up a bit. Today I've washed the blanket in Rhea's bed, and made a little basket of bath time goodies for Susan, which I've placed by the bath with some candles. I found the huge stash of cosmetics and skincare that she's bought from me over the years, hidden in a kitchen cupboard. She must have intended them as gifts, and then forgotten to give them, so I've made certain that she will treat herself instead. I'm not sure how long I will stay here, but for the moment we are comfortable enough as house mates , and the idea of going anywhere else is highly unappealing. She and Rhea come back across the lawn when I'm outside having my fourth fix of the day .

'Wipe her paws!' I say, handing her an old tea towel. I've cleaned the floor.

December 6 - Frankie

'Everyone seems to need work finished in time for Christmas!', Angel says, when I'm surprised that Lee isn't yet home. It's dark at five, and it's so cold.

'He can't possibly be up on a roof, can he?' I shudder at the thought.

314

'He knocks off before it gets dark' she explains, 'then he usually goes to the Brico, or the roofing supplier place, often via the déchèterie, with a trailer full of broken slate and rotten wood'

She makes chamomile tea while she's talking , and hands me a mug.

'Let's leave it to cool down a bit, and please come and look at this'. I'm impatient for her to see what I've brought her, and anyway the tea is too hot to drink. Outside, I open the side door of the van . I wanted them both to be here really, as it's a joint present. I found the cot at the brocante on Sunday. It's old and solid. I stripped a few layers of paint off with the sandblaster, then simply waxed it. The old wood has such a lovely patina that I couldn't wait to show it off, and I'm fresh back from Ikea, having driven all the way with the cot in the back so that I could put the new mattress straight in it. It fits perfectly. Angel is speechless, and when Lee arrives a few minutes later, she is crying and hugging me.

'It must be the hormones !' I explain to him, as he gets out of the car, and he nods in agreement, but then he sees the cot, and his eyes well up too.

'That was a result!' I say to myself as I get back in the van to drive home before it gets any colder. 'I do like to make my friends cry'.

December 7 - Heather

I put a couple of warm sweaters on the bed, ready to pack, then swap one of them for a lighter one. It's very warm in Sophie's house. I put half of the socks and underwear back too. I can do laundry while I'm there . Thug watches every move. He will go to Alan tomorrow night, and I've not yet decided whether I'll stay the night too. It's not been mentioned at all, and I'm wondering if that's because he's taking it for granted that I will, or if he hasn't even given it a thought. We are seeing more of each other than we originally said we would . Three or four times a week, instead of just a couple of times. We will spend Christmas together when I return from England. I'll be a grandmother then though, and perhaps he won't fancy me any more. I throw everything in the suitcase, and zip it up. I can always buy anything I've forgotten. I unzip the side pocket and tuck the Agenda in there with a couple of pens, noticing guiltily the pile of black notebooks . The ones I use for writing. I've gone back to the idea of something autobiographical, but the ink won't flow, and those virgin notebooks, neatly stacked on my bedroom bookshelf, ready and waiting should inspiration come to me in my dreams, stare at me accusingly. Oh well, maybe once this baby is born, I'll fall back into creativity mode.

December 8 - Susan

Relief washes over me when Charlotte stands up and says 'Right, give me ten minutes and I'm ready to go!'

We're going to make a start on some Christmas shopping. This would have been yesterday's plan, but yesterday was a bad day for Charlotte. I think there are bound to be bad days, and there will be more like yesterday, when she got up as usual, but then went back to bed , saying that she felt too alone in herself. I think I understood what she meant. It was later on in the day that I checked my phone, and found a group chat that I'd been added to on Messenger.

' Please come for housewarming Pre-Christmas drinks on Saturday', the message said. It was from Hope Hill, and had been sent early that morning, to a group of us locals that included

Maisie, Angel, Frankie and me, and of course, Charlotte. 'Insensitive!' I mutter to myself.

'If she hadn't been pushing him to get everything moved out of the garage....' Charlotte has often said, though I don't think she really blames Hope for what happened, if anything she blames herself, 'If only I'd gone to help him, instead of just leaving him to it', is the alternative lament that she frequently utters. I read again Hope's message while Charlotte is upstairs putting her face on. Nobody has replied yet. I hesitate, but then put my phone in my bag, and go to check on the kittens.

'They'll be ok for a few hours won't they?' , Charlotte asks anxiously as she comes down the stairs.

'They will' , I reply, and when she still looks concerned I take her arm, 'and so will we!' . I lead her out to the car before she changes her mind.

December 9 - Angel

Every time I go upstairs now, I stop in front of the nursery door, and gaze at the little cot. It's just so beautiful, and Bington sits there on the bare mattress in all of his freshly remodelled glory, waiting for a new child to love him. I stand there for a couple of minutes breathing in pure joy, and love, and hope, before my phone vibrates in my pocket and I pull it out, to see Heather's message in reply to Hope Hill's invitation. It simply says. 'Sorry but I will be in England'. Nobody else has replied, and Frankie has removed herself from the group. I feel a bit bad, so I commit to 'passing by for a quick apéro' , and apologise for my late response. A couple of minutes later Maisie does the sam , after all, what happened to Tony wasn't Hope's fault . We should really give her a chance. Back in the kitchen I stare at the piles of stuff on the table. I'm having a Pre-Christmas sort out , and Lee said I can

317

throw out anything I don't want. He has so many pans, plates, and glasses that I barely know where to start. If I had some boxes I could take a load to the brocante. Inspiration strikes, and I realise who may have boxes to spare. Hope Hill of course! For half a second I consider this idea, before deciding to go to Susan's. She will probably have some empty ones from the pottery supplier.

December 10 - Charlotte

Susan and I stand on the doorstep of my old house. It feels very odd to be knocking and waiting. I'm glad that I was persuaded to come. Susan was right. The sooner I forgive and forget, the easier it will be , and after all, Hope didn't actually do anything wrong. There is no answer, and Susan knocks again. We aren't early, in fact we are bang on time, so it's a little bit weird that she appears to be out. I open the door then, and call her name, while Susan looks at me, eyes wide. The house has that feel of being completely devoid of any human presence. There are glasses and bottles on the table though, and packets of crisps and snacks, that look as though they've been put there ready to empty into the bowls that are stacked next to them.

'Have we got the time wrong, somehow?' Susan checks her phone, but says she is sure that we haven't. Another car pulls up behind us and I recognise Alan as he gets out, but with him, in the passenger seat is not Heather, as I'm sure it really should be, but Hope, wearing a man's padded jacket that completely swamps her tiny figure (Alan's?) , with her bare legs and feet visibly covered in goosebumps, and her wet hair hanging in ratty tails down her back. I feel a nudge from Susan, but neither of us say anything, other than 'Bonjour!'

December 11 - Frankie

'So Alan was just leaving as I arrived', Angel says.

I hand a mug of hot chocolate to her, and then stand by the fire as she recounts the tale . It's a strange feeling when I have been holding so much negativity towards a person, to feel that person suddenly rise so considerably in my estimation. Hope had been gathering some ivy and mistletoe from the trees along the canal path, to decorate her table with before welcoming her guests, when the sound of something thrashing about in the water caught her attention. A dog had caught his paw in a tangle of weed and fishing line, and was desperately trying to free himself and clamber up the bank, but all of this heavy rain that we've been getting has increased the flow of the river, and the dog was struggling to keep his head above water, while being slowly dragged towards the weir. With no hesitation Hope jumped in, fully clothed, to rescue Thug, just as Alan appeared on the path with the lead in his hand.

' Oh my god! It's so cold at the moment, even I won't go in!' I shudder.

'You would though! If you saw an animal struggling.' Yep, Angel's right. I would!

We sip our hot chocolate, and Angel continues

'And Alan was on the phone to Heather at the time….she was reminding him to keep Thug out of the woods and away from the chasse, as they are always such a danger on a Saturday afternoon!'

'Ironic isn't it, that on this occasion it was the fishermen who proved to be the real danger!' I put my mug down 'so Hope 'Hero' Hill it is then!'

December 12 - Heather

'Well it's only one day late, so far' we've all said it, several times over, at different times throughout the day. A brisk evening walk around the town might get things moving, a cup of raspberry leaf tea, or a large gin and tonic? Sophie is only half joking .

'First babies are often late' Paddy yawns knowledgeably . He has been staying over every night since Friday, just in case, and he doesn't get much sleep, waking every time Sophie shifts about in the bed, thinking this might be it, the start of labour.

'Have an early night, Paddy '. I suggest.

'Actually, I thought I might go home for the night. If anything happens I'm only five minutes away?'

He aims this statement at Sophie, and makes it sound like a question. She shrugs sulkily, and I excuse myself from the room, saying that I need to phone Alan. I've not heard from him since the river incident, and I need to check that Thug's ok. I sit at the top of the stairs where the signal is good, and tap the green phone icon by Alan's name . He picks up almost immediately, and we say our hello's and how are you's? while Sophie and Paddy say their goodnight, sleep tights . Paddy waves up at me before Sophie closes the door behind him and leans against it, waiting while I finish a very quick conversation about the weather and the lack of baby news. She stands there for maybe fifteen seconds before I notice her expression, and the puddle of water at her feet.

'Paddy!' We both scream.

December 13 - Susan

320

There is snow forecast. We need to nip to the supermarket, but Charlotte is engrossed in playing with the kittens, and I don't want to spoil things. There is enough food here really, and I could feed a small army if I had to. As long as I make the bread from scratch, and we drink our coffee black, we'll be ok for a while, unless of course we drink all of the wine. This last thought has me reaching for the car keys. Charlotte's not a baby. I can leave her for an hour or two and she'll be fine.

'You stay here in the warm, while I just go and get a few bits from the shops. We don't want to run out of anything if we're going to be snowed in'. I mentally add cat food to my list, and then cigarettes. There are baubles all over the floor, and the black kitten is running around with a piece of tinsel around its neck like a scarf. Charlotte has her phone out, and is taking photos, when we both get a message at the same time. Heather has sent us all a photo of her newborn grandson. A tiny screwed up face in a white hat, tightly swaddled in a crocheted shawl. 'Willoughby is here!' , she writes, 'all eight pounds of him! Mother and baby are doing well' .

I look at Charlotte. There are tears in her eyes. I think I'll give it an hour or so before I go out.

December 14 - Angel

So much for the snow! It's raining again. I've one client this morning, and then Lee will come home so we can have lunch together. I'd hoped for a snowy walk this afternoon, but it's not to be, and Lakshmi and I will have a wander down the lane and back instead, before lighting a fire and selecting a Christmas movie to watch. Corinne arrives, with the remains of a cold, evident in the way she speaks

'I've got so much shopping still to do' , she says, and goes on to tell me that her family arrive next Wednesday, two daughters, a son in law, and the tiny baby who is her first grandson, together with her own mother and sister.

'Quite a houseful!' She blows her nose before settling on to my couch. She will cook for nine adults on Christmas Day she tells me, as I put a blanket over her and make her comfortable.

'There's just so much to do!' she says again, as I warm the oil for her massage. I feel a stab of envy at the thought of that huge family. It will just be Lee and I on Christmas Day here. Frankie and Ross are expecting Henry, and we could join them if we wanted to, but Lee thinks a romantic Christmas, with just the two of us, while we can still do that, will be absolutely perfect. I feel the tense knots in Corinne's shoulders as I begin to massage, and I wonder if Lee might be right! Keeping Christmas small and simple does have its advantages.

December 15 - Charlotte

I want to buy a Christmas present for Susan. It's not easy. Everything she wants, and everything she needs, she buys herself. In the kitchen she's making mince pies while I clean up after the kittens. I look about me for inspiration, and what I see is every appliance anyone could possibly ever need, all of them top brands too. In her studio everything is brand new and sparkling. There's literally nothing she hasn't got. I take the cat litter out to the compost pile, and stop for a quick smoke before I go back inside, flicking through Facebook on my phone as I puff away. As I scroll down my page, something catches my eye. An advert for fake fur duvet covers, that look wonderfully warm and cosy, flaunts its luxuriousness across my screen.

'Perfect!' I say to myself, checking that the delivery time is sufficient, and clicking on the 'buy it now' button. I walk back in with the empty litter tray and a satisfied smile on my face . She looks up.

'You ok?' She asks, obviously mystified by my expression. I pretend not to hear her as I pour a cascade of fresh cat litter into the tray. By the time I look up again I've managed to wipe the grin from my face.

'What?' I ask innocently. She goes back to her mince pies without another word.

December 16 - Frankie

I smile at Hope, and wish her a good day, when I see her for the third time this week, walking alone, along the canal path. Artie is off somewhere chasing a scent, so I look like I too am on my own. I briefly wonder if Hope is lonely, but I don't invite her over for coffee or anything. Even after her heroic dip in the river, I'm not sure that I like her. My gut feeling still tells me to keep my distance, and when I look at her this morning, in full makeup with matching scarf and gloves, and what are probably 'designer' boots, I'm pretty convinced that she's not going to fit in here . Who is she out to impress in all that gear? I wonder, and then it all becomes clear, as coming down the path from the other direction, is Alan , walking Thug. The look on his face as he spots Hope, further along the path now , but walking very slowly, tells me all I need to know. He's obviously looking for a way to avoid bumping into her, and when Artie comes bounding back, and the two dogs run off together, we get into a conversation about the weather, and Heather and the new baby. Further down the path, Hope stops, and turns towards us, flicking her hair over her shoulders as she does so. A look of panic flashes across Alan's face and he takes my elbow, steering me swiftly back the other way.

'Come and have a coffee with me!' he says, and I fall into step with him , trying to look as though we do this all the time.

'I'm sorry but that woman is an absolute predator!', he confides quietly , when we are far enough away.

December 17 - Heather

We all spend a lot of time staring into the bassinet. Willoughby is awake for such a short time, normally every couple of hours or so, though sometimes he sleeps for four or five hours at a stretch. Sophie is content. Paddy is here every day at the moment, and he stays late into the night so that Sophie can go to bed and get some sleep. I do my bit, but it's necessary for the two of them to establish a routine. Paddy goes home at around one am, leaving the sleeping baby with Sophie for the rest of the night. It seems to work. I am cooking for the freezer, so that they don't need to worry about meals at least, and I'm shopping, and in between times I'm trying to write a bit, but there's so much going on that I only manage a word or two before I'm distracted. Alan phones every other day, and makes me laugh with his tales of adventuring with Thug, and the necessity of changing his walking times in order to avoid the attentions of Hope Hill, who seems to be looking for some kind of attention herself. I will have to pass by her house, with some kind of Christmassy gift, to thank her for her doggy life saving efforts. It's not really a visit that I'm looking forward to.

December 18 - Susan

The only problem with this cleaning spree that Charlotte is on, is that nothing is sacred. She's been going through every cupboard, and it occupies her mind in a weirdly therapeutic way, so my house has never looked cleaner, but she wants to tackle my walk-in wardrobe next . It's true, it's rammed with clothes I don't wear, shoe boxes I haven't even looked in for years , and other assorted debris. It also hides though, a big box containing a lovely soft fluffy duvet cover which I've just bought for her Christmas present. There's nowhere else in the house to hide it, now that Charlotte is in full Marie Kondo mode. I am enjoying myself though, having her here. She's someone I can spoil at Christmas, and it's kind of fun, being a bit secretive, and planning surprises. I wait for her to go outside, as she normally does, with the litter tray that she empties onto the compost heap at the bottom of the garden . She always takes a few minutes doing this, so it gives me time to stealthily grab the box containing the duvet cover, and the other various items that I plan to fill her Christmas stocking with, and stash the whole lot in my studio, amongst other boxes which contain pottery supplies.

'Just checking the kiln!' I say, as I return to the house and find her on the doorstep with a cigarette in her hand. Looks like I timed that well!

December 19 - Angel

Ok, so France lost against Argentina. There are more important things to worry about, and this is what I tell Gilliane's husband, when he comes to pick her up after her hot stone massage. Gilliane can hardly walk, because of an old injury which has left her a bit stooped and arthritic. Their daughter is getting a divorce, and Gilliane worries about the effect on her granddaughters, and on top of that, this heavy rain has brought the river to their door, where at the moment the sandbags are only just stopping it from entering the house. They need to get most of the furniture upstairs just in case, but her husband is in a terrible mood because France lost the football match yesterday. England lost against France just a few days ago, but life goes on…

'It hardly matters though does it? In the grand scheme of things?' I get no answer to my question as Gilliane smiles and thanks me for the massage, and probably for the way I stood up to her husband, who mutters something unintelligible in French, and drives away without a backwards glance. I close the door on the torrential rain, and check my phone for messages, in case my next client has cancelled due to the inclement weather. The first thing I see when I open Facebook, is a post about the football result.

'Sacré bleu !' I say to Reiki who has curled up on the warm towels. She looks at me and yawns.

'Yes you're right, it's very boring! '

December 20 - Charlotte

Some days I am just sad, all day. This, unfortunately, is one of those days. Susan's present arrives, while she's out, and in plenty of time for Christmas, then I discover that the money from the house sale is now in my account. I should feel a bit happier but I don't. She arrives home from the supermarket with a fresh turkey and a box of English Christmas crackers.

'Eric and Michelle will join us for Christmas dinner!' She announces .

I sit here with a kitten on my lap, and the dull ache that comes from missing Tony, wondering what the point is in doing anything at all this Christmas. Everything reminds me of him, and of Christmases past . The tree that he would 'borrow' from the forest.

The tins of Quality Street that he would ask clients to bring back from their U.K. trips, even the bacon rashers that Susan waves in front of me saying that she'll make 'pigs in blankets '. She puts a mug of coffee in front of me with a good glug of Baileys in it, then asks Alexa to play some Christmas carols.

'There you go!' She says 'You sit and cry for a bit, then we'll go for a lovely walk in the rain when you're feeling a bit better!'

I do as I'm told. Nobody could ever take as good care of me as she does. Not even Tony!

December 21 - Frankie

Henry is being Henry. I hadn't heard from him for a couple of weeks, so I sent him a text yesterday to check that he still has plans to join us for Christmas. Then I wrapped his present and put it by the tree, while I waited for a response, refusing to let the seeds of doubt, that had begun to sprout, take hold, until I knew for sure whether or not he would be here. We have had many Christmases without Henry over the years. It's no big deal, except that he promised, and we were looking forward to it . A couple of hours later, his message stated that he was trying to find an affordable flight from Hong Kong. I didn't even know that he was in Hong Kong, or what he was even doing there. So today I wait , and that's the difficult thing, not knowing which way it's likely to go . I've packed up my atelier for a little Christmas holiday, clearing my bench, and sorting through a few boxes of collected items, ready to start afresh in the New Year . I hover in the doorway, wondering about starting on something now, but I don't feel the necessary creative spark, and really I'm just looking for something to occupy my mind, while I continue to wait to hear from Henry. Ross is moving the fence, where the overflowing river has flooded the lower paddock. Boris is upstairs on her perch in the barn. I decide to go and chat to her. Owls do have the reputation for being wise. Artie cocks his head to one side , as if saying 'what about me?'

'Come on then!' I tell him, and he does the little circular dance that he does when we're about to go for a walk. I pick up my phone. No message yet. Ok Boris, I hope you have some good advice.

December 22 - Heather

My car edges forward a little, but I can see from the amount of tail lights in front of me that I am still a long way from getting on the boat. I watch as the line of lorries next to me, slowly creeps ahead of us. At least it's not wet and windy tonight . The crossing should be calm. This trip home is definitely feeling bitter sweet. I can't wait to see Alan, and spend Christmas with him, and I'm dying to give Thug, an almighty hug. It will be wonderful to catch up with all my friends too! But then there is Sophie and darling Willoughby, the dear little soul . It was so hard to part with them. We will share a drink, by video call, on Christmas Day, and after that, I'm sure it'll be a regular thing. I will pop back to see them every couple of months, for a few days if I can afford to, then in the summer they will come to France. The car in front inches forward a few feet and I realise our line is now moving .

'Go on, go on! ' I mutter, under my breath. It won't really make any difference at all, whether I get on first or last. I have a plan to sit in the bar with a gin and tonic , and start making notes for a new book idea. There's no hurry though. After all I'll be on this boat all night!

December 23 - Susan

I let Charlotte decorate the tree. It's been there, with the decorations in a box next to it, for a couple of days. I've been hoping that she would galvanise again, and this morning she made a comment about it looking quite Christmassy, as she stood with the door open . There was quite a heavy frost, no snow of course, so I hinted that once we have a decorated tree, I have a couple of presents to wrap that I might place underneath it. Now, having had a second cup of coffee and another cigarette, she's opened the box of unbreakable, kitten friendly baubles and tinsel. I heat up some mince pies, and ask Alexa to play some Christmas music, and by the time Heather knocks on the door, a little before lunchtime, with our English Christmas shopping , we are indeed looking very festive. She comes in and dumps the heavy box on the table.

'Is it too early for a glass of wine?' She asks, getting ready to show us the latest baby photos on her phone.

'Surely it's Christmas already! ' I say 'so it's never too early'

December 24 - Angel

I put a couple of bottles of non alcoholic bubbly stuff into the trolley with the two chickens (I couldn't find a turkey, and one chicken doesn't look like enough for two men and Frankie). I'm making a nut roast too, and a traditional trifle. A bit naff, but once we'd decided to forego the romantic Christmas, and invite over our best friends, for a bit of fun, I decided that the tiny little verrines of raspberry coulis and limoncello sorbet wouldn't cut it.

'How can we not invite them?' Lee said, when we heard from Frankie that Henry was no longer coming.

'They are the only extended family that this baby will have!' He placed his hand protectively over my stomach then, and I felt the 'little chap' , as we've taken to calling him or her, move in response. It's something I've been thinking about more and more as Christmas approaches, the idea that good friends are indeed better than family really, and auntie Frankie and uncle Ross will be perfect as substitute family members. I push my trolley to the checkout and end up in a queue behind Susan who has only some brussel sprouts and a punnet of prawns in her hand. We both talk excitedly about our plans for tomorrow. She has quite a day in store for Charlotte

'You will call in over Christmas and have a drink with us, won't you?' , she asks, then places her hand on my belly and says in a squeaky voice

'Auntie Susan and Aunt Charlotte might have a little surprise for you under the tree!'

Ok then, so that's two sets of aunties and uncles already. I can feel myself getting emotional again.

December 25 - Charlotte

I lie awake for a few minutes, checking in with myself, trying to decide whether I feel flat, empty, scared and alone, or if this is going to be a good day, one where I can believe in a future of some sort. A moment later I sit up, and put on the furry slippers that Susan gave me, and a fleecy top. I actually feel a bit excited, and when I open my bedroom door the feeling increases, as the first thing I see, propped against the stair rail, is a Christmas stocking stuffed with goodies. I wish I'd thought of doing one for

Susan, but unfortunately I didn't, and she will have to make do with the one large box that I put under the tree, containing the fluffy duvet cover. I pick up the stocking, and go down to the kitchen where Susan already has the coffee on.

'Merry Christmas!' , she says, and tells me to start delving in . I look over at the tree where even more presents are now stacked. There is a box very similar in size to the one that I've got for her. She follows my gaze, and we both smile. The first thing I pull out of the stocking is a miniature bottle of Baileys.

'Shall we put it in the coffee?' , I ask. It's nine a.m., but we do it anyway. The second thing is a tiara, made of twisted copper wire with red glass stones woven into it. Its intricately woven with finer copper threads and tiny jet beads, and it's just too beautiful! I put it on and Susan picks up a pair of reindeer antlers, similarly exquisite, and obviously made by the same artist, and puts them on her head.

'Frankie made them for us!' , she says. A genuine smile comes unbidden to my lips . Not like the fake one I've been using lately to reassure people that I'm doing ok, but a real one, a little sadder than the one I used to have but that's only natural I guess. Today will be a good day.

December 26 - Frankie

Ross holds my flask of tea, and my DryRobe. (the perfect Christmas present that I can't believe he managed to secretly buy), and I run into the sea, ignoring the cold, and the fact that my feet and legs are almost immediately tingly and numb. I duck my shoulders under and actually swim a few strokes before surfacing and splashing my way back out and up the beach, quickly donning the DryRobe . I'm not cold as I stand there drinking my tea, while normal people walk past, dressed for winter with their hats and scarves. The natural high that I feel whenever I come out of the sea after a cold swim, never gets old. Ross lights a joint and we spend ten minutes or so just feeling quietly content. All traces of the hangover from yesterday are now gone, and I feel happy that this has been a great Christmas. Another one without Henry, but hey, if you can't be with the ones you love, love the ones you're with. The only tiny issue though is all that food I bought! Loads of cheese, wine, and snacky things, thinking that we'd get through a mountain of goodies with Henry being there, and then Angel and Lee, insisting we weren't to bring anything.

'How do you feel about having a party on New Years Eve?' I ask the question as it occurs to me. Ross shrugs noncommittally, but as I wander amongst the pebbles on the edge of the shore, looking for sea-glass, I piece together a party plan that I will put into action as soon as we get home.

December 27 - Heather

It saves on fuel costs to heat just the one house over Christmas, and my house was the obvious choice, having been empty for a while,and in need of a good fire anyway to drive the damp away from stones and bones. This morning I wake with Alan beside me again, and I wonder if today is the day that he'll finally go home. We've kept ourselves to ourselves, walking Thug in the woods, cooking nice meals, and then chilling out with Netflix. It's been one of my most favourite Christmases, and so different to last year. Lying here looking out of the window at the trees swaying alarmingly in the storm, and the rain pounding on the velux window, I start to get the seed of an idea for a story. It's been such a year, that if I did write my life story, 2022 would stand alone as the all singing, all dancing, glorious technicolour year, after years of mediocre, bland and beige, preamble. For my new friends too there have been changes this year, and many of them I have unwittingly recorded in my beloved agenda. Alan yawns and stretches, and my thoughts change tack for the moment, towards breakfast, and Thug's bathroom requirements, but I file this idea for a new book away in my mind, just behind my conscious thoughts, where I can pull it out again later. I visualise it sitting there inside my head, a gem of an idea, lighting up my mind and filling me with the inspiration thats been so evasive of late.

December 28 - Susan

I'm a bit surprised when Charlotte suggests that we find some clothes to dress up in.

'Wear all of your finery, like a seven year old raiding her mother's wardrobe!' , Frankie's message says.

'It could be fun!' Charlotte puts down her phone, happy to have received an invitation, and if she's happy then I am too, so we spend the morning trying on hats that I've worn over the years, to various weddings, a ball gown from about thirty years ago, and a whole suitcase full of glamorous outfits from the seventies and eighties that were just too flamboyant and fancy for me ever to discard. She decides that rara skirts and lacy tights are the way to go, and wonders what she can do with her hair. I decide that I need to lose weight, but my wedding dress does indeed look fabulous when teamed with Paul's old top hat, tuxedo, and bow tie. By lunchtime we are all set for Saturday night, with two days to spare, and Charlotte is busy scribbling something in a notepad while I rustle up a turkey omelette. I put the plates down with a flourish, and discover a sheet of paper next to my knife and fork . It has my name at the top , and 'New Year's Resolutions' written next to it. I look across at her own list . At the very top, underneath her name she's written

'1. Lose this sadness ' , with a sad emoji face .

I know that she is going too fast, and not allowing herself time to grieve, but I don't say anything. Instead I write

'1. Lose the fat', at the top of my face, and then draw a stick lady, with a big belly. It makes her giggle.

December 29 - Angel

This New Year is blowing in with a force. I know it's going to be a huge year for me! The hugest in fact! Mercury is in retrograde again though, and I'm going to need to do some work . Lee comments when I begin to take down some of the decorations.

'It's a bit soon isn't it?' I feel the need to clear my space though, and remove anything that no longer serves me. On New Years Eve there's a big party at Frankie's. She and Ross are getting the barn ready. We will go of course, Lee in an old suit with an enormous kipper tie and an outrageous waistcoat, Me in a sari with butterfly wings, and a tiara on my head, but before any of that I will cleanse this house and clear it of negative energies . I will place a candle in each room, each inscribed with an intention (to bring peace, to bring success, to bring abundance etc) . I don't need to ask for love, as I'm overflowing with it already. I place the baubles carefully in the box, knowing that next time I take them out there will be an extra little person here to enjoy them with us. This thought alone makes me smile, and I look over at Lee. A smile, is evidently contagious.

December 30 - Charlotte

I can't wait for this year to be over . If only it would just stop raining ! The kittens are asleep as I sit by them, trying to cheer myself up. The temptation to return upstairs to that fluffy duvet heaven, is great, but I must snap myself out of this melancholy mood before it descends into true depression. When Susan suggests wrapping up and going for a walk along the canal to see how fast it's flowing now, I can't help grimacing . There is nothing I would less rather do than head out into the storm, but I do it anyway, half listening as I pull on a woolly hat and scarf, to her encouragements about a little fresh air, and something about cobweb blowing . I light a cigarette while Susan calls Rhea. She doesn't come though, and Susan kicks off her wellies again in irritation, so that she can go and find the dog, who is probably hiding out upstairs .

'She doesn't like to go out much in this weather', Susan states unnecessarily. She's not the only one, and I look longingly over at the sofa as Susan goes from room to room calling her name. As I blow my cigarette smoke out and waft it into the wood burner, I catch sight of her tail. She is hiding under the Christmas tree, curled up in the bucket it sits in , her body wrapped tightly around its trunk, trying to avoid discovery. The tail wags slightly, and one eye peeps comically out at me from a head that's tucked under a front paw

'Bring your phone!' I call excitedly, not wanting to miss this photo opportunity. I feel my mood start to shift slightly.

December 31 - Frankie

'So how was your year really?', Heather asks . We are standing on the mezzanine in the barn, looking down at a crowd of about thirty people, drinking, dancing, and generally partying. Ross is deep in conversation with Alan. Lee and Angel are smoochy

335

dancing. Hope, (it felt wrong to leave her out) , seems to have designs on Didier.

'Oh you know, same old, same old!' I tell her. But, for me it has been a good year, one of many good years. I think for a minute or two, and come to the conclusion that I just never have bad years.

'Life is what you make it I guess, and we are lucky, all of us living here with such good friends around us'.

She nods in agreement and we stand in silence for a while, people watching. I have one eye on my watch, as it's getting close to midnight, and she begins to tell me of her big idea for a new book. It's a partly fictional tale, of a year in the life of a handful of expat women, inspired by those same friends who are here with us tonight . There's a lot to write about . Angel, her new man, and their surprise baby, Charlotte's rather sad rollercoaster year, Susan's success with her pottery and her newfound happiness with her live-in companion.

'Your own year's been quite eventful too!' I point out, and she agrees, throwing her head back and laughing. We look down at Alan and Ross , and I glance at my watch again.

'I would say, that I myself have had a successful year, even quite a magical one'. I tell her, and then add

'I can't wait to read what you write about me! '

I look down at the dragon's head I've made, that breathes a cascade of laser lights down over the floor beneath, and as the hour advances Heather leaves my side to go and join Alan for the countdown. I wait there, and as the clock strikes twelve I switch on the machine that sends a million bubbles floating down from above, while projecting at the same time the words 'welcome 2023 ' on to the far wall of the barn in gold and silver lights .

'So this is 2023!' Ross says, creeping up behind me with 2 glasses of champagne, and nuzzling my neck. Heather catches my eye and raises her glass, so I raise my own, and watch as the champagne bubbles dance and mingle with the machine bubbles that float between us, a beautiful metaphor for the bubbles of inspiration, that flit spontaneously in and out of each of our creative minds .

'Bring it on!' I reply.

Printed in Great Britain
by Amazon

26962386R00192